The Labyrinth of Tender Force

THE
SEAGULL
LIBRARY OF
GERMAN
LITERATURE

The Labyrinth of Tender Force

166 LOVE STORIES

ALEXANDER KLUGE

TRANSLATED BY WIELAND HOBAN

LONDON NEW YORK CALCUTTA

This publication was supported by a grant
from the Goethe-Institut India

Seagull Books, 2022

Originally published as Das Labyrinth der zärlichen Kraft. 166 Liebesgeschichten

First published in English translation by Seagull Books, 2018

ISBN 978 1 80309 179 2

British Library Cataloguing-in-Publication Data
A catalogue record for this book is available from the British Library

Typeset by Seagull Books, Calcutta, India
Printed and bound by WordsWorth India, New Delhi, India

CONTENTS

FIGURE 1. 'Love as meaning that by wanting to receive something from another person, one gives that very thing oneself.'

FOREWORD

Whatever one says about loving relationships, their natural richness in casuistry refutes it. Love is a millipede. When telling stories about it, circumspection, pacing and assertions are the weakest of virtues.

Alexander Kluge

I

IN THE TANGLE OF CIRCUITOUSNESS

Tender strength is confusing, and active everywhere. There are as many love stories as there are stars in the sky. But in them, states Sigmund Freud, tenderness is only ignited in a particular mixture, namely together with 'sensual strength'. Presumably the circuitousness with which love expresses itself has something to do with this. This tangle is one of the brightest, most love-able features of human beings. 'Love makes you clear-sighted . . . '

In the Tangle of Circuitousness

She, the correspondent at the *Neue Zürcher Zeitung*, was sitting opposite one of these older researchers from Stephen Gould's department at Harvard. Instead of concentrating on the subject that she was covering in her newspaper's series, he was courting her. It cost her some effort to direct his attention back to the topic.

–You're saying that people are playthings of their genes? That they're not in control of their own decisions in matters of love?

–Genes are interested exclusively in their own procreation. Everything goes back to that elemental position. For humans and animals. Though only on an evolutionary scale.

–So not today, the way we're drinking tea and rum here?

–It applies to an extent.

–And genes aren't interested in the details of our LOVE LIVES, in love stories?

–I don't think so.

–Would our genes also consider violence, greed or revenge useful vehicles for procreation?

–Certainly. For the human race to multiply, our correlation to 'love' is only a circuitous one. That's equally true of animals.

–You mean, Tristan and Isolde don't have children. Romeo and Juliet are also childless. Just like the majority of 'young lovers' in literary art. You're saying that deviates from the instrumental logic of genes?

—The only people left over are those who didn't follow the famous love stories.

The rum in the tea and the sweetness of the sweetener (no regrets) were seductive. The other's eyes: a dark bluish-grey, 'steely'. These eyes captivated her, but at the same time the 'subject-focused' character of his gaze bothered her. As long as his eyes and his words seemed to contradict each other, this man barely had a chance of putting her in an interesting erotic mood. In practice, he continued, one could not 'see' the 'persistent work' of the genes. To disguise their plans they needed digressions, follies, human actors. Without these digressions, the genes know they will not reach their goal. Their intrigues work: they are impeded by the power of the genes themselves, as they try somehow to outmanoeuvre their opponents, and need the TANGLE OF CIRCUITOUSNESS for that very reason.

That was an expedient title. After their fourth tea with rum, they agreed that humans would not have survived evolution without circuitousness: the thing we call love. It is not only tolerated by the genes; they need it as a LANDSCAPE.

Love Triumphs

It was coincidence that the 'eternal couple' ever met at all. Had the Chevalier Des Grieux reached the carriage alighting point an hour later, he would never have encountered the irretrievable Manon.

–You think that destiny brought them together? Providence?

–Neither of us believe in such a thing. The encounter wasn't based on anything like fate.

Coincidence had bound them together; henceforth, the couple stayed together. Des Grieux made them a living from cheating at gambling and other trickery; Manon pulled the wool over old men's eyes and robbed them. Soon they had vengeful victims and the police on their trail.

For Manon there was only *one* law: her love. Feeling, affection, concentration, sincerity. But all this only applied to the *one* question of whether she loved Des Grieux and how she could ensure that he must love her again. The constancy of this was legendary.

We know that Grieux followed his beloved when the court sentenced her to deportation. They sailed to the penal colony in Louisiana. After duelling with the governor's nephew, the couple saw no other choice than to flee across the desert. We know how Manon died in the desert night. All that was left for Des Grieux was to tell humanity the tale.

'The violent colours
in the sky abruptly vanish.'

She Never Had Any Doubts

'She placed both hands on her bosom and gazed into the night with hot, fanatical eyes.'

Let us suppose that Manon Lescaut awakens one September morning and no longer senses any of the emotions she has felt for her lover Des Grieux in the last days, and which constantly made his presence inescapable for her. Suddenly she has tired of him. What should she do?

–She'll wait. She'll test it. I don't think she'll waver.

–But what should she do? She tried all day long, but couldn't find that feeling again. She had always been sure that the 'feeling of the first moment' would never fade.

–Not even after a bout of pneumonia? Or from an intestinal colic? When the body draws all sensations to itself as if it had gone bankrupt?

–No. She would still have had the memory of the 'first moment of acquaintance'. And that was her faith. The only thing she saw as incorruptible.

This persistence or underlying force, which is so rare and which marks the strength of Manon's character, would lie in tatters. The observers of the young couple, who would have liked to share some of that mysterious certainty about love which they had observed for so long in the young woman, asked themselves how they could help.

–You said yourself: 'let us suppose'. It didn't actually happen.

–Because the young woman died early and young. She carried her obsession, her certainty inside her like a demon.

—Why are you speaking in such a faithless, in fact faith-eroding, way about the novel, when nobody knows what Manon would have felt if she had reached the age of 40? I think what you're saying is out of jealousy, out of envy.

The doubter gave himself away as soon as he accused the couple's observers of wanting to come to their aid, even though they were only discussing a hypothetical case—a case in which Manon's feelings, at the limits of the novel, so to speak, had failed. In fact, there are no reports of this. Such a failure would have revealed itself in some second or other of her life. Were there always observers present? She herself was the observer, and she never had any doubts.

A Lucky Charm

The lawyers of the Federal Republic of Germany, represented by the Foreign Office, which was represented by the so-called legal representatives and lawyers of the family of the 'bride', quickly reached an agreement. After losing once in court, they waited until the end of the two-year period which had to pass before the young Iraqi could acquire legal citizenship. The marriage had to last two years for there to be considered a 'lasting bond' between the German woman and the immigrant; mere marriage was not enough. They assumed that the 'bridegroom', a 25-year-old young man from the Orient, would divorce the far older 'bride' the day after the two-year period ended and be on his way in full possession of his civil rights.

–For a man from that kind of Middle Eastern culture, his own self-image would prevent him from marrying a woman who couldn't bear him any children.

–He'll only take a virgin from his own country. As soon as his citizenship is secure, he'll bring one like that over here.

–With her parents and relatives?

–His own and the virgin's.

The lawyers wanted to wait for that moment, then strike. The files were ready for resubmission. The 'bride' had the rights to a large fortune; so far she had not claimed it. The unequal couple lived in a modest flat. The woman was divorced, childless, 35 years older than her beau. Her relatives said she was disappointed by her two previous husbands, who were considered upstanding in their social class but had been unpleasant in their private lives and taken to the bottle under stress.

–She has a sixth sense for choosing the wrong men.

–You're not in a position to judge that. You don't have any psychological training.

–But don't you see anything wrong with the way she made her choice?

With this marriage, she seemed to be continuing an established pattern among the female members of her family: it seemed that the women in this amply propertied clan had sought out unhappy liaisons for generations. The pinnacle of this, the observers believed, was the marriage of

Bettina-Elisabeth G. to the 25-year-old new arrival. Where on earth had she found him? What did the two of them do when they were alone? How was the 45-year-old going to look after the 80-year-old in 20 years?

Month after month went by. The two-year period ended. No crisis, no preparations for separation. Reports by private detectives sent to spy on them spoke of a 'harmonious overall situation'.

On the contrary, said the 'bride's' former lover, a certain Dr Arentz, who had remained friends with her. The two of them loved undertaking things together. Was it possible that the 'bridegroom' was not an adventurer, that the marriage was not a sham? Was he transferring some of his good luck to the older woman? Jokes about the 'merry widow' were met with silence.

'Lights shine
Violins weep
Please love me'

And so it went on. The couple adopted a child, supposedly unknown to them, but it later transpired that the 'bridegroom' had fathered it before his marriage. Now there were three of them. She outlived her 'young friend', as she called him, by three years; he died in an accident. After his death, which she mourned for a long time, she claimed the fortune to which she was the rightful heir. Its beneficiary was the 'Oriental's' child, which the old woman brought up with care. For its facial features reminded her of her lucky charm, to whom she was grateful until the end of her life. The lawyers were left empty-handed.

Beauty Is Flawless

The beautiful Greek woman from the Waterloo Institute fascinated the physics community at the well-attended annual conference in Hawaii. Her head was wreathed in thick black hair. The tall figure strode up to the blackboard that was set up in the background of the lectern. With firm, screeching chalk strokes–that is, in a conventional way compared to the opulent electronic facilities of the giant hall, she elaborated equations that connected the INFINITELY SMALL and TEMPORALLY SHORT with the COSMICALLY LARGE (for example, a proto-galactic group, located in the constellation Coma Berenices, that had once spread out only 300,000 years away from the beginning of the world). One equation followed another with no complications. The majority of specialists in the hall considered both this woman and the formulae she was writing down 'beautiful'. But the Greek reserved the word 'beauty' exclusively for the cosmos and the world of nanospheres. Her lecture proceeded from the axiom that the beauty and simplicity of equations, when they referred to such extremely disparate realities, were the correct indication of their coherence.

–Do you speak of 'beauty' or 'splendour' when you refer to the long-expired galactic group?

–Beauty.

–In the sense of regularity?

–There's nothing regular about it.

–So it's complicated?

–It's not that either; it's autonomous.

–In the sense of rebellious?

–Not towards my equations.

A young physicist, who was attending this congress for the first time, would not have wanted to miss the moments he shared with the enchanting scholar over a cup of tea after her lecture. The goddess remained unattainable for him–not only because she was married and had no interest in adventures in the middle of the Pacific anyway. Rather, this untouchable character seemed to the young man like a prerequisite for beauty. And how could he have installed the beauty in his laboratory or his bachelor's quarters anyway? Only if she had been a statue.

The Imperfect One

She had an unfavourable pelvis. Its halves were wide apart, creating a hollow space between her thighs. Though advantageous for giving birth, this was unusual, and met with disapproving gazes. As she rarely looked at herself in the mirror (and when she did, it was not at her whole body) she would not have dwelt on it, had not one of her 'boyfriends', who made no further advances after that, pointed it out to her 'comfortingly'.

So she no longer presented her 'inferior' self actively any more, and hardly went to any dance events or 'occasions for meeting people'. Should she have been on the lookout for a 'partner with blemishes'? 'Young, passionate working woman with widely spaced thighs (otherwise intact) seeks cross-eyed or otherwise impaired boyfriend.'

'You are my man
My life
The sight of you
Makes me blind'

She could not pluck up the courage to put the ad online, as she feared impostors who might have seen her as easy prey. She could already see herself as a slave, sold somewhere far to the east.

So she abandoned her efforts in that direction, towards a life partnership, and became sufficiently qualified in her profession that she was soon considered a rich woman. Now she could have travelled abroad and made half-starved men dependent on her money, finding opportunities to satisfy her lust. But she was too proud. And too inexperienced to know how one should go about such dealings without danger. She would have liked to have a child; in the end she adopted one from São Paulo. The adoptive mother and her foundling were inseparable. No problems.

Wildness as a Requirement

When I come to the subject of love in my evening classes, I encounter resistance as soon as I formulate these two demands:

–sense of proportion and predictability
–reliable repeatability

Love, my students tell me, needs to retain a certain wildness, its own special kind of excess. Its principle is boundlessness. As soon as one sees boundaries ahead, one has already overcome them. Love is thought to be UNTAMEABLE. So if it were repeatable, that is, at all subject to force of will, it would lose its magic. It would lose all value.

'So,' I respond tenaciously, as I am not only a woman who researches education, but also a love economist and a Marxist, 'it is meant to stay at a barbaric level of gathering activities, or battles between clans for prey. That hardly corresponds to any modern stage of production.' I add, 'Small wonder that this ubiquitous social power, the most significant power of production available to us humans, has almost entirely drifted away to advertising and the media? That's where the great passions, the magical powers of love, are displayed: the ability to gain permission for intimacy with another person.'

My courses last three months. Two hours four times a week. I have not, however, arrived at a MODERN-AGE VIEW OF LOVE (in keeping with the conceptual blueprints of the Bauhaus) with the participants. It genuinely seems to be an OLD FORCE, held tight by a vehement interest among the students of which, for all my reading of economic texts as a Marxist, I cannot make any sense.

My Maternal Grandfather

> 'With a beautiful woman, you have to find
> the right second.'
>
> *Wedding Night in Paradise*

FIGURE 2. My maternal grandfather. On the right is the ear, the organ that controls the sense of balance and the ability to distinguish. On the basis of information with a tonal shading. SENSE OF PROPORTION. The radiant eye transmits seductive power, assuming a partner responds. If the partner does not respond, the gaze is lowered. But if they respond, an inaudible conversation follows.

He knocked. His heart stayed calm, it certainly didn't beat any louder than before, but it was biting. One could see over the wooden door into the changing room. The woman moved about near the door. Outside, the shuffling sounds of the ice skaters. Dusk had fallen, and the lights were opening the ice-skating evening. The sounds mingled with the music, a potpourri of works by Emil Waldteufel. She opened, he entered. Now the whole thing was already an illegal situation, the way the two of them had acted so rashly. What was he doing in the ladies' changing rooms? Why didn't she scream? Why had she unlocked the door? There was no use of force involved.

A few months later he asked for her hand in marriage. Negotiations with Martha's father. A factory owner and experienced businessman, he assumed he had been duped. The suitor had a horse with him, on loan from a livery stable; he gave it to the servant to look after. He was unable to ride it himself but had brought it along as a sign of wealth. Martha's father, who saw through this disguise, wanted to see financial documents and sought information about the suitor's income. Nothing was decided at once. The suitor still had his main negotiating advantage up his sleeve. He only ever spoke of Martha's will, of his intense desire to join with her, and of her consent. But he actually had a guarantee: she was pregnant by him. In that sense, Martha's father believed in a negotiating position that he had long ceased to have. In the end my grandfather received the consent of Martha's father, who took revenge by disinheriting his daughter. Not one iota of his fortune would go to this son-in-law, the upstart.

Later, Martha's father would often sit at my grandfather's summer residence, and was happy to accept the hospitality offered by his son-in-law, who turned out to be successful. This did nothing to change his decision about material benefits. For all forms of balance in this marriage, which produced five children, that was a favourable circumstance.

Thus my grandfather had gained a wife ON HER OWN MERITS: the fate of a spontaneous decision at the entrance to the changing room, in a twilight he would never forget. He had already taken the forbidden path. Before that, he had seen little of the young woman's details; she had come with an entirely different companion. A sudden idea. He was curious by nature.

–His self-confidence was his capital, is that right? A self-assured body? A spirit that trusted in the moment?

—That was his capital.

—Her capital was a decision that even surprised her?

—Yes, in later life she would never be that spontaneous again. The man appealed to her.

—What happened to her father's capital?

—It dwindled. Each of the four sons received part of the fortune; then they lost it.

—And what he kept?

—Didn't survive the First World War.

—And your grandfather lived until 1936?

—He died of pneumonia. His respiratory system was his weakness.

—And Martha?

—Lived to the age of 101 with his help.

—Help in what sense?

—He had equipped her.

—And all in a moment of perhaps 16 seconds, in which a decision formed with the setting sun and the shuffling of ice skaters?

—There is no greater investment than that.

The Hour in Which the 'Self' Is Born

> 'The origin of the ego in presumption and mourning.'
>
> *S. Freud*

In response to complaints from the populace about the presumption of the two friends Enkidu and Gilgamesh (two epic 'super-humans'), the gods sent a winged bull with

FIGURE 3. A group of 'egos' 6,000 years ago. They lived near Baghdad. Each one of them an 'island defending itself'.

a human head to the city of Uruk. An immense animal with special destructive power: the bull was capable of splitting open the ground so far that the spirits of the dead could emerge from the underworld and annihilate the living.[1] Hundreds of the city's youths fell into the abyss ripped open by the bull.

The hero Enkidu also fell into one of the cracks in the ground but leapt out again and grabbed the bull by the horns. Unless Enkidu and Gilgamesh put a swift end to the raging of the WINGED BULL, the people would no longer accept them as magnificent heroes (they were tiresome enough as tyrants). So Enkidu forced the bull to its knees and Gilgamesh plunged the dagger into its neck. They tore

1 *The Epic of Gilgamesh*, Tablet 6, ll. 96–100.

out the bull's heart and sacrificed it to Uruk's male protective god.

Enkidu mocked Ishtar, the goddess of Uruk. He tore a leg off the divine bull and threw it onto her lap. For the community of gods this was intolerable.

At the height of their fame, Gilgamesh and Enkidu marched triumphantly through the streets of Uruk lined with people. No one could oppose them, they boasted. Little did they know that the curse of Ishtar would begin to take effect that very night.

Enkidu died of a fever. Gilgamesh was disconsolate; he had his splendid hair cut off at his friend's deathbed. He cast off his royal jewels 'as if they were cursed'. His wild desire for battle, play and pleasure disappeared.

That is the hour in which the SELF is born. In the battle against the gods, whose true power cannot be assessed. It is not even adequately clear which of the gods deserve sacrifices. At the same time, the SELF is born from mourning a friend and the loss of ingenuousness.

FIGURE 4. 'The self'.

'None will ever see death
none will look death in the face
none will ever hear death's voice
and yet grim death
is the reaper of mankind.'

The First Seven Seconds

–In the first seven seconds after meeting someone, the woman determines what will happen next.

–Through glances? With her eyes?

–From within the eyes. It's impossible to say exactly what it is. A posture, a word. Some women are mistaken for being passive because they take control of the situation imperceptibly.

–There can't be many words in seven seconds.

–Unspoken words.

–From a position of defence?

–An attack is loud. In that sense, I couldn't imagine any intimate regulation of events coming from a man's broad frontal attack.

–Isn't that rather a generalization? After all, there are girly men.

–Not in this role.

–What's that supposed to mean? I've seen men who knew how to use 'feminine wiles'.

–I don't know where you saw that. I'm not familiar with it.

–Well, how could you know everything? We're talking about encounters with the opposite sex, right?

–Exclusively. And I'm saying that with these encounters, the first seven seconds decide what will happen next.

–Except when there's a use of force?

–I think it still applies then.

–With a random attack?

–Not in that case.

–You haven't experienced that yourself?

–One doesn't need to have experienced something if one knows it.

In the Magic of Haste

An international arrest warrant had been issued for a former US president because of his involvement in 'handing over a delinquent to a willing foreign power for torture'. The former president was in an aeroplane when Interpol agents tried to enforce the warrant in Athens. The well-known man was flown by his crew (all US reserve officers) to Sicily, and from there to Dublin. His lawyer, who was fighting for the president in an Irish court while the defendant was still sitting quasi-exterritorially in the secure custody of the aeroplane, fell in love with the assistant who was accompanying the senior politician. What moments those are, when two people send each other the first signals of attraction! It is a point outside of reality. There was no time to perform any acts of love during those exciting days. The fugitive president succeeded in escaping on a regular flight that took him back to the USA. The assistant accompanied him. The lawyer stayed to ensure the correct processing of the case in the Irish courts. Promises in the eyes of the two lovers that they would see each other again under victorious circumstances.

–Will you call me once you've landed?

–Yes, of course.

Later, once the dramatic rescue operation was over, it was impossible to reproduce the magic of haste, of COMPRESSED TIME, a form of parallel world of emotional appetence. Left alone, without the driving force of current events, the two of them sat in front of each other inattentively in a New York cafeteria and could hardly imagine any more the 'daring moment' of their parting and last eye contact in Dublin.

A Late Application of Immanuel Kant's Natural Law

In the mysterious time after the upheaval in the Soviet Union, the division into separate states by the 'bush robbers of Minsk', there were civil courts in Russia that considered themselves independent. Near Smolensk, a judge who had read some literature from Brussels applied 'international natural law'.

A woman had travelled there from the territory of the former GDR. She said she had been 'raped in 1945 with resulting childbirth'. She had brought the child, meanwhile a grown fellow, along with her. By that point she had traced the child's presumed father. The archives of the Red Army regiments that had been stationed in the environs of Berlin in May 1945 were open. Police authorities in Smolensk were helpful in exchange for bribes.

The judge decreed that the child's father, a widower, must take his victim, now 62 years old, into his home. While the deed had not brought about a marriage, it had established a situation of ownership with the woman and the begotten child. Ownership has its responsibilities. This was a new approach to the law.

The educated judge based his decision on a sentence from *The Metaphysics of Morals*, §25, by Immanuel Kant, on p. 389 of the collected works. It reads:

> 'But acquiring a member of a
> human being is at the same time
> acquiring the whole person'[2]

Why, asked the defendant's lawyer, was a member acquired during the incident? There was physical contact and an ejaculation. But the defendant had not taken possession of his victim's skin, limbs, private parts or bones. Every part of the body, responded the judge, and if necessary the sight of the plaintiff's shocked face, which had 'aroused' the defendant, was also a form of 'appropriation'. Members in the sense meant by Immanuel Kant, that resident of Kaliningrad, were not a narrowly defined concept. To that extent, the perpetrator of 1945 had acquired property. One cannot 'acquire members of a human being' and then make off. The consequence that a child was begotten was the natural law's indication of ownership, which in personal relationships cannot be documented by any contract or land registry. Here it was documented by the consequence instead.

---

2 Immanuel Kant, *The Metaphysics of Morals* (Mary J. Gregor ed. and trans.) (Cambridge: Cambridge University Press, 1996), p. 62.

But if the acquisition of the whole human being takes place by acquisition of a member, then this applies for all time.

When the festivities were held to celebrate the 'marriage', which the Russian pensioner did not consider outlandish, the judge was a guest. There was caviar, cucumbers, potatoes, pickled cabbage. The couple's place of residence was still undecided: either Zwickau or Smolensk. The unemployed Russian was not displeased that the assets of his 'late bride' and his son were enough for all parties. The 'bride' was a tax consultant in the west; only her sense of order, not an interest in profit, had sent her eastwards in search of the father. She considered it 'natural' for him to acknowledge his fatherhood. Much as the judge who followed 'international natural law' was following a sense of proportion that is specific to humans. Two years later he was dismissed. But still often invited to visit the happy crowd that had enthroned itself in Smolensk. Thus an act of wrongdoing in 1945 found a happy ending late on.

'For Anna Karenina'

1

'Several young men, ugly, impertinent, intrusive, but at once closely observing the impression they were making, drew closer'

What are the essential facts? The young men form a group. Each of them is entangled in establishing his 'value', that is, observing the impression he makes (intended: terror). They tried to establish this in the station district of a

German city with a woman, a person currently weakened in her individual will, a destroyed lover, a 'stray object'. As if a human being were a measuring instrument, or a kind of mirror. Only the latter is true of people; they are not devices, however. The group of men could not make this distinction precisely.

They were terrorists. They wanted to perceive themselves as 'chosen'. As beer-drenched as they were that night, that was practically out of the question. Nonetheless, they attempted to extort an 'impression of themselves'. And so, despite being warned by their foreknowledge of culpability and their consciences, their brazen hands grabbed the chubby lass they had chosen as the mirror of their souls. They dragged the girl to the backyard of one of the office blocks that belonged to the station district. The buildings seemed deserted now, at this late hour. The group of young men revelled in their victim's resistance. They enjoyed the reciprocity of their joint enterprise.

An elderly bookkeeper was leaving the office block at this time. He watched the scene for a brief moment and wanted to leave, to disappear into his section of the building. The association of perpetrators saw this as an attack; they seized the witness and smashed his body, leaving him lying in the backyard.

Now the young woman, multiply penetrated (she wanted to drag herself up and was searching for a gap through which to escape), was also doomed. She too was a witness. There was no telling if the joint crime had not already organized a trail of semen with a multi-faceted future inside of her. So much had happened.

The gang, having set off in the early evening to have a beer together after a hard week, with no intentions regarding the WHOLE COURSE OF EVENTS, made sure to leave no traces at the scene of the crime that would point to them. Then the group made their way through the station district to the bar Luxor. There they numbed themselves with Mexican alcoholic beverages, though without becoming too talkative–their consciences were still that much awake–and mentioning their preceding activities. It was difficult to keep this oath, which they had wordlessly sworn to one another, never to mention the event with a single breath. It was supposed to have 'never happened'. They wanted to stay loyal, and be hopeful.

This band of young men was a late successor to that other group of youths who had aggressively observed a lady, Anna Karenina, on the platform of a Russian train station some 140 years earlier. Tolstoy describes it in the last few paragraphs of his novel *Anna Karenina.* It is not out of the question that this band too, aware of their victim's diminished will to resist, would have boarded the train and committed an act of violence against the woman in the middle of the first-class section (without going through the proper ticket-buying procedure). They would have alighted at the rail junction in Volkhov, located in the middle of the swamps, and would have been able to catch the train travelling in the other direction to St Petersburg; they would have had to buy tickets at the station in Volkhov first, as the small numbers of travellers would have made it impossible to board the train unnoticed. But the train would already have been en route to Moscow by the time the gruesome deed was discovered by the train conductors, regardless of whether the victim had survived or been killed.

Assuming the beautiful woman, abused by the terror group, had not died, could the life of this desperate person been saved? By overtaking one cruelty with another? Through a sharper form of cruelty? Resurrection through cruelty: what is the indifference of the cavalry captain Vronsky, which made Anna Karenina doubt her own worth, compared to the reality of the terror-seeking group of young men? The description of the scene contains the words: 'closely watching the impression they were making'. People who feel thus observed *urgently* need to make themselves blind as mirrors.

2
Generosity

> 'My love grows evermore passionate and egotistical, while his grows weaker and weaker, and so we are separating.'

Once she was divorced from Karenin and her heart was now 'legitimately' in Vronsky's hands, Anna Karenina's behaviour became petty. Generosity would have been what she needed. She counted the glances Vronsky cast at other women, in fact other people in general, and then the days he spent without her. While he took pains to manage his country estate, she enumerated how he had been neglecting her in that time. It was difficult to tell how far the no longer infatuated man could endure this form of tyranny. And indeed, it was inevitable that the increasing wilfulness of this beautiful woman would widen the divide between them and thus, as described in the novel, lead to her death.

In a parallel novel, a verse epic, a similarly beautiful Russian woman was suffering because of the fickleness, in fact, the fundamental inability to commit, of the man she idolized. A long time passed. She chose another man, even though she did not feel the same signs of intense devotion to him as to her idol. Her body and her character (all the faithful hounds of her self-esteem) came to the fore. When it occurred to Onegin, the idol, that he actually desired this devoted young woman (he saw the memory of her before his mind's eye) more than anything else, and that it would perhaps be good for him to bring her home, and he met Tatyana–who had become a princess in the meantime–at a festive occasion in Moscow, she refrained from entering a new round in this hopeless game of love and inadequate capacity for devotion. Her self-confidence was sufficient for her to spurn him graciously; she explained why she no longer trusted his 'love'. Thus both sides had their share of bitterness. This self-confidence saved Tatyana's life.

–A person dies of a lack of love?

–Like a cold.

–Only slower?

–Sometimes faster.

–Though men like Karenin, Vronsky or Onegin are armoured. Do they simply refrain from giving themselves up so completely and make do with a modest dose, what one could call the mere notion or demonstration of love? The way certain plants develop spores that can withstand drought and cold for decades because they only live in rations, not truly.

—You believe in that kind of male virginity, and that it protects?

—At least some people think it has a use.

—And haven't they, like Karenin, practically died already, despite still being alive?

—Onegin and Vronsky get their ration of love by the grain.

—They're omnivores.

—Karenin is the only one who starves. If need be, Vronsky can fall back on the love of his fellow officers. Perhaps what he needs is really something different from love? He needs social contact. Maybe people need to feel a 'touch', not 'love'.

—You think Anna Karenina's demands of her lover Vronsky were dogmatic?

—Yes, terroristic.

—She had no means of terror at her disposal.

—Because she killed herself?

—Yes, she wasn't generous.

3
The Story of a 'Magnanimous' Love

The director Peter Konwitschny did not believe in the 'pathological tendency towards benevolence' attributed in Mozart's opera *La Clemenza di Tito* to said Roman emperor who had the temple in Jerusalem destroyed. He considers 'kindness' a characteristic 'mask of the Caesar'. It presents the illusion that the emperor can ruthlessly pardon any foe without endangering his own rule, thus demonstrating the harmlessness of the opposing public and robbing his enemy of more than his life: his identity. This is an illusion to the extent that a ruler can only ever feign such 'proof of his absolute power', but not offer it in reality. In fact, a number of emperors died precisely as a result of their pardoning practices. Caesar, for example.[3]

Mozart, Konwitschny continued, saw through the emperor's mask. That is why he relates it to a peculiarity: the emperor behaves privately. This drama is about the emperor's personal attachment to his friend Sesto. Both amorous partners have attempted to approach women. Sesto's efforts to serve Vitellia unreservedly (like a subject, devoid of his own will) are in fact meant to force him into the vicinity of the emperor–which is where Sesto is drawn anyway. And how could he come closer to his beloved than with the knife that opens the monarch's heart? The attack fails because the emperor himself is controlling it.

The results are equally pitiful when the emperor seeks to elevate the 'simple girl' Servilia to an empress. He abandons the plan immediately. He decides to place Vitellia, who he knows planned the attempt on his life and is the daughter of the toppled emperor Vitellius, on the throne as his wife. Those are attempts. They aim for something libidinously impossible and fail. Mozart, Konwitschny argues, marvelled at the fact that in the inner circle of power, there were such artificial attempts to make love win out even when it led to absurd deeds.

The whole time, Tito and Sesto beguile each other with the murder weapon in the roles of policeman and

---

3 The fate of Gorbachev also shows that the non-punishment of serious opponents punishes the merciful one.

assassin. For the executioner who wields the imperial sword is himself an instrument, a murder weapon. He only acts when the emperor commands it. The intimacy of the dialogue between the emperor and Sesto tells us that it is sadly impossible for the emperor and his assassin to behave personally, that is, privately, towards each other. There is no privacy in the centre of power. An elegy.

So that, a wishful fantasy of Mozart's from the eighteenth century that rulers too should participate in the new privacy spreading through society, and not some renunciation of urges by 'the robber baron Rome', is the subject of this 'drama with the comforting music'. A 'misapprehension of actual circumstances' fuels the conflicts and ultimately puts the emperor in the position of confidently pardoning those whose lives he has already destroyed.

4

The Deceased and I

I lost my 'secret sweetheart'. He collapsed around midnight in the town square of a South German city and died of a heart attack. Some passers-by managed to carry him to the hospital. He breathed for a few minutes thanks to the machines, then crossed over to Mount Parnassus.

I bid him farewell 'anonymously'. None of the mourners had an inkling of the feelings that we, the deceased and I, had carried within us year after year.

The widow sat one row in front of me, still a young woman. The child too. But I was the light he had prayed to. One cannot 'see' that kind of light.

Strict secrecy was part of our 'conspiracy of two souls'. Abstinence too. For I would have lost him if I had gone against his conservative views and his religion by practising sexual intercourse. What is physical contact compared to the intoxication of the soul! I think there have never been two souls that met each other as we met each other. I know that's just a claim. But I feel it strongly.

Days later I received a letter from the deceased. A final letter. It contained passages that would have exposed us if read by others. The postmark showed the hour of death: 12 a.m. He had put the letter in the letterbox in the town square, where he collapsed minutes later. By no longer having the letter on him, he saved our 'silent marriage'. What if this letter had fallen into the most foreign hands, from my perspective–those of his wife!

So he had still managed to post the letter, which I held in my hands and burnt shortly afterwards. Then he had died without further ado, beyond saving, in intensive care.

Will I see him again? Or will he reappear in Kazakhstan while I'm resurrected on a Caribbean island? The traffic connections between the two places are completely inadequate.

The Reckless Dog

'Once upon a time there was a faithful hussar.'[4]

He felt he was too good for just *one* life. He was a Wagnerian, a conductor. And he was prepared to faithfully keep a serious emotion, that of being in love, safe inside

4 'Der Treue Husar' [The Faithful Hussar] is best known today as a carnival song in Cologne but is originally based on a ninteenth-century folk song. [Trans.]

himself and to see it in another person. An abundance of mirrors; they reflect their light back to one another. Diving into the ocean or the calm see or such enchantment, which can last for up to three weeks–or, in a certain case, 'an entire year'. At every moment the prospect, the expectation of 'and much more'. Then the spell was usually broken. One of the two woke up as a land dweller. Far from the waters, the radiant shores.

That happened to him time and again.

–Your beloved goes by different names, but isn't it always the same one?

–The same basic tendency.

–And the same basic pathology? 'You can't be faithful, no, no, you can't be'?[5]

–It's a shame to leave out all the others for the sake of the one.

–And what if this kept repeating itself for ever: you'd be punished for your infidelity by having to repeat the same thing again and again?

–You mean for ever?

–Yes, terrible–unfaithful for ever.

–Alive forever? That'd be something!

–With the same indispensable ambition. Just for a taste of something new.

–In the name of the law.

---

5 A reference to Hans Otten's waltz song 'Du kannst nicht treu sein' [You Can't Be Faithful], which became a great hit in the 1930s. [Trans.]

–Do you know if your activities have produced any offspring?

–I can't say.

–Do you want to know?

–'Unconscious, supreme delight.'[6] I don't know if I want to know.

–And once again, eternal repetition wouldn't be a punishment?

–It'd be the only thing that *wouldn't* feel like a punishment. Erotically, there is no such thing as repetition.

–You read that in Nietzsche?

–I read a lot of things in Nietzsche. But he couldn't convince Richard Wagner.

Love—Dispensation from Work?

People come to me for advice when they have no idea how to sort out their lives. What interests me is the quality of my work. An appointment begins at eight in the morning, I counsel without interruptions (I listen first, that is). Often the session will end with my advice around midnight. I don't need much sleep, as I don't let the worries that are presented to me get under my skin. I am content with a few morsels of white bread dunked in tea, then in the late afternoon some raisin bread. Some clients and some young women who come for advice nip around the corner to buy a snack or refreshment. This way I never solve more than 365 crises per year. Holidays are alien to me.

---

6 From Act III of Richard Wagner's *Tristan and Isolde*; the original words are 'unbewusst, höchste Lust'. [Trans.]

Formerly Hildesheim, now Zurich, Bahnhofstrasse. My quarters consist of my counselling office, with a large table, and my bedroom, which also contains a water boiler. I can't travel any more, nor do I want to. I place my extensive body in my armchair in the morning and stay seated like that. I eat the tiniest amounts, yet seem to be expanding.

I'm an early bird; I work on my personal reports from four to five o'clock at night. In 30 years, I had the chance to give advice to 9,000 clients. My statistics show a success rate of 92 per cent. Accordingly, I have to turn down most of the requests that reach me via recommendations. I can't change the fact that the quality of my work demands one day per problem or person. I won't budge on that.

How life repeats itself! After 40 years of experience, I can point out the central errors within 5 minutes. The fact that I can endure the rest of the day, listening to the details, stems from my insistence on quality–not from delayed insight. The most difficult cases are based on errors about the nature of love. What can I demand when I love? You can see at once that this is the wrong question. It strikes me as a very resilient prejudice that love cannot endure any effort of the will, cannot tolerate any work. Those are deeply etched 'inscriptions'. A mother spoils four sons; she has conveyed to them that her love can replace all efforts. Now she is burdened with four emotional sluggards and finds it hard to love them. What advice can I give when it is too late for advice? You can see why I need a whole day of intense intimacy and counselling to find a way out. It turns out like this: 5 minutes of insight, 15 hours and 55 minutes looking for tracks.

He makes me work for him, he doesn't love me, says G., the wife of a pimp. After 16 hours of questioning, I'm in a position to tell her: I can assure you, that's exactly why he loves you, because you work. In the circus, one female client laments, there's no time for love. I didn't know that. I had thought that while the circus is travelling, that is to say during the transport phase, there would surely be time and opportunity for moments of affection. No, I now learn: that's precisely when the hubbub is at its greatest. It's impossible to find a quiet place anywhere. I find out how much detail work, how much attention with all the senses is focused on the other person during this artiste's trapeze acts, from the partner to her and from her to the partner. For over 16 years. She spent her youth with the partner. What could be more beautiful than such exchange? Is her profession her passion? Is her partner, to whom she is not married (but they have not spent a single day apart in years), a passionate artiste? I can only advise this client to continue this life. She has always done so anyway.

Work is attentiveness, changes in one's state. How is love any different? I'm rather like a woman translating from a foreign language, translating misunderstood and internalized words into one another. What do my clients pay (125 euros an hour), why do they recommend me so urgently? Where does the wisdom of my advice come from, when I never even went to university? Coming from the provincial town of Hildesheim, where all I learned was procuring on a local scale? It's the strength of my principles that makes me equally thorough in every consultation, even in cases that seem easy to disentangle. Even if I often think of other things, I then concentrate all the more on the client. I have only brought people together, that is, acted as a procuress, in two cases. I don't have to use my enormous collection of addresses, because the solutions to problems can't be found by creating new bonds. So now I put in order what I thought I was bringing together when I chose my profession.

Mignon

Born in a small northern Bavarian town, she had marched a mile ahead of her motives and desires, which hurried and grew after her. She presented herself as a rebellious, vital type of person, assembled from a hotchpotch of information and histories taken partly from her imagination and partly from her environment. She tried out intersex, drugs, exhaustion and adventures, as far as that was possible out in the sticks. Her zeal was a great obstacle. It was stress.

At the Frankfurt Book Fair, this bundle of excitement met one of the Great Men whom our republic has to offer. She changed her programme. The fact that he paid attention to her, who was like a show-woman of her own life—he was deeply impressed by her—touched her. She saw a purpose in returning his affection. For how many years did he have left, the Great Man?

She provided him with skin contact. Her arsenal of youthful boasts had the function of suggesting to him a kind of belonging, a third youth. How would he know what youth is today? Within a few days she got the apartment of a deceased composer in Venice into shape to serve as their abode. Venetian nights and days. Four weeks. She was soon pregnant.

The comedienne: now her body was getting serious. With a belly like a ball, she moved to the countryside with her celebrity. The excitement of a premature birth bound them together, the three of them a single person.

The ugly days: on telephones, at counselling sessions, at drinking bouts. She felt attacked by it but he showed no visible effects. The causes of the trouble were accusations in major papers that the Great Man had served the Stasi as an informal collaborator (IM). What secrets was he supposed to have revealed? Had he read them unpublished texts from his poetic reserves? What was Schweiger claimed to have said during meetings at various theatre cafeterias? She advised her man to tell the *Spiegel* editor everything, the way in Hanseatic cities one could one could confess to Roland, a cynical, unanswering stone (with the city councillors listening behind it) and be exempt from any punishment. The advice was right. Where did she get this wisdom? She had never encountered such a situation before.

The malicious rumours exhausted themselves. What was important was for the Great Man to continue writing, unperturbed: on the backs of beer mats, on loose sheets, napkins, hammering away at the typewriter at night.

A simple schema: he sought to protect his growing child, which remained one of the three of them, hungering for the young woman who placed him in a generation to which he certainly did not belong, in an unknown land. He benefited from what she had thought up and tried out at an early age, a virtual generation, a hybrid youth.

No causality between DELIGHT and DEATH. For two years, he waged war against the REBELLION OF HIS OWN

FLESH. She took up residence wherever he went to clinics for operations. He, convalescent, had more operations, waited. The gypsy child always in the vicinity, firmly holding their shared daughter.

She wanted to do it particularly well. Because the unexpected affections from a generation walking far ahead had surprised her. Even after he died, she went to see him in the storeroom of the clinic complex (she was a professional photographer) and captured the dead man on film. His was already a destroyed body. She could not read its features.

For many years, she did not understand that he had left her. She was meanwhile a grown woman, her soul matured.[7] But she could not find the time in which she belonged. The dreamt-up time of her early days, then the birth, spent on an island of love with the Great Man, of whom the child remained–neither was her time. Was the time she rushed through always faster than she was, unreal? To whom could she have displayed, at whose feet could she have laid, like a show-woman, the props, costumes and roles of her 'life'? There is no stage on which people stand to make an effort, and that was exactly what she wanted.

Negative Imperialism

It is not easy for a feminist to find the best answer at once amid the stress of the media. What I convey are attitudes.

---

7 She read in a periodical that every person in Central Europe decides on 'their goal' by the age of 35.

It's not about factual questions with four multiple choices each. The only really adequate answer is the one developed jointly by feminist women in dialogue and subjected to formulation. But this is not how we are asked questions in the shows.

So I think for a moment. The face is soothingly covered with powder; a mask places itself over the tense features. The warmth of the lights on the skin. As a Hindu, Gandhi strived for *moksha*: liberation from the cycle of life, death and rebirth. This is the topic of discussion. Accurate enough, because it's not worthwhile to criticize a religious error. But one can use it to show the total egocentricity of the male search for sexual asceticism. Did Gandhi ever ask the female partners whom he commanded to lie next to him at night in the service of chastity? Publicly and in the awareness of being seen? And then the criminal overestimation of semen itself. Why does ejaculation cause cowardice? Using the semen for any other purpose than procreation, according to this Hindu, was a godless waste of an elixir of life. Don't make me laugh! How much embrace, body heat, sweat, speech and answer, blood and ovula do we waste? I knew a Hindu feminist who carried a preserving jar with eggs with her. It festered like a fruit salad.

First it's the turn of the discussants on my right. To lay out the feminist position, we, the women, need the whole speaking time of this debate to ourselves, not the time for a fragmented interjection. It's about countering an entire false world.

After marrying at the customary age of 13 years, reports Gandhi, he took every available opportunity day and night to have intercourse with his wife of the same age, and thought about *it* in school and during every other activity. When he was keeping watch beside his dying father at the age of 16, one of his father's brothers took over for a while and, in 'obsessive sensual desire', he slept with his wife; in the meantime his father died.

This gave him a lifelong sense of guilt that he sought to preserve and expound in public. This was a sign of the Indian rebel's greatness, said one of the discussants. A silly overestimation of men's secretions, I respond, interrupting the speaker. A guilty conscience over an imagined guilt, that was a distraction. In the biography by Nirmal Kumar Bose, *MY DAYS WITH GANDHI*, one reads that Gandhi saw himself as the product of the marriage between an 'old lecher' and an 'inexperienced' 18-year-old. Then why did he love his father so much that missing the last gasp of the 'old lecher' left him with a lasting sense of guilt?

Men lie. They lie to themselves. The lies serve to mark their domain. Thus Gandhi thought he could prevent the partition of the Indian subcontinent through sexual abstinence, that is, something personal. A nocturnal, controlled ejaculation, he said, would foil the plan.

Brahmadaya, a staff member and resident at his ashram, reports that 'at the age of 66, in Bombay, he suffered an ejaculation in broad daylight at the sight of a woman, even though he was not thinking of such matters'. I had meanwhile taken up seven minutes with my interjection, in addition to the speaking time still to come, before the presenter managed to put an end to it. Let me emphasize that I am not concerned with debating how one should assess Gandhi, or how oppressively the Hindu religion deals with the senses and bodies of women. I am not at all concerned with India in the present moment. Rather, I am concerned with showing how men turn their sexuality as a whole, wrapped in cement bags (much the way the New York mafia encases corpses in cement and surrenders them to the Hudson), into a vehicle for seizing power. We need to work out how domains of this kind are not consolidated affirmatively through appropriation but, rather, negatively through renunciation, by prohibiting touches. I think I have found a secret of imperialism here, following on from a line in Rosa Luxemburg's diary from 1917. It reads: 'Negative imperialism, more frightful than positive. First robbery, then disposal. The latter leaves the terrain devastated.'

How many slaves are seized, taken onto ships and sold at auctions? And how many perish and are thrown into the sea? How many slave ships are abandoned once they risk discovery? Rotted, deserted by the slavers, the shackled inmates in the hull, stranded in swampy bays? Nothing is worse than an imperialist who abstains.

Violent Achievement of Willingness

In 1940, Oliver Petzold, a French citizen of Alsatian descent, founded a system in French Somaliland to provide brothels around the world with the highly valuable material of Amharic girls in flower. Preferably by capturing the offspring of nobles. First the young animals were given such a shock that they were prepared to do anything. Then bribed with 'kindness', allowing them to regain a piece of their own will. That was taming, so to speak. Into this vessel of a manipulated individuality, that is, one suited to the sale of the commodity, the PRAETOR, as Petzold made them call him, poured knowledge about erotic interaction and sensual-social intensification, with the aid of a number of women which his business had at its disposal for teaching purposes; thus, for a time, the brand 'fresh goods from Somalia' was the most profitable in the brothels of the East. This ACME (peak, sharpness, time of bloom) initially applied to Indian, Bengali, Thai, Vietnamese and Japanese brothels. Soon afterwards the goal was sexually supplying the gigantic armada and the USA's bases extending across the Pacific. The candidates had initially learnt French, and had to be retrained to communicate in English (at least at a rudimentary level), which was difficult without the organizing power of 'terror and kindness'. They did not prove willing to learn. Some of them had learnt Japanese, however, so they could also be used as agents.

The Schoolmistress and Her Prince

In many stories and fairy tales, it is a prince who takes a girl of low social class, a swineherd or a maid, and later makes her his queen. But love also knows another way. A Chinese schoolmistress from a rural commune near Suifenhe, on the Russian border, made the acquaintance of a Russian who often crossed the border for trafficking purposes, and they fell in love. She bore him two children over the years, but then the young father was killed on one of his border crossings. One of her sons died. She moved to Shanghai with the remaining son, to the safety of cities.

Schoolmistresses were not needed here. She fed herself and the child in the rapidly changing city, whose speedy reconstruction led to much valuable demolition material and disused technical devices being left in publicly accessible places, by sorting discarded goods into wood, glass, metal, household effects and technically usable machines, and guarding them in places that would only later become building sites. No one paid her for this sorting and guarding activity; but if the forgotten material was needed after all, she delivered it for money. This is how she earned the money for her son's education. One could say that she threw her beloved child over the fence between societies (the society of the expansive country and the society of the megacity), a boundary that separates people in China. Behind this fence, the assault run into the 'new time' begins.

The son is now a high-ranking functionary (a manager). She often walks past the tower block where he lives. Occasionally she brings him a parcel with supplies. Little presents, like in earlier times. She made a prince of her son. Now she can devote herself to her teaching job once again. In the border area directly adjoining Shanghai (provided the booming city does not swallow up this patch of ground soon). Teaching is still of use here. The high takings from her scrap-guarding and scrap-sorting service are no longer needed. Her prince, 'created by her', takes care of himself. And the demolition material is no longer around in the places where she could still find it two years ago. There, green areas surround a high-rise district that does not house people but, rather, provides services.

Faster Than Fate

A man, a slave or prince, threatened by a prophecy that predicts his demise and (worse for him) disaster for a woman he loves, can run faster across land and sea than fate can follow. This can be observed in CHEN KAIGE's film *The Promise.* This was the most expensive film ever produced in the People's Republic of China. Where does the ability to run so fast come from in this case? In one scene, the hero looks through a veil separating worlds into an earlier time. The 'people who came from the snow' (he, the observer, is one of these) were once rounded up and murdered by the archers of a tyrant, the DUKE OF THE NORTH. One sees them being carried off and shot. Their blood colours the snow. Through the visual wall separating the different realities, the hero follows the events but cannot help, as he is on the side of the future. But he owes the miracle of his fast feet to the earlier world from which he came. There is pain and longing in his joints. Protest drives a person's feet in a way that no doping doctor could ever achieve.

The party censors had a problem with this major film. It was a LITERARY FAIRY TALE. In China, there had never been a legend like the story of *The Promise* before. A single man, art-obsessed, a prize-winner at Cannes and thus impossible to dismiss in his projects, had conceived something individual.

–The censors of the People's Republic had problems with the work?

—Not only them, the economists and auditors too. The film was expensive.

—What was the problem for the ideologues, the censors?

—It didn't show anything forbidden. But it was difficult to make out any social relevance.

—Because one should only spend so much money on something socially relevant, something factual?

—That was what the economists and the ideologues argued about in the party and in the government bodies.

—It was too expensive for a fairy tale? The film is full of elan and cinematographic beauty. It has chances of being nominated for Best Foreign Film at the Oscars. That could enhance China's standing in the world.

—The criticisms of the ideologues also overlook the fact that Chen Kaige views his 'Chinese interpretation of the world' as a prophecy. He considers the stories realistic.

—For example, the starving girl at the start, whom a sorceress turns into a princess on the condition (or prediction) that she will always lose the man she loves? What's realistic about that?

—You mean, does it happen every day?

—It's a story that grips me. It transfers the story of the dwarf king Alberich, who renounces happiness in love for gold to a young woman. To the Old European mind, this is unusual.

—The story of Alberich the dwarf was unknown to the censors and ideologues.

—But actually, can't economic success ever be connected to happiness in love? That's an interpretation which seriously damages the words 'economic' or 'gold'.

—That itself is ideology. And Chen Kaige turns against that.

—You think he considered all of that?

—He's a trained Marxist.

—So what's he doing with all those stories about ghosts and magic?

—What are ghosts?

—Fateful predictions that gather into swarms.

—Meaning that one needs quick feet to escape them? That's what Chen Kaige means?

—He thinks that only the kind of films he makes can have any realistic character.

—And how did the censors help themselves? They couldn't simply ban the great artist's work.

—Only if they had formed a united front with the auditors and economists. But they were worlds apart from them.

—And how did they help themselves?

— 'There is always a way out.' They invented allegorical interpretations in the press releases and promotional brochures for the film *The Promise.* The 'general'—he loves the princess but doesn't get her; the hero of the film is his slave, later he kills him and thus frees himself and the beloved princess—this general means either Korea or Japan, the ideologues claimed. The princess, on the other hand, was either China or the Indian subcontinent. The 'people who came from the snow' could, as a METAPHORICAL PARABLE, be Korea. This is suggested by the fact that the part of the slave or prince from the tribe of those 'who came from the snow' is played by a Korean.

–Are these interpretations compelling?

–No. But they would suggest that one is dealing with the representation of a 'social relationship'. It is not that an artist had captivating, magical images and a cinematographically excellent sequence of scenes paid for by the state, an obsession, so to speak; rather, a brilliant member of Chinese society gives an expansive description of relationships between powers in greater East Asia from the perspective of the People's Republic.

–Such a view is bolder in a film than the Republic itself and its inhabitants could express by themselves? The ideologues and the economists were equally able to accept this perspective?

–The ideologues rejected the objections of the economists.

–What's realistic about that?

–You mean, the struggles among the party comrades or governmental representatives in the calculating and justifying departments are a construction, removed from the reality in China? That may be so, but what about Chen Kaige?

–You mean, can an aloof artist present himself as both a realist and a fortune-teller?

–Perhaps this work he set down 'with the blood of his heart' is genuinely something real.

–Let's take an example. A tyrannical ruler, accompanied by superior archers (as in Shakespeare's royal plays), known as the Duke of the North, threatens the legitimate king of a country. To save himself, the king agrees to sacrifice his daughter (the princess). Disguised as a 'foreign general', the slave ('he who came from the snow') sneaks up to the king and shoots him, then puts the princess on the back of his horse and escapes. In what sense is that unrealistic?

–It's not unrealistic at all if you think of the cities of Mesopotamia. Nomads besiege the city; to avoid destruction, the king hands his daughter over to them, resulting in an ambiguous ('unrealistic') relationship. The nomads thought that after the deaths of the king and the high priest, they could take over the city together with the princess. The civilized city and its government, on the other hand, assume that they have pacified the nomads with the forced marriage, the sacrifice of a single woman, and essentially made them vassals. In fact, what happens is this: subjugated by the nomads' leader, the woman teaches her children (thus governing the future of the nomadic tribe and the entitlement to the city) to follow contracts that have been made–but, in the subtext, to fight tyrants and strive eternally for autonomy.

–A marriage of two worlds.

–The birth of two worlds. Only the line of descendants is real.

–And you think Chen Kaige wanted to express something along those lines?

–So he claims.

–But he doesn't know Mesopotamia at all.

–How would you know what Chen Kaige knows?

Secret Love

'Fear in the blind wall
a gaze that looks for you.'

Nerval

The affection which the chief director of the national-political schools felt towards the boys that were entrusted to him (though this affection was concretely focused on one or two characters, not the crowd) was not visible on the outside, as he never physically approached any of the ADORED SPIRITS (he treated those whom he loved like all the other students); indeed, he would have recoiled in shock if one of the beloved had touched his body. Nor did he write a word about it in his diaries or in letters.

He brought some of the young companions who had gone through his hardening course to safety, arranging army positions for them in Greece. So that they wouldn't be shot in the cold on the Eastern Front, after he had selected them and refined them through physical and intellectual education.

Quite unlike himself, who could only nurture his inner libidinous fire in solitude (hermit and monk of his emotion), these noble youths could reproduce. They had no reservations about forming couples with women. He looked with satisfaction on what was alien to him.

Here, in a 'political garden', a tree nursery, a new, more resolute race was growing up, a clutch of SLAYERS as he imagined them: WHOSE CHILDREN'S CHILDREN WOULD BE IRRESISTIBLE IN THE WORLD. Though he had already observed 'softness' and 'good-naturedness' in some of his pupils when he caught them behaving spontaneously. He still intended to overcome that. Purity is the goal.

Then She Called Out: 'Homeland, Sweet Homeland, When Will I See You Again?'[8]

A Girl from Poznan

She had a sweet tooth. She enjoyed life. She was considered seducible, which she truly was not when awake. Rather, she was determined to save herself for a man who loved her with all his heart, who was capable of looking after her. In that sense, she was merry, but also calculating.

But one night, tired from all the dancing, she was no longer in control of her senses. A LIEUTENANT FROM THE GUARD surprised her in this state and 'stole her innocence'. He stole the core of her firm intentions, a piece of her self-confidence, a faith that her contacts with men would ultimately be successful.

'She wanted to tear herself apart
To walk into the deep water
But the river was frozen over
With no opening in sight.
Then she called out: "Homeland, sweet homeland!
When will we meet again?"'

Poland had been her homeland. Now it was the German Reich, because her clan had found work her. She

8 This story draws on the folk song 'Der Leutnant von der Garde', sometimes known by its first line 'Sie war ein Mädchen voller Güte' [She was a girl full of kindness]. [Trans.]

was glad to be here, but at once full of longing for home. What did she mean by 'homeland'?

The lieutenant from the guard appeared to the girl in a dream shortly after the deed. He comforted her in a cynical fashion: she should wait until the ice on the river showed cracks. Until then, she couldn't kill herself. And she wouldn't fit through narrow slits in the ice, not least because of the increase in her girth due to pregnancy. It would take a larger open stretch in the river to absorb her. The encounter with the lieutenant (whom she had barely made out that night, tired and weak from dancing) proved to be a phantasm. She had neither his address nor any notion of how to find him.

'Now all her happiness was lost
Now she returned home to the fatherland
And there she bore the child
Whose father she never knew.'

The home to which the young girl occasionally returned had meanwhile become the district capital. But there were enough relatives who had come here from the villages for someone to take her up. Two aunts, keen to look after the newborn. Neither of them had managed to get hold of a beau, whether a guard lieutenant or a workman. And so they adopted the 'Christ Child', which the young girl had brought into the world during the Advent season. No cause to drown herself.

The families were still commuting between the Rhineland and Poland. The child was admirable with its straight legs, which it had perhaps inherited from the lieutenant. It had integrated itself into the extended family. The young girl did not even have to relate how intoxicated she had been; robbed of her reason by liqueurs, known as 'petticoat stormers', when the guard lieutenant 'grabbed' her in 1912.

Even if he was an aristocrat, he was a cuckoo to her. She despised her impregnator. Although her aunts did their best to keep her away from the child, she still had so much influence on this 'sword of her will' that (after resettling in the Reich for good) he became a National Socialist, and formed a splinter group within the Rhineland-Westphalian NSDAP for the 'true implementation of the people's will of 1934'. In keeping with his mother's views, he asserted that one must TAKE REVENGE FOR ABUSE. The goal was not the 'night of the long knives', but rather 'the establishment of a new world'. Thus, after 1942, he followed the deviousness of the Prussian nobility (it was obvious that they had designs on the Führer's life) with eagle eyes. This son, like an Oedipus, would almost have stumbled on his unknown father, if the guard lieutenant who had once impregnated his mother had still been alive.

Hence the only object of retribution (who did indeed belong to the circle of conspirators against Hitler) was a cousin of that 'seducer', though the 'son of the impregnated woman' did not know him. By August 1944, after the assassination attempt, the progeny of that 'night of 1912' had already ceased to be a faithful Hitlerist. As a consistent National Socialist, his view after Stalingrad (and especially because no deeds followed Stalingrad) was that the German Reich was more corrupt 'than a guard lieutenant in 1912 could ever have been when least in control of himself'.

'Homeland, sweet homeland
When will we meet again?'

Behind Every Indignation There Is the Image of a Woman

In a lodging south of Algiers, commissioned and non-commissioned officers of the Foreign Legion, all of them Poles, prepared for the forceful landing in Paris. They had experienced Dien Bien Phu. They had been in action in the Sahara, where there had still been hope of preventing a spread of the national uprising. They held their beer glasses in front of their chests, standing at the bar in the mess tent. They sang:

'In a little Polish town
There once lived a girl
She was so beautiful!'

After becoming pregnant against her will, this girl had the decency to fasten stones to her body and drown herself in a lake in her home country. She chose this over dishonour, though it wouldn't have been dishonour if the gamblers singing here had been in the vicinity. They would have protected the girl from all insults. Anyone giving her so much as a dirty look would have been killed. And, if necessary, they would have known how to help her find a husband who wouldn't cheat on her, who feared and respected the comrades.

Honour of this kind wasn't to be expected in Paris. The changing governments of the citizens' republic viewed all world matters from a *practical* perspective. They would be in for a shock in the public bars and the Champs-Élysées when the men, waiting for the command, landed and took over the state. It was a miracle that General de Gaulle managed, at the last moment, to tame this wild band filled with martial vigour.

Illusion and Reality in Operetta

In 1943, the German occupation forces in Krakow, the capital of the General Government, allowed themselves a joke. The occasion was a gala performance of Karl Millöcker's operetta *The Beggar Student* for heavily wounded soldiers. The plot features a German colonel who, during the Saxon rule over Poland after 1697, makes erotic advances at a Polish noblewoman and is spurned with a slap in the face; thus shamed, he recruits a convict from one of the jails under his control, who passes himself off as a prince. The colonel pairs him off with the noblewoman to shame her in return. For its 1943 performance, this meagre intrigue was 'spiced up' in the light of current events. The local police commander made an authentic prisoner of limited vocal ability available for the occasion. Count Czatorski, the prisoner, who sang in an inadequate, that is, caricatured manner to the amusement of the heavily wounded audience, genuinely held the high rank claimed by his character in the libretto. The soprano, who recognized this, shuddered because of the proximity of the real events to the intrigue in the piece (conceived in an earlier century). She, who was playing a high Polish aristocrat desired by the commander of the occupation forces, and who would thus (in the operetta) have been entitled to a wish in exchange for relinquishing her innocence, was unable to save the borrowed prisoner from the real Krakow prison. She would have done anything, would have risked losing her voice; when the performance was over, she went to the German commanders' box, fell to the ground and begged for the count's life. The merry group of officers did not react.

Later on, those responsible were unable to explain to the inspector appointed by the high command, who appeared together with a head inspector from the SS security service, why this had been an amusing idea. The two considered the scene 'entirely inappropriate'.

It remained an eerie thing to have a condemned man appear in a musical comedy that served the purpose of amusement. In the difficult vocal passages he was pushed on stage by the guards, doing what he was supposed to while his part was sung by Polish singers from the side of the stage. The head inspector of the SS, a Flag Leader[9] and the representative of the general headquarters, a lieutenant-colonel, agreed that it would have been in keeping with the 'spirit of the operetta' to exempt the convict (making use of the twists in the operetta's dramaturgy) from the death penalty. Examination of his file revealed that he had

---

9 Nazi paramilitary organizations such as the SA and SS introduced various new ranks and titles. As these do not have established equivalents in English, the translator must choose whether to retain the originals for the sake of historical authenticity or to find adequate descriptions with no claim to absolute validity; the latter has been attempted here, consistently using capitals to distinguish the titles from ordinary descriptions. [Trans.]

not been charged with any capital crime, but that his death was part of the general policy of exterminating the Polish-Austrian nobility (for security reasons). One could not make a joke, said the SS Flag Leader, whose name was Dr Hans Rudolfs, and then kill someone with deadly seriousness.

After the conflict became known, some of the heavily wounded men who had been in the audience wrote petitions. They were highly decorated, bearers of the Knight's Cross. But even that was no use. For a moment, the world of the stage (the director's jocular idea) and reality came into such close contact that the plot could genuinely have led from the 'mustiness of the eighteenth century' to the 'National Socialist present'. That would have meant releasing the man–and even letting the count marry the soprano if he had so desired, and if she had been willing (which she was). There was no real reason not to do so, except for the sluggishness of the overall circumstances. Count Czatorski was shot three days after the premiere. Only 12 days later, the lieutenant-colonel and the SS Flag Leader obtained a certificate of exemption from the Reich Leader SS and the supreme command of the Wehrmacht authorizing them to release the prisoner. Flag Leader Rudolfs had convinced the Reich Leader SS by pointing out that according to traditional Germanic custom, a blunder by the executioner (that is, a missed blow to the neck) renders execution impossible. An analogy in the case of a 'misappropriation of the prisoner' struck the Reich Leader as plausible and he gave his consent. Consent by telephone in matters of life and death was excessively frequent at that time.

Death in Theatre and in Reality

'Noble freedom, O my life
How sullenly you walk along.'

Bajazzo

Time and again, the pretty SOPRANO who had come from the Magdeburg City Theatre tried to bring the events on the provincial stage in order, supported by the ensemble, which seemed appalled by the outbursts of the jealous BARITONE. His jealousy was justified. The audience had observed how the young beauty exchanged intimacies with a boy from the country, how she 'gave herself away'. That was terrible. One could see how the actor, to whom she had been unfaithful in real life, tried to 'pull himself together' in front of his young wife in this play, which in turn attempted to present a tragedy of jealousy in a humorous form, as a popular farce; but there was no possibility of self-control, no chance for him to integrate himself and 'play'. Every masking attempt failed.

The woman in the third row could see that, as she knew the problem from her private life, which she did not want dragged into the city theatre. She could have formulated the problem more succinctly: sitting here in the audience next to her cheated husband, she felt directly threatened. Even without music, she found what was presented on stage dangerous. Her own indiscretions had not yet been discovered. She considered her partner capable of 'sensing' something.

Accordingly, she was only happy again once she had survived the tragedy and was sitting with a large group at

The Sour Snout. The beers were flowing effortlessly. A circle of officers on leave for a few days. 'Shot by Thirst Tomorrow', they kept singing that. Even to them, without any personal connection to the plot, the tempo of the drama had seemed 'paralyzing'–on the one hand captivating through its diabolical consistency, and on the other hand thirst-inducing in its hopelessness. There were longer waits in war than at the theatre, but also very rapid, deadly events without any dallying; this affected the evening when the time was approaching twelve o'clock. The pealing of the bells of St Martin's Church, only a few steps from the pub, was gruesomely loud. They were a reminder that we do not have long to live: individual death comes considerably more quickly than the bells exhaust themselves. 'Cheers everyone!' called out the theatregoer who, less than two hours previously, had feared for her life when she thought of her husband sitting next to her. She was at pains to liven up the mood. It was extremely hard work.

A Sudden Transition of Power

The second wife of Emperor Severus, Julia Domna, came from the provinces. She insisted on having a political role.

She was unable to bring her sons Geta and Antonius, who was later known as Caracalla,[10] to work together after the death of Severus. She tried to separate the jealous brothers. Antioch and the east would be the domain of Geta, the west that of Caracalla.

---

10 After the cloak worn by Gaulish warriors, which he wore for reasons of fashion. The cloak was known as the *caracalla.*

Caracalla's plan to murder Geta at Saturnalia was foiled; his brother was protected by guards. Days later, the two of them (both unarmed and without guards, it was agreed) met at their mother's palace for a reconciliatory dialogue. But six centurions were secretly in position (which Caracalla later denied) and stabbed Geta. He fled, mortally wounded, into his mother's arms. She commanded the centurions to stop, but they added blows to the thrusts. The body of the young emperor, hanging on Julia Domna's neck. That was the turning point. Henceforth, the empress had to act a part; the power was in Caracalla's hands.

The Story of the Vengeful Medicine Man

It is known that R. W. Fassbinder punished a lover who had played a part in one of his films, and then left him, by having the negatives from the relevant two weeks of shooting, which were stored at the film laboratory, destroyed.

However, as in the fairy tale about the hunter who is meant to kill the king's child, but instead only exposes it, that is, entrusts it to a hind, because he cannot bring himself to kill the beautiful being (and brings home the heart of an animal as proof of the completed murder), the film-laboratory employee charged with this work of destruction did not actually eliminate the material but kept it in a cellar that he believed was dry enough to act as a storeroom for tins of negatives. He labelled the tins with an imaginative description. He later changed his profession and address, and is now untraceable.

–Did he do that because it's so hard to destroy 35 mm film material? It's barely flammable. One can't shred or cut it easily either. Was it sloth that saved the material?

–It's very difficult to destroy such film material. Time destroys it. So does the wrong storage. But it's not really there to be destroyed.

–Or did the photo-lab worker appreciate its value? Two weeks of Fassbinder! That's an element of film history. Perhaps, for example if Fassbinder later regrets his decision, reconciles with his lover and searches for the material, the lab worker could even get a finder's fee?

–It does have a value. Its market value as a fragment of a Fassbinder work would be immeasurable today. Perhaps not back then.

–And how was the material found?

–When its hiding place was cleared out.

–How do we know that it's Fassbinder material?

–The negative bears the date on which it was sent in. On the rush prints one can see Fassbinder directing for a moment–the cameraman had accidentally turned on the camera.

–What was known about the conflict with the actor, the man for whose sake the material was supposed to be destroyed?

–That hasn't been researched.

–What did the material show?

–It was an independent film within a film, grown to a length of 25 minutes. When shooting a film, Fassbinder would sometimes start shooting a new one if he felt like it.

—Out of calculation?

—That's exactly why. The second film was paid for using the cost calculation of the first.

This movie had the following plot: an Indian medicine man has the head of a white man murdered in 1944 put on him. This medicine man takes revenge on one of the British families whose ancestors once exterminated his tribe. The end of the story and the dramaturgical connections could not be ascertained from the fragment.

—Would Fassbinder have connected the parts with a commentary?

—Nobody knows. But the material wasn't set up so that everything would be illustrated. For example, one doesn't see the head of the white man being surgically attached to the medicine man. One only sees a photo of the process in the protagonist's hand.

—The medicine man is the protagonist?

—No, a member of the family on which the medicine man is taking revenge.

—What happens to the material?

—It belongs to the finder. He hasn't taken possession of it so far.

—And who was the finder?

—A building contractor who had been hired to clear out the storerooms.

—Why hasn't he decided what to do with his find?

–It's not clear whether he or the student helping him is the actual finder.

–Is there a dispute?

–No. But the contractor and the student assistant were evidently seeing each other. Now the affair is supposed to be kept quiet, which is preventing everyone from resolving the question of who the finder is, and who is allowed to take the material.

–That's similar to how it was before that with Fassbinder. There seems to be a curse on this story.

–Well, it has a strange plot too.

The Cinema Programme for December 1917 in St Petersburg and Moscow

In the two capital cities of Russia, as in the district capitals, the melodramas of previous years were shown without paying particular attention to the revolution outside. The populace showed considerable affection for these programmes. In a colourful mix of classes, they sat in seats arranged in different price categories. These buyable differences of rank were abolished on 17 December 1917. An attempt to intervene in the programme itself in the same month would have toppled the young revolution.

At the CAPITOL, *The Waves Swallowed the Secret* had been showing since September. In December it was followed by *The King of Paris.*

–*A Life for a Life* at the METROPOL?

–With Vera Kholodnaya. A magnificent film.

FIGURE 5. Vera Kholodnaya (1893–1919), the queen of melodrama.

—What's it about?

—As the subtitle says: *A Drop of Blood for Every Tear.* The mother tells her son-in-law: 'Don't make my daughter unhappy. You will pay for every tear she cries with a drop of blood.

—Will she demand the blood herself?

—She is a millionaire's widow, a modern woman. She loves her daughter Musya. She has brought up a foster daughter, Nada, played by Vera Kholodnaya. Both girls fall in love with the same young man, an impoverished prince. He falls in love with the foster daughter. But when he realizes that she won't inherit anything, he instead chooses the Musya, daughter, whom he doesn't love. The mother, having recognized this, speaks of the drop of blood at that particular moment.

—Is he unfaithful to the young woman, Musya, with Nada?

—Constantly. He also bets on the horses. Spends his wife's money. Fakes a bill of exchange with the signature of his banker friend, who married Nada.

—Now the mother comes on the scene.

—She hands him the revolver; he must kill himself as a man of honour. But he has no intention of doing so.

—She shoots him?

—If nobody is going to uphold honour, what choice does the mother have but to shoot? The film went through all the cinemas of Europe.

—And *Martyred Souls* at the ARCADES CINEMA? Also with Vera Kholodnaya?

—An engineer loves a married woman (Kholodnaya). While hunting, this engineer accidentally shoots dead his godfather, who, unbeknownst to him, is also his biological father and has bequeathed his entire fortune to him. The jealous husband denounces the engineer in court. He claims it was deliberate, not a hunting accident.

—And now the woman steps in for her lover?

—She publicly declares that he is her lover, and that her husband has accused him in court purely to destroy him. Her reputation and life are destroyed, her lover saved.

—Those are the *Martyred Souls*?

—They are indeed.

On Madame Kollontai's recommendation, Jonas A. Zalkind goes to see the movie melodrama *The Fiancé* at the MAXIM. A merchant's daughter called Natasha loses her way in the forest and stumbles on a robbers' drinking hole.

An orgy is in progress there. In the course of events, the bandit chief's mistress is murdered. When the drunken brigands go to sleep, the merchant's daughter pulls a ring off the dead woman's finger. She finds her way back to her parents in the city. One day a handsome young man appears, rich and wasteful. The merchant's daughter recognizes him as the bandit chief; he had barely noticed her the last time. Enchanted by her beauty, he sends wooers to her parents.

A marriage contract is drawn up at once. According to traditional custom ('one field marries another, one fortune the next'), the merchant's daughter would have to obey. But she will not marry a murderer. No, SHE AVENGES THE MURDERED MISTRESS OF THE BANDIT CHIEF OF HER OWN ACCORD. She produces the ring (during the marriage feast) and announces who her husband really is. The man is arrested and killed.

ZALKIND: What was the reason, comrade, that you sent me to watch this melodrama?

KOLLONTAI: That the young woman defends herself—not for her own sake but for the INNOCENT DECEASED.

A Case of Class Struggle Within the GDR

She came from the village of Klein-Quenstedt, north of the Harz Mountains. Before the Second World War, she married Fritz Lehmann, a railway worker with a permanent post at the railway repair workshop H. Later he joined the Western Border Patrol in the Saarland, then he was conscripted to the 12th Infantry Regiment, which fell in Stalingrad. She had two children from this marriage. Her mother looked after these children when she had to work. Even before the 12th Infantry Regiment met its demise, except for 17 men, Corporal Lehmann died of pneumonia while on leave in Klein-Quenstedt.

With a calm spirit, equipped with much misfortune, Lisbeth–that was the name of the woman from Klein-Quenstedt–joins the canteen staff at the airport in H., which is used by the Russians and was once a renowned base for the German Air Force. The buildings are still the same. She meets her future boss on the way from this workplace to the station. He employs her as a housekeeper. For three weeks she is a mistress, and useful after that.

The children of this boss take to her with enthusiasm. She is undoubtedly indispensable to him, even if this man is fickle with regard to erotic preferences. At least he does not make any promises of status based on his urges. Because of his prejudices, the man is indifferent to women and class-conscious. Like many bourgeois characters, however, he is many other things too. Some afternoons, for example, he is devoted. When he is drunk, he can be very relaxed.

She has the idea that something favourable could result from this unplanned, unchosen 'position' of hers if, for example, she could bring together her two children and her boss', who are roughly the same age and will soon be sexually mature. A family association could be formed above the level on which she and her boss stand; that would turn the erotic connection, which the boss appreciates from case to case, from a private fact to a social one.

After all, it is not as if her boss' prejudices constant the prevailing doctrine in the country.

The boss promises something, then he promises nothing. She performs her duties. She tolerates no insults. She decides to complete a two-year course in midwifery advertised in the district capital. Her boss is a doctor. As a midwife, she could work together with her boss in his function as a doctor. Then the connection between the children, the reality of their coexistence and the functions of their occupations would be linked–what obstacles to an equal footing would remain?

Her suggestion of a two-year leave of absence for training purposes incenses her boss, who rages inwardly. As if the power of a 'bourgeois collective worker' had taken effect inside him (more strongly than in Othello, Rigoletto, Alfredo or William Tell), he puts her in her place. In so doing, he removes the trust which, in defiance of all practical experience, had grown within her during the years in which she had lived with him according to class. This trust would be a capital. Blind to class, he is incapable of seeing it. Because she is still not irrevocably disappointed in him, she takes it with her to the midwifery academy in Magdeburg. But he, left alone (he did not realize that his inner powers had already become rooted in this other person; now these roots seem to have been cut off), falls ill. Suspicion of hepatitis A or B. Under the centralized conditions of the GDR, where anything can be ascertained in Berlin or Magdeburg but almost nothing in H., it is impossible to tell which it is. His medical practice closes. The child looking after him, 14 years old, believes she will soon be abandoned by this father; a divorce 10 years previously had already cost her her mother. If this daughter does not believe in his recovery, he will be unable to recover. She would rather die than lose him. It is winter. She sits down on the balcony and undresses her upper body; let pneumonia put an end to her suffering. Healthy nature does not become ill.

The blind faith in a Western medication obtained by a doctor friend helps the class warrior to his feet. Gradually, with exquisite nutrition by the spoonful, the skeleton regains body mass. The mistress, still training, knows nothing of the crisis. Spurred on, even vindicated, she would have taken the 50-kilometre train journey back and looked after him by cooking soups, placing her hands on him, giving him comfort. No; he had forbidden his daughter, whose heart tended towards her class enemy, to speak a word about it. She had been won over through warm-heartedness.

Now, returned after all her examinations, she found that the earlier sides could no longer be restored. The recovered 'hero' fended off temptation with mockery. The parvenu, who still had feelings for him, offered herself with 'restraint'. If only it had been possible for her boss' sympathies, which had long grown within him, to clear the fence of prejudices, as one says of show-jumping jockeys—throw his heart over first, then leap after it (with the self as the rider). This was not in keeping with the individual situations in which they met again. She sat in her place, ready to jump, while he, split into two people, was ready to jump and greatly inhibited.

–Do you want to stay for dinner? Nothing special.

–If you like.

She came for a visit. He had laid the table. But the dinner was not the setting for a decisive expressive leap of the kind that becomes possible in some scenes at the theatre. The boss' daughter tried to bring them together. The duration of the meal was limited. Barbed remarks that had built up inside him (and were potentially the prime weapons of his class status, meaning they rested on a lifetime of armament) required a larger span of time. There was a remainder of affection within her, hidden beneath a layer of insults; bringing herself to have a suitable conversation while their mouths chomped away would demand further time. Meanwhile, it was time to watch the western news together.

–In Richard Strauss' *Der Rosenkavalier*, a young count marries a commoner without any problems. Under the premises of the GDR, surely a relationship between a proletarian and a bourgeois person would be possible.

–The GDR supported it; the midwifery course is free. There is a considerable social gap between an untrained woman from Klein-Quenstedt and an established doctor in H., but a midwife has the same standing as an ageing doctor. He's not what he used to be.

–Why can't the parties see that themselves?

–That's just what they call the class barrier.

–A barrier of prejudices?

–Prejudices as hard as concrete.

–None of the GDR's efforts can help in the face of such a barrier?

–Nothing can help, except forcing them.

–But the world which the boss' prejudices came from had undoubtedly ceased to exist by that time.

–No. Like others, this boss didn't believe in any other society than the GDR.

–To which he had completely conformed?

–Yes, as a doctor and a bourgeois.

–Not as a man?

–No. As a man he was class-conscious.

–But with a masculinity that's especially fragile among doctors with their delicate, even feminine hands.

–You're quite right. And he was never sure if he should have desired men instead. But it was dictated by custom, class status, that a man should go after women.

–Class prejudice, like a virus, concentrates on fragile conditions?

–Evidently. To the detriment of our 'hero'.

–You mean he's a bourgeois who lost his capital?

–Several times.

–Something about the class instinct is incapable of recognizing what has value?

–As strange as it sounds, that's the damage which class consciousness rests upon.

–If one had mentioned class consciousness to this boss, what would he have replied?

–He would have denied it.

–Is class consciousness subconscious?

–Strictly separated from the subconscious, it's unconscious.

–And the subconscious itself?

–Is classless.

–So it would be a possible arbitrator between the parties in this association through destiny, or, rather, 'failed destiny'?

–It could have been. It would have had the power for it. Often, when each of them was alone, they swore their love to the other. When they were together, they were lost for words.

A Flying Visit to Davos

Zalkind was carrying bundles of roubles in large denominations. He had the assignment to deliver them to a sanatorium in Davos where three comrades lay. He spent the night in a maid's chamber and, handsome as he was, made conquests for the night. The next morning he set off on his return journey, crossing the Rhine to East Prussia and from there to Petrograd.

The delivery of the bag with the rouble notes had been registered by the management at the sanatorium (and once again by the three comrades who received the gift). A sentence had been added to the receipt: 'The revolution has not yet forgotten the people.'

During the First World War, the only connection for lung-diseased Russians in the sanatoria of Davos to their homeland was along the Astrakhan–Tehran–Aden–Suez–Italy–Little St Bernard Pass route. But money transfers worked directly via wireless telegraph. During the provisional government, the sick were virtually forgotten. The young commissar's assignment came from the short-term memory which the revolutionary government had for a few months. This conscientiousness disappeared after the move to Moscow.

For a while, a member of the ancillary staff at the sanatorium in Davos still remembered the visitor.

'Two blue eyes
A muddled mind–'

A Strong Motive

His head had been shot apart in Flanders. The surgeons at the field hospital had patched him together because he was the son of a famous anatomist, the author of the textbook which the army doctors had used in their training. Upon learning his name, they placed a piece of metal on his exposed cerebral membrane, his face was pieced together and a face mask was sewn on so that he would still resemble a human being. Later, many people took him for a madman simply because of his appearance. Any other officer in that state would not have been cut into shape. The result looked alarming.

The wounded man had just joined a radical leftist group in December 1918. He had done so in the belief that one had to 'prevent something even worse'. Because the world war, he claimed, would inevitably be followed by a world civil war, a war of all against all.

He actually had many other reasons to join this group, to participate in their struggle (errands, joint reading, shared meals, secret contact, collecting weapons, setting up arms caches, etc.).

He sought the company of his comrade Harry Egenwolf, who had recruited him for the group. He would have followed this comrade anywhere. With his special appearance, he could not hope to appeal to this friend as a lover. And so, from a greater distance, he wanted to be close to him as a comrade and participant in the revolutionary movement that was taking hold of the century.

—Is L.'s motivation sufficient? Is it enough to love someone (hopelessly) and have a good reason for hating war? Is there is a key to what kind of revolutionary motivation is enough?

—*One* motive is enough. Further ones aren't a hindrance.

—And if someone wants to do business, let's say because he's an arms dealer; he joins the revolutionary group, proves especially useful and practical at work, but his motive is that of a black marketeer. He constitutes a catalyst in the group. Other groups envy this group because of his achievement. But his motive is born of entrepreneurial spirit. He's not guided by hate for the class enemy or compassion for the oppressed. He has a strong, useable motive but not a good one—is that enough?

—I suppose the group wasn't in a position to choose. Practically speaking, he was useful.

–And does it harm the revolutionary movement if his motivation does not stand up to a revolutionary test?

–Well, he was later shot as a counter-revolutionary.

–After that the group was poorer than before?

–It had became poorer.

–To return to the hopeless lover, the one with the shot-up face: some thought he was mad, some saw that he was in love. Nobody knew if they could demand anything of him. But what should they do with him?

–He was one of the most faithful of the faithful. What more can one ask?

–But he failed every cadre selection. None of the examiners trusted him.

–But there shouldn't have been any examiners. There were none while the revolution continued.

–And when the revolution collapsed, there was no use forming cadres anyway?

–No. Now L. wasn't needed any more either.

–Was it about the social revolution in December 1918? Oder was it about an anti-war movement?

–An anti-war movement. And that, the group believed, was why the social revolution had to happen. What better reason to oppose war than L.'s shot-up head?

–And his love? Didn't it bias him? One has to carry out the revolution for the sake of the revolution, not to appeal to one's beloved.

–But what better motivation could you find for L.? As awful as he looked, there was no hope of putting his infatuation into practice; he devoted all his power to the struggle. What more do you want?

The Siamese Hands

The doctors in this Spanish district hospital, despite lacking any legal training, had voiced reservations. They did not dare to take their scalpels to the bodily integrity of the couple brought in by the police. They kept them in one of the patient's rooms and demanded that the police officers obtain a chemical solvent capable of separating the two people's hands, which were glued together.

—So they had joined their bodies at the instigation of the man arrested in Cádiz, using glue smuggled into prison by his girlfriend?

—A glue for car bodies. The palms were stuck tight, his right to her left.

—No amount of pulling would help?

—People were constantly pulling at them.

—That ruled out returning the man, who was in detention pending extradition, from the visitor's room to his cell? The woman would also have been taken there?

—And that would have been UNLAWFUL DETENTION IN OFFICE.

—And if the doctors had cut through the mass of glue with their knives?

—They would have had to cut into the skin. That would have been assault.

—And what about driving the two of them to the airport immediately and putting them on a plane?

—Not without the woman's consent. There was no extradition request for her. It would have been kidnapping.

—The actual gluing of the hands and bringing the glue to the prison, was that an offence?

—That wasn't punishable.

—Aiding and abetting the freeing of prisoners?

—She didn't free her lover. At least, not by joining their hands firmly, more strongly than any wedding ring. This state of affairs is unknown to the law.

—It could be a form of assault if she 'tied him to her' in this manner.

—You mean, is it damage to property? It would be punishable if it were a vase but not with a person's body part.

—But she did make his hand functional?

—With his consent.

It was not entirely clear from the file why the young man had been arrested in Cádiz. Pimping, human trafficking, smuggling. Supposedly he is also wanted for manslaughter. Crossing the border to Gibraltar. Was the woman whose hand he was stuck to besotted with him? Was she his creature, his 'hooker'?

—Did they find a chemical solvent that could separate the hands?

—Not in Spain. The glue for car bodies was a type sold in the Ukraine. Nothing came from there.

—In the meantime, a press conference with the couple.

—The district hospital's management had no experience of how to prevent a press conference.

Headlines came to mind: 'Hand in Hand', 'Inseparably Joined', 'How Leonore (the young girl's name) Finally Got Engaged' or 'Instead of Rings'. A detective arrived from Germany. He was supposed to justify the extradition request in person. Meanwhile, the couple's popularity ('Siamese hands') was growing. It seemed as if the Spanish side wanted to release them.

—What were the doctors supposed to do? How would they continue to accommodate the couple? The hospital didn't have any double beds.

—They belonged in prison.

—Only one part of them.

—Do you think she did it out of love or calculation?

It's impossible to say, replied Detective Superintendent Dr Schlensag. The two stayed together, at any rate. Taken to Germany, 'the bond of their hands' freed from the glue, they proved inseparable. There was a connection between them that could not be explained by glue.

Two years later they were arrested again in Frankfurt. They were legally convicted for numerous joint offences. Even imprisonment could not separate the two. The judicial authorities could not handle the couple.

A Friendly Story

'You'll only find that once
It'll never come again
It's too good
To be true.'

The song was playing during the world fair in Hanover. The exhibition wasn't making enough money. But he, Eduard Schwenke, could not escape from success in his management in a major north-west German city. Bypassing the usual jurisdiction, staff were turning directly to him, asking their boss for advice. He, on the other hand, in the most experienced period of his life, was able to delegate. Often he sat at leisure for a quarter of an hour, dozing successfully in front of the unused telephone. So much power is rare.

He fell in love with Vera, a young woman working in the bookkeeping department, who had been hired on her second career path. She wanted to make something of her life. No one in the firm was supposed to know that the boss was having a liaison with a young employee (she had narrowly escaped minority). The secrecy intensified their happiness. The hiding places they found contributed to that feeling. When a child came, there was no longer much they could hide.

Then a dispute with the woman who owned his company. Uproar among the staff. Betrayed by people he had trusted. Holding on to the victorious feeling of the last two years, he gave up his position. He would still make something of himself. He felt strong with his young wife and new child.

The couple moved out to the country. Years later, when their beloved child had grown, it was back to the city. In the fervour of that joyful year, his last before he became a 'consultant', he had gone somewhat too far for his age in the assessment of his powers. He liked to read a book in the evening, went to bed early, got up early, he loved quiet hours in front of the fireplace. There was nothing in this daily routine that might have entertained or even occupied the young woman, who still showed him all the love she had in her. The inventive man had been WEAKENED BY AGE. At that point he gave himself another six years. He invested time and energy in looking after his child and wife.

Then six years became nine, and the prospect of further years seemed to have improved. He was tough. A mentally powerful old man. But it also transpired that even when they first met, Vera, who stayed very close to her child when abandoned by the waking body of her husband (though not his affection), had quite different interests from those that occupied his generation. She had grown up with different goals, in a different time. The popular songs in their respective ears were different ones.

So now he stood there like an impostor. There was a way out: to pass himself off as something other than what he was. But his supply of openness when he was tired and his supply of contemporary interest could not be hidden, not from the person closest to him, who shared every space with him daily, the bathroom too. Less and less often he found pretexts to go to some 'important session' or 'meeting'. This would have kept something secret: that he was different when he was away or at home. No, anyone could see that he had gone bankrupt for reasons of age.

In the forms of his youth, that is, the style of the war or of the dangerous years of Germany's reconstruction, his alert spirit (though it had quickly become exhaustible) might have produced some ideas about what to do in this marriage as a couple, and with their beloved child. But where, for example, was there a bar in that yellow Viennese light (snowing outside), filled with quiet sounds spreading atmosphere? He had his doubts whether Vera would even have liked such a 'hideout for two'. A visit 'to the common people' at a station restaurant at New Year's? To real life? When he tried that, the station bistro turned out to be a room full of vending machines from which one could pull out food, the same one finds standing at any petrol station. Having set out for an adventure, the three of them quickly found themselves at home again.

He *had to* do something to free his beloved child and his admired wife (and, as he very well knew, once 'ardently loved' and now his 'closest confidant', 'the person for whom he would sacrifice everything'). He owed them that. In his aged existence, after all, he was empathetically enclosed by the two of them. Like a ball and chain shackled to a dangerous criminal's foot, he was preventing the two who loved him from escaping on their own strength. He sought advice.

At any rate, he thought, the child, which had now grown up and was looking for partners, should not be held up by having to take his place with the young mother.

One option was to let Vera go her own way. Twice she met with a possible alternative partner, a younger one. That proved complicated, because Vera was unwilling to accept such 'happiness' under his supervision or with his involvement. She didn't even try it. Right after he had assured her that he knew this younger man: he would be the last to destroy the triangle of such a relationship with aggression. His attempt was clumsy. Actually, Vera resented his suggestion. Her own character prevented her from working on such a way out, which they, in the jargon of their marital discussions, had called 'French marriage'. And he would have forbidden it if it came to that. Torn apart by jealousy, he would have started fighting for solo power, and in this case, precisely because of his weakness, he would have been victorious.

So the only remaining option was for him to die, thus clearing the way for those whom he wanted to care for honestly. He was decisive. He knew doctors whom he could ask for effective help. But it had to happen in secret, otherwise these beloved beings would have been enslaved even more strongly by a guilty conscience than by the 'bullet in the leg' which he represented while alive.

So it was a stroke of luck that, during a snow-filled month of March, a bout of purulent bronchitis carried him off within a mere two weeks. Raging fever. Everything possible was done to help him. In the end, he did not die from the infected, phlegmy vessels of the lungs but, rather, because his heart failed. All right, he thought. He observed his active decline with benevolence. It solved a problem that he, an experienced manager after all (not only of his businesses but also of his life thus far), had created himself in the exuberance of his most successful year.

FIGURE 6. Republican wedding at the 'Altar of the Fatherland' (1792).

To What Extent Is Love a Republican Virtue?

In the time when Königsberg was occupied by the tsarina's army (for seven years), effusive Russian officers with a philosophical orientation often visited Immanuel Kant. One Saturday the question came up: Can love (*l'amour*) stand alongside the powers of the mind, which join to form the cognitive capacity, in supplying the laws for life? Then the motivation would be the strongest imaginable. The tools of reason bestowed upon the human race by nature would then not only have an observing and judging but also a DYNAMIC effect.

The young officers, personally in love and projecting their subjective experiences onto the totality of the world, talked themselves into a state of great enthusiasm. 'Always act in such a way that your desire could be the measure for a universal legislation!' What energetic ideas pour from the swelling hearts in this 'matter' (or, rather, in such an Arcadia of subjects). For an amorous relationship, claimed the young captains and majors, usually feeds off the reflection of the other: I see that you love me and consequently I love you all the more!

This was a challenge for the philosopher. He would have preferred simpler examples from sensory experience. Thus 'finding one's orientation in thought' first of all means determining the points of the compass at sunrise (at night too, the rising of the stars provides information about the direction of the horizons). At the same time, however, the 'perceiving subject' knows which of its two hands is the right or the left. A person knows this through sensory experience, but also because the hands and the points of the compass orient themselves by each other. If I see the sun rise in the east, the right and left hands have their certain place. It is a matter of *ensuring* the cognitive allocation between subject and object.

There was no guarantee of such a thing in matters of love. Rather, the philosopher began his response, love, as the MOST OVERBEARING COMPONENT POWER OF THE CAPACITY FOR DESIRE, tends to make itself the highest precept. By no means does reason do that; rather, it acts as an arbiter between the different powers of the mind, the concert of the feelings–the conductor, so to speak, and certainly not the trumpet.

'But you cannot, Herr Professor, compare the most delicate and quite emotion, that of incipient infatuation, with a trumpet. Experience does not confirm that love, in its beginnings, immediately drowns out everything else.'

'That has not been my experience,' interjected Captain von Löwe-Danilow. 'Love strikes like a lightning bolt, usually between strangers who do not understand each other, as we read in French novels. Like Phaeton's sun chariot which crashes. Arcadia lies scorched and the nymph Callisto wanders about thirsting for water. Thus she falls prey to Jupiter who provides water. An awful story. I know of no undergrowth more impenetrable than the world of love.'

Immanuel Kant expected fun and good cheer from an evening gathering; this time of day struck him as inappropriate for the pursuit of knowledge but highly rewarding for so-called 'games of the mind'. For a person cannot be disabused of the enjoyment of letting their thoughts and words wander, without any direct need to acquire knowledge, much like the sounds in 'musical games' or the rapid flashes of coincidence in 'games of chance'. Here we have an echoing world of cognitive capacities; by no means does the enjoyment of conversation, of unforced evening exchanges, stem from an animal nature. The philosopher had just been arguing about this in his correspondence with Johann Gleim, who—entirely on the contrary—called *animals* 'chatty and sociable', that is, 'music-playing and gambling creatures'.

'Goodwill,' the philosopher explained, 'has a repellent power in matters of love. Goodwill in love excludes all third persons from sharing in the mental powers of the lovers and is concentrated on the one person who is meant to respond to such one-sided amorous desire: an excess of affection to which the beloved other cannot by any stretch of the imagination yield, as it would at least have to resist it with its own expression (the autonomy) of their amorous capacity, and thus first expound to the other how the grammar on both sides of the "unspeakable", this relationship intensified with much ecstasy and intuitive capacity, should be understood.'

The officers found this response dry. They immediately began recounting matters of love again; one example followed another in quick succession. If it were impossible for them to follow their inclinations, they would rather dispense with philosophy than with the interesting topic to which they held on so intently. Kant, a polite host, did not insist on clarifying, on untangling the different concepts. He was content if no one expected to be granted their happiness in love by supernatural powers, from 'the space of the supernatural, filled with thick fog'. Let them seek well-being or create mischief in worldly practices. He found the view that a single power of the mind should rule over all the others, just as the affection of one particular god in the Greek pantheon had caused the undoing of Troy, dogmatic. What ghastly presumption to say, 'through this temporary surge within me (unguided by stars or laws) I determine that I *love* this one other (or perhaps only one leg, their beautiful hair, one of two radiant eyes, some madly adore feet) whom I have met by chance; but I firmly reject all possible others beside this one. Such a judgement, Kant argued that evening, could only produce misfortune. He considered it worse than the religious misjudgements that triggered the murders of the St Bartholomew's Day Massacre: because Protestant and Catholic families mixed through marriage, the massacres already began on the wedding night.

One could not tell from the outside what the scholar was thinking. Independently of the machinery of his thoughts, he made polite conversation that pleased the guests, the occupants. The company thought of themselves as metropolitan, in so far as they enthused about the novels of France, represented the power of the Russian Empire, yet they knew that world philosophy was present in this small town. The handsome philosopher embodied an invisible republic of scholars that kept a network spread around the world. He did not consider love between the sexes a republican virtue.

'The Company Thought of Themselves as Metropolitan, Insofar as They Enthused about the Novels of France'

–Did the novels of France have an influence on the Great French Revolution?

–Certainly. There are 80,000. Two-thirds of them are romantic novels.

–Novels like *Dangerous Liaisons, Manon Lescaut* or *Emile*?

–The last of those certainly had an influence. Especially on the evidentiary procedures in the trials conducted by the revolutionary tribunals.

–In what sense?

–It was a matter of credibility. In the relationships described by the novels, a person was honest if they were sure no one would learn of their statements. What they said in public depended on the interests they were pursuing.

—So then private letters, especially 'stolen letters' in the big lawsuits against the king and Danton, were the main pieces of evidence?

—Because they're documents from the intimate realm. These letters weren't intended to be read by a third person.

—Isn't that a paltry harvest from the great wealth of intimate experiences and proofs of love?

—Paltry.

—Is it true that the Thermidor which ended the Great French Revolution was a conspiracy by couples?

—The conspirators were erotically connected to one another. For the first time since the Women's March on Versailles in 1789, women played a central part in the overthrow.

— 'Decisiveness' is a republican virtue. The revolution could have used this virtue. It's more present in amorous relationships than in state and constitutional conflicts. Would the revolution have needed some better raw material? Would it have lasted longer if it had learnt from the 'logic of love'?

—What logic of love are you referring to?

—To the emancipation of love. What use are the sections of the constitution and the principles of liberty, equality and fraternity for the liberation of love?

—Liberty ('free as a bird') is part of love anyway. It's not interested in equality.

—And fraternity?

—What love are you referring to?

—Evidently brotherly and sisterly love are trustworthy.

—But they aren't treated much in the romantic novels from before the French Revolution.

—'Decisiveness' remains a republican virtue. What's more relevant than the distinction: I love or I do not love?

—You mean, the revolution should have based itself on amorous relationships, on the roots of intimate trust, not political conditions?

The historian Carla Hesse, University of California, Berkeley, became known in Europe with her research on 'stolen letters'. Working near the Pacific Ocean, she was nonetheless close to the events from 1789 to 1795. The French Revolution, she stated, continues to this day. Not only do we still feel its aftereffects, it also lies ahead of us. We don't know how it will end.

—Do we know its raw materials?

—Not even those.

A Person Wants to Be Rewarded for Their Own Sake

The role of the East German who marries the daughter of the Chicago meat millionaire was based on an authentic case. The producers had high expectations for this story of a social climber.

In the real case, a young officer from the National People's Army had gained entry to a Rhenish-Belgian industrial clan after German reunification. The lucky devil had met the company boss' daughter on a trip to Spain.

After some initial hesitation, the clan gave its blessing to the relationship. The rich family hoped the stranger would provide 'new blood'. They thought there was every reason for the young man to make an effort to show his best side.

But the man from Halle, a graduate of the workers' and farmers' faculty and most recently a frigate captain, proved to be a freethinker. The daughter who had been placed at his disposal only met his standards for a certain time. He took a mistress. He was interested in support for museums and foundations, in long-distance trips too, but not at all in the balances and day-to-day work in the firm.

He wanted to be loved for his own sake. That was human nature, and explained in the work of Immanuel Kant. One had to do things 'for their own sake'. That applied not only to himself but also to the achievements of the family into which he had married.

In fact, the young woman was still infatuated with the outsider, who did not treat her well; she took him as he was. As she told the doctor who was attempting to cure a rash that was afflicting her neck, she scarcely had any hope that he would better himself. Her devotion, however, proved to be the precondition for the couple to grow closer after their first year.

She Lived in Restlessness

The courses she had to apply for now would start in one or two years. Whether she decided to study at an English-speaking university or take up a practical profession in her own country, she would be setting the direction for the rest of her life. A choice like that only exists once. The choice determines whom she will one day meet, what offspring they will have, how she will feel in 30 years. She was supposed to take a position on such decisive questions within 14 days. That entailed preparations. An application for admission to a course or for a professional shift depended on documents.

Really, she felt, it would have been right to leave it to nature, to 'development', the way destiny plays out, instead of risking the presumption of deciding her own destiny.

She could not know anything this week about a future two years away. How could she say what she would feel in two or five years? That depended on whom she would live with in the meantime and in the future. No one can say of themselves, like some Robinson, how they will feel. And Robinson can only do so as long as he has no hope of being picked up from his island. He is filled with that hope every day.

What will happen to me? She lived uncertainly in a life that was located two years ahead of hers, and which she already had to fill out with all her vital energy–on credit, so to speak.

If someone had come and said to her–'Enough of the planning. Let us take these days, with the nerves and blood coursing through us in the now, as our fate. We will accept them without any further examination'–she would gladly have joined them. She would have crossed over from the absurd time in two years, the tomorrow of the world, to the year of moments. It was a gloriously sunny day.

The Mermaid

She was born as a 'mermaid'. The phenomenon is called sirenomelia: the girl's legs were grown together from the pelvis to the soles of her feet. The child was 13 months old when her parents decided to have the legs separated. This was carried out successfully in a 16-hour operation. In two years, the doctors claimed, the creature would be able to walk 'normally'. In Russia, there were top-class surgeons after 1917. Trained by masters of the scalpel from the West, who had been lured there for a hundred years by the ample wages of the tsars. This 'plantation of medical skill' coexisted with the reforms of the revolution.

–Don't the child's spindly limbs look funny after the operation? It was impossible to make her legs look as if they hadn't operated on them.

–What do you mean by 'spindly limbs'?

–The child walks as if it had spider's legs, one calls that spindly.

–Everyone knew that the surgery wasn't 'natural'. But the parents found her 'conjoined legs' unsettling. They couldn't imagine that kind of 'new human being'.

–And the legend will follow the child around. Her future fiancé will shudder when he touches the two human rods she walks on. Will he be able to love her unreservedly?

–You mean, he would sooner be inflamed with passion if she had stayed a mermaid?

–Then she could have grown up in the moist element as a swimmer and lived there, for example, as a swimming champion.

–Yes, that would have been something special.

–And one needs people with different qualities under socialism. One needs different abilities that complement one another.

–The need for individuality becomes greater under socialism, is that what you mean?

–Considerably.

–The parents denied their child that.

–Without asking the child.

–They couldn't really have asked the 13-month-old child what she wanted.

–And couldn't they have waited?

–The operation would have become more and more difficult. And the medical team was dying to start the interesting operation.

–Were the genitals and anus normal?

–Everything as usual. Only the legs were grown together. Into a 'plate'. A 'unileg'. With a lot of imagination, one could call it a 'fish tail'.

–Unique!

–The child lost this uniqueness.

–Was the political revolution innocent of that?

–It was about the medical revolution.[11]

---

11 Zalkind was asked, 'Who would have supplied care for the creature if there hadn't been an operation?' 'That is precisely the nature of the political revolution,' Zalkind replied, 'it solves unusual supply problems.' *From each according to his ability, for each according to his need.*

'Imagine,' says the leader of the group therapy session, 'that two of you'–there are 17 people sitting in front of him, so the row is not divided evenly–'are on a desert island. There's only a boat that will carry *one* of you; two people and it will capsize. This is the only way to leave the island. Whoever stays behind will die from poisonous fumes. Do you decide *which one* of you should leave?'

The group leader motions to a couple on his left; he knows they are together, and that they use this psychological session because they can't bear their life together but can't bring themselves to separate either.

It does not take long before the rest of the group starts interfering in the couple's attempts to make a decision. On the one hand, neither of them wants to stay on the island; but on the other, neither wants to sacrifice the other or give them priority. It is a confused state of affairs, as it remains doubtful whether they will endure staying there together, or would both be better off dead. They say they would rather die of each other than of the island sickness.

Alternatively, say other couples, one could–perhaps there are several boats waiting on the shores of the desert island–put one person in the boat while the other swims along beside it; then, when the latter is exhausted, they swap. The key is to wait for the exact moment before the outside swimmer is too exhausted for the person in the boat to pull them on board; there has to be strength left over for the changeover. Perhaps the danger of missing the right moment will bring the two closer. But what shall we do with the seventeenth in the group? He would have to rotate. He could get on one of the couple boats for a while, then swim to another one and so on. But one would have to make sure the boats did not drift too far apart.

For a while, the fleet rowing across the ocean in this rotation procedure is content. As the whole undertaking remains a hazardous assumption, however (it depends on everyone believing in it, otherwise the same battle of decisions would ensue that was avoided when leaving the island), one couple-partner interjects that he definitely wants to abstain from his departure for the sake of the other partner; he would rather die himself and let the other partner take the boat. For in spite of everything, he says, and a number of people in the group sense that, there is something hopeful in this question of life and death (which remains an example), there is something attractive about leaving the island without the other.

Without anyone saying anything, two factions form: those who are happy to survive by staying on the island (one can get used to the fumes, they argue) and those who want to achieve it by boat; the main thing is for the partner to disappear.

This makes one of the younger men in the group think that he would actually like to be more ruthless. He says that through his greater physical strength, he would definitely occupy the boat and quickly row away from his companion and the island of death. 'What good is a conscience if it leads us into a crisis but has no idea of what could lead us out? We can't afford that kind of fair-weather conscience,' says the young man, 'because when it comes to an emergency, no one will follow it.'

Outside the windows of the meeting room, gusts of wind blow across the lake. It is warm indoors. The month is October. The group leader tries to control his face and make sure that it gives no information about TRUE–FALSE. Because the discussants, even as they struggle for survival, are dealing with an exemplary chain of imagined decisions, a test of their actions, there is a part of them that is constantly trying to work out what the group leader expects as correct, as if it were life-hygienic answers. They want to learn those but avoid any dangerous experience if possible. Are we saved from forming couples in a benevolent fashion? Or is there some formula to turn us into a true couple? The urgency of this question leads the couples to examine thoroughly the inscrutable expression of the group leader and the supervisor.

He does not smile but they read a hint of a smile into his features, or perhaps an increasing hardness. One thing is certain: the group leader is getting tired. He feels like a quizmaster but needs a success in guiding souls, as the objective course of the session has led to the development of lines from the battle ruins of the couple, lines—seven women against nine men, plus a single man—going through the entire emotional terrain. This is a promising change. If the group leader were not too tired. The supervisor is no good as a helper, as she is too gripped by the events to utter a word.

The couples read the hardening in the group leader's features as a *lurking gaze.* But they have no desire to be his prey, and so they return to the starting position: ballet students standing at their bars, exhausted, resting for a moment; they still have the experience of work in their muscles. They feel as if they have made a great effort. They have grown hungry, they have a non-physical appetite, they would like to have the island on which they could die. Or which one could leave by boat. Or there would be balloons that took off. It would be possible as soon as the interests of the seven women set themselves against those of the nine men who felt they were capable of being ruthless.

The arrangement of the chairs in relation to one another–no one setting them up could foresee it or come up with it afterwards–keeps up the tension between the participants, who are feeling the urge to get their coats, even longer. Only the cleaners will push the remains of the imagined islands back into place, in the way that least obstructs their mops.

Addendum to I

IS THE LABYRINTH A SUITABLE METAPHOR FOR LOVE?

The genealogy of the tender force, to the extent that it is described in literature, suggests that its beginnings lie in a relationship of violence. In generous fashion, love 'forgot' the horrors of its origins. But, because emotions in particular cannot forget, this tender force lives in a certain nervousness to this day . . .

Sir Arthur Evans in Knossos

It was during the hot August of 1909 that Sir Arthur Evans unearthed, in the north-west pillar vestibule of the palace district he ascribed to King Minos, a stucco relief bearing a coloured bull. He gazed at the image of a magnificent animal which he took for the one that had aroused Queen Pasiphaë, or perhaps, rather, the one transported across the sea by Princess Europa. His imagination got the better of him. At no point, however, did the seasoned archaeologist confuse this bull (and others he later found on vases) with the Minotaur, which he did not even consider a bull but actually a god.

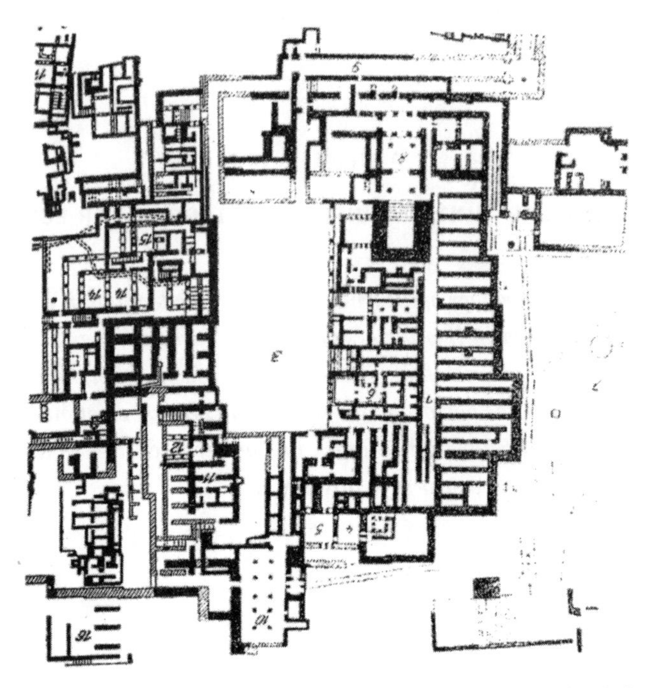

FIGURE 7. The excavation site at Knossos. Sir Arthur Evans believed the whole of Minos' palace to be the labyrinth.

The Most Beautiful Treasure of Evolution

The sociologist Karl Otto Hondrich, to whom we owe the essay collection *The Most Beautiful Treasure of Evolution: Love in the Age of Global Society*, speaks of the ECHOES OF DISTANT TIMES with reference to his object of research, namely, the tender force. In every successful amorous relationship today, Hondrich states, there are overtones; by this he means resonances from before and after past events that point to horrors. In a sense, amorous behaviour consists of this substance. The 'tender force' repeats its entire genealogy in a flash: that is the 'experience', regardless of what the participants in this 'miracle' know about it or how they make sense of it. To that extent, amorous behaviour does not consist of the present.

One could question, Karl Otto Hondrich adds, whether there is, or ever was, such a thing as an intact tender force. It consists of splinters like the libido, of echoes. It is precisely this not-consistent quality, however, that forms a highly substantial foundation, that is 'influential'. He observed this, albeit not under laboratory conditions.

–Can one reproduce what you examined?

–Barely.

–So how can one grasp your hypothesis in scientific terms?

–One must wait.

–Until something comes along?

–Until the thing I am referring to takes place. The tender force reproduces itself.

Hondrich likes to use the word 'original' in this context: original curiosity, original honesty, an original attracter, a first glance, etc.

Yet this distant cousin of the Frankfurt School's critical theory could not be induced to give any definition of the word 'original'. 'I only use the term as a word,' he said.

The reason, he claimed, why the tender force had become so strong and invincible, why it showed its wild force, is that it sensed hot lava masses of violence, suffering and powerful pasts beneath its ground. It constitutes the negation of all that. One could view it as a synthetic product; that makes it especially viable.

That was all the scholar would say about it.

The 'Original Accumulation of the Tender Force'

Sir Evans was a thorough man. Excited by the image of the splendid bull's head, he travelled to see Schliemann. Was there a connection between the relief of the bull and the ability to love, or to remember horror? There were no parallels with the pictures to be found in Troy. The two excavators had to consult Mesopotamian finds in order to have any representations of bull's heads at all for comparison.

Sir Evans travelled to Spain. Going by the experiences of bullfighters or bull rearers, was it possible that a female fighter could hold the bull by the horns while one male and one female fighter danced on the animal's back? One can't dance on a bull's back, answered the Spanish experts. Even arrows with tassels hanging from them could only be attached to the back of a bull's neck with some effort. Were the Cretan bulls of antiquity different creatures from the overbred Spanish animals?

Sir Evans travelled on to London, to the treasures of the British Museum. Nothing suitable for comparison. But the tracker felt that the depiction he had found pointed to the 'original accumulation of the tender force'. Why did one need a dancing bull to express the transformation of destructive force into desire? What sort of production was taking place there?

Stones from the Labyrinth as Mementos

In 1942, a group of academic speakers gave travel lectures in Crete, organized by the monthly journal *Kosmos* (edited by Bruno H. Bürgel), to the occupation army provided by the 22nd Infantry Division. The speakers had told of Daedalus and the labyrinth, which was located on the island. In the subsequent weeks, Lieutenant Colonel Paetzold in the general staff found out that infantrymen were taken the tram to Knossos along the Evans road and returning with stones and pieces of a wall. They were also sending these stones home in field post parcels.

Questioning some non-commissioned officers revealed that they ascribed an effect to the finds, which they believed to be stones from the labyrinth; it remained unclear, however, what this effect was supposed to be. The lieutenant colonel banned this practice, as it constituted an activity with no military necessity.

FIGURE 8. The Minotaur looks with longing into the distance.

A Female Sacrifice in Antiquity

It did not cost blood but subjugation. Because no other sacrifice was available, the princess, 12 years old, was handed over to the conqueror. It was feared that the nomad ruler would attack the city if he were not appeased. The young woman, practically still a child, resisted. She was inexperienced in defending herself (it would have taken an entire life, a throng of helpers and sufficient time for any defence to be possible in this situation). The

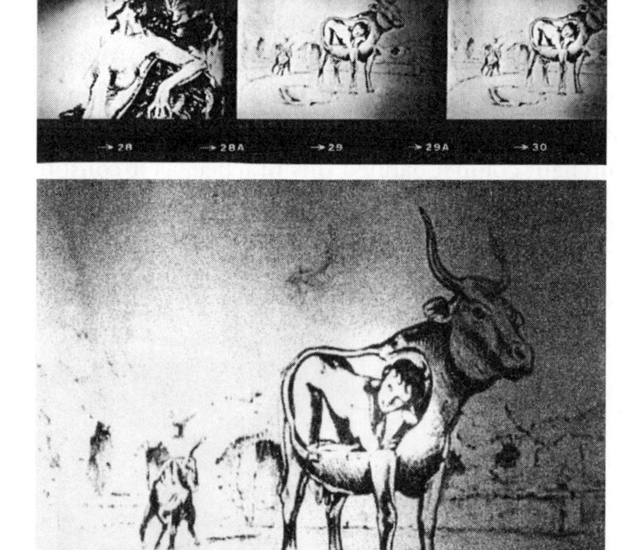

FIGURE 9. Queen Pasiphaë with the model of a cow built for her by Daedalus. In the background, the divine bull.

sacrificial victim was put on a beast of burden, fastened to it like a piece of baggage and tied up. According to reports, the girl, still resisting and seeming quite unsuitable as a gift of appeasement, was straightened out and prepared by the recipient and his servants. The ruler was moved by the young thing; hence no blood flowed. Nor was she beaten cruelly. But she was not asked whether she would voluntarily do any of the things that were demanded of her.

The child treated in this way later called herself a princess, as she belonged to the ruler. She had also been born a princess but in a different sense. She later had 16 children and many grandchildren. After the death of the tyrannous rapist, she was considered a great lady and helped subjugate numerous cities.

The story of her life survives in inscriptions found in the city of Uruk. The head teacher and reserve major Dr Rolf Hartung, stationed in Thessaloniki, examined these texts in 1941; they had been carved into earthenware shards and were available on the Greek black market. They were of certified Mesopotamian origin.

A Female Sacrifice in 1944

In February 1944, a German couple with three daughters was accosted by the Red Army at their mansion in Poland. Of their three daughters, the firstborn and the youngest were the parents' favourites. So the circumspect parents gave a Soviet officer the middle daughter as a gift in exchange for the assurance that this high-ranking man would effectively protect the rest of the family. They had learnt Russian before the war. Nonetheless, because of the special nature of the matter, it was not easy to find the right choice of words during the negotiations.

The middle daughter was dragged there and handed over. The officer seemed well disposed towards her, a polite man.

Amid the social chaos of this transitional time between two ruling systems, the rescue of the remaining family was actually successful. They made it to the river Ems in Western Germany.

The sacrifice of their daughter almost proved to be in vain, as the Soviet officer to whom she had been surrendered was redeployed earlier than expected. But the paths of the rapists–all of them lower-ranking than this officer–were already well established in the area through sluggishness and habit. That protected the family. The middle daughter (the sacrifice) had also been handed on by the Soviet officer who was initially chosen as a protector to another high-ranking military functionary who, like her first owner, felt a sense of responsibility for the 'gift' and her relatives.

Were the parents and their child, whom they had given up for lost, reunited? Shortly before the currency reform of June 1948, the young human being reached home by an adventurous journey passing through Greece (from Crimea to Thessaloniki, stopping for a while in Athens, via Italy). The family never spoke of what had happened.

FIGURE 10. Marx, Engels, Lenin and Ovid.

Murder in the Wedding Night

Hyginus (168) and Horace (*Carmina* 3.11.22ff.) report:

King Danaus had 50 daughters and his brother Aegyptus, who was an enemy, had 50 sons. Aegyptus forced Danaus into an agreement that their respective children would be married to one another. But Danaus commanded his daughters to kill the enemy husbands already in the wedding night. With one exception, they all followed their father's command. Later, in the underworld, they were condemned for all eternity to fill water into a tub ridden with holes.

The Beauty in the Voice of the Nightingale

After Ovid (*Metamorphoses* 6.24ff.):

The Thracian King Tereus, after five years of marriage with Procne, an Attic princess who had borne him a son named Itys, was meant to collect her sister, Princess Philomela, from Athens. After returning home, Tereus raped Philomela and cut out her tongue to prevent her from speaking of the outrage. He hid the mute in a cabin in the woods near his capital.

But Philomela sat down at a loom and illustrated her story on tapestries. Thus Procne learnt what had happened to her sister. In her anger, she killed her son Itys and served him to the unfaithful king as a dish. When Tereus had finished eating, Procne revealed the true nature of his meal. She summoned Philomela, who threw the bloody severed head of little Itys in Tereus's face. Tereus, enraged, reached for his sword.

But the gods immediately transformed all three of them into birds: Tereus into a hoopoe, Procne into a swallow and Philomela into a nightingale. She the mute, has been mourning at night with a beautiful voice ever since, even though it was her sister, not she, who lost her son.

The *Metamorphoses* of Ovid

In his research into the poetic aetiology of Ovid's *Metmorphoses*, the classical scholar Niklas Kaminski was most interested in fractures. He described the surface as smooth. It was logical and consecutive, for example, that not Procne but, rather, her sister Philomela was turned into a nightingale: the tongueless one was turned into the most beautiful singer of the night. She could not be that as a swallow, only as a nightingale. This made the story smooth but also pointed to the fact that the subtext of the narrative, the historical events of which the narrator was aware, told of something different, something secret. Why was it concealed? Ovid's *Metamorphoses*, he said, were full of such irregularities and fractures. Indeed, the quality of this classical author lay in the fact that he permitted them. One could almost say that the fractures formed the heart of the narrative.

Book I and the beginning of Book II of the *perpetuum carmen*, the 'uninterrupted poem', deal with the origin of the world, with chaos, cosmos, eros and renewed chaos. In Book I, there is initially a confrontation between gods and humans, the Great Flood (ll. 5–437). The new beginning of life on earth after this flood sees the appearance of a monstrous creature, Python, a terror of entire peoples. Thus a god, Apollo, has to kill it.

This deed is followed directly by a love story. The god is seized by greedy desire for the nymph Daphne; but she has been made immune to feelings of love, even before a god (ll. 452–567). Apollo chases Daphne, prepared to rape her. While running, he begins to speak; the young woman answers him. He asks her to run more slowly, promising to pursue her more slowly too. Before moving on to the use of force, he behaves like an elegiac lover, describing possible peace agreements. In the very moment he attempts to seize Daphne and do violence to her, she flees to her father the river god. He transforms her for ever into a laurel tree. Future heroes and Caesars will form their headgear from its leaves, documenting their power with it:

unspoilt, incorruptible. The attempted act of violence is peculiar, writes Kaminski; as if Saint George or the dragon-slayer Siegfried von Xanten had followed the killing of the dragon, an act of liberation, with rape. A generosity of fate prevents the deed and gives the endangered nymph eternal life through metamorphosis. Daphne does not reach the starry heavens but, rather, settles ubiquitously along the coasts of the Mediterranean.

The first five stanzas (pentad) of the 'continuous song' provide a number of further love stories. The one that stands out is the myth of Perseus: he risks his life to save that of Andromeda, whom he finds in chains and under threat from a great beast, and marries her at a magnificent celebration. During the banquet, Andromeda's original betrothed, Phineus, appears with a band of armed henchmen. Perseus succeeds in petrifying his opponent by showing him the face of Medusa, who is depicted on both his shield and a mirror. This terrible image shows a head of snakes, as if Python had been multiplied. The love story of Perseus and Andromeda is constructed over an abyss where monsters dwell.

The errant path of a handsome young man called Narcissus (3.339–510) is rather different. He lives under the delusion that he can take his own image, reflected in the water, as his lover. It remains unreachable.

'[. . .] for whenever I lean forwards to kiss the clear waters he lifts up his face to mine and strives to reach me. You would think he could be reached–it is such a small thing that hinders our love.'[12]

---

12 Ovid, *Metamorphoses* (Mary M. Innes trans.) (London: Penguin, 1955), p. 86.

Another quite different tale is that of Callisto (2.401–532). This huntress and virgin is completely unaware of her ability to love. The god Jupiter plans to use force. He seeks to create an opportunity for rape through deception, by adopting the guise of the goddess Diana who is also a huntress. Callisto falls prey to him without understanding what has happened to her. She becomes pregnant. Despite her attempts to resist, she is punished by Jupiter's wife: she changes her 'rival' into a bear. Through joined forces of love, namely, that of her innocence and that of the mighty leader of the gods, Callisto is placed in the sky as a constellation, the Great Bear, while her son becomes the Little Bear. Now these constellations eternally guide ships across the sea at night.

At the transition from the second to the third pentad (in Books X and XI), Ovid deals with the fate of Orpheus. Because he cannot cease from mourning his beloved Eurydice, and due to the beauty of his singing, he is torn to pieces by the Thracian maenads while still alive. His head alone is left drifting in the river, still singing its 'endless song', and crosses the Aegean Sea before finally reaching Lesbos.

None of the stories in books VI–XV lack a fracture marking the subterranean flow of the narrative. Even the consoling tale of Philemon and Baucis draws from such a 'well to the underworld', as the gods received by them as guests also buried all their neighbours in a swamp (to reward the couple and as the foundation of their eternal happiness). The latter are punished for their inhospitality, as they turned away the gods, whom they did not recognize owing to their disguise. In their underworld beneath the swamps, Kaminski claims, they will never rest.[13]

Nothing Is Simply Routine

In 2009, a head was observed in a tributary of the Euphrates floating slightly beneath the surface of the flowing water. According to the report of the US Army medical officer responsible for keeping the waters in this area clean, it belonged to a bodyguard shot by insurgents.

At least, that is what the officer concluded from a missing-persons report. It was not necessarily true. But the body part could be seen at the site of the find. Dusk fell, and one could hear a humming–other witnesses spoke of a continuous note–that could not come from cicadas or some other known sound source. The officer William Feddersen (family from northern Hesse, immigrated to the USA in 1830) was confused for a long time by the simultaneous impression of a 'singing note' and the perception of an underwater head that was in the process of dissolving yet still had all its contours.

---

13 In Goethe's *Faust II*, Act 5, Faust drains the swamps that came about in this way. On that same occasion, the property belonging to Philemon and Baucis is destroyed, along with the trees that have grown there (and also the guest, present as a god disguised as a student). Thus the combination of chaos and eros, divine anger, as well as the rewarding and rebellion of those harmed, is an urgent matter in the present. The 'uninterrupted song' from 2,000 years ago continues to this day, even if no one seems to be singing at the moment.

Amazons in the Northern Aegean

A group of 26 women, reported the vice-chief of the Greek naval police who guarded the small northern islands facing Turkey, was committing acts of piracy in the area in 1947. They attacked cargo ships. They deposited their prisoners on uninhabited islands. They maintained 'men farms'.

–They captured men but didn't give them the status of prisoners or hostages?

–They kept them as slaves. None of the women were allowed to lay hands on them, except once a year for reproductive purposes. Then the prisoners were locked away. The women were militant; they were pirates. Considerable losses for merchant shipping. A real nuisance.

–Difficult to fight?

–We couldn't find them at all. They had either a special sense of intuition or excellent informants. Struck exactly where we weren't.

–Heavily armed?

–With everything one could buy after the war.

–Greeks? Where did they come from?

–From the coast of the Black Sea. Supposedly they were recruited by force to an officer's brothel, close to the swamps where partisans operate.[14] Then one night they

14 The officers, said the police chief, apparently belonged to a brigade fighting the partisans alongside the Germans. Ukrainian patriots.

collectively murdered their tormentors and left in a south-easterly direction. At some point, they arrived at the Turkish border.

—Were they let in?

—Arrested immediately. They escaped from custody and hijacked a ship.

—No one knows more than this beginning?

—Not even their whereabouts today. They never put their weapons down again.

—Could attacks in the China Sea or off the coast of Somalia be connected to this group of pirate women?

—If they've reproduced. People say they killed the male newborns. The same with men they don't need. Private 'relationships' between pirates and men are punishable by death.

—That makes reproduction harder.

—It seems to be true. We found bodies.

—Newborns?

—Dead men on an uninhabited island. Gunshot wounds.

—And suddenly they disappeared?

—We were glad.

—Why? It was a promising enforcement project for the naval police. What's more important than having a mission?

—We weren't sure who would win in combat.

—You feared the high motivation of the fighting women?

—We found it unsettling how little we knew about them.

Do People Confuse the Minotaur with an Entirely Different Construction by Daedalus?

Walter Benjamin did not find the Minotaur *strange*; he considered such a monster *improbable.* How was the oversized human-animal body supposed to have passed through Queen Pasiphaë's birth canal? Assuming the other legends concerning the bovine construction in which she was supposedly mounted by the bull were true. Other details of the account also bothered Benjamin.

–The impenetrability of the walls?

–The technical ability to build an edifice which stimulates the desire to lose one's way, yet prevents people through terror or panic from seeking the exit; there is always a way out, according to Benjamin.

–The annual sacrifice of seven girls and seven boys, considering the high civilizatory standard of Minoan Crete?

–But especially the involvement of Daedalus.

It was this engineer, Daedalus, that captivated Benjamin most. He was a master of artefacts; according to Ovid and Hyginus, he had been trained by Hephaestus himself. Benjamin argued that either the whole of Knossos was the labyrinth, and then the Minotaur was a screen memory or altogether superfluous, as it was in the palace, the hermetic realm of Minos, that prisoners were kept; or the monster was something other than the creature we imagine. He believed that only Daedalus the engineer was real, and that he had probably built something.

Benjamin compared the labyrinth, the tower of Babel and the defence machines in the land of Medea, which were built deep into the earth and served to defend the coasts of the Black Sea against intruders.

Benjamin was unable to complete this research using the resources of the Bibliothèque nationale in Paris, as he soon found himself in Marseille and, a short time later, on the way to the Pyrenees, the place of his demise.

In the meantime, Benjamin's confidant and student, the Frenchman Julian Dimitri Czernowitz, had continued the research project. He examines another of Daedalus' artefacts: the giant Talos, whom the engineer fashioned from pure iron. This giant figure moves along the coasts of Crete with 'loudly singing hinges'. Every day (or every month, according to other sources) he walks around the island on his mechanical legs. He fends off foreign intruders and throws pieces of rock at approaching ships.

If invaders manage nonetheless to land on the island, this giant leaps into fire until he is red-hot, then welcomes the strangers with an embrace. That is, he presses himself against them so that they burn up. Their features freeze in a 'sardonic smile' as they are clasped by the scorching iron claws.

Czernowitz was fascinated by this source, written in Linear B script. This giant, he believed, was actually the Minotaur; like the golem, the artefact was ensouled. That was precisely the art of Daedalus: he crafted the latent power of self-defence that every Cretan, indeed every person, arranged by clan, carries within them, into a technical product. That which is dearest to humans acts as their defence. In this respect, the giant Talos (that is, the Minotaur) is identical to Medea's machines, which–buried up to their chests in the earth–were unable to repel the thieving Greeks who landed in Abkhazia.

He considered the legend of the annual group of human sacrifices devoured by a man-eating monster, on the other hand, no more than an expression of the Athenians' guilty conscience. It was correct that the cunning Theseus–already one of the foremost destroyers on Thessalonian soil–broke through the defences arranged by Daedalus. The simplicity of his aggressive intent was superior to the accumulation of sophisticated countermeasures. It was an illusion that technical ingenuity (erotic level 1) could paralyse the combinations of the 'will to power' (erotic accumulation level 7). Technical ingenuity had to participate in such an increase itself (and would, in the process, separate from the erotic basis that makes it inventive).

Czernowitz further developed this line of thought in his essay on the myth of Princess Turandot, published in Paris in 1947. He argued that she responded to the mechanical wilfulness of invading, masculine conquerors by setting them in competition with one another. Through his egocentrism, each of these conquerors guaranteed the fair distribution of chances when the suitors courted the princess.[15]

Each one who failed to solve the princess' riddle was beheaded. The completion of the process was guaranteed

---

15 They desired not her but the kingdom.

by the competitors, frozen in their waiting attitude. Daedalus, Czernowitz concluded, must have devised such a mechanism in the palace of Minos to deal with greedy strangers; the Minotaur was exactly that and nothing else. In this sense, the 'tender force', when guided by an intelligent engineer and master builder, displays the attributes of a scorpion: at its heart lies the sting. It also means that love is free ('*comme un oiseau*') and 'incorruptible'.

But why is the labyrinth considered a confusing edifice, a system of paths leading nowhere? Why is orientation ruled out in the areas of the tender force? Because, Czernowitz replies, this irreplaceable force is only a compound. Daedalus had to borrow a solid material like iron, because love itself is composed of numerous conflicting components, meaning that if one left it as it is, it would be more likely to spin around than to defend itself or act. It has no nature.

—Why are the walls of the labyrinth so solid?

—They consist of human flesh.

—But that's not solid.

—Once it becomes spirit, it's more solid than concrete.

—Or plaster?

—More solid than plaster.

—Denser than a diamond?

—Harder.

—We know little about the basements and catacombs of the subjective world on which our houses stand.

—The bottom breaks open faster than anyone can think.

—Why are the exits of the labyrinth blocked, and why are they so difficult to find, considering that barriers indicate an exit?

—You have to see it negatively; they don't find out because the labyrinth doesn't exist. The whole of Knossos is the labyrinth. It's about an image.

—With no horizon?

—If we don't have a horizon, that's equivalent to a wall.

'One Can See from the Start That It Will Come to a Bad End'

King Agamemnon, the butcher of Troy who sacrificed his own daughter Iphigenia, returns to his palace years later. He is led into the bathroom, where he is hacked to death with axes by his wife (and her lover). A trail of blood trickles from the bathroom, crossing a terrace and running down the splendid steps at the entrance to the palace. This red trail, said Ernst Jünger, was the first of the red carpets. They are rolled out to welcome foreign rulers, a document of the trail of blood.

Collective Erotic Groundswell as a Cause of Increased Impregnation During a Parisian Night

Marcel Proust, influenced in his judgement by the fact that he believed he loved the descendant of one of Napoleon's colonels, Count N., defended a pronouncement allegedly made while visiting the battlefield after the battle of Borodino, in which he suffered heavy losses. According to rumour, he declared that the number of those who had fallen for France that day could be balanced out through reproduction in a single Parisian night of love.

The pronouncement was decried as cynical. But Proust considered it quite correct. He wanted to incorporate a justification in one of his texts: in some nights, the French capital is seized by a ZEAL OF THE TENDER FORCE kindled in ghostly fashion by new arrivals (soldiers on leave from the front, young women coming from the provinces), such that the diverse society, gathered at all manner of soirées, balls, in ballrooms and taverns, decides to enter unions that would not come about in such numbers at other times, even over many years. This was a ghostly movement, Proust said. In this way, he continued, in the water molecules so abundant in the English Channel, the oxygen atoms lust after one another. One molecule is drawn to its neighbour by such an illegal yearning, though without destroying the form of that molecule. Thus the behaviour of the oxygen particles, each of them guarded and held by two hydrogen atoms, leads to the formation of HYDROGEN BRIDGES, like crystals, which a cricket could traverse as if it were solid ground in the water, if the waves did not conceal this reality. Invisible to our eyes, parts of the personality, the SELVES OF PARIS, break away in their greed like the oxygen atoms, which only constitute a third of the water; they lean out of their bodies (invisibly) and turn towards others. Precisely this erotic curiosity, almost like a chatter of souls without the barrier placed by the concrete touch of desire, allows the real couples to create the life of future generations if they remain faithful, if they stay together in this night.

This is what characterizes the groundswell of a Parisian night to which, Proust states, the emperor was referring. In that sense, the compensation for the dead at Borodino in just *one* Parisian night is neither cynical nor unrealistic. Rather, the connection of amorous relationships to procreation is nothing individual, but depends on such an underlying current in which large collectives, the same as a capital city, wrap themselves as if it were a cocoon.

The Labyrinth as a Pit

In his 42,000-word tact *Heath, Nothing but Heath,* Arno Schmidt directs the reader's towards the conventional depiction of the labyrinth. We look at such a construction from above, he notes, and thus see the paths and walls. We view it like inspectors. No one perceives the edifice like that once they are in its clutches.

'I do not know,' Schmidt writes, 'what these drawings are based on.' He claims that after 1909, they were copied from the plan of the excavated palace complex of Minos published by Sir Arthur Evans. But that does not explain why the pictures of the labyrinth I see before me now should come from the sixteenth and seventeenth centuries, not from supplementary Volume 6 by Sir Arthur. It was published in 1936. Admirable: southern English garden labyrinths. And here, once again, a labyrinth made of tiles in one of the Gothic churches in France. One could try to play chess in such a 'plan' but one could not lose one's way.

In fact, Arno Schmidt continues his observations, the labyrinth is not a construction that extends horizontally; this is shown by Egyptian sources. Rather, labyrinths are built *downwards*. That is what shocks the intruders in the labyrinth: they are moving to the centre of the earth with no end in sight–not even straight, but along a slope.

If one could see it clearly, one could compare it to a mine or a catacomb. But there is no suitable term for the place because in the dark, one ultimately cannot know if one has gone uphill or downhill. The situation is made even more difficult by the fact that an escape upwards to the light is prevented by the will to finally explore the secret of these depths. One cannot tear oneself away from the labyrinth; therein lies its fatality.

II

DEAR ANGELS, OPEN HEAVEN'S GATE WHILE ON THIS EARTH I STILL DO WAIT

The harshness of time shapes emotions. Often there is no space for the tender force. But how unwaveringly it finds its ways . . .

Betti's Aversion to False Harmony

K. stopped to apologize, with the politeness of the Old World, for bumping into a girl by chance. In the meantime, Betti came along behind him and made up for the damage of staring (for K. would never have bumped into a girl deliberately, or even dared to look at her for more than a moment, if she had been there) by pushing the girl's hat down onto her nose. At least that left a conflict behind, something real.

Love in 1944

The uncertainty, and most of all the impossibility of influencing whether or when someone will be struck down by war, makes the soul bold. There is nothing left to lose.

And so Gerda F. stopped saving herself for anyone after the hours-long air raid on Ulm. No question of waiting for one of the returning fighters whom she still knew, and who would ask for her hand in marriage. She had no desire to get any closer to those left behind in the city's arms factories. They were all looking for closeness. So she took a passing traveller up to her room. They never saw each other again. She did not regret anything.

'For a night
Full of bliss
I would give up everything.'

The Wedding at 'The Steed'

'I was here at six o'clock this morning and had a look. Didn't want you to come here with nothing prepared.

Flowers and everything.' That is what the bride's mother said when they came here from the cathedral and saw the makeshift breakfast laid out: the row of Harzbräu beers, four bottles of Mosel wine, the things the hotel people had brought from their stores; the bride's family had added ham, butter and two ring cakes.

Then, at 11.20, the emergency alarm. The waitress on duty said: 'You have to go to the basement immediately.' The wedding guests had realized that anyway. They chattered their way through the door, down the hall, down the beige basement steps: the bride (from the lower city), currently working for the Junkers, the groom (a heavy concrete engineer), the bride's mother, the groom's mother, four sisters of the bride's mother, one sister of the bride, her brother, who only went with them as far as the basement door, because he was on duty as an air raid warden and had to go out again, four children from the bride's clan who scattered flowers. Twelve minutes later, they were all buried.

'I hope they suffocated immediately,' said the bride's brother, who searched through the mountain of rubble the next day.

After the ceremony at the cathedral, which took longer because there were two couples before them, the wedding guests had around 40 minutes at the Steed. The brother of the bride had brought along a suitcase gramophone and played the bride's 'favourite song'.

'Dream my little baby,
you'll be a lady,
and I'll be a rich cavalier.'

After that, the mother of the bride pointed to the set table and handed out plates. 'And if you don't want any, it's your loss.' 'And if you don't have any,' countered the groom's mother, 'you'll get some.' The witnesses presented their empty plates.

'Lissy can stop that!' said the mother. 'And if I don't hear anything from Edeltraud, I'll take it with dignity.' The groom's mother supported her: 'You're not going there. You're not budging an inch for her.' 'And as for the flat,' the bride's mother continued, 'I'm not cleaning it once. Not even the windows.' 'That's right,' said the groom's mother.

'What are you reading?' said Gerda, one of the sisters of the bride's mother, a teacher, to the eight-year-old flower child, Hanna's boy. 'Oh, you're reading the opera guide? That's good. The child is always reader.' 'What's he reading?' called out the groom's mother. 'The opera guide!' The child had already been reading in church, and for the last few minutes he had been reading one opera synopsis after another.

'I put away the garlands.' With those words, Hanna touched on a danger that could ruin the atmosphere that day: there had been a death in the bride's family only two weeks previously. 'Got rid of the garlands,' Hanna said, 'and put some petunias there. So they suit the occasion better. I sped that up. We're not allowed to put any gravel there. But they'll pile on some fresh earth in September, then that'll be out of the way too. They're a few days apart.'

She wanted to lighten the mood, so she said, 'Cheers.' 'The lovely wedding presents,' said Gerda.

They wanted to be finished there by 1 p.m., then have lunch at the flat in Gröperstrasse and coffee at the home of the bride's great-aunt, who was unable to walk, and tables were reserved in the evening at the restaurant the Sour Snout. The next day, Monday, the bridegroom was set to be in Barby.

The bridal couple barely spoke to each other. The atmosphere was awkward. That had to change within less than an hour; the bride's and groom's mothers were working on that. For there was a genuine danger: the bridegroom came from a propertied family in Cologne. His bride, from Halberstadt, came from a family with no assets in the lower city. The informal *du* did not yet come naturally to the opposing families (except for the bridal couple, who had instigated all this but were now silent). The bride's family were hoping to have an untroubled day until they dropped off the couple at their room at the Steed at 1 a.m. (or gave them a bedroom at the flat in Gröperstrasse, that didn't matter now). Then this celebration too would be over. They had only just mourned before that, for such a short time. As mentioned earlier, no one escaped.

Not Public—Public

[Café Hundt, 12 December 1944, Zurich] The record player was going all afternoon; one had to put five rappen in the slot at the side, at the request of Diana the waitress, who had a day off.

'Oh you dear, oh you clever,
oh you sly, sly rascal!'

How clever they were to find each other! And then this record:

> 'I have a man, a real man,
> the snappiest cavalier!
> No one believes it, they just look on,
> he's more *dashing* than anyone here!'

Those were the wonderful days in Vienna, so before 1914; there were a few pieces of cake and the cafe's lamps as reminders. Five steps away from the door, the *Swiss surroundings* again.

She, such a hard businesswoman, would have liked to be sentimental. She would have liked to have the cleverness of the two 'sly rascals' (in a single person!) or a man with whom she could play dolls as long until her free time was over. A slave at her disposal for two hours, one might say.

That was only possible with music and many glasses of wine, sugared and paid for with a headache. But everything was still blurred. Exactly on the hour: a moment. 'Her compassion embraced the whole world.' She wished for something all afternoon. She turned down every man who tried to chat her up. She would never have assumed there would be a rascal among them or someone that could be described as 'dashing', a word she knew had still meant something to her mother.

[40 steps from Café Hundt, figure-skating stadium, Zurich]
The stadium band played 'Très jolie' by Emil Waldteufel, then the ice-skater waltz. The official figure-skating couples

were to be announced in a quarter of an hour. Snowflakes slowly landed on the heads of the spectators, who sat there in thick coats between the twilight and the floodlights.

[A person with a reason for consciousness and special access to news sources] Christl Mehnert, sports reporter at the *Züricher Zeitung*, tried to look up to the sky that had to be above the edge of the floodlights. She associated the general weather situation with the brother of whom she 'knew' that he was carrying out drilling work as a 'forced labourer', in a camp near the Harz Mountains, because of political crimes. What did the wind, the flakes, the twilight look like in the Harz? What effect did 'the circumstances' have? Now clowns were dancing on the ice; there were sweets on offer.

Going by the city map, she knew which way was north-east; that was where her feelings searched. But what feelings did she have? To have feelings one also needs knowledge. But she knew what her brother had looked like last time, in 1938, and she knew words. What was consciousness about the fact that she imagined he would come to this event? Sit down next to her? But she was at an advantage, as a reporter, sitting at the source of the news that Switzerland received.

> 'White children shuffle quietly
> through the snow on thin ice . . . '
> Dance: march-fox.

[A desperate attempt at public protest] The night shift leaving the tunnel entrances of Malachite found the Baptist preacher Busch hanging from a lamppost next to the freight cars, about 930 metres from the cave exit. They took down the body, still warm, and brought it into the daylight in front of the cave entrance. Madloch noted this protest death for his report. He estimated that the essentially incalculable 'mental confusion' and conversational exchange about the incident among the convicts would use up 10 million ergs of work (which would thus be lost). Tscheu, the camp commandant, viewed the deed as 'the most intense incitement'. He saw no way to report it to Senior Assault Leader Lübeck, who would have directed his anger at him. They tried to prevent the kitchen patrol, the most important disseminator of news within the secret restricted area, from finding out about the event.

[A more intuituve measurement by Madloch, Christmas Eve 1944] If one was Madloch, who–reasonably well nourished and enthusiastic about his measurements–walked towards the exit through the warmth of the cave systems with the additional rows of lamps on each side of the tunnel, one saw gangs of waiting workers standing in the snow, wearing their thin, blue-and-white-striped coats and caps, though he was not cold, then the apt description of the camp, which corresponded to its location (for it was in a valley, and on the mountaintops there was a rough wind that swept the snow in streaks like torrents of rain, but here on the gravel paths the snow had been trampled flat, and the flakes were falling slowly), the workers wandering back and forth or standing there as if for a roll call–Madloch, measuring, not only saw what he saw but knew what no one knew deep in the tunnel (and far above it a quiet, snow-topped mountain forest and an excessive amount of air–**then it could be classified as an illustration for a fairy tale in which good mountain spirits and gnomes mine ore in the mountains.**

Madloch was not sentimental. 'Why are the people standing around here?' he barked at the Luftwaffe soldiers waiting with the workers in front of the cave entrance as guards. They hadn't lined the gang up close enough to the rock wall to make use of the leeward position. They didn't know why they were standing here. Freezing for an hour cost each man 800 calories, out of 1,100 calories available for the entire day.

Furthermore, after Madloch had moved the gang further towards the tunnel entrance, out of the wind, the 'woodland terrain' began to take on a Christmas feel.

Memory of a Romance

In Sydney I met F. At the time I was still a young, enthusiastic person. She secured a few days off for me through her connections in the company, and we spent some unforgettable days together. Then she flew back to Europe. I received a telegram from Alexandria asking me what she should do: a fly or something similar had bitten her while she was swimming, and she wanted to know if she should follow the doctors' advice and have her leg amputated. She wanted me to decide the matter. As I found out later, her life had already been in danger for hours by that time but she was waiting for my answer. Naturally I telegraphed that she should amputate it as the doctors said. I also asked the doctor I was seeing back then. I met her again years later.

A very young woman, perhaps half a year younger than myself. She could still swim, despite the stump.

Manfred Schmidt Visits His Former Girlfriend L. in the Hour of Her Death

One first-class blue-skied Sunday–after the morning snack he had already obtained around seven o'clock, even though most establishments only opened later–Manfred Schmidt had the idea of visiting L. The air was still cool. He went to see L., with whom he had recently spent an enjoyable few days on holiday in Trident; but she was rather sick now. Nonetheless, he hoped she would not cause him any difficulties.

L. opened the door wearing a silk gown tied with a cloth belt, white with cherry blossoms; she had worn it in bed because she was cold. A pretty face, much too small, around which the head had grown to normal adult size. Small hands, body, limbs of different age groups. Her attention was claimed by the telephone as soon as he had entered, so he had time to look at her again and imprint her on his memory.

After the phone call (she was back in bed, a fold-up alarm clock set up next to her pillow in the bed, and everything else arranged nicely too) he tried to start something with her, but she would have none of it. He had probably been out of touch for too long. He got up from the edge of the bed and switched on the little Philips radio in the next room, then spooned the coffee she had put there for him. Shortly afterwards, for the second time that day, he had the thought that maybe he could start something with her after all. But this idea dissipated as a result of the earlier rejection. Before he was finished with the coffee–and when he looked at the radio again–the screen with the stations on it was illuminated.

He made himself comfortable in the flat. When the doctor came, L. asked him to go to another room. When the doctor had left, he wanted to give her a cold shower, a useful old-folk remedy for stomach aches, but he had no luck with that either. He listened to the radio programme and told her that she should call him if she wanted something. Later on, he went to her again and asked if she even found him likeable, if his presence there meant anything to her. He reminded her of the days in Trident. She groaned, lying on one side with the blanket almost pulled up over her head, at least the thin, sheet-covered end of the blanket, the way one puts a handkerchief in one's mouth and bites on it. He tried to massage her stomach but she fended him off when he became too forward. He criticized her attitude and her coldness.

Her condition grew worse in the course of the afternoon. She had cramps but he was too sulky to notice. He simply didn't go to her. He only called the doctor when she was still groaning after a considerable while. He tried to distract her by trying to cheer her up. But she was grumpy and everything he did was painful for her.

It proved difficult to get hold of the doctor. Initially, because of all the injuries she had inflicted on him, Schmidt had not made enough of an effort. He tried to comfort his friend, who was feeling worse and worse, and to kiss her; she didn't understand him, didn't know what he wanted and reacted clumsily when he placed her lips on hers. It was only considerably later that he realized he was dealing with someone who was just in the process of dying.

He was afraid, and had the idea that she should have an experience with him before her death. He began an attempt but the conflict of emotions inside him brought it to a halt. He ran a fresh bath for her and carried her around the room. She whimpered incessantly and stayed squatting while he pulled back the old bedsheet and let in some air. Then he laid her down on the fresh sheet; he phoned various doctors and called a hospital too, but they were unwilling to send anyone. She died just when he was getting a proper grip on things. And with the necessary energy on the telephone, success eventually came. The doctor was there only a quarter of an hour later.

Example of a Love Story

(The Time with Gitta)

Gitta as the Young Lover of an Old Farmer

She is embarrassed by her partner's teeth and keeps her mouth closed for that reason. She sticks her tongue into a bottle of Coca-Cola but can't get it through the narrow opening and bursts into laughter. The tongue disappears inside her mouth. Very pale arms with vaccination scars, muscular beneath the white skin, bluish where the veins are: like a dog, she pushes her head towards the fancy-dressed farmer to tell him something; a fairly high voice. With a large gap between her front teeth that gives her a pretty mouth; she narrows her lips so that no one can see the gap.

She yawns, narrow mouth, she wants to say something to this man, but the sight of his unpleasant front teeth interrupts her and it takes some time for her to laugh again. The yellow-brown, slightly reflecting eyes, looking around calmly, moving over there, until she pushes her head forwards again like a dog and says something in a high voice.

She was ashamed to be seen by Schmidt in the company of this farmer, who was wearing a Pierrot costume. The man tried to grope her while taking the odd sip of wine. Naturally, Schmidt rescued the girl from this impossible situation immediately. He took her to his flat. This first night spent with Gitta was a complete failure. She became cheeky. Even as she was making an effort to be nice and pass over his fiasco, she became cheeky.

The Trip to Sylt

It rained all day. Just once, very early in the morning, they ran down to the beach through the rain in their swimwear. Murky grey sea with very light spray on the waves. They just splashed around a little at the water's edge, not daring to go in the sea because of the wind. Oddly enough, there was no sign here to warn bathers.

They spent the rest of the day lying in bed and reading, each with a few books and magazines spread out around them. From time to time, one of them would read something out. In between that, Manfred Schmidt slept for long periods while his girlfriend Gitta read her novels. He wasn't very interested in reading. Still, he too found this rainy day more pleasant than the previous tiring sunny days, when one always had the feeling of missing out on something.

Attendance at a Not-Insignificant Party to Which He Is Taken by His Pretty Girlfriend Gitta

Everyone knew that Schmidt knew something about Emperor Frederick II in Sicily (from some trip to Sicily). To impress the board members who had also come to the party, he brought up that very topic. Gitta was very embarrassed. But she didn't want to interrupt him, as she didn't know how he would react.

With his intensely blue eyes and hard black stars in his eyes. His head looked good and no doubt functioned fairly well but seemed to be used in a very one-sided way. He had some kind of inhibition about using it. She brought him cigarettes and a glass of the champagne that the waiters were standing around holding. She tried to get him out of the circle where he had got stuck in conversation.

A bone of contention between Gitta and M. S.

I can't stand it when he says:

That's not official yet.

Tomorrow's another day.

We don't even know if we'll still be here tomorrow.

Let's just wait and see.

That's still a long way off.

We don't know yet what'll happen between now and then.

There's some inbuilt inhibition that prevents him from using his brain, except with things he can see. His brain is completely dominated by those eyes.

Reconciliation

A crisis between Manfred Schmidt and Gitta dragged on for almost half a year, though neither of them became genuinely aggressive. Neither of them blew their top, and it was virtually over by the time Gitta had the felicitous idea of taking a trip together. She would have come up with all manner of ideas if it had been a whole series of afternoons rather than just one. But the exception was already enough for the travel project.

A stopover in the mountains, because they found the mountains impressive and wanted to make decisions. So they climbed up and looked for a hotel. They couldn't get a room, but there was a vacant bathroom in one of the big hotels. They took the bathroom, and the staff arranged some makeshift facilities.

They had a large meal–there were no other choices available–but were compensated for the uncomfortable expenditure by the fact that they had found an empty tin can from England while getting dressed in their bathroom, and were happy to take it with them. They felt richer than they had during the train ride and were completely reconciled before the second course had even arrived.

Later on they tried out whether they could both fit in the bathtub, which took up the most space in the bathroom. But it was two tight for two, so instead they chose the operating table that had been set up for them to sleep on. It was an absolutely clean room, white linen with the scent of detergent, fresh, very hot, giving them red ears; they cleared up the black clothes that were lying around. It was all so clean and tiled and overheated in this bathroom, with only artificial light, they were pleasantly full from their large meal and occasionally heard people walking down the hallway outside, it was so hot that they didn't want to be cautious too. They knew of no better way to show their reconciliation than this. They would have liked to devour each other, but contented themselves with not being cautious.

Gitta's Monologue

Should Gitta become a mother? Should she do something? Take matters into her own hands or ask Manfred Schmidt? The latest time is the end of the third month. In those days of doubt, Schmidt sent Gitta three red roses, delivered by a Fleurop courier.

A Side Trip by Manfred Schmidt During That Time

The young girl Carmela Pichota, known as 'Lastics', was born in 1926. At the age of 16 months, she fell into her mother's washing water and received light scalds, then skin transplants; the child got through it all well. No further incidents until the age of 17. As a 17-year-old nurse at a military hospital, a romance with a considerably older married man who had been sent there to recover. For him, it was over as soon as he left the hospital. For her it was a shock. Four abortions within a year, now she was 18. In the next few years she studied economics.

I shouldn't have started anything with her. I actually had an aversion to her. When I looked at her, I hadn't seen what an unlucky person she is.

His Girlfriend Gitta Doesn't Become a Mother Yet

This time she came back to the pub completely transformed and whispered to one of the people sitting there. Something secret. The skin of her face was different, slightly pale: white, olive. She lit a cigarette.

Can Love Be Aborted Too?

He brought his filled-up emotions to her in this unfamiliar town. Gitta had been waiting at the hotel since his message arrived. She had gone shopping in town during the morning hours. In those days, he came to her from drawn-out, smoky morning meetings. As soon as he was with her at the hotel, he drew a line separating the tiresome morning from their time together and gave himself up to her. He repeated that so often, trampling about on the one point where new emotions revealed themselves, that there was soon nothing left.

(When he arrived, he was overflowing with sympathy and completely wrapped her in it. He shone on her almost all afternoon, only just back from his unrewarding morning activities. Her brain was like a freshly raked garden, but not only her brain–her arms and legs were willing too, and she surrendered them to him. Such warm, soft lips. Then he stopped shining on her.)

Separation

Schmidt and Gitta withdrew for a week to Krefeld, where there was not a soul who knew them, to bring their separation into the world in peace and quiet. Gitta took care of that for both of them. She was exhausted when the result produced by the retreat, for which she had hopes, proved to be separation. Schmidt paid for her to take a trip to the North Sea and joined her for a few days; he let her get burnt brown by the sun in Rantum. He was content with this solution, but still only half-sure about the separation, as he still had Gitta close to him every day; he enjoyed freedom as an idea and their bond as the reality. He was already looking forward to a winter with Gitta, for he assumed that their relationship would now reawaken. Much to his surprise, however, the separation proved to be a fait accompli once he had left Rantum. One gets entangled in guilt. But what else can one do?

A Sudden Recollection of Gitta

A line of hair going from right to left under the kneecap. No resemblance otherwise. The woman had her legs crossed and wondered, albeit without raising her eyes from her newspaper, why the man—they were the only two passengers left in that carriage—was looking at her knees for so long.

Portrait of a Woman Happy to Have a Cold (G.)

She was freezing her socks off, which made her speak more than usual. The metamizole-quinine tablets were no use at all. She had borrowed a men's pullover that had to be fetched especially from the cloakroom and wore a fur coat over it, but she was still freezing. In front of her were several glasses of mulled wine that the gentlemen had ordered her. Each of them wanted to buy her something, and before they had all reached an agreement that just one would order—or a few take turns—it was there. She sat there, wrapped up as if it was deepest winter.

Past the World City

After the long journey through the night from the country to the city, she has to wash her entire upper body. She has the feeling that she must to do it to be fresh and cool. The sinks in the entrance area of the station toilet are under surveillance, so she does it in the toilet with the water that comes out freshly to flush the toilet bowl; one can lift the lid off the water tank. She washes herself, and once she is dry she puts her clothes back on. Now she is strong, she has some small chance of a future ahead of her. Her path leads her to Bockenheim, on the edge of the metropolis of Frankfurt. She regrets that.

The film and TV production company whose job advertisement Rila answered, and where she is now going, is located in the backyard of a two-storey building. The street is as provincial as the one Rila comes from. The two-storey building has a modern annexe consisting of cabins, leading to a garage. This is where the production company is at home. Rila has to wait.

Later on she can judge it all much better. She has to face being told that they already decided against her the previous evening, while she was still preparing for her journey. The role has been cast. They will cover her travel expenses if she insists. In spite of all this, they ask her some questions.

DIRECTOR: What have you done so far? Oh yes. Here are your photos. Who photographed you?

Rila answers all the questions; she is hoping for the role, for her breakthrough. 'The film is about relationships with women,' says the director, who is also in charge of the production. 'Yes,' answers Rila, 'I've had relationships like that, several of them.'

DIRECTOR: In what sense?

RILA: Pretty much the way you mean.

DIRECTOR: And what was your experience?

RILA: I'd already had that experience.

DIRECTOR: I mean, what's your attitude towards it?

RILA: Positive.

DIRECTOR: The film is about one woman gradually getting closer to the other one. One feels a kind of magnetism.

RILA: As often happens.

DIRECTOR: But in this case, it's something special.

RILA: Aha.

DIRECTOR: The two women become closer.

RILA: That has to be expressed well.

DIRECTOR: Yes, it has to be acted!

RILA: I could . . .

DIRECTOR: Don't you go for men at all?

RILA: Do you mean privately or professionally?

DIRECTOR: Privately *and* artistically.

RILA: Well, artistically I'm supposed to act the other way here.

DIRECTOR: Sure, but we do also approach it in a documentary way.

RILA: Then I just have to imagine it intensely enough . . .

DIRECTOR: I mean, inwardly? Really?

RILA: The camera can't pick that up, I've heard.

DIRECTOR: Just asking.

Later, as already mentioned, Rila, who was now waiting again, had to find out that this conversation, which tried to probe her inner emotions, was completely superfluous (the questions were so hard to answer because it wasn't about whether the answer was true or untrue but whether it would lead to being hired). The production company lacked the professional knowhow to formulate a rejection in time, and wasted the day by putting questions to the people who had been summoned and acting as if the role still had to be cast.

Rila also felt they knew nothing about the subject they wanted to make a film about. She had the impression–and it took a great effort for her mind to refute this impression–that the whole production company was a facade and they actually intended to do something quite different from making a film.

She became restless. She ran to the toilet and vomited. It seemed to her that she had bad breath, she felt herself getting weaker, so that the men plucked up the courage after all to tell her that evening that they had already decided against her the previous day. She grew angry. Most of all because she had attuned herself to the artistic questions for nothing. She should never have thrown herself at the job, and the follow-up to the conversations would probably have involved spending that very night giving her body and soul to one of the directors, who would have probed her willingness to say risqué things on the pretext of testing her 'playfulness'.

Rila walked briskly to the train station, then drove past the world city and back to the country, stinking calmly and uncaringly.

A Learning Process with a Fatal Outcome for Otto Laube and Fritz Brink

I

In 1938, in the small towns of Gröningen and Egeln, near Halberstadt, lived Fritz Brink, formerly a journalist in Magdeburg and the son of a major in the First World War, and Otto Laube, owner of a garden centre. Laube had gained attention as a jockey at various riding and driving shows in Halberstadt. As soldiers of the revolution, they had been marching at the front of their SA company since 1931. Their wives, Rose Laube and Dagmar Brink, were friends. Their shared work towards great political change drove the men together. 'And fresh sustenance, new blood, I draw from the wide world.'[1]

After the successful revolution in March 1933, Brink took the position of SS Local Group Leader in Gröningen and Otto Laube did the same in Egeln. This was not simply a change of government. This revolution was total, in the sense that it encompassed the 'whole human being'. Overturning the education system, overcoming the terrible

1 From Goethe's poem 'Auf dem See' [On the Lake] (1775). [Trans.]

cowardice, doing away with property restrictions, at least to the extent that Laube and Brink took control of and redistributed certain properties and assets (Tacke Grain Company, Jewish property, Münemann and Gresinsky, etc.) within their range of influence.

'Behind the last house, all alone,
the red sun goes to bed,
and stern closing octaves intone
the day's rejoicing's end.'[2]

They thought, now it's the revolution and then everything will be overturned, our private lives too . . .

An elderly journalist, W. Jattmann, worked for a Magdeburg daily. He visited Egeln in 1938.

Since 1934, the friends Brink and Laube **had often swapped their wives, Rosi and Dagmar.** Frequent 'parties' together. Jattmann heard about this. He reported Brink and Laube to the *Gauleiter*; his motive is unknown.

II

[Laube Otto was his motto] In his initial panic–upon hearing the news of his denunciation–Laube drank a brandy, then took tablets that he found in his wife's bathroom (their villa had three). He lay down in bed, curled up, and pulled the blanket over his head. That was the state in which he was found by the maid who was about to clear up. In the twilight of that April day, the maid ran to the

2 From Rilke's poem 'Abend' [Evening] (1895). [Trans.]

Egeln physician, Dr Gerti W.: 'Madam doctor, please come quickly, Mr Laube is lying there and we don't know what's the matter.'

The doctor followed the girl. It was known in Egeln that she had been engaged to Laube between 1926 and 1928, during her time at university. She found Laube curled up in his bed, a position often assumed by those with appendicitis. Laube was speaking unclearly. The doctor sent the maid out. 'Where is Mrs Laube?' 'She isn't here.' 'Gerti,' Laube stammered, 'the glory is over.' The experienced doctor presumed poisoning by alcohol or tablets. She pressed down on his stomach. She left Laube's house to fetch a few instruments from her surgery. She wanted to try pumping his stomach.

The maid caught up with her halfway there on her bicycle: 'Madam doctor, you must go to Mr Laube at once, he's shot himself.' The doctor found a bullet lodged in his brain and a shot in the stomach. Only now did she realize that Laube had, partly in her presence, attempted suicide. The patient was unconscious, breathing feebly.

She felt the entry wounds. 'My Ottokar, it can't be true.' She gave him a slim chance but at that moment it occurred to her that perhaps he had no wish to be saved. She tried to dress him in the uniform that had been laid next to the bed. She wanted to be faithful to his idea: 'A death that befits the overall picture of Laube in life.' But the shirt was missing a piece where the second bullet had entered, around the stomach; he had probably intended to hit the chest. Take off the clothes again. She changed her mind: she wanted to save whatever could be saved of Laube. 'Hopefully Otto still has a mind.' She said to herself, 'The bullet that entered his head is subject to gravity, meaning that it will gradually sink and affect further parts of his brain. This process occurs very slowly. So any movement of the head is extremely dangerous.'

She reflected that admitting Otto to the district hospital in Egeln might not be in his interests. She sent someone to search the town for Mrs Laube, her successor at Otto Laube's side. Around 9 p.m. she reached Fritz Brink, the Local Group Leader in Gröningen, who instructed: 'Wait until I come.' The doctor examined 'Ocka' Laube's breathing, his eye responses. She sent the maid to bed and prepared one of the bedrooms for herself.

III

Fritz Brink's sports car, approaching from Gröningen, was stopped by officers from the Halberstadt Criminal Investigation Department at the entrance to Egeln. 'Local Group Leader Brink, we learnt from your adjutant that you were on the way here and came to meet you so as to avoid any incident.' Fritz Brink followed the detective to the district court jail. Other detectives appeared at Laube's villa. As everything seemed to be out in the open now, the doctor instructed that Laube be taken to the district hospital. Rosi Laube, who returned from a trip to the Harz Mountains around 11 p.m., was taken into custody by the detectives. Around 1 a.m., someone with a voice unknown to the doctor called on the telephone: 'Dagmar Brink sends her regards. Green Minna was there, keep mum at all costs!' The doctor was unable to pass the message on, as Mrs Laube had already been arrested; the unconscious Otto Laube was carefully taken away.

A tall, handsome officer type. 'Shall we go to the Oker Valley dam? We've got four trays of plum cake in the car. We'll stop at Pfeifert's on the way and pick up some drinks. Come on, it's Tuesday afternoon. They've forecast lots of bad weather coming from Iceland, but it's all sunshine here in the Harz!'

Fritz Brink said to the prison guard, whom he knew and whom he brought a bottle of liqueur, 'If Ocka Laube kicks the bucket, I'll be looking after both our wives from now on. No one admits to anything. It's still not clear whether the arrest happened because of confiscating some flour from Tacke & Co.'

IV

At four in the morning, Mrs Brink called on von Schwertner, her lawyer. Schwertner spoke on the phone with friends in Magdeburg and concluded these conversations that it was a matter of **moral misconduct**. He let Mrs Brink explain it to him.

Mrs Brink: 'So if we said that Mrs Laube and I were lesbians, and that wouldn't even be true, we just would've been trying to get our husbands going–that wouldn't be punishable, my husband's adjutant said.' Schwertner: 'You, my dear Dagmar, can do whatever you like. All that matters is that the men didn't touch each other.' Dagmar Brink: 'But they did!' Schwertner: 'We have to forget about that right away.'

The head of the Egeln district court had joined the consultation. He said, 'They were all totally drunk, and whatever the comrades do when they're drunk can't be reconstructed. The only mistake was letting anything get out at all.'

V

[Exchange and absolute value] The greater habitat of Germany (initially within the borders of the Old Reich but feeling like a greater habitat) is full of **exchange possibilities.** Between them, like mined terrain: **absolute values** (criminal law, moral order). Values like 'An official does not swap his wife' bring death on those who break them. This is where the exchange possibilities end.[3]

1. Absolute values, easily understood: Criminal Code §181 I 2: 'Severe sexual procuration, if the guilty party is the husband of the procured person, a) he must intervene in her indecent behaviour' (Reich court ruling 58, 97). Compare Criminal Code §180 A 2: 'The offence can equally be carried out by omission, if there is a duty to prevent fornication, unless there is no abetting, but that is not the case in practice' (Reich Court Ruling 58, 98 established law practice).[4]

2. Absolute values, difficult to understand (Hegel): 'Marriage, and essentially monogamy, is one of the absolute principles on which the ethical life of a community rests.'

---

3 *Gaurechtsführer* Jordan: 'Our victory is the sharpest and most instantaneous establishment of absolute values (such as blood, purity of family, inheritance)–in brutal violation of all values if need be.'

4 *Established Law Practice of the Reich Court in Criminal Matters,* VOL. 58, p. 98.

‘Because marriage contains the aspect of emotion, it is not absolute but, rather, fluctuates and contains the possibility of dissolution. But laws must hinder this possibility to the highest degree.’

‘In modern dramas and other artistic representations, however, where love between the sexes is the primary object of interest, the element of pervasive frostiness encountered there is brought into the heat of the depicted passion by the attendant, complete **arbitrariness**, the fact that the entire interest is imagined as resting only on **this**, which can certainly be of infinite importance for **it** but is not so **in itself**.’

‘Love is therefore the most tremendous contradiction, irresolvable by the understanding, and in it there is nothing more resilient than this punctuality of self-consciousness which is negated, yet which I am nonetheless meant to hold as affirmative.’

3. Further values (as of 1929ff.): forcefulness; awareness of ownership; self-sacrifice; doggedness, hardness; cleanliness; being decent; identifying oneself through knowledge; the way one sits; quality of craft; curiosity; kindness; ataraxia (unshakable calm); sensual joys, or rather: a certain sensuality and imagination, scepticism, letting things go, leading calmly, command of eating and speaking apparatus; ability to discriminate, understanding of values; understanding of the world, mobility, family orientation, love, normality, moderate warmth; quick reactions, homesickness, rootedness, natural and national consciousness, sharpness of mind, heart, heartiness, elegance; polyvalence, realism, search for truth; right, culture, sense of military honour (discipline), duty. Essentially, it all comes down to one thing: **the will to persevere.**

Popular leaders in the provinces like Otto Laube and Fritz Brink, resting on an emotional foundation of millions of 'like-minded' people (thinking alike in their conflicted emotions, which wanted 'different' and 'manifold' things), thought they could help themselves as part of a 'revolutionary change' in 1929–38. Laube knew a tune from the opera *The White Lady* by heart; he sang it when he was drunk. Gottschalk the Jew always ate caviar with potatoes. He sent a plate of it over to Brink, who was also at the Sour Snout. Brink ate it, pretended he hadn't received it from the Jew, and in return gave Gottschalk, whom he was unable to save after all two years later, some Limburg cheese in his side pocket. Whenever Laube left the Sour Snout, he said, 'I'm not driving down Schmiedestrasse, I'm taking the Martiniplan steps,' then drove his Opel down the near-vertical steps from the twelfth century. 'Women are my weak point, that's where I'm mortal. When I kiss the first, I'm thinking of the second and already sneaking a glance at a third.' Brink had a 'fat cough' at the time. The brigade drove from Egeln to Halberstadt with a flat plum cake and two crates of beer on the back seats. '*I'll pull out an eyelash and stab you dead, then I'll take my lipstick and paint you red, and if you're still angry you're pulling my leg, I'll douse you in spinach and order an egg.*' A brickyard owner 'wanted to drill his way into Laube's heart'. This rich man came from Brazil, where he had 'put the slits in coffee beans'. At a garden party in Egeln with the theme 'An evening at Maria Theresa's court' they 'built more arbours than there were couples'. Laube and Brink had to go to Halle on a deployment. There was going to be a street battle. Brink: 'Either I'm coming back or I'm coming in a little bag.' What he meant was that he wanted to be burnt, definitely not buried with the worms on the Egeln cemetery, the soil was 'too fat'. On this emotional foundation: the energetic will to prevent any static battle, to break through the front of 'antiquated values'.

VI

Interrogation of Fritz Brink before the party's head inspector, the comrade District Court Councillor Paul from Halle. Brandy is served. The question is whether to get party comrade Brink out of jail, whether the party should discipline him or expel him on account of violating party rules.

DR PAUL: Party Member Brink, you have been friends with Otto Laube since 1932?

BRINK: Longer than that.

DR PAUL: You've known Mrs Laube just as long?

BRINK: No.

DR PAUL: If you could answer more precisely . . .

BRINK: The Laubes have only been married for four years.

DR PAUL: Your wife is also friends with Mrs Laube?

BRINK: Yes.

There is no denying it: Local Group Leaders Laube and Brink occasionally swapped wives. The women were not used to such things; they reacted with silliness. 'So we cracked jokes for about four hours. Gradually a certain atmosphere developed. We were all good friends, after all.'

'Those are secondary circumstances,' said District Court Councillor Dr Paul, 'but I need to form a precise idea of this, so these secondary circumstances are also relevant for the larger picture in order to establish the type of deed.'

BRINK: So one word led to another.

DR PAUL: What does that mean?

BRINK: First of all, I felt up Rosi Laube to find out where she was sensitive. I reject any kind of inconsiderate approach.

'The women', said the head inspector, 'had not had any "experiences" before getting married to you and Laube, had they?'

BRINK: No.

DR PAUL: So they were especially used to each of you as their first men, in a sense even dependent on you.

BRINK: We'd spoken to them beforehand and agreed on the matter.

DR PAUL: Were there any difficulties?

BRINK: I had to intervene when I saw that Laube was treating my wife in completely the wrong way. A woman is a highly valuable instrument, the same way one doesn't just grab a horse. In my view, promiscuity has a detrimental effect on a woman if the respective other man makes mistakes. That doesn't apply to Otto Laube in general. But that first evening, I had to stop him. That created some resentment.

DR PAUL: What was the result of this resentment?

BRINK: Nothing. We took two hours to get over it, because naturally, I couldn't just carry on with Rosi Laube after intervening with her husband on behalf of my wife. We opened a few bottles, after that the atmosphere was fine again.

DR PAUL: And you had intercourse?

BRINK: Not on that evening. My bladder too full.

DR PAUL: You have been in the party since 1932. With this matter, you are causing the party some difficulties. Word has spread in Egeln and in Magdeburg. I saw you in 1934 when you were arraying your men in Magdeburg-Buckau. That looked good.

Now Laube's interrogation at his hospital bed.

DR PAUL: Your name is Otto Laube and you are a Local Group Leader?

LAUBE: Yes.

DR PAUL: A party member since 1932?

LAUBE: Yes, since 1928.

DR PAUL: Cavalry captain?

Weak nodding.

DR PAUL: You are known as 'Ocka' and are the addressee of this postcard written by Dagmar Brink, the wife of Local Group Leader Brink. 'Dear Ocka, I long for the three of you and embrace you all together. Dagmar.' Why did she have to write that on an open postcard?

Laube's ADJUTANT, who was sitting beside the bed, spoke on Laube's behalf: We didn't expect any consequences because of postal privacy.

DR PAUL: Now the postcard is in my hands.

ADJUTANT: Can one really conclude so much from the postcard . . . ?

You can't be serious, said the head inspector.

'It is undeniable,' said Dr Paul, 'that Laube and Brink believed the boundaries of moral law had shifted as a result of the National Socialist revolution.'

The head inspector wanted to know whether the 'sessions' with three or four of them had involved any masturbation or paedophilia. Laube's adjutant confirmed: there was nothing except severe sexual procuration.

BRINK'S ADJUTANT: An occidental, Christian prohibition.

DR PAUL: You see, dear comrade, I recently went to my wife during her period. There is an old Jewish prohibition. I made a deliberate point of ignoring that. But afterwards I had a burning sensation, and then thought: there's something in it after all. It's simply not healthy.

The head inspector, Dr Paul, recommended a temporary expulsion from the party for Brink, loss of all party offices and later the transfer of both leaders and their wives to locations far apart from each other.

Laube's adjutant and the head inspector drove to Halberstadt for a drink at the 'Hacker'. Laube's adjutant later fell near Kiev.

VII

['Dragged into her lap yesterday, today from her bosom cast away'][5] The Chief Prosecutor in Magdeburg misunderstood the decision of the party's head inspector: for him the most important fact was the replacement of Brink and Laube as Local Group Leaders, which he took as their 'neutralization' by the party. He brought charges of severe sexual procuration against them. The indictment read: 'Brink carried out sexual intercourse with Mrs Rosi Laube orally and in unnatural fashion continuously and in several individual acts, as well as exchanging affections equivalent to sexual intercourse in 17 cases while maintaining full marital sexual relations; at the same time, Otto Laube did likewise with Mrs Dagmar Brink in various locations (Oker Valley dam, parts of the Harz Mountains, Laube's villa and Brink's home); evidence to follow.' The four defendants were found guilty of severe sexual procuration by the Magedeburg Regional Court and each sentenced to five

5 From the poem 'Abschied von seiner untreuen Geliebten' [Farewell to His Unfaithful Lover] by Johann Christian Günther (1695–1723). [Trans.]

years in prison and revocation of civil rights. After the verdict became known, a higher party authority stepped in. The sentence was quashed by the Reich Ministry of Justice; the new sentence was death for the men involved, while the seduced women were acquitted.

Otto Laube was in a semi-conscious state at Egeln District Hospital. He could move his hands but not speak. It needed to be established whether he should be nursed back to health, or at least a somewhat conscious state, before his sentence was carried out; the idea of punishment required that the condemned man feel something. A further basic principle was that acts of justice could only be performed on a legally capable person. In this state, however, Laube was only partially capable. But if these principles had been applied properly, he should not have been sentenced in the first place. The prosecution decided on a compromise: temporary stimulation followed by execution in 'the most near-conscious moment'.

The members of the SA company in Egeln, mobilized by the desperate wives Dagmar Brink and Rosi Laube, wanted to march to Magdeburg Prison under their new Local Group Leader, SA Cavalry Captain Pfeffer, and break in to rescue Brink. The men were stopped in Heudeber-Dannstedt by a higher SA leader. 'Comrades, don't make a scandal of this. We can't help these two former comrades any more. Don't get yourselves into dire straits!' Soldiers had been deployed to the suburb of Magdeburg in case the men got through. So the company turned back. 'We sang a battle song underneath the hospital window for Laube, who didn't notice anything.'

After the sentences of Brink and Laube were carried out, their wives were sent to separate places in the Reich and given work. Even without the order to keep apart, they were much too terrified to want any more contact with each other.

An Attempt at Love

In 1943, X-ray treatment seemed the cheapest way to carry out mass sterilizations in the camps. It was doubtful whether the resulting infertility was lasting. We once brought a male and a female prisoner together for a test. The designated room was larger than most of the other cells and was lined with carpets belonging to the camp management. Our hope that the prisoners would comply with the test in their maritally decorated cell remained unfulfilled.

Did they know they had been sterilized?

That was unlikely. The two prisoners sat down in different corners of the room, which had floorboards and carpets. We couldn't tell through the bull's eye in the wall, which was there so that we could watch from outside, if they had spoken since being brought together. At any rate, they didn't have any conversations. This passivity was especially unpleasant because high-ranking guests were expected to observe the experiment; to speed things up, the camp doctor in charge of the experiment ordered the two prisoners' clothes to be removed.

Were the test subjects ashamed?

One can't really say that the test persons were ashamed. Even without their clothes, they stayed more or less in the same positions as before; they looked as if they were sleeping. 'Let's wake them up a bit,' said the supervisor. Gramophone records were brought in. One could see through the bull's eye that both prisoners initially reacted to the music but they returned to their apathetic state shortly afterwards. It was important for the experiment that the test subjects finally begin, as this was the only way to be sure whether the inconspicuous sterilization of the persons who had been treated would remain in effect for longer durations. The groups taking part in the experiment waited in the hallways of the castle, a few metres from the cell door. They kept quiet. They had been instructed only to speak in whispers. An observer was following the events inside. In this way, the two prisoners were supposed to believe that they were alone.

But no erotic tension developed in the cell. Those responsible almost felt that a smaller space should have been chosen. The test subjects themselves had been carefully selected; according to their files, they should have taken a considerable erotic interest in each other.

How did people know that?

J., the daughter of a Brunswick government councillor, born 1915, so around 28 years old, with an Aryan husband, A-levels, studied art history, was believed in the small town of G. in Lower Saxony to be inseparable from the male test subject, a certain P., born 1900, no profession. It was for P. that J. left her husband, the one thing saving her.

She followed her lover to Prague, then to Paris. In 1938 the authorities succeeded in arresting P. on Reich territory. A few days later, J. entered Reich territory in search of P. and was also arrested. In prison and later in the camp, both of them tried several times to find each other. Hence our disappointment: now they were finally allowed to meet and now they didn't want to.

Weren't the test subjects willing?

Generally speaking, they were obedient. Willing, I would say.

Were the prisoners well nourished?

For some time before the experiment began, the persons chosen as test subjects had been nourished especially well. Now they had already been lying in the same room for two days without any attempts at contact. We gave them protein jelly made of eggs and the prisoners took it greedily. Senior Squad Leader Wilhelm had them both hosed down and then they were taken back to the room with the floorboards, freezing, yet even the need for warmth didn't bring them together.

Were they afraid of the libertinage to which they felt they were being exposed? Did they think it was a test in which they had to prove their morality?

Did they know that both their bodies would be dissected and examined if impregnation ensued?

It's unlikely that the test subjects knew or even suspected that. The camp management repeatedly gave them positive assurances in case of their survival. I think they didn't want to do it. To the disappointment of Senior Group

Leader A. Zerbst and his companion, who had come especially for the experiment, we were unable to carry it out, as none of our methods–including those using force–led to a positive result. We pressed their bodies together, kept them in contact while slowly warming them close to their skin, coated them in alcohol and gave them alcohol, red wine with eggs, even meat to eat and champagne to drink, we adjusted the lighting–but none of this caused arousal.

Did you really try everything?

I can guarantee that we tried everything. We had a senior squad leader with us who knew about such things.

Bit by bit, he tried out all the things that usually work without fail. We couldn't go in there ourselves and try our luck, as that would have been racial defilement.

Did we become aroused ourselves?

More than the two in the room, at any rate; at least, that was what it looked like. On the other hand, that would have been forbidden. I therefore doubt that we were aroused. Perhaps agitated, because it wasn't working.

If I give my heart to you,
will you come to me this night?

There was no way to get a reaction from the test subjects, so we broke off the experiment without any results. Later it was resumed with other persons.

What happened to the test subjects?

The rebellious test subjects were shot.

Does this mean that at a certain level of misfortune, love can no longer be brought about?

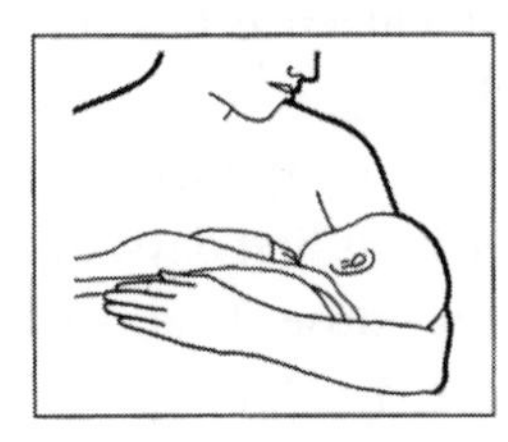

FIGURE 11A. The ball.

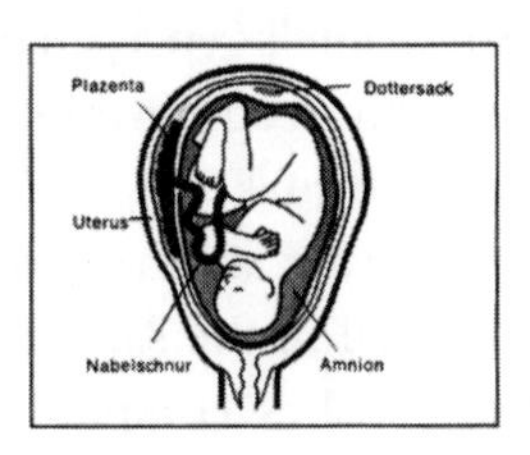

FIGURE 11B. Months earlier, completely different bloodstream.

FIGURE 11C. Baby anteater, embryo

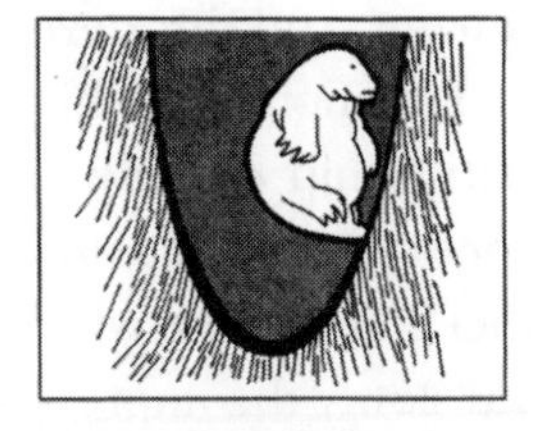

FIGURE 11D. Somewhat later, still connected to the mother's bloodstream. In the wall there is warmth, a teat.

The Robot as Emotional Intelligence

Everyone is born. One can't remember the first days, people say, though I think there are memory traces that we simply cannot read. Robots with artificial intelligence are being built. One woman, a scientist at MIT, is developing a beautiful robot creature programmed according to the behaviour between mother and child during those first days. It can recognize a large face, and as soon as the face disappears, its cardboard ears droop, it assumes a sad expression and thus seems more intelligent. The robot is a social intelligence, an emotional intelligence. It is of little use to this cognitive intelligence that it can count; that is not what makes it intelligent but, rather, the fact that it starts loving another living creature in its first days, that it is shaped in the same way as a grey goose. That is what distinguishes computer intelligence. Its developers are convinced that there will be a new intelligence in 40 to 80 years, emotionally capable and intelligent computers and robots; in a sense, they will continue the better part of humans. And this development starts from the mother–child relationship, which all of us have experienced. This relationship develops pre-linguistically, as in a musical process–through mumbling, humming and a thousand other sounds with which parents interact with their child. And slowly the impressions are channelled, then at some point the child learns to differentiate. At first it would be unable to differentiate between its own bowel activities and its mother's face. If something is no longer there, if it is tormented or deprived, it will become aggressive but also develop trust. This wonderful process takes place in a musical fashion, with both hemispheres of the brain. That is how a human learns to swim in the world.

The Concept of Self-Regulation Is Unsuitable for Affirmative Assumptions

The principle of self-regulation became an object of affirmative hope in the protest movement. It seemed as if self-regulation existed as a substance. If one examines the things that perform self-regulation, they are **laws of nature** as opposed to those of society, **things and furniture**, namely, the element of dead work that does not deviate from its own independent law, **generic-historical** and **historical capacities for work** like **autonomous reserves**, remembering and forgetting, quite manifold aspects of **co-operation** in the inner sensory community, self-regulation of social **associations**, the mode of action of **history**, aporias, protest, the action of wishes–that is to say, **contradictions** that permit no affirmation. Self-regulation is a comprehensive order that, under the conditions of alienation, usually appears as a disturbance in organization, not an organizing factor.

Birth

We encounter self-regulation once again at a different level, namely, in the birth of a human being. One can follow what happens here, what we call the birth and the first weeks, the first impressions between the child and the world, from an entirely different perspective: from the immediately effective reduction of what the child expresses as a body and as movement on all sides (the two are identical as ciphers but not necessarily appreciable to the adults). The child's 'programme' that becomes apparent in the first phase seems, as a whole, richer than everything that will later come about through growth and upbringing. Compared to other life forms, humans are born especially naked and helpless but have not yet encountered the reality principle. It is probably inaccurate, however, to describe birth as the birth of the 'animal human' for which there is no place in society, for it immediately finds itself surrounded by adults, in divided spaces, in social organization, in organized time scales.

Social Second, Third, Fourth, etc. Birth

One can therefore only understand biological birth in conjunction with a form of social second birth in which the human sets about coding the goals that inhere in them, and coding the processing of their earliest experiences (this is the original language of its self-regulation), then abandons them and leans those of its social surroundings. This second birth encompasses the period of basic fault (up to the learning of language and a modicum of physical control) or, at most, the development of the psychological agencies that, according to Freud, is completed by the age of six. In this time, they can be 'born complete as a social human being' or become an 'incompletely born human being'.

In all processes of first and second birth, as well as all further developments that build on this objectivity–third, fourth, fifth birth, what we call 'upbringing'–the natural law of the available energies (the economy of drives) and their transformations into human or social forms are always determined by the underlying self-regulation. In truth, one cannot understand the hard, energetic instructional intervention, the most successful result of self-control, without examining how it came to be that the self-regulating drive energies and their will could be built up and organized in such a way. The mechanical outside pressure of upbringing, as found, for example, in the devices of Dr Schreber or in practising mechanically, only becomes effective because it appropriates such self-regulations despite the senseless method of intervention.

Michel Foucault described the institutionalization of domination in the microphysics of bodies using examples of the earliest physical education. He speaks of the **politics of the body** and the **political economy of the body.** The child's body wants to be active on all sides–with all its skin, all its muscles, all its joints, all its brain impulses and all that its eyes or hands can reach. But even benevolent adults will not respond to this universal interest. *For the good of the child*, they are interested in ensuring that it learns to sit, stand and walk. They do not necessarily wash its entire body, perhaps only where they suspect it is unclean. A selection takes place. This selection is constraint; it creates movements or regions of the skin that do not receive this attention. One is not yet dealing with further 'punishments', power relationships or barriers like those triggered, for example, by the incest taboo, or the fact that the child is not only supposed to walk but also one day to become an adult who is willing to work. Each of these levels of confrontation between the child's own will and the barriers that cause it to learn and to suffer, which enable it to find its form and restrict itself, is a battle between self-regulation and an opposing objectivity (those who bring it up, after all, are conditioned by reality and act like objects in relation to self-regulation). In this battle, upbringing only wins to the extent that it inherently appropriates automatic energy into its forms of upbringing. It is utterly false to say that upbringing does anything; the children do it with their own powers.

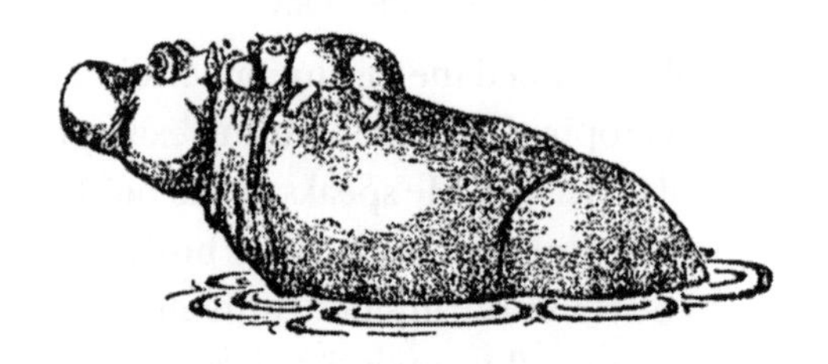

FIGURE 12. Drawing from P. C. Mitchell (1983), p. 185: 'Hippopotamus with offspring on its back'.

An Unusually Difficult Birth

> Every birth and every death, far from being a protracted gradualness, is rather its breaking off and a leap from quantitative to qualitative alteration.
>
> G. W. F. Hegel, *The Science of Logic* (George di Giovanni ed. and trans.) (Cambridge: Cambridge University Press, 2010), p. 321.

On 18 December 1944, the second day of the Battle of the Bulge, an American doctor from Wisconsin set up a makeshift military hospital in the community hall of a village in the Eifel. The tanks of a German Waffen-SS division had rolled past his quarters at a distance of a few kilometres, heading for River Maas; it was snowing. An iron heating stove inside. Attributes of a field hospital.

A pregnant local woman arrived after dusk. She complained of pains. The contractions had been going on for days but she had been unable to give birth.

Strictly speaking, the doctor had been tasked with treating the wounds of his US soldiers. In his bag, due to an interest in the subject, there was an obstetrics textbook.

News from the old Europe. He had another look at the text.

The examination revealed: a breach presentation.[6] The child's bottom was in front and the legs, folded backwards, obstructed childbirth. Outside, gunfire was coming closer. After patiently washing his hands, the doctor 'developed' the walking tools for the incipient little human and then, although he had nothing with him for the operation except a doctor's natural sensitivity and what was in the textbook, written by the German obstetrician Bracht, he held the young creature on his forearm, the back turned upwards and the navel downwards. Now it was a matter of quickly withdrawing the head of this child, whose body was lying in its mother's womb the wrong way around. A difficult task, as the head is by nature too large to make enough space for itself around the chin. The doctor must therefore put their middle finger in the child's mouth and carefully guide the head forwards.

German soldiers entered, a reconnaissance party. The doctor did not let it influence his concentration.

Afterwards, the child, with an unusual bulge on the back of its head (the child was in good voice), lay on a disinfected cotton cloth. The enemy soldiers, impatient, had left again. They hadn't dared to disrupt the operation. Outside it was Christmas.

The next day, the 'US military hospital', consisting of only seven people, headed west towards the Maas, moving

6 A breach presentation is critically dangerous for both mother and child; the doctor's equipment was insufficient for him to risk a caesarean section.

in parallel with the German advance troops. The young woman's relatives had arrived and taken over the community hall. The 'field hospital' had left behind tins of food as well as disinfectant and medical supplies. Christmas Eve with child.

Original Property

One of the mothers in the shared flat was breastfeeding her five-month-old child. The 13-month-old daughter of the other mother—they were all sitting together with macrobiotic food on the table—was crying, as she was watching her fellow child suckling calmly at the other mother's breast. Both of her own mother's breasts were at her disposal; she needed only to turn towards one, then the pullover would be lifted up and a breast would fall into her mouth, so to speak. But the basic property of this 13-month-old also included both of the other woman's breasts.

The mothers usually swapped children. The piece of property belonging to Miriam, the 13-month-old daughter, extended—crawled along one half metre at a time—from the shoulder and breast of one mother to the outer breast and shoulder of the other, wherever they happened to be in this community's spacious living area.

And so Miriam crawled away from her mother, accompanied by the mockery and gazes of both mothers, and reached towards the rival baby with the intention of pushing it away, crying and screaming.

'Let's swap,' said Anne. She gave her five-month-old child to her good friend, who took over. The child did not let the brief changeover disturb it. Now Miriam was also happy. She could assure herself of her endangered property and, while suckling thoughtfully, reached towards the other mother-person with her hand outstretched and an index finger in her mouth; all this was hers alone. Until a sideways glance revealed the betrayal at the other end of her paradise: there lay the baby with her original mother smiling at it. Nervously the 13-month-old turned around for battle, moved down the woman's lap and let her guide her towards her mother's legs. She wanted to restore the correct order, that is, to push the other child from her mother's arms, from her breast.

The maternal friends, far from breaking or manipulating this furious will, which would have been in their power (they were not royal gentlemen or legal advisors), did not stop communally satisfying the five-month-old. So they swapped children again.

A brief moment of victory for Miriam. Then the attentive Miriam once again noticed that her fenced land was being developed by someone else, her presumed reserves being used, firmly refused the breast in front of her, looked to the other side, whimpered, her back leaning against the warm belly of her taller mother, which she explored with her hand. She could really have settled into that position for the afternoon. A walk in the forest was planned. But she could not tolerate this use of her property by another, had to abandon all contentment to go and fight.

'This suffering is necessary,' said Miriam's mother. 'Yes,' her friend replied quietly. 'You can't do anything. She has to bear that suffering.'

She Had Resolved That Her Child Would Want for Nothing: Decidedly Special Treatment

It baffled her endlessly how this living creature reacted to her good intentions. Like someone leaping from the 10-metre diving board, it dropped onto her chest with its nose, cheek, forehead, indeed its entire head, suckled, took a break, then went to sleep. They understood each other without making many sounds. She maintained this intensity for around two years. Then she once 'failed' out of weakness for two or three weeks. And now, for this failure, her little son will always extort her 'love'.

To escape this terror, she stores up 'love' at times when the child does not want her, simply from the perspective of gathering up her entire capacity for love in order to compensate for her failure (which has meanwhile been followed by a number of other failures). The battle between the two revolves around the moment of love, namely, the moment when she feels it, or has it at her disposal, or thinks she must give it in payment, or love at moments when the child demands it, but the mother happens to be bankrupt. Or love when she finds him especially appealing or is embracing him, but he has no wish to be embraced. A tremendous 'mass' of 'love' is redistributed in this fashion. It is not a matter of quantities, however, but of moments: the organization of this 'supply'. It is a glimmer of hope in this unequal battle (at times the child is as big as a tiger, reaching up to the ceiling, at times there is this worm and the mother, an adult giant) that this relationship only influences the child superficially. Underneath this system of terror lives another life, a real life, and draws a part of its sustenance from this underside of its dual attitude.

Nothing Could Be Simpler Than Controlling Gizella

She, for whom men paid everything, met someone who wanted money from her. She didn't know how to turn him down. She gave the man, who had introduced himself as Pit Schwieters, a dishonourably discharged trainee policeman, all that she had on her. For a while she believed it was a 'great love'. Until he got into the habit of poking her in the kidneys, which she didn't like. When he tried this again while she was walking down the steps to the

'Amusing in the Evening'

in front of him, she kicked him in the shin so hard that he fell and tore a bloody wound in his mouth.

During this time, however, her parents were trying to bring her back home. But as soon as she arrived at her parents' place, they started quarrelling about the child. Soon the word 'whore' was spoken. So she went back to Pit, who had settled in the bedsitter she had booked for four months. He had covered everything 'in disorder', that is, his possessions lay strewn over her things. What an amateur. She left the flat on the pretext of buying cigarettes and spent a night in her childhood room (she always had the key to her parents' place with her). Morning surprise. Her son's voice: 'Mummy.' She knew her parents were waiting behind him, that they'd sent the child ahead and were keeping quiet.

Gizella got dressed and briefly picked up her little boy, who had been instructed by her parents, and then left the house without looking at them; but she did return with some shopping around lunchtime. She was easily influenced and now had the will to stay here for good. But when they had finished eating, the dispute began again: she had to decide, the child needed his mother, etc.

There were rum pots in the kitchen cupboards, 26 bottles of elderberry juice, etc. for the winter. Now that she was willing, they wanted to work on her, make her come back by making preserves intended for her return.

As she found this manipulation unbearable, she packed a few things in a carrier bag and went to the bed-sitter, where Pit initially left her alone when she came through the door.

Her happiness only lasted a few days, until she found out that her lover had a little horse running around for him: Angela Schweitzer, who told her. She confronted the man, whose defence was that he wanted to convince her to work for him too. This suggestion, he claimed, was a sign of his 'love'. She didn't actually have anything against him bringing this Angela into their shared 'context'. They could have discussed the possibility of her helping out occasionally as far as her work allowed. When he cornered her and told her how he felt about her, she turned him down. He beat her. She couldn't move around the way she wanted to because she wasn't dressed, and this exposed state limited her movements. She tried her best to fend off his punches, and was glad when the punishment ended the same way every beating ended when she wasn't wearing anything.

In the evening, she was supposed to accompany him to a party. He didn't trust her for a moment and assumed that she would do something like report him at the police station and show them her bumps and bruises. She saw the situation: Pit had invited a gentleman to this party, which was taking place at his sister's place, and promised him something that she could easily imagine. As she definitely didn't want to, there would be trouble later on. She confided in Pit's sister. The two women got on well. The sister might have been able to convince her but now the conversation was already heading in a different direction. She gave her the key to the flat, as Pit had locked the door after they arrived. On the pretext of going to the toilet because she was feeling sick, Gizella left the party room and then ran out of the flat and the house. She heard Pit's sister call after her from the window: 'Run!' She started running, but after two blocks she could already feel Pit catching up. She was hardly afraid. Her one thought: don't get close to the water. She kept decidedly away from the riverbank and the railing, even if the railing looked precisely like something firm to hold on to. She came to the park and threw herself to the ground when he started hitting her, and screamed because she didn't care about anything any more except for it to stop. A few people passed but didn't dare intervene. Her lover dragged her up and stood her up against a tree so that he could reach her face better from both sides, to prevent her from falling sideways from the rapid impact of his blows. She wished it would stop. Because he was thrashing her so frantically, not least to prevent her from being knocked to one side, there was no time for her to change her mind, for example, to agree to his initial intention after all. No one was asking her. She hardly felt any relief when the police patrol arrived. The officers, holding her lover, asked if she had been beaten. She felt the skin inside her mouth with her tongue, worn down, it was bleeding slightly, and said 'No.' As this contradicted her appearance, one of the officers asked if she wanted to press charges. 'Yes,' she said. She wanted the violent bastard put away and later gave her signature at the police station. The officers beat up her boyfriend as she watched and dragged him to the next room as he screamed after her.

Her father appeared at her workplace in uniform the following day; he was a senior patrol officer in the sixteenth district. She intercepted him in the lift but couldn't prevent him from entering the office, pushing her in front of him with his chest, and speaking to the boss. He spoke of a whore and a whore's child but that didn't get him anywhere with Gizella's superior. She was proud of her boss and willing to take him as her new lover that very evening, and subsequently risked a great deal for him, emptying her post-office savings account because the company was in financial trouble.

After work, Pit, who had been set free after coming up with the right pack of lies, came across her in the street in front of her little bedsitter. They had an exchange of words and immediately started punching each other, until a police patrol separated them and took them to the station. As a fellow police officer, now in civvies, Gizella's father had an advantage. Gizella had seen the two of them, who had wanted to catch her outside the flat when she got home from work, from a distance. She ran to the police station and secured police protection to influence the course of events. The chief officer tried to convince her to go home with her father, who had assured him there would be no punishment. She said 'No.' After all she had been through, she didn't feel like going with anyone. She wanted to be alone. Now she thought she could see her father crying; she changed her mind and went with him. After a short time at her parents' house, their supper in the kitchen wasn't ready yet, it was the same old talk about a whore's life, 'Don't you look after your son at all?', which she couldn't have done in the short time since her return anyway, as her son had been with neighbours. She left the house and moved back into the bedsitter; Pit hadn't given back the key and was already waiting there. Now her father, who had drummed up a few colleagues, came and rang the doorbell. That way Gizella's lover didn't dare touch her. She had a vague feeling that her lover and her father might reach an agreement to haul her over the coals together. At that moment, she had no idea how to thwart this version. Why did these life partners always have to oversteer when they controlled her? She submitted just to keep the peace.

In Her Last Hour

I

She had absolutely had enough. Fleeced by P. for six months, then thrown away. She had taken pills. She managed to drive as far as the outward road that led to the suburbs in the Taunus. Then she parked under a pylon. Her eyes became blind.

Kudelski, a sales representative by day and entrepreneurial in the evening, in the time that belonged to him, noticed the half-dead woman with her head resting on the steering wheel. He stopped and dragged her out of the car; she was dazed and puked on the brief way to his Ford. He could tell that this person was only a little leftover of a life. So he 'borrowed' the female part of that leftover on the backseat of his Ford; he had no qualms about violating her right to drift towards death in peace, 'the right of human beings to end their lives as they themselves decide' (though then she should have locked her car). By day, he upheld people's rights; after dark, he didn't.

He should have been quieter, less conspicuous; his hectic movements were noticed by a passer-by, Fred Hirsch, who took down the Ford's registration number.

Kudelski, who was unable to ask for any kind of consent from this woman who was whimpering and dirtying the backseat, saw nothing wrong with raping her–she would soon be dead, but there was still warmth emanating from her body. He had had a tiring day and, as the woman had done something worse than this rape (which wouldn't have been one anyway if she had agreed) by her own hand, he didn't want to let the remainder go to waste.

The direction of Kudelski's intentions saved the woman's life. The police patrol, alerted by Fred Hirsch, blocked Kudelski's path as he was trying to find a spot for consummation in the southern part of the city forest. They took the semi-conscious woman to the university clinic with their blue light flashing. Kudelski was taken to a cell at the police headquarters. He could not even claim he had been driving under the influence, as he was stone-cold sober. He was punished senselessly, when he should really have been honoured for saving the woman.

II

The woman testified in the main trial that she had given up her resolution to end her life. She could no longer 'relate to' the way she had acted. P., her lover, a pea-brained dog, was not worth an uncompromising deed of that kind. She was therefore grateful to the defendant, Kudelski, that he had roused her from her sleep. She did not really hold his malicious intent to use her in her capacity as a woman while she was slipping away against him. She considered herself attractive. She let P. grab her any time. Nor did she have any reason to turn down the defendant, as she would not have recognized him. She was neutral. She was unaware of any basic right to determine the end of one's own life; if need be, she would do without it.

She had been restless, not calm: 'completely beside herself'. Wouldn't she have objected to the defendant's deed if he had carried it out?–The way the judge asked the question, she made it seem frivolous if the witness replied, 'No, I wouldn't have minded at all.' The witness referred to her oath to answer truthfully and said that the hard-heartedness and deviousness of P., who hadn't done anything to her, hurt her more. In any case, the deed hadn't been carried out. So her response to the judge's question was, 'Don't know.' 'That's no good,' said the judge. The sentence she had in mind for Krudelski was either two years and six months or three years and two months, taking into account the man's far-from-exemplary history and his somewhat disreputable occupation, which had been investigated in detail. She believed the defendant to be capable of anything and wanted to prevent further harm.

Researching Weak Points Based on the Work of Beate G., Doctor of Natural Sciences

'There might be a gigantic flash of lightning or a love story, a change of profession, an upheaval, an end of the world, or she might conquer Meier after all . . . '

I

Bold or discrete: but more and more herself. More and more herself, which meant she could not get close to H. Meier.

Reading, creeping about, combing her hair, observing, examining scientifically, wanting something, apologizing, not shying away from severity. She wants to be like Meier. But she is very glad that this lying whore has weaknesses which she would never allow herself. Weakness in this world is strength in another. No: because she doesn't have him. She moves towards him as if he were a haven, follows him like a lapdog and now belongs to the three unfortunate women mourning for him. The only one with dignity is the one who *doesn't* have him. The one who has him, only ever for a short time, seems like a lapdog. Only the misfortune of being left by him throws her back on herself.

'And do not turn away in brooding from the bitter riddle of love, the white breast of the murky sea and every confused wandering star.'

II

At least she knew, whereas Meier did not, for he had only read about it and had a burning interest in it, what such a wandering star might consist of: celestial mechanics, the scale of elements, the plausibility of hypotheses, the genesis of planets, etc. While she was being attentive, or saying something, or keeping still or standing there, her fingers took hold of a piece of wire or a paperclip that can be opened up, or a bit of paper, and bent it, arranged it, with the same intensity with which the woman who was currently all over the papers as a political prisoner repeated her words in short commands. The secret messages had been smuggled out of prison until recently, but this hammering with words is not the correct way to approach mesons, which demand the stone- or hammer-swinging of the Iron Age, that is, an unsuitable tool, an inadequate force to penetrate the determinants below the atom. Thus her fingers conducted a violently productive energy 'sideways', involuntarily, into some waiting process. 'One could operate an electric power plant,' said Meier, who was sitting opposite her in the canteen, 'with the nervous energy of your fingers.' She wanted to reply and her face suggested she would. 'Spit it out,' said Meier.

She was not in the mood for such acute observations of her facial expressions, which Meier tended to make when he had nothing in particular in mind. For five minutes she kept her nervous fingers still (by force) while her feet started drumming in an irregular tempo, which Meier did not see from his position at the table, and even if he heard something, he did not associate it with her.

III

Female scientist, 39 years old, concentrating. The spring convention of the German Society of Astronomy and Astrophysics. She is taking the minutes of symposia III and IV. They are dealing with something extremely distant and precise: the detection of what are termed 'dark holes' in outer space, that is, stars with such an incredibly high mass that their matter becomes 'stingy' and no longer radiates any light waves, radio waves or X-ray waves (the compact mass holds back any that move outwards). These 'dark stars' therefore give no indication of their existence, meaning that they challenge natural science to submit precisely to the unending, the immeasurable.

The symposium consists of a less important official part, filled with presentations, and a second part for informal exchange among the scholars, which is the most important aspect of the spring convention. Beate notes:

–I can't make much sense of that.

–So things are pretty simple in a neutron star. The particles lose their angular momentum by connecting to the magnetic field, and then they go in, but if a black hole can't have a magnetic field, that's why I asked you before, then this process completely disappears, and then one only has this . . .

–No. Wait a minute. Let me just add something here. The one thing I could imagine is that the light emission needs to have a characteristic which diverts the angular momentum. Isn't that the case?

Mr Vogt, an astronomer, joins in:

–It can be accelerated. That could be.

–Yes.

–What Mr Hörterich had considered was . . .

–The energy must radiate . . .

–Yes, that's right.

–But then it would have to, that's amazing . . .

–So a neutron star?

–Then, of course, one can introduce everything . . .

–But when does one really speak of a black hole? Effectively only when there are no photons coming out, or . . .

–Yes. Yes.

–What does compact mean?

–That's right, what does compact mean. What kind of diameter does a white dwarf have?

–10,000 or 20,000 metres?

–Yes. The diameter of a neutron star is normally 10–20 kilometres, and I think the boundary between non-compact and compact lies between those values.

For over 52 hours, Beate G. has been behaving 'purely businesslike' manner. When asked how she is she responds, 'I'm well.'–'One can no longer use big words, but the small ones are inappropriate.'

IV

Whether she intended to or not, she expressed 'misery'; she looked a 'picture of misery' sitting in the frame of leather and iron in this airport lounge next to her departing idol Heinz Meier. One of her large hands on her left thigh, the other leg thrown beside the seat at an 'awkward' angle, just as it had developed historically–as the body part of a former child–the same way entire fronts were left there, 6, 8, 18 divisions in the winter attack of 1941, the way they lay there for one or two years in these awkward random positions until they were scattered or destroyed by some gust of wind. Thus completely on the level of 'destiny', 'con-destined', 'condensed'. The various attributes, not held together by hope, slung over one shoulder like a sack, but who could act as such a shoulder? In other words, laid there sliding, somehow a sack full of attributes–that, to a special degree, was supposed to be a person.

She stood up again after all when the soldiers on guard searched her idol's suitcases and bags. He was the last to board the plane. She lifted her bones and waved time and again, half back turned towards him–that is, she perhaps raised her arm above head height once. She continued this motion while taking the conveyor belt another two to six times towards the airport exit, where she felt no inclination whatsoever to go. Beate G. had a soft spot for Meier.

V

Meier

Every time he left her he became ill. A rising cold, moving from the bronchia up to the nose, to the frontal sinus and back down to the bronchia. His wish to go back: thwarted by his sense of realism. Yet he did not follow this realism willingly, but hampered by accidental damage, for example, cold draughts.

VI

Being Unfaithful in an Unfamiliar City

The unknown woman had claws on her freezing hands. These hands occasionally raised the coffee cup, the rest of the time they remained on the marble table; her fingernails, slender and long, filed, considerably exceeded the fingertips and were painted with blue polish. Her dark eyes hidden behind cheekbones. As she had sat down at Meier's table in this cafe of her own accord, he assumed that she meant him, that he could get something started here. He thought about how to talk to her, as it seemed she was only waiting for him to do so. She sat there tensely, freezing and trembling in the poorly heated cafe. Meier urged her to take her hands off the marble. She could put them in front of her stomach (her dress had no pockets), then they would be warmer. A few moments later, her arms trembled and she threw herself to the ground, saliva dribbling from her mouth. A guest leapt to her aid–Meier watched, mesmerized–and forced a napkin between her convulsively clenched teeth. She thrashed about on the floor. And so this adventure took an unexpectedly negative turn for Meier.

VII

Meier was in a gentle mood for a few moments when he returned from his trip. Dr Beate G. transported him to her flat. At such moments he tried to make him understand that the line he was taking was unrealistic: 'If war breaks out in three years and seventeen weeks or in four years and eight days, then all you are working for so hard will be interrupted.' As if reciting lines he had memorized, he responded: 'This external violence, war, is surely not omnipotent; one shouldn't overestimate it.' He surely didn't mean that seriously, he had just read it somewhere. It was precisely when he truly believed something (I want it to be, yes, I am sure it is true) that he said nothing about it. That was a leftover of superstition in him.

Meier was stubborn. In those days, he would have liked nothing better than to start anew, to sever all ties. He formulated a text in which he asked to be dismissed 'from duty', but then he cut these tangled intersections with reality, with 'women's thoughts', which Beate recognized as weak points and which she had momentarily penetrated.

After this (ultimately futile) conversation, an embrace of a few hours, they first of all fortified themselves with coffee and cake. She was wearing a baggy raincoat, but with a hood like those worn by little bear monks or beer angels or children in bathrooms. 'If you need men, I know one for you. We could do that.' In his presence she was hungry for novelty. That only lasted for a brief moment–as long as he was there. Now she felt nothing, not even the nearness of Meier, who was next to her, rather exhausted, waiting for some connection after she had inhaled five cups of coffee in order to be awake and not miss a moment of this happy constellation. She took his hand, then let it go again because he might find it 'too direct'. She wanted them to have '**robust relations**'. Now, because he was tired, she had him at her disposal for roughly another five or six hours, which did not happen often, and didn't know what she should do with him. 'For the effort necessitated by everything leaves no space for stimulation effects of any kind.'

VIII

Fourth day of the spring convention. Beate G. notes:

–Hm.

–Near Centauri X, observed.

–Yes.

–I don't understand that at all.

–I have this crazy notion that in 1908 a pin-sized black hole just slipped through Earth; it must have been one of those originating from the earliest phase of cosmogony . . .

–Crazy.

IX

Meier's strength is what he does 'on duty'. As for his weakness, she still wanted to investigate that. They have known each other for two years. She was unsure whether to agree to the rendezvous with him in Innsbruck, as he demanded it so vehemently; that didn't suggest he would treat her tenderly. But as it was already thawing in Seefeld and there was nothing to do, she agreed on the phone to meet him. Innsbruck was cloaked in fog. The Easter holidays would most likely bring things to a standstill in the city and environs. As both she and Meier, whom she had only seen for four whole days (if one added up the hours of numerous individual meetings), could not stand being in their little hotel rooms any more, they wanted to take some lovely walks along the riverbank while it was still light. But they never found the riverbank. Walking along one of the streets in the old town (after stopping off at a cafe), Beate was crapped on by a pigeon. On her black outfit, which was really too conservative for the occasion of a spring rendezvous (at home in Osnabrück she was in the riding club, it would have been suitable there, but her riding boots were at home), the whitish stain became more obvious the more she rubbed. So that was the modern substitute for a pregnancy. Until then, being together had been hard work without success for them. The brandy they both poured into their coffee didn't bring them any closer. Beate was tired from driving there, getting to know each other again, removing the unfamiliarity. The city of Innsbruck, feeling like it was in a cauldron. Now being soiled erased the estrangement; she took the stain to their hotel. Unfortunately they no longer had the nerves to 'cultivate' the relationship after the Easter holidays. Meier's strength . . . That's been dragging on for two years.

X

While he placed his hands in front of his face (elbows on the armrests on either side in the train compartment) so that the balls of his hands were touching the corners of his mouth, the side of the hand covering his eyes and his fingertips sliding back and forth between the temples and the ears, he occasionally allowed the sun, which cut through the trees like a knife from outside, to hurt his eyes whenever he uncovered them for a moment; this convinced him that he was really sitting there. Sooner or later he had an idea, and realized (once again shaded and protected by his covering hands) that this skull, which was now also shielding his eager brain activity from the day, would one day be all that remained of him–as bones, and not incalculably long. He felt his cheekbones, his temples and the bones at the back of his head, trying to imagine the skull base bone, which he was unable to touch. It would not have taken much of an 'impact' (a car, not even an act of war) to shatter this magic, for which he would have liked to find some convincing plan, into its component parts, leaving nothing but his skullcap. Near Mannheim he saw a graveyard chapel from the train window; even on the Rhine plain, viewed from the train window, one could imagine a tree-covered place; the Rheingau would make a nice burial ground . . .

This crucial point, which he could only discuss with himself–for it would be embarrassing to seem sentimental if he spoke to colleagues about it–filled him with pleasure and could spur him on to work just as much as making plans. That meant not thinking forwards the way one is used to doing from school, simply because unexhausted time promises surprises, but instead measuring the extent of the available minutes backwards from the endpoint. Then it was clear that there was not much time left. That could just as easily make him helpful, talkative (in all matters except this central question of 'restlessness'), needy for contact and affection.

XI

Her hair was a frizzy mass around her head. Either she nibbled her cake in the canteen, sucked on her cup of coffee or gnawed on a necklace that she held against her mouth, and above that her vigilant eyes, focused on her partner, which looked 'debauched', that is, there was something laughing in them that 'knew the score'. She sat hunched, her legs placed next to each other. Her body was generously wrapped in a thick, light woollen pullover. A herd of sheep had gone into making it. Only the best sheep's wool. She did not feel well. That was why she bought such valuable encasements.

XII

This was her twelfth year as a physicist. She was working in basic research. In a test group that fired elementary particles into a gaseous magnetic field. She never saw these elementary particles; one can only render their trace in the smallest space visible as a smoky little field on the photographic plate.

Punished by the fact that none of the things one wants to have can be bought with money. A feeling of great insecurity.

A particular problem, a research topic she had 'discovered', was preoccupying her. She would not have thought of it if her nerves had not been so torn and tangled by such contrasting activities as 'research' and 'love' for Meier. In that sense, it was difficult for her to judge whether she should approach her research topic as a 'reflection of her self-relation' (poetry) or an astrophysical hypothesis that she could present to her superior (science). It was about three observations that, if they could be verified, constituted a law of physics:

'The elementary particles sometimes break laws of behaviour, but they do this so incredibly quickly that they hardly break them at all.'

'They do the things that are forbidden for the laws of physics at lightning speed, as if nothing were happening, and then they immediately subordinate themselves again.'

'Meaning that certain phenomena on the smallest scale come about in what one could call a loan-like manner.'

That was what she noted down. She was concerned with the behaviour of individual particles on a tiny scale of 10^{-18} centimetres, and this loan-like use of a physically different world was measured for part of a millionth of a second. So nature, Dr Beate G. concluded, makes debts with its laws, or it participates in its own counter-nature, or is 'nature' itself merely a loan from an actually real 'counter-nature'? subversive. Dr G. extrapolates this radically over a total of 80 A4 pages–filled with her tiniest numbers–for example, for 13 billion years and the mass contained in the cosmos, as the cosmos had to behave in that forbidden manner for an appropriately longer time.

Certainly she doubted the objectivity of this promising hypothesis, which seemed applicable for the negative definition of cosmogony or any other purpose; but she had doubts, for she felt that the hypothesis overly mirrored the twofold programme of her own situation: mourning for Meier and her 'businesslike' work for the institute, for which she borrowed the energy from her mourning.

On the other hand, she felt a deep attraction to this hypothesis. After all, all kinds of things could pass through the weak points in nature she had discovered!

Everything is shaky. It's on the brink. There could be a gigantic stroke of lightning, or a love story, a change of profession, an upheaval, the end of the world, or she might win Meier's heart after all. 'She was never scientific in her feelings.' You are never scientific in your feelings, my dear Beate, said the head of the institute, who one could say took part in her experiences through short questioning phrases and remarks. On the other hand, as a weak point researcher, she was convinced that these feelings–'They do the things that are forbidden by the laws at lightning speed, as if nothing were happening, and then they immediately subordinate themselves again.' These phenomena came about 'in what one could call a loan-like manner'.

1. So doesn't the head of the institute know my feelings at all?
2. What if one views not the lightning-fast deviation from the laws but, rather, the laws themselves as depending through a loan on an entirely different physical world? Then all reality is merely borrowed. And now to extrapolate that! She liked that passage.

'The Sensuality of Having': It Doesn't Have to Be the Whole Gerda

Since eight weeks ago he had an achievement to his name: he had taken an attractive personality, Gerda, into his home. He often marvelled at her merits. Her breasts, when he first met her, looked exactly like those of the model on the front page of *Quick*. That showed 'spirit'. She quite clearly thought he smelt good, and practically sniffed his skin, his mouth, his hair, ears–she found the smell 'manly'. Another time she mentioned that men stink. That wasn't very clear. He liked the way she deposited her clothes and things modestly in one corner to avoid creating disorder in his quarters.

He didn't really need a *whole woman* of this calibre. After all, he wouldn't have ordered 1 duck, 1 deer or 1 goose with dumplings and cabbage, only a quarter duck, one goose leg or piece of breast or some saddle of venison. Five to six friends could have joined him in nibbling on the inductee Gerda. But he didn't want to suggest it to her, as he feared she would take offence.

'I have to pull myself together,' he said. He often wished she would be quiet when she kept on at him.

He tried it with some mental emergency relief. He imagined intensely that he was alone, no one had spoken to him in three-fourth of a year, it was cold and draughty, no skin warmth near him, and then a sexual pressure seized him, leading him to roam through parks with binoculars to see if he can espy any girls' skirts in the distance. That was imaginable, even if it had never happened in his lifetime. The conclusion from this situation was meant to be: how happy I am to have Gerda, this striking figure, within my reach now.

While he was trying to *concentrate* in this way she started speaking to him, which disturbed him. He could not simultaneously stoke his appetite and listen to her. Making something that he had more valuable by imagining that he did not have it was possible with food, for example. If he imagined it intensely, the notion that the bread rations had been fixed at 180 g, barely one and a half slices, or, looking at a juicy steak, the thought that this steak would have been unattainable for a soldier near Tula in the winter of 1941, had repeatedly led him to eat more. He had eaten up just as if that would really make him grow up big and strong. Obviously he didn't believe in children's fairy tales. When it came to Gerda, however, he quickly found himself daydreaming. In his special situation, complete solitude seemed attractive. He could only feel in the moment, not in the form of building up reserves.

He Wanted to Keep Her for a While Like a Preserving Jar and Then Exchange Her for Someone Better at Some Point

He was not up for many future things, many surprises. From the start, he couldn't say whether he loved Gabi. What does love mean anyway? He felt fear more often than love, which is a code word for 'various things'. He had long been planning to exchange Gabi, and provoked arguments in order to have that breaking-up energy at his disposal at the right moment. By now a hatred had accumulated between the two of them, but it could not survive before Erwin's 'loving eye' and was transformed into love, that is, a sticky substance that held both of them tight. Each of them assumed there was still something to be had from the relationship before any separation. The thought of separating warmed his heart; that drew him to her every time. Then Gabi drove to Stuttgart around 5 p.m. in late January. The accident left her paraplegic. Now Erwin could no longer leave this paralyzed woman. That would have made him a deserter. He had underestimated how dangerous it could be for his life if he kept drawing out this relationship, which was actually unwanted, day after day.

Any relationship can be patched together, especially one that never had a reason. She gave him a furniture suite for his 55th birthday 'out of gratitude', as she had brought her accident benefit into the marriage. For his 56th birthday she gave him the book *Great Surgeons* (he was a GP) and wrote in it: 'Your eternally faithful Gabi.' That made them both cry, because they knew it was terrible.

The Bed Warmer

I

Minguel Ozmann, from the Yellow Antillean Island—women's escort for money. I would never give up my independence. I earn it every day with my sweat, even if I suppress it in bed by limiting my movements so that I don't make an unpleasant impression. It would be shameful for me if a client had occasion to say, 'Minguel, you're sweating.' Or, 'Kurtchen, dry yourself off with my towel.'

Early in the morning I go to a woman from Boston and give her a massage at her hotel; then I visit my corpse, a Belgian lady to whom I am contracted for the entire day. In that sense, seeing the woman from Boston is already moonlighting. I go swimming with my contractual partner, hold her dead paw in mine on the beach chair and rub her arm, all the while letting the Antillean wind blow around my muscles in beautiful freedom. Then, in the afternoon, I have to 'ambush' Micki–that's supposedly her name–in her room, which means that she says to me, 'You'll phone me first, Kurtchen, you can't just ambush me, I want to know when you're coming.' That's why I say ambush, because I have to think of her forewarning after the call, when I work my way up from my room on the fourth floor of this big building to hers on the sixth.

I got the fright of my life this morning when her ancient fingers touched me on the beach, rousing me from a brief slumber. 'Don't touch me, you old corpse!' I called out. She pulled back her fingers in alarm. While swimming to an offshore sandbank to tire myself out, to get through the day somehow, I called to mind her merits. I need a fixed point to concentrate on. Everything else is a question of attitude. So I make an effort with this client, who is supposed to receive a real product as promised in the contract, which is not purely physical work, as it also demands an inner concentration on the object of effort; that is, at some point I also want to give her some inner feeling that she can take back to foggy Belgium from this sunny beach.

In the afternoon, I found help in the following comparison: I established that the skin on the back of my hand, probably under the influence of the sunscreen, felt similarly sticky to my Micki's skin, so it was clearly a reaction so sun, water and this cream, as my 32-year-old nature undoubtedly has no corpselike attributes–in this respect too, we were two *equal* persons and there was solidarity between us, once I had taken off her clothes, her suspenders and bra and driven her towards a beach chair. I had her eating out of my hand, meaning that she would have agreed to anything, even annulling our contract, if that had reduced the astronomic distance between us–that she would have said, 'Kurtchen, or Minguel, never mind all that, just lie there and have a good sleep or get yourself a chubby girl from downstairs, at least let me watch, or forbid it, then I'll go and have a coffee in the meantime, no conditions, you don't have to cast a grateful glance my way . . . ' While she was in this mood, which touched me and won me over once and for all, I asked her to write me a one-off cheque for 4,000 dollars, which I later found in my suit trousers. She was obviously a rich heiress or widow. I didn't want to ask, as it would have looked greedy.

II

Right now a thunderstorm is pouring its rain over the gardens and terraces of the luxury hotel. Dishes and tablecloths blown off the tables. The decorations for the 'Southern Ball Night' have been destroyed. I hope there'll be quite a lot of destruction in this luxury district; that would give it a news value which can be spread across the whole world and spread the reputation of our Yellow Island on a planetary scale. Only then would the storm have any value. There's no hope of that today, unless a plane attempting a blind landing crashes, as this pattering rain doesn't destroy anything worth mentioning.

'If one has character, one has one's typical experience that keeps recurring.' Thus I argue time and again with my comrades who do the same work I do. My comrades

Charlie and Alfred Duhamel call me a strike-breaker because I fulfil my contractual obligations in all their implications while they just keep to the letter of their contracts. They maintain a distance from their work by denigrating the objects of work, that is to say, their employers. They pinch the women in public to show that they have to put up with this. Until they've been paid, they see themselves as above it all. Alfred Duhamel recently informed his brother of a client's wishes. On the telephone, Charlie replied, 'Don't move until you get the money.'

Here I must defend myself against the accusation that I have no character, or that my devotion to my work harms my independence. Alfred Duhamel: 'Minguel, it is honest and sincere to show one's aversion to this work.' I answer, 'No, there's a conflict there. One should either choose a different job or devote one's entire life to this one.'

Duhamel: 'If you've got 40 clients a day like us, you have to keep your personal side out of things, otherwise you can't get through it.' Me: 'I do one, two at most, but thoroughly.' Duhamel: 'But you look for your own advantage just like we do.' Me: 'Naturally.' Duhamel: 'So why so blockheaded?' I reply that it's a matter of character, refuting his argument. It's not because I have no character but because I do have one that I take this *path of infinite devotion* with Micki, for example. Duhamel: 'That makes problems for us. If one watches you at work, it makes it look as if we're not giving our clients *our all*.'

With my handsome income I could choose or keep one or several girlfriends. I already dislike this form of abstract affection, which is not based on any contract and thus wasted aimlessly; it's a luxury that our hard-working island population, who are defending nothing less than our independence with their working productivity, can't afford. If we want to remain independent of the dollar we must learn to work. A lady from the United States tried to treat me like a gigolo today. We had not even finished luncheon but she already wanted to give me instructions on where and how to wait for her, what I should bring along and what wishes I should fulfil without any further conversation. I paid for the luncheon out of my own pocket and went, leaving her sitting there, bewildered. My ancestors were Indians. Apart from my professional interest, this is the only genuine interest I have: how to defend my independence in keeping with my ancestors' intentions (which I can only imagine, of course). I probe each woman who is given to me to look after to find out whether she knows anything about this. It would give them an additional attraction for me. But they're too hasty. 'People of deep sadness give themselves away when they are happy: they have a way of grasping happiness as if they wanted to squash and suffocate it, out of jealousy–oh, they know all too well that it will run away from them!' Though I would not run away at all but, rather, listen attentively. No collaboration ensues.

III

After spending a few weeks on the Yellow Antillean Island–yellow because of the advertising slogan referring to the sand of the island's former beach–Ms Veronique Clermont, who had introduced herself to Minguel as 'Micki', began to feel unwell. Her paid lover's diligent hands found signs of weight loss and emaciation. She now refrained from all spa treatment and lay calmly in a beach tent. Minguel felt a bulbous swelling on the left side of her neck. There was a palpable growth above one of her teeth. She complained of pains. Minguel, being helpful (partly hoping for a special reward, perhaps a share of the sick woman's fortune), called a specialist. He established contact in the local language, so the doctors saw him as the client.

One afternoon, Minguel found Veronique coughing and gasping for air. He tore open the balcony door. He put her close to the draught, propped up on cushions, and rubbed her neck. The old lady wheezed. Minguel could not help putting himself in the dying woman's position (previously, Alfred Duhamel had warned him, 'You have to keep in mind that this lump of fat has nothing to do with you, otherwise you'll be harmed'). He presented the half-dead woman with a list of her shares and insurance papers that he had found in a box from her bedside table, and had her sign a note on which he had written his first name and surname. He later referred to this note as her *will*, which he intended to have recognized in Belgium. The trusting Micki scrawled her name underneath his.

Minguel then summoned the specialists. Dr Scelinski dragged the croaking woman onto the bed and put his knife to her throat in order to prevent her imminent suffocation with a tracheotomy. At that moment, Ms Veronika wheezed and slumped back. The doctors stopped what they were doing, checked her right pupil and established her death.

The bill for these medical efforts was addressed to Minguel. As the doctors had recorded his details, the authorities instructed him to have the body transported at his own expense (as the *host*). This required Minguel to fly to Europe. The relatives of the deceased accepted the death certificate and let him attend a small ceremony, but refused any further conversations. The 'will' was not recognized. Minguel had to pay for the flight and the Grand Hotel in Brussels. His money was used up. A bout of flu forced him to have himself admitted to hospital, where he was unable to communicate in words. As he did not pay the hospital bill, he was expelled.

If one makes the greatest possible effort with the object of one's work, one will ultimately be rewarded. 'The problem,' says Minguel, 'is that I can no longer say what such a reward might consist of. That's how rooted I am in my work.'

Accuracy of Measurement

The barmaid weighs up how much, very roughly, this guest's wallet contains. She stops serving him once the last significant sum has been spent. That's the art of her gaze. Maybe leave a bit for a taxi ride, 20 marks. If she overestimates by 20 marks, it's bad for business, as it means serving drinks that the guest can't pay for. If she underestimates, the bar has lost potential profits.

A Woman Whose Signature under the Social Contract Is Forged

She comforted the tired businessman's balls, rod, thighs, chest, armpits, etc. and, once he had calmly fallen asleep, stole his wallet and left the hotel. She works as a housemaid and only ever stays with each employer for a short time, stealing entire warehouses; she gives away a large part of it, doesn't use much herself.

In West Berlin, employed by a doctor as a housemaid, she steals large sums in cash, buys two fur coats and a bracelet that she means to give her sister, though she never does. This time she has grabbed so much money that she can afford a tour of various South German spas.

At the spa house of a city in Rhineland-Palatinate, she encounters the owner's son, who wants her to be his wife. She steals what she can find and leaves town. Her relationship with this man has consequences. While serving a prison sentence of two years and six months, she gives birth to twins. Once released, she takes them out of the children's home. Now there is nothing keeping her in any one place. She leaves the children at a forest inn and disappears with two duvets, a pillow and DM 140 from a guest's suitcase. Travels, cons, steals and serves her sentences. Sent to a mental hospital. The hospital management grants this clever woman leave. She takes a cleaning job, steals jewellery worth DM 10,000, fur coats, two cameras and a brocade dress; after she is admitted to the hospital, one of the other women being treated there buys it off her for DM 15 and immediately cuts it up.

'Is her mental faculty impaired?' asks Judge Rehgut. Dr Brille, MD: 'No, no. Neither is her ability to understand the criminal nature of her deeds. Now, I could say that the accused was missing maternal partnership, or that one should speak of an experience of lack. But none of that would be correct.' 'So what would you consider correct?' asks the judge. 'How do you assess the young woman?' Dr Brille: 'Essentially a very capable and clever person. There's nothing missing. She is located precisely on the seam. An interesting product of nature.' Judge Rehgut: 'Come on now! Let's not blur things.' Dr Brill: 'But yes: this is a one-person minority that simply lives like that. We are looking at a remarkable natural phenomenon. She lives off violating property, just as others live off acquiring it.' Judge Rehgut: 'I can't believe that. That would go against every legal order.' Dr Brille: 'Not every one. Think of the Indians on the Orinoco, for example.' Judge Rehgut: 'But she's not an Indian, is she?' Dr Brille: 'I could give you a report now detailing how her father died when she was seven years old, and four years after starting school her mother died. Hostile environment, etc. But that wouldn't clarify things.' Judge Rehgut: 'You mean, this is just her way of seeking contact?' Dr Brille: 'Yes. She either lives like this or not at all.' Judge Rehgut: 'Now, now. She just has to learn to control herself.' Dr Brill: 'She completely controlled. How much control do you think it takes to carry out these acts without letting anyone bribe her or hold her up? To keep leaving like that demands control. If you can't leave her the way she is, you might as well sentence her to death.' Judge: 'It's a mystery to me. So you think this is a kind of foreign one-person tribe. Like gypsies? At least there are several of those.' Dr Brille: 'Certainly a bit more foreign than that. She's not one of them at all.' Judge Rehgut: 'And against the regulations. I'm sorry, then I can't address it, even if you bring in Dr Grzimek as an expert witness. I can see that this is a person, not an animal.'

The court draws up a plan of treatment: two years of prison, then admission to a closed mental hospital. Dr Brille: 'And what result are you expecting?' Judge: 'Improvement.' Dr Brille: 'And if I tell you you'll be waiting a long time for that?' Judge Rehgut: 'You should be helping me here, instead of making trouble for me too. What am I supposed to decide in a case like this?' Dr Brille: 'No decision. This person can't live any other way. Her acts aren't theft, they're expressions of life. The way you or I draw breath.' Judge: 'That wouldn't be forbidden.'

The judge cannot be persuaded to act against his duty, not even by a cunning female doctor.

Regine Feiler of the Moonlighters' Brigade

'She was the only woman I've ever seen cuffing a man with her left hand after feinting with her right.'

Regine Feiler defends herself. But the man she was hoping to bind to her by cuffing him (the way one tries out a steam iron with a loose connection first, maybe it'll work after all) never came back.

Regine Feiler, 26 years old, from a village near Brunswick, maidservant in Brunswick, later rose to laundry and ironing specialist. 'What I imagine as the meaning of life is never having to go back to the flat country.'

Regine considers herself ugly. Skirts or trousers 'tighten' around her overly fat bottom. Her nose is 'fleshy', eyebrows 'too hairy'. Regine: That's because of my environment; if I kept completely different company, then I'd be 'as beautiful as a mannequin'.

'On the prejudice that a woman markets herself well by having a certain balance of proportions, certain normalities, even though love is the last thing that sticks to norms.' A 'lover', sweaty, her face dirty, working hard, dragging objects, stirring a large pot from which steam is rising. Two living eyes gaze from a dead, mask-like face. Half a litre of tears flows from her eyes onto the doughy material, creating a deep furrow. Here one can see the (still dirty) living skin underneath. One can reach in. A man's two fingers test the firmness of the skin.

In contrast, the 'sales' woman from the big wide world: a 'mannequin face' with extremely long eyelashes, weeping. **Because she always wept so much, her eyelashes grew more quickly; they were 'watered'.**

A 'tennis player'. After playing tennis she takes a shower. Through a peephole in the cubicle a voyeur–her tennis partner a moment earlier–watches her as she showers. 'He compares and assesses the objective value of his partner.' The woman's head. Her head alternates between black-haired and blonde. Which suits her better?

Beautiful women on beautiful horses. The furious Regine pulls down a 'mannequin doll', bound to a white steed with ropes, into the dirt and drags it behind her for a while. To reach into a pretty face, fashioned out of putty by a make-up artist, with all one's ten fingers! Now the face has ugly dents. 'It's not real, but it's more real than the pretty face made of putty was before.'

'No Flow'

Steffie Haseloff has a curved forehead. Her hair ends in thin blonde fluff. There is a mirror at the pub. From her seat, she can watch the wire brush running through her new floppy hairstyle, with two little tails fastened by clips hanging down at the sides. Her eyebrows are emphasized with strong black lines and her eyelids covered in thick green make-up. Now she stands in front of the pub's mirror with her legs apart and continues brushing her hair, simply because a girl who had just arrived said she had 'such cool hair'. A boy from the same group is holding two rings he asked one of the girls to give him, and trying to bend them together into a *single* ring. One of the girls says, 'If Marie-Lou gave you her ring, that means a lot.' Steffie has cuddled up to her boyfriend and whispers in his ear: 'I love you.' He: 'You can keep that to yourself.' She: 'Then you can look for someone better.' Despite all the joking, things are not going well at the moment. He is indifferent, and her laughter, displaying of teeth, frowning and eye movements are either too fast or delayed; badly timed. 'No flow.'

One just has to wait for this Easter Saturday to pass.

Dr Friday Took His Young Girlfriend, Miss Illig, to His Room on Easter Saturday

The automatic Sony radio alarm wakes her. On this Easter Sunday there is no production; Dr Friday has no contact with his school and his girlfriend can't go to work because the stone in front of Jesus's tomb has suddenly disappeared, causing the guards to cast themselves down, shaken to their core, and become believers. Sony's voice: '. . . to **believe** that the stone had been rolled away, that it has been rolled away! My dear listeners, you know the myth of Sisyphus. This world wants to choose the rock itself. With a stubborn effort, it seeks to be its own god. What does Easter say to this Sisyphus? Easter says to Sisyphus: You have a misconception of yourself. Look up: the stone *has* been rolled away! . . . ' Mousie Illig asks Dr Friday: 'What stone? Dr Frank Stone?' Dr Friday: 'What about Stone?' Mousie: 'You're too lazy to speak or think.' She only wanted to see how talkative he was. In fact, Dr Friday is currently not interested in any other person, only his own need for sleep. Mousie, on the other hand, is wide awake because she usually starts work early. Dr Friday (lying): 'I'm listening to you and will answer all your questions.'

(Voice on the radio:) 'This stone must be saved from itself. But then stone is no longer stone.'

The girl insists: 'That's stone in the sense of rock.' Dr Friday murmurs: 'That's because of Easter.' Mousie: 'The reason we're all celebrating is the cross.' Dr Friday: 'But not at Easter, there it's about stone.' Mousie: 'Dr Frank Stone?' This room, which cannot be darkened properly and has only been rented by this teacher temporarily (for the duration of his placement in this little town), is far too bright for his tired eyes. She puts on the kettle for coffee.

(Voice on the radio:) 'And what you'll hear next is perfectly suited to the mood of this Easter morning. "Ave Maria" by Charles Gounod, sung by Professor . . . (inaudible), with Professor Sedebour and Charles Richter at the pianos and Professor Schnicki on the violin . . . '

While they have breakfast, Miss Illig describes how a hotel owner from Bergen-Enkheim flew to South Africa a few days earlier–ahead of the Easter rush–and was eaten up by sharks near Durban Harbour. The sharks, in turn, were hunted by dolphins near the coast. With their snouts, dolphins can strike hard blows feared by the sharks. Dr Friday answers: 'The hotel owner had a strong sense of purpose to meet chance, as it were.' 'And what's that supposed to mean?'

'When production halts, accidents increase.'

Teatime with Academics

She arrived on time, as we had told her. The man who had followed her here from the tram stop was standing close to her back. She sensed the threat behind her while asking at the reception desk. She let a student pass who was in a hurry and asked her question, then let the man waiting behind her back pass too, because she couldn't stand having something behind her like that, and then she waited until it was her turn again. The porter let her pass when she asked her question and she went up to the student accommodation, where she searched the dark, echoing hallway with monk's cells on both sides until she found his name and knocked. He called her by name from inside, then turned from the table where he was working to face her. She had known what he wanted from her as soon as he invited her. But she hadn't imagined it would be so cosy, with this little room and the beds in the wall that looked like caves. She sat down, as he wanted, and had to drink some liquor he had in his cupboard. He wanted to see a big gulp. He grimaced as he took his own gulp, and she had to put her fingers in his hair right then because it looked so pretty. There wasn't even any tea there. She had expected as much and hadn't taken the invitation literally anyway, but she was a little disappointed.

She didn't have any time to occupy herself with that, because now the bottle came back to her. She protested, but didn't want to make trouble. They were sitting on the floor and she complained that there was no tea–how was he going to make any? But she held him tight and told him that he should be a nice boy, after which he passed her the bottle and urged her to take a swig. She sensed the uncertainty raging inside him, even though he had calculated everything precisely, which she also sensed: the alarm bell inside him and his orchestration of both their actions. She gripped his shoulders and showed him that he could be quiet, running her thumbnail down his spine from top to bottom. He tried to reach the bottle again but she pushed it away and sat against the wall facing him, forcing him to look at her. They talked a bit about the cafe where they had first met, then got into bed.

Later he put on his dressing gown, naked underneath, and went out. She waited for a little while, as she still wanted to have him. She would have liked to see his face, and asked him to turn on the light when he came back and cast off the dressing gown. But he held her tight when she wanted to go to the light switch herself and they wrestled, which aroused him immediately, so she crouched down and prayed, and as soon as she felt something hard she was his. She didn't understand why he had to get up straight away and leave the room again. There was something that bothered her, but she let it go. She would have liked to watch a film now.

She heard 'You Are My Special Angel' coming from the room next door and reflected on the text until he returned. She wanted to talk now, and found it stupid that he wanted to start again as soon as he took off his dressing gown, without saying a word. She sat up and slapped him when he tried to use force, but then she was so sorry that she gave in, even though she didn't feel like carrying on and wanted to talk to him instead. She thought about what she wanted to say, but was suddenly somewhere else without wanting it. The third time felt like an excess and she was scared. She tried to hold him tight when he wanted to pull out again, but she was still too soft and he escaped. She was afraid, so she turned on the light and tidied up the bed, which calmed her a little. At the moment she didn't feel like doing anything. She had forgotten whatever it was she wanted to say. She waited and hoped that he would think of something to talk about when he came back.

When the door opened she saw at once that it was an Iranian wearing his dressing gown. She tore open the door, which he tried to shut again when he saw the light, and took a big swing, hitting the Iranian on the ear and slamming his head against the wall in the hallway where he had tried to escape. It was a dry, hard thud that sounded pretty horrible in the narrow corridor that came after the monastic cells. The Iranian stared at the woman, who went back inside, and then he fled to one of the doors.

Later, when it was talked about, people said she had screamed in the hallway or run down the stairs naked and screamed. In fact, after the blow–her hand had automatically lashed out–she returned to the room and locked the door.

She turned on as many lights as she could and washed herself over the sink. It took no great effort for her to work out that after he had left, it had been someone else each time. She washed herself in the unfamiliar room, going through her hair with his brushes. She felt sorry for that nice boy. But as soon as she had that thought, everything came back and she was afraid. It occurred to her that they might have ambushed him when he left her, then come to her in his dressing gown while keeping him captive in one of the adjoining rooms. She was on the point of going next door to get him out. But she didn't really believe in his innocence, any more than she believed in the tea. When she was finished she went through the men's corridor, which was quiet again, and then through the women's corridor, because she missed the exit. In the stairwell, she remembered that she had seen a sign for showers. She went back and took a shower, putting her clothes in the front part of the room to stop them from getting wet. Some students from the women's corridor saw her while she was still in the shower and made a scene right in front of her, ruining her enjoyment of the water that was splashing onto her shoulders, and alerted the house management. The young woman managed to get past the front desk before the students returned. Feeling warm and clean again, she went in the direction where she supposed there was a tram. Still a little woozy, a ball of warmth with her little bag, accurately folded umbrella and round shoulders, she walked away from the academics.

Frankfurt/Kaiserstrasse

1. Bettine G.

Bettine G. wore 'her marshal's baton in her knapsack'[7]. But because she generally never read books in which words like 'knapsack', 'marshal' or 'baton' appeared, she said, 'I have to go to the city. I have a chance there.' She had reasons for being entrepreneurial: her absolutely unbearable situation in northern Hesse. But as long as a picture of the world still has blind spots, regions of society that remain unexplored, that is where her expectations are concentrated:

1. that something real will happen
2. that one can have an enduring love of something
3. that one gives oneself up and is not deceived for it.

7 This quotation comes from Napoleon Bonaparte. [Trans.]

*
* *

Bettine G. went to Frankfurt to make money. She had spent 26 years of her life in her birthplace, the large village of W. in northern Hesse. She never wanted to go back there. Why didn't she want to go back? No comment. She was bored of the place. Someone could have promised her an estate, which she could have afforded with the money she planned to earn, but even the prospect of becoming a lady of the manor and being allowed to bully the other villagers held little attraction for her.

She wanted to draw a line under this life, which had no real advantages as far as she was concerned, whether one had to work for them or not. She would have liked to emigrate, for example; but for that she needed a certain sum of money. Marrying her way to America was too uncertain for her. Nor was she willing to sacrifice her freedom in New York before she even arrived there, and she knew how hard it was to get rid of a man if one was indebted to him. How were her looks? Advantageous.

So she went to Frankfurt.

She left her handbag, which contained everything she needed, at the storage facility at the central station, then chose a restaurant in Kaiserstrasse and ordered some food. Someone approached her and she couldn't get rid of him. She absolutely wanted to be alone now, as she didn't want to mess up this beginning. She said 'yes, yes' and drank up whatever the man ordered. She regretted it in the same moment, as she didn't want to drink anything and didn't want to accept anything from him—aside from his hasty departure. The man was determined to see her again and acted as if his fate depended on it, and she gave the intrusive man her ID card as a pledge to finally get rid of him. She promised to be in a particular place at a particular time. But she didn't even remember the time and place; she was just waiting for him to leave her at last.

*
* *

At the Kaiser-Lichtspiele cinema she met her later friend, Sadie Hellmann, who was also spending her first night in Frankfurt, and they stayed together that evening, forming a certain bond of friendship. Then the men sitting with them wanted to go. Once she was alone with her customer, Bettine had to admit that she didn't have a room of her own. The man found a hotel room for them, and accordingly paid her less than agreed. She demanded the money up front, as she didn't know if she'd have reservations about accepting it afterwards. Later, the man wanted his money back. He threatened to call the police and report Bettine G. for what she had done. She asked him what it was that she had done. She took her chance and gave him nothing, nor did she let him take anything away when he tried to get it by force.

After that experience she felt more secure on her feet.

She usually worked at the Café Royal together with her colleague Sadie Hellmann, though Sadie was reckless and occasionally stole things from the customers. That was why Sadie had to go to Hamburg after a few weeks, as aggrieved customers came back and asked after her. The work was clearer and more straightforward without Sadie, as there were no webs of lies that had to be kept intact. Sadie had the habit of making it look as if it was still her first night, which she had to make up for when the customers didn't dare approach her. Bettine was glad that Sadie and the whole complicated friendship system were in Hamburg, where they could be appreciated from a distance.

She had principles to which she clung firmly, like a kind of chastity; she didn't drink, she didn't tolerate any special requests and she insisted on cleanliness. Unwashed customers were sent away, and she paid back the unspent fee for her time. She took great care not to catch anything, including on the toilet. She once read that the head of the medical academy in Düsseldorf had said in a lecture that there were virtually no illnesses any more; they had to explain venereal disease to the students using pictures because they couldn't find any sufferers. She made a mental note of the professor's name but kept the knowledge to herself, as she saw that the fear of disease secured her business, which rested above all on her cleanliness.

2. Semm

On the Corner of Kaiserstrasse and Elbestrasse

Semm sees Charles with Angélique, whom she doesn't know. Charles was sitting at the Narrow Towel, just as Fricka had said. Semm didn't look properly; she took a few steps back, closed the restaurant door and started crying without a word before running to her workplace, the cafe Mario, where she put two coffees and one sweet wine on the bill. She had to get the orders off her tongue. Until 3 p.m., she rushed about between the seven tables that formed her territory, her whole body tense. This time the lunchtime rush brought four travellers who blocked the way with their bags and didn't order much.

Work: A Cave or a Harbour

Semm waits for commands. The guests are quiet. Semm belongs to anyone who looks after her, who finds themselves prepared to exploit her. She is so geared towards exploitation that it is impossible not to exploit her. Semm demands a new kind of exploiter: one who can bear to keep up their exploitation continuously. The disasters occur at the times when exploitation ceases.

Can One Breed Misfortune?

Semm, a showman's child, born in 1938. Her family broke up when she was three years old. The children were spread between the villages in Thuringia. Semm ended up with a farmer. After a few years, her grandmother opened a business; she gathered the children together again and trained them–with a whip–to perform certain fairground tricks. The training and performing career lasted until the age of 18. Then Semm went to Frankfurt as a waitress.

The Other Waitresses Have Valkyries' Names

Fricka, Albertine. Leaving the narrowness of the bar like two departing battleships: Albertine. Fricka. Albertine: as if the middle of her body had exploded–arms, legs, big hands, neck. She should have worn a belt around her waist but instead she had a broad ruche going from her navel to her breasts. Today the two girls left Semm alone. The bitch Semm, sitting on her black chair next to the till, guards the skewered receipts. Semm, who scours Kaiserstrasse in search of Charles, who is spoken to from the side by a passer-by and moves away, who is stopped by police officers, who–when she sees police–immediately abandons her plans and runs back to her working corner: who has no feelings except for Charles, out of her mind with attachment.

Puritanical

With a strong aversion to fat women, who are corporeal. Rose, hell's rose, marzipan rose. One must never eat marzipan. The whore Gilda once asked Semm if she wanted to come along for an afternoon nap. As she asked, Gilda stroked a jukebox she had fed with pennies. Semm: No.

Love Out of a Need for Reality

Because one has to submit to a man, because some would be afraid of losing touch otherwise, because it's the way one does things: she finds Charles, a 'good' man. The fear of finding one who was worse. Love and misfortune are so intertwined that Semm can't say whether she wants love or misfortune; and the choice only exists purely theoretically. Like a dog that sits down where it is bound to be kicked, she sets traps and catches misfortune in her traps.

Charles is looking for fatter people, greater stimulation. Loves what's behind: behind the ample bottom of his current partner, who is not Semm. Lets himself be exploited to stay on the case–fear that reality will slip away, just as his fleshy companion will disappear once his cash supply is exhausted. Perhaps Charles would have been better off skipping the adventure with the fat Angélique? Matter-of-factness and decency, but also uncertainty in

Charles and Semm's relationship, drinking alcohol instead of talking. Crying instead of talking.

The Situation at the Time of the Meeting with Charles

Semm was held up and was therefore late to the corner of Weserstrasse and Kaiserstrasse. She waited when she couldn't find Charles, then started scouring Kaiserstrasse. She wasn't let into the *Reichshof–La Plaza* because of her somewhat shabby blouse, so she could only ask at the door if Charles had been there. But as she herself didn't think Charles had been there, she didn't ask assertively enough and received (although Charles had been waiting at La Plaza since lunchtime and had left a message at the reception) a negative response.

First Search

So she kept walking, with her characteristic gait, her legs straight, and scoured the restaurants in Kaiserstrasse. Her high heels stabbed into her abdomen. Her back hurt and, as she thought she was bleeding, she went home, where the landlady asked after Charles and demanded that she return the coat she had borrowed. Semm put on different shoes and got changed, then went back to look for Charles. She found him at La Plaza when she tried again there. The tall, dark man leapt up as soon as he saw her coming.

Second Search

Semm was too hunted. She didn't know how to respond to his 'joy'. She ordered drinks and went to the toilet to freshen up. But that didn't bring about the change she was hoping for; she was still too fearful that she wouldn't find him. She said she still had something to take care of. When she returned, Charles was no longer at La Plaza.

She waited where he had sat. Later the vice squad appeared to conduct and check; they do that in the late afternoon, as it gets in the way of business in the evening. Semm was scared because she had no red card and didn't think she would be able to explain the true reason for her presence at that restaurant to the officers (search for Charles). So she went to the toilet with a few other girls and paid the toilet lady a mark to bring her to the neighbouring Roxy cinema. She cried, and when a man tried to approach her she smacked him on the neck with her handbag, then searched the restaurants.

Charles, Found Again

She found Charles in the evening at the Fischerstuben with a sergeant. He ran all five fingers of one hand through his messy black hair out of tiredness. He was trying to describe a bar to the sergeant. While the men were speaking, Semm sat there next to them without saying a word.

When a prostitute finally picked up the young sergeant, Charles didn't want to let him go. Semm felt better once he was gone. She tried to convince Charles to leave the place. She would have been happy just to be allowed to walk along next to him or do something together, but she was also happy to sit here next to him, although she didn't know what to talk to him about in his drunken state.

Semm didn't know how to prevent Gitti and Kitti from sitting down at Charles' table. They were among the few wealthy prostitutes who frequented the Fischerstuben and were wearing elegant black dresses. They had young, pale skin, white and without any spots on their forehead, neck and shoulders; fair hair that stood out to all sides in its weakness and surrounded their heads with a ring of wan curls, in the artificial light with their pale, bright necks. Semm sat at the table wordlessly.

Semm lent Charles the money he needed to pay for the drinks. She would have liked to go with Charles and the two rich girls. But she didn't ask for fear of being turned down. So she went to the nine o'clock showing at the Kaiser-Lichtspiele with four prostitutes.

Third Search

After the film, she cried, because she was tired and couldn't forget the two rich girls, and started looking for Charles. She was approached in Kaiserstrasse and had a drink with a man who insisted on it–a black-currant juice–because she couldn't find Charles, but she left immediately and found Charles at a pub in Münchener Strasse, robbed. They had taken money and valuables.

Climax

Semm was angry and threw down the money demanded for Charles' release by the landlord of the dive, whom she blamed for the theft, and then took Charles with her, who was fairly drunk. She walked up Kaiserstrasse at Charles' side. She had waited all day for that. At Gallusanlage, they found an unlocked American car and sat inside it. She longed for her work and had no idea what to talk about, despite being 'happy' that she no longer had to look for Charles. She had stomach pains. She took Charles' hand and wanted to say something, but didn't dare. Charles undid her dress and she immediately tensed up again and tried to fend him off but without success. She didn't resist Charles, because she didn't want to do anything wrong. She lay on the backseat naked with her eyes closed and waited. But Charles just made her wet, then lay cuddled up against her side.

She was freezing, but didn't dare pull her clothes out from under Charles' large body. She kept her eyes closed and was happy to have him next to her but was freezing. Later it occurred to her that his permit expired at three in the morning.

Day's End

She got dressed in the cramped car and walked home to get some money. She brought Charles to the camp in a taxi. Charles, who had slept in a taxi, went over to the camp's guarded gate. Semm could still see him talking to the military-police officer when the taxi started up again and she looked for Charles through the rear window. So the day did end relatively well.

The Taxi Driver's Account

'I'd never have thought', said the taxi driver, 'that I'd have a black girlfriend some day.'

We drove through the Brandenburg Gate, along Unter den Linden, along the model castle made of cloth that was on show for 100 days; the Christmas market was also underway.

–How did you meet your black girlfriend?

–Here in the taxi.

–You spoke to her first?

–No. *She* said something.

–And you got the conversation going?

–That's not quite the way it happened.

One could no longer drive to the Volksbühne theatre in Rosa Luxemburg Square the way the taxi driver was used to doing in the past.

–I have to say, of course, if I can just say this in a way you can't really say it: it's like you sometimes think–you've got a monkey in bed with you.

–Because of the skin colour? Where is she from?

–From Zimbabwe. It's not because of the skin colour. But something what here (that's me) and something black there (that's her), strange.

–Not unpleasant?

–Not at all. She hums sometimes.

–Why is it strange?

–Not because she hums.

The taxi driver had to concentrate on the traffic.

–The best thing is that she's at her flat and I stay at mine. We both have jobs.

–What's so good about that?

—You're not in control if you're living together in one flat. You can control the relationship as long as you're not living together. Otherwise it's over.

—So is it good, what you're experiencing now?

—Stunning.

Now we had arrived in the street that leads to the theatre, which has stood in this square like a battleship or a big cruiser since the 1920s, a square named after a revolutionary.

'The Tree That Greens, the Peaks of Branches . . . '; Smoothing Down

Alice K. had an inclination towards cutting down trees. Her relationship towards sun and shade was different from that of her husband. Her husband, Ernst K., liked to have the canopy of leaves above him—'well-arranged oaks', or else a chestnut, a walnut or at least a fast-growing poplar. Until 1936, for example, one such high tree had stood by the garden pond: an ash that placed the conservatory and northern part of the garden in its shade.

> 'The tree that greens, the peaks of branches,
> the flowers around the bark of the trunk,
> come from divine nature, they are like life,
> for heaven's air leans over them.'[8]

And it was the city air. A view of the backs of house rows.

---

8 From Friedrich Hölderlin's poem 'Die Zufriedenheit' [Contentment] (1811). [Trans.]

Ernst K. had to worry for years that the roots of this tree might burst the concrete foundations of the pond. One day there will be cracks, the water, 50 centimentres high, will trickle away and the duckweed and water lilies will lose their home. One morning, the fat goldfishes, the size of men's hands, will be lying on the stone slabs at the bottom of the pond. But the disaster could just as easily come in the daytime. The staff run over from the kitchen, see the cracks in the pond's foundation–there's still water–then run back and report the falling water level.

According to Alice's logic, one should chop down the ash tree, or whatever it was, then dig up and clear away the rest of the trunk and the uncontrollable roots attached to it. That would make space for a few stone tiles, and on those one could place a little tea table, two chairs and around them a flowerbed close to the pond. And then she could also have placed her sun bed on wheels, which could be rolled out of the conservatory, out in the sun and the air to assist the tanning of her skin, with a view over the garden and into the air at her disposal.

'Don't you go destroying the garden', warned her husband before he travelled. In the autumn he returned from Madeira, Benghazi, Tobruk, Alexandria, Rome and Florence. In the meantime, Alice K. had hired men to cut the tree down to a height of 2 metres. The branches and piece of trunk were stacked at the back of the garden. Alice did not get around to actually removing the tree.

Flying back from Italy over the Alps in a Ju 52, Ernst K. started to feel sick. Transported home like a suitcase by plane, car and train, none of the curiosity and hunger for innovation that had departed southwards a quarter of a year earlier returned to the villa intact. And so his shock to find this central garden tree chopped off did not go deep at first. Ernst K. looked and cursed. But then his anger took root for days, and he would have had to cut off his wife at the feet, as it were, the logical and cheerful Alice, to 'express himself fairly'. Now, however–for even in distant North Africa she haunted him–he has settled in her shade, as well as that of his trees, and nothing could have been further from his mind than to summon men of the law and file for divorce or to destroy her Sunday elan in some other way. For it was not just about chopping down the tree in his absence; he feared for her.

> 'I fear for you,
> you hardly bear the fate of these times.
> You will yet try a variety of things,
> will . . . '

Chopping down the tree was certainly not the only thing Alice had done in the last three months. Ernst couldn't talk about that at all. Don't be 'grumpy', Alice said. Come on, sit over here. But he wasn't 'grumpy'; he no longer had his tree but instead a dump of sellable branches, as well as two large blocks of chopped trunks. His authority, which clearly meant nothing to his staff or friends, could be added to the pile.

At least the rest of the trunk was still there. One could treat it like a shortened pillar and put a potted palm tree on the surface of the trunk or use it as a tea table, and at least it hadn't been smoothed down, so one could see all the different directions of the axe strokes. The danger posed to the pond foundation by the roots of the former tree persisted, for these roots subsequently continued to grow. Secondary shoots sprouted from the remaining trunk, forming an ash bush. Later on a representative of the law, disguised as Alice's lover, cut this young woman out of her environment comprising the garden, house and children: a bomb attack devastated the garden and razed the house. The shortened trunk, too low for a pillar and too high for a table, remained there for years next to the ravaged pond. Ernst K. could not live there now, unfaithful to the former giver of shade, which was now only a memory; but probably he hardly thought of the tree anymore. 'As if it were a piece of him.' Then Alice's daughter, already living in the new house, left for the West. In empty barbarism, though still surrounded by the tools of the medical practice and a few antiques, he lived a more relaxed, less rooted life. After all that, it didn't really matter if he kept on living.

> 'But when the tree grows old . . . ,
> so the juice can no longer rise,
> then there grow underneath, around the trunk . . .
> and finally on the roots too,
> and transfigure the old tree . . . ,
> for nature or juice defends itself . . . '[9]

But without effect.

---

9 An abridged quotation from Jakob Böhme's unfinished work *Aurora: Die Morgenröte im Aufgang* [Aurora: The Rising Dawn] (1612).

Addendum to II

DERIVATIVES OF THE TENDER FORCE

What emboldens love—considering it is a labyrinth? Perhaps it is not itself but, rather, its offshoots, its side-lines and margins, that embolden it? Nothing can prevent love from betting on its happiness . . .

The following are emboldeners:

1. Matter-of-factness, making an effort
2. Close quarters
3. Blindness and incorruptibility of libido

A Remark by Richard Sennett

In the twenty-first century, according to the sociologist Richard Sennett, the tender force, overwhelmed on one side by the chemical, wild sexual nature that is its carrier and, on the other side, disturbed by the modern demand to compensate for the missing validity of the self in every-day social life, survives more in its *derivatives* than in the desert of the sexes.

What Are Derivatives?

In economy, derivatives are bets on so-called underlying assets, future share prices, averages, probabilities, deficiency and surplus, or the weather. Derivatives can also become the underlying assets of other (second-degree) derivatives. Derivatives are the most rapidly growing and changing element of the modern financial system. They cover risks and produce risks. Here one distinguishes between risks that can be established through probability calculations and uncertainty that, because it constitutes 'ignorance', cannot be determined by any mathematical method. Economic derivatives have a leverage effect. The investor in a derivative participates disproportionately in both price rises and price drops.

The meaning of the word 'derivative' for love is different than its meaning for the economy. The French word for derivative in the sense of 'derivation' or 'offshoot' would be *dispositif*. The meaning of this word in French philosophy is close to the original semantics of 'derivative': 'Shifting the boundaries of a shore', 'diverting water into a channel so that it goes where it is needed', and irrigation in general; all of this is covered by the Latin *derivare* and would be a meaningful image in the context of love.

There are evidently two different directions for such a meaning in this context: (1) love bets on an underlying asset, that is, its happiness; (2) the tender force expresses itself in neighbouring areas or uncharted territory if it cannot adequately articulate itself on its own terrain.

Examples of the first case include: a young woman binds herself to a man on her mother's advice (like the

Princess of Cleves); I make an effort to get good grades in school, then later to be intelligent, because the person I love most expects it of me. I make an effort by using the abilities I have. Referring to a person who began a relationship with a man because she trusted in the plot of a novel (she had watched its film adaptation), the marriage broker Ingrid Bärlamm said that the chance of becoming happy after doing this is no less than if the person had 'chosen'. In all these cases the tender force manifests itself indirectly, that is, as a derivative.

> The derivatives of love
> differ from those of the banks:
> when they plummet,
> they fall back on the hardness
> that forms their raw material.

FIGURE 13. Ingrid Bärlamm

An Observation by Niklas Luhmann as a Response to Richard Sennett's Remark

According to an observation made by Niklas Luhmann, one of the differences between the seventeenth century (the beginnings of *Homo novus*) and the twenty-first (the helplessness of *Homo novus*), that 'self-realization' can only be experienced inadequately in today's everyday social reality. The system environment (occupation, career, achievement) only demands parts of a person; it would be tiresome if someone came along with their whole person (all their needless and boundless attributes) and held up the others with their totality. Luhmann states that the whole person, who continues to be a subject, that is, the property of the one going through a career, must prove and confirm itself in intimate relationship, specifically in the narrow area of sexuality. This is a burden upon the tender force, and one can thus observe a kind of flight from overtaxing, a flight from the *property of love.*

'Love relationships, because they are the only context in which the involvement of the entire person seems possible, become a stage, that is, less real. Social relationships, on the other hand, lose value and gain realism.'

The marriage-broker Bärlamm points out that the only possible solution is to integrate libidinous needs (she studied sociology in Bielefeld) into the partial relationships of the system environment. How happy it makes Doctor Mansfeld when the trained employee with whom he spent 20 years of his life smiles at him; on the other hand, the smile of his wife, whom he has only known for two years, when he leaves in the morning seems to have a different meaning than mere friendliness. He thinks this smile mirrors the expectation that with his help, the new day will be different from the preceding days, something which is beyond his control. Many people today, Bärlamm adds, marry their secretaries. As soon as that happens, the old familiarity at the workplace is lost. Then there is a new employee at the office endeavouring to please the boss. The result is unease.

Matter-of-factness
Making an effort

A Libidinous Reason for Matter-of-Factness

The evolutionary biologist Dr Erwin Boltzmann claims that the majority of people throughout history who survived had an 'unwrought goodwill', a surplus force that did not quite correspond to any of their other 'useful' abilities. One can, he argues, observe this 'special admixture' in the agricultural revolution of the last 7,000 years. There was no evidence that it was causal for reproduction, that is, for direct offspring. People who entirely lacked this attribute, however, had not reproduced a great deal. It appeared as something 'derived' from other, paid services. For example, the story about the à 'Bed Warmer' Minguel Ozman: his behaviour went beyond his purchasable services as a gigolo. He carried out unpaid work; his actions were a matter of self-respect, not his profession. In addition (likewise as a surplus, for he was selling an erotic service), according to Boltzmann, this force was characterized by functionality and matter-of-factness.

FIGURE 14 (ABOVE). While he was unemployed, the blind Mirko Wirschke drove his truck for half a year with the help of his son. The son told his blind father where to drive. One could call the trust they shared love.

FIGURE 15 (BELOW). Some children got a tractor going. Their parents wanted to rescue them; Vera F. Succeeded in pushing the youngest away but was fatally injured in the process.

He claims that functionality, that is, utility for third parties, was a derivative of Narcissus (who desired a relationship with his reflection), Daphne (who would rather be turned into a laurel tree than let herself be raped) and the huntress Callisto (who did not want to be a traitor and was placed in the heavens, proving indispensable for a long time as a navigation aid for sailing ships).

Someone asks Dr Boltzmann what he would call this millennia-long force of attraction. 'To repeat myself,' says Dr Boltzmann, 'I call the libidinous reason for such matter-of-factness self-respect. It stands out especially in a milieu dedicated to earning money. Someone who comes into conflict with their self-respect can die of it. (→ 'Doing Something for Its Own Sake', p. 239.)

Figaro's Loyalty

We know that Figaro, the protagonist of Beaumarchais' hit play *The Marriage of Figaro* and the later opera by Mozart based on it, was not of noble descent, nor was the countess. The two had evidently been childhood sweethearts before she married the count.

Since then, Figaro had caressed this young woman's hair and cosmetically prepared her face for each day. He always felt attracted to her. He provided her with advice, as we know, on maintaining her marriage. He did not make use of his intimate position by her hair and her ear, by her side and at her back, for any intrigues. The tenderness of his hands and his senses was always restrained (unlike the taboo on incest, but like a taboo based on loyalty that is both well known and novel, yet rather ill-defined in literature: you must not betray the interests of those you love). Figaro's marriage to Susanna, organized by the count and the countess, which seemed perfect in the finale of Mozart's opera, did not survive the revolutionary chaos of 1789. Susanna began a career as a scribe at the Committee of Public Safety. The count and countess were imprisoned in a Parisian jail. Figaro had become the head of a revolutionary tribunal, and the count and countess now faced him as accused parties. Figaro could easily have condemned his rival, the count, to death and made the countess dependent on him. None of that occurred. Soon afterwards the count and countess, having escaped across the Ardennes, settled in a private house on the other side of the Rhine in Koblenz, where a large colony of émigrés were waiting for a change in current events.

After a short time, Figaro–the powerful man, the achiever–followed his former superiors. His services as an advisor, barber and costume designer were sought after in Koblenz, in German circles too. Thus he provided for the count's household with his income as a 'servant' or a 'lord'. Soon that intimate feeling of the morning hours, caring for the hair and face of the countess, tenderly returned.

After the king's return (for the turbulences of the Napoleonic Wars were over), the count and countess, who were no longer so young, went back to their restored properties in France. They did not take Figaro with them. Because of the frequent changes of governance, where he had often found himself on the wrong side because his actions were not based on political advantage, he was considered used up in aristocratic circles. He had not adapted sufficiently to the current fashions either.

He remained a provincial barber by the Rhine. He had learnt some German. He had three sisters, something Mozart's opera does not mention. He himself remained childless but his sisters had a total of 16 children. The name of the family, who were originally Spanish, became famous.

Additional Note by Dr Boltzmann:

In evolutionary-biological terms, Dr Boltzmann states, the positioning of Figaro in this true sequence of events initially seems negative. With his superior physical strength, Figaro could already have beaten up and chased away the count, who was courting Susanna, as a young man. That is what an animal would have done. Later, as the head of the revolutionary tribunal, he should have bitten the count in the throat. He should have taken the countess and thus the chance of having his own offspring.

But in fact, according to Dr Boltzmann, Figaro's behaviour, the underlying principle of his actions, can tell us something. He developed a new kind of terrain for the workings and multi-faceted expansion of the tender force (a terrain created in antiquity but lost in the eighteenth century). This innovation has a similar effect to a newly discovered star that enriches a constellation. It results in new contradictions but fewer than the old ones it resolves. Nor can it be ruled out that such a positioning, that of a 'lucky accompanying star', can produce children too.

FIGURE 16. A philologist. She reliably accompanies foreign texts. She finds them, reconstructs them and saves them from misunderstandings. Without appropriating the texts herself. A public-relations worker.

The Frontline Fighter

Marie-Luise Girkenson, from Upper Hesse, had been infected by the frenzy of the search for oil south of Svalbard. After all, what else was one supposed to do in the little backwater on this island except get straight to work? She had a boil on her bottom and her manager, who felt affection for this hard-working woman, insisted that she should not work until she was completely cured of it, and should thus stay home for a few days. 'You know as well as I do,' Fretty answered, 'that I do most of my work on my knees. The boil won't bother me at all.' She could not be persuaded to spend several mornings, afternoons, evenings and nights bored in her cabin room, without any social interaction. 'Then you might as well throw me in prison.' But her manager insisted on having his way.

She still refused to stay in bed, and wandered up and down in the icy air in front of the cabin. As it happened, a new girl had been flown in that morning, and the manager assigned this young Frankfurt woman, who still had to get used to the northern climate–her name was Erika–the task of keeping Fretty company, and perhaps even inducing her to lie down on her stomach somewhere so that her boil, which he still considered harmful to business, could fully disappear. Every now and again he sent the doctor from the main settlement in Svalbard to examine his best worker. Erika did 'her best' to calm Fretty, to 'take her mind off things', but Fretty 'went on and on' about her work. If there was nothing concrete for her to do, she at least tried somehow to keep her steady concentration on the job–not because she was afraid of losing her work if she was unwilling (the manager's personal affection protected her from that), but because she did not want to slip

FIGURE 16. Marie-Luise Girkenson, known as Fretty, the frontline fighter.

into a kind of weekend up there, and because she felt she was losing the 'social context' if she did not stay close to her real tasks.

She kept stomping around the cabin over the frozen ground–the wider surroundings were rocky and inaccessible–with Erika walking behind her. 'As I say, I don't mind. But you'd be surprised how many people insist that I have to swallow the stuff. On a long day one swallows a lot of it. They've been given instructions so that I just need to push them and they'll come. That has disadvantages too, of course. Like that pathetic dummy who was flown in from Diomede Island, he probably hasn't taken a bath in a month. I washed roughly 14 centimetre of him. That was the last bath he'll be having before he comes back. The other day I worked out that on a single day I swallow 8 metre of cock, that's about 54 customers, because they usually just want a blow job. I give them that. It's because they fly down to Germany every few weeks, and I don't think they want to take the clap with them when they're on home leave.'

There was no tiring her. Later she sat in one of the cabin rooms and had a few glasses, but was still not tired until 3 a.m. At six, she woke up again, roused the sleep-deprived Erika and wanted to talk about her experiences on the job again. The manager then decided to put Fretty back to work after all, as the inactivity was not good for her. Instead of a medal he gave her two 100-dollar notes, which she didn't attach to her dress as he suggested, but stored in her box of possessions.

Doing Something for Its Own Sake

In the short time when people were saying that there would be 'blooming landscapes' in the states of the former East Germany, the West German business consultant Horst Ziegler had more assignments than he could handle. He had barely finished analysing various aspects of a beer brewery before he had to drive on (usually at night) to a special construction company, a machine tool factory and from there to an electric power plant that used coke. He always had to structure, exclude, prepare layoffs and drive on. Although the experienced Swabian knew that his suggestions were only had any value if he implemented them himself or had someone he had trained do so. (But how would he make the time to train them, where was he supposed to find such a person? How much time would it take to look for them?) That was special about him, the fact that he demanded this of himself. Ultimately this inner conflict was bad for his health. He tended towards high blood pressure.

He was particularly hindered, both at the brewery and the machine tool factory, by individual employees who cultivated a particular level of quality in their work even though nobody was paying for this quality on the market. Egon Fritzsche, for example, was unwilling to discontinue a particular lemonade in cans that combined vanilla flavour with the taste of fresh cherries, as he found the combination successful and it struck him as profitable for summer parties. It was impossible to convince this man, who was a chemist on the one hand and a member of the works council on the other, that the necessary marketing

FIGURE 18. Horst Ziegler.

costs for the previously unknown product would exceed the company's means. The zealous Fritzsche never looked at things from the perspective of a consumer who was willing to pay, he only spoke about his 'successful product'— which admittedly came fizzing out of the can in pretty colours as soon as one opened it. The seal suited the barrel-shaped tin can especially well, as it imitated a stopper and thus hinted at a transition from a tin can to a traditional bottle. In future, this 'innovator' wanted to add a free screw-mountable cup for the 'user'. Fritzsche was concerned with the matter itself, and another seven similar characters made life difficult for the business consultant Horst Ziegler. They had no inhibitions about consuming his time, which he could not multiply. Should he have declined or postponed assignments? He couldn't imagine that. What narrowed his capillaries and veins, sending him to doctors and thus absorbing further time, was the fact that in his heart he felt much like these meticulous makers, whose advantage over him was that they stayed in one place, had plenty of surplus time and would probably soon become superfluous themselves.

He was on their side 'as if it were a piece of me'. That is an especially dangerous conflict for a 'flexible mind', which was the mask Ziegler wore. Being in his mid 40s, he could easily work for 12 to 14 hours, but not with an unresolved conscience. He wanted to do his work because he considered it valuable, not because he was paid for it. He cursed the scrupulous makers who 'wanted to do their work for its own sake' as 'fusspots'. In the same moment, he thought to himself that cursing only proves one is in the wrong. The inflexible seven were the first he recommended for dismissal. And that was especially painful for him.

What emboldens us?

Eros and Thanatos

Other emboldeners (derivatives of eros) are: **intelligence, revolutionary elan, pleasure, art, lightness of touch, cooperation, friendship, generosity, indomitability of libido, loyalty.**

All these basic values, which the tender force and goodwill rely on, have a light and a dark side, depending on whether eros or thanatos were dominant in the genesis of the derivative.

The insistence on the value of suffering and gloom, the valorization of the 'sombre passions' (Nietzsche), belongs to the dark side of intelligence. In a revolutionary movement, the establishment of liberal rights, that is, a phase of light, is followed by the guillotine, a period of dark energy.

The climax of the novel *The Princess of Cleves* is the chapter in which the princess confesses something to her husband which she believes to be the truth of her heart. In the static courtly society of France this is uncommon, even forbidden. Whatever one feels subjectively must be masked. It is forbidden to reveal subjective realities and thus draw the surroundings into one's own confusion. This imperative of dissimulation (developed to stem the civil war of emotion) is violated in a revolutionary act by the princess. She goes about it clumsily; she uses the truth, a sharp instrument, clumsily. The result of her confession is her husband's death. The courage to break with convention and strain her relationship with the princess is light; the great self-love expressed in the hastiness of her confession, the lack of empathy with her husband, is dark.

In art, the relation between dark and light forces is inverted. A lament, an expression of sorrow, can spread more light than a bright C major.

But all these things are only seemingly 'bets' and 'derivatives'. They are disguises of eros. In the end, however, eros itself emerges from its costumes and all the emboldeners transpire as part of an encompassing capacity for love. The definition of the antagonistic driving forces as eros and thanatos is also imprecise. We are not dealing here with unified phenomena but, rather, projections and survivals that disintegrate into new figures at every moment and consist of billions of libidinous particles: residues, echoes of former longing. Some of them come about in this very second, others are 6,000 years old; one cannot see this in the swarms of such forces from the outside.

FIGURE 19. Lust is a goat.

The Conviviality of Transgenic Mice

On the day of our visit to Rockefeller University in New York, the voles, elegant prairie animals and to their left the mountain voles, only managed to go forwards with a halting, stumbling motion. In separate cages. It was the week in which deformatory genetic experiments were being carried out on the animals' cerebellums. How much of it can be dispensed with? What still functions after the procedure? We, the sponsors, were to assess whether a publication of this research would have any promotional value. We considered the mice's demeanour entirely unsuitable.

The head of the group of professors said:

—In mice that lack a molecular antenna for oestrogen, one can't see anything at first glance after our procedure. It's only their mating behaviour that proves deeply disturbed.

—However much oestrogen you inject?

—Yes, however much.

—They behave like innocents? As if they'd never heard of sexuality? As if it were a sport?

—Not like sport. Like with a broken telephone line.

—Where one can't hear anything?

—Yes. The animals are agitated, blundering and uninformed.

—Aroused?

—Yes, in a monstrous way.

We returned one of the following weeks. The director was hoping for funding from the university and the associated research company at all costs.

This time vasopressin. A hormone not originating from the sex glands but, rather, a product of the nerve cells. The voles in all the cages and the running area were not staggering; they were sitting in groups, practising starts.

—Normally vasopressin makes the kidneys use water sparingly. We've found that it also makes the animals sociable.

—A social hormone? You've discovered the genetic makeup for 'conviviality'?

—In a monogamous species of American vole!

—The bond between couples grows stronger?

'Do you know that particular bond between men in urinals?' I interjected. 'High-ranking jurists, guided by their bladders and under pressure from their kidneys, reach intimate agreements about their judgements at pink basins.' 'That's not vasopressin,' answered the director of the pilot project. 'But it's kidney plus conviviality,' I insisted, 'and if I understand you correctly, that's what this is about.'

–So far we're only examining prairie voles. They don't at all produce more vasopressin than the mountain voles in their small bodies. The difference lies in the antennae: the mountain voles don't react with a sense of community. They lack the antenna for vasopressin.

–You're talking about molecular antennae? Like last week?

–The molecular antennae for vasopressin are distributed completely differently in the brains of the two species. We equipped mountain voles with the gene of the prairie vole and their behaviour changed.

–The gene for the antennae in the brain?

–If one treats a transgenic animal with the hormone it reacts convivially, even though it's a mountain vole.

–Independently of its surroundings?

–Quite independently. And if we increase the hormone sixfold, they become six times as sociable. As if they'd been drilled.

–A nerve hormone?

–It's produced in the brain and the lymph gland. The mountain voles become outgoing. Biologists just don't want to believe it.

—In a mountain vole without such a transgenic antenna, one can't achieve anything with an extra dose of vasopressin?

—Nothing at all.[10]

—If one gives aggressive Muslims food containing hidden vasopressin, will they become more convivial?

—Only if we've transgenically placed an effective antenna for the substance inside them. We could try it with the sons and daughters of the next generation.

—Only if it works the same way as with the voles.

—If it even works on the mountain vole!

—But convivial doesn't mean friendly and peaceful?

—It means sociable among themselves.

—Whoever passes water together gets on well?

—Something like that. First of all, the genetics of behaviour.

—Could one develop an antenna and a nerve hormone for the human race 'globally'?

—In mountain or prairie voles?

—In general.

—We can only test it on rodents at our institute. There's sure to be some substance. One can only explain mass migrations of animals in evolution if there are substances that drive the animals to gather in large numbers.

---

10 Neurotransmitters function locally. Hormones rush through every corner of the body; what effects they develop depends on the receiving antennae.

We restructured the funding measures of our company to incorporate the research complex 'conviviality, social behaviour, coupling'. The director and public-relations department were overjoyed. After all, we're advertising men. Just imagine if one could improve a consumer trait through transgenic receptors! A long way from Hans in Luck to the modern transgenically boosted consumer of 2032!

The Nature of Love

In his essay 'The Nature of Love', Harry F. Harlow examines the 'question of primary drives'. According to the established theory, he says, the basic motives are above all hunger, thirst, loneliness, pain and sex. The mother–child relationship is interpreted in the sense that it satisfies the primary drives, and secondary reinforcing mechanisms bring about the mother–child relationship. What is true about this observation, he continues, is that no other bond influences the later course of a person's drives and its generalization as intensely as the mother–child relationship. It is conspicuous, however, that when tested experimentally, all secondary reinforcers connected to satisfactions of the aforementioned drives or needs disappear after a certain time. By contrast, the affections that form part of the mother–child relationship never disappear; in fact, they showed a tendency to become more generalized.

Harlow proceeds experimentally. In so doing, he encounters the problem that among human newborns, experimental examinations come up against an inadequate development of motor abilities. The human child

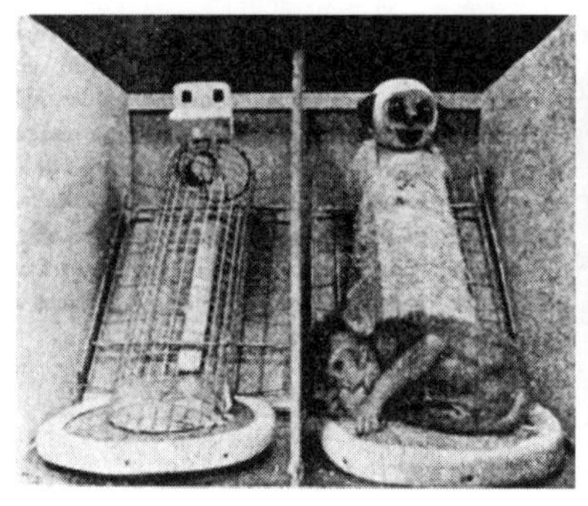

FIGURE 20. Wire mother, cloth mother.

FIGURE 21. Monkey clings to cloth mother, 'response to cloth'.

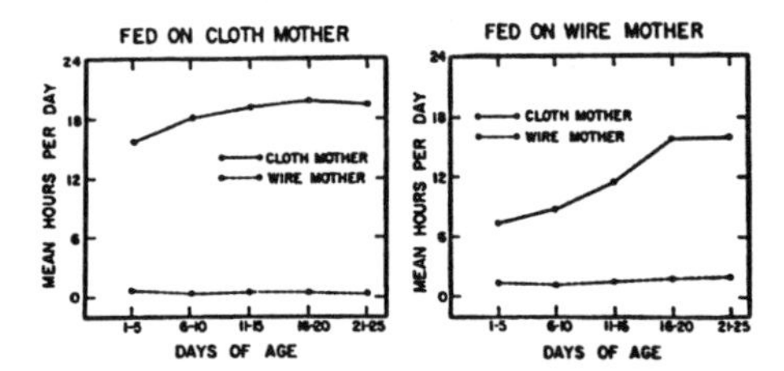

FIGURE 22. Diagram: 'The monkeys reject the wire mother because she does not allow any skin contact.'

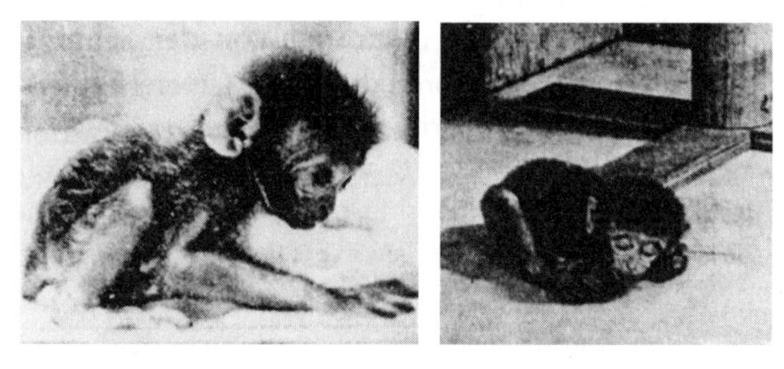

FIGURE 23. Abandoned monkey when only the wire mother is available, even if she provides milk.

initially has no adequate expression. That, says Harlow, is not the case among newborn macaques. Their motor skills are more mature directly after birth and develop more quickly. The 'basic responses' relating to love ('affection, including nursing, contact clinging, and even visual and auditory exploration'), on the other hand, show no fundamental differences from those of human infants. Harlow therefore began by studying this infant monkeys in a three-year experiment. He offered two surrogate mothers to a group of equally strong babies: one mother made of cloth and one made of wire. **In the experiment, the wire mother and the cloth mother alternated in providing milk.** In all cases, even when the cloth mother could not still their hunger, the babies concentrated exclusively on the skin mother.[11]

What Does Lust Know About Good and Evil?

'Oh, reason! I'd gladly live
Without it, I'd manage well–
How much I often pity it.'

A. Pushkin

11 Both mother machines had a fan in the background providing warmth. But it was not the same warmth when it came from the wire. The experiments including the introduction of a 'typical fear stimulus': the babies fled to the cloth mother, but almost never to the wire mother. The face of the cloth mother consisted of a wooden head. After a while, the same cloth mother was offered with a painted face. The babies rotated this head by 180 degrees; they didn't want to see a face but rather the wooden head, which matched the mother's warm, vibrating but otherwise immovable skin body.

She was always attentive to 'signs', and read them too. When he touched her hips while she was on the phone to her husband, she 'understood' this sign and breathed more heavily. Her husband asked, 'Why are you wheezing on the phone like that?' She answered, 'Oh nothing, dear.' Her husband thought he had said something fitting that aroused her. After hanging up, she wanted to throw herself into her lover's arms. She did not *understand* that; she knew it.

Blindness,
incorruptibility of libido

IN THE SHADOW REALM OF THE LIBIDO

Invisible Images

No one has ever caught a glimpse of the death drive or the god Eros. For a hundred thousand years (an estimate), both have been concealed in amalgams, in particles of bodies and spirits. One only sees this evidently very compartmentalized part of humans, the LIBIDO, in its effects.

It consists of 'signs' or 'forces', energy-carrying images. We deduce such 'splinters of which humans consist'. 'If we assume', said the tall man whom the congress participants addressed as 'Herr Doktor', 'that we can name these images, it seems to me that they consist of DESIRE AND DISAPPOINTMENT, of radiant, uncontrollable elements of the life drive (of curiosity, of upheaval) and the dark battalions of the SUPEREGO. Once brought together, they produce the ferment, the 'energetic pole' of which we are speaking.

–The SUPEREGO is an apparatus?

–It doesn't exist only for itself.

Thus every element, and also the assembling of such elements in books, generations, great kingdoms and pictures, has a special history. It cannot be transferred or inherited. At the same time, it is inexorable. It bridges morphological chasms.

Improbability clouds circle the planet. One should not take them for gods. They are shadows of the LIBIDO, which we cannot see where it comes into being.

–Can one see the improbability clouds?

–Only in events.

Psychoanalytical Congress in 1917

The 17th of November was a Monday. Someone who knew nothing about the matter, and had not received a sketch or more precise plan from one of the other members of the Psychoanalytical Society, would not have found the location of the congress in the centre of Budapest. It was a ballroom. A podium had been set up in one corner.

They were all dressed as military doctors with the exception of Sigmund Freud himself, who was wearing a suit of dark British cloth. Doctors practising psychoanalysis had performed astounding acts of healing on war-wounded patients. They were considered sorcerers. The military psychiatrists, soul technicians, were defeated. Our psychoanalytical movement, said Sigmund Freud, is the WAR PROFITEER OF THIS WAR.

'When we now return from our daily agenda to the war,' he said in his speech, 'we find that the adaptation required of people in the trenches is difficult to achieve, albeit far less difficult than often in the various situations of sexual life. [. . .] More fear of death comes from them (scenes from sexual life) than from war, whose sign the inner eye often reads; it is indifferent to the state of war . . . '

Now, the year before the war's end (which no one knew yet), vital forces were stirring that, because of their indifference to losses in war, demanded individual happiness. Even as the sequence of speakers at the PSYCHOANALYTICAL CONGRESS continued, enterprising couples ventured into the ballroom, where a dance was to take place late in the evening.

There is something nonsensical, said Sigmund Freud, in the fact that this favourable situation for analytical matters is triggered by the struggle of worlds, that is, through 'murderous events'. We do not condone any of that. All of it furthers our form of work. 'Our cause' could not have become as influential and impossible to dismiss in 20 years of peaceful practice as—like shamans—we have become through a few 'miraculous healings in the military hospitals'. But the twenty-first century began here, on 12 November 1917, with the words of Sigmund Freud:

'Those of our memories most deeply embedded in us are themselves *unconscious* [. . .] what we call our character rests on memory traces of our impressions, and it is precisely those impressions which affected us most strongly [. . .] that *almost never become conscious . . .* '

FIGURE 24. Sigmund Freud with one brother and five sisters. © Imagno Vienna

A Child's Lie

One of Sigmund Freud's patients had been caught lying at the age of seven. She had been punished for her lie, which she referred to as a 'turning point' in her childhood. 'Until then she was a wild, confident child, and from that point she became shy and hesitant.' During her engagement, Freud continues, she falls into a rage she cannot explain when her mother procures the furniture and the dowry. It is her money, she says, and no one else must buy anything with it. In her marriage, she then separates 'in a superfluous fashion' the expenses for her personal needs from the household expenses, for which she receives money from her husband. It was because of such annoyances that she underwent psychoanalytical treatment.

The maid of the family, who had cared for Freud's patient during the latter's childhood, had become erotically involved with a doctor in the neighbourhood. This relationship was pursued in the rooms of his practice, which the maid visited after going for walks with the child. Thus the child was taken along to the rendezvous, waiting in the meantime and gaining a few insights. She was given coins by the maid, who seems to have received payments, and by the doctor, in the expectation that it would ensure her silence.[12]

Some time later, the child asked her father for money in order to buy paints for Easter eggs. Her father refused her the money. The girl framed her request differently the next time: in school, each child was required to bring a donation of 50 pfennigs to contribute to a wreath for the deceased princess. The father gave the child 10 marks; she paid her sum, placed 9 marks on her father's desk and bought paints for the remaining 50 pfennigs, hiding them in the toy cupboard. Her father asked what she has done with the missing 50 pfennigs and whether she might not have bought paints with them after all. She denies it. But her brother, who had taken part in painting the Easter eggs, gave her away. Her father gave her mother the task

---

12 See Sigmund Freud, 'Two Lies Told by Children' in *The Standard Edition of the Complete Psychoanalytical Works of Sigmund Freud* (James Strachey ed. and trans.), VOL. 12 (London: Hogarth, 1958), pp.303–9.

of beating the lying child. The mother was shocked when she experienced her child's reaction to the strokes; she sought to comfort her but to no avail. In psychoanalytical treatment, it transpired that the child wanted to receive the 'love wage', which she knew from the doctor and her beloved maid, from her father. According to Freud, the seven-year-old girl lied because, as a well-behaved, sensitive person, she could not formulate the reason for her request (namely, to win her father at her mother's expense). The issue in this case was not a lie but, rather, the inexpressibility of the truth. One must distinguish between a lie and indeterminacy, says Freud.

There is a relativity within the reality principle, adds the sociologist Dirk Baecker. All speech has a vividness that reshapes the expression according to the circumstances. Here the objects, time and location were dependent on the subjective circumstances. That chameleon, reality, not only seems to change but genuinely does so as a result of the subjective power of those present.

The child, says Sigmund Freud, was rejected in her longing for her beloved father and humiliated a second time by the thrashing which her mother was instructed to give her. If one views the existence of the family, its forms of equilibrium, as a republic, this was a breaking of the constitution, not merely of the child's will.

The generosity of all emotional events became apparent in the further course of the treatment. When the–normally passive–therapist told the patient never to bring flowers to their sessions again (thus provoking her), the echoes of that old conflict erupted vigorously. Like the subterranean pool of a volcano, the 'bubble of refusal' was emptied. Now her pain was gone. On a single morning (in a similar space of time to that in which events had once taken a turn for the worse). The child's confidence could not be restored. But the compulsion to continue the conflict in her new family in a thousand differences had disappeared.

The Testicles of Eels

Phillie Sophia Jonasson had been working on her PhD at New York University (NYU) for two years. The topic of her dissertation was Sigmund Freud's earliest research object, which he had pursued even before his own doctoral thesis. The objects of Freud's interest were the testicles of deep-sea eels, that is, their physical traits and metamorphosis during the long journey from the streams and rivers of their home, across the ocean, to the Sargasso Sea near the Bahamas.[13]

The eels had begun the journey equipped with immense fat reserves. They reached their mating ground,

---

13 Ms Jonasson was surprised by the term 'deep-sea eels' used by Freud. The early forms of the later eels move through the seawater as *leptocephalus*. Having reached European coasts, they swim into the inland waters. Here they are referred to as 'climbing eels' or, owing to the colouration of their bellies, 'yellow eels'. After six to nine years, they are ready to mate. On their way through the ocean up to the coast of the USA, they swim at depths of up to 600 metres by day and not far below the surface by night. Mating takes place at a depth of 2,000 metres. Once mating is completed, the animals die of exhaustion. Only now, says Jonasson, do they sink to the deep sea.

emaciated, with the last of their strength. The EVOLUTIONARY COMPETITION was not decided by duels with rivals, Freud noted, but via this stamina.

Freud found it interesting that those eels which succeeded in becoming parents of future generations could be recognized by their skinniness, yet their sexual organs were not affected by this degeneration. Phillie Sophia Jonasson could reconstruct all of Freud's observations. The distance of their journey (towards reproduction and death) was 5,000 kilometres. For half of their underwater journey, the rectums of the male eels were drawn inwards. As they operated without nutrition (for over a year), their digestive organs withered away. Their abdominal cavities (except for a small remainder of their fat reserves) were completely filled out by their sexual organs.

Ms Jonasson summarized Freud's research approach: what erotic elan leads the eels to faraway places with such accuracy? The eros of these animals, according to Freud, is expressed in the rhythm of fat absorption and fat emission, the work of navigation and the enormous duration of their migration tradition.[14]

Their virtue, he argues, is PERMANENCE. It is about the fidelity to a place, not a subject. It is not through

---

14 The annual migration begins during bad weather (that is, there have to be rainstorms) in the first days of November. The animals shorten their way out of the steams to the next-largest rivers by moving through damp grass. Conserving energy and bent into an S-shape, they swim in the slack tide of the large rivers. As soon as they come into contact with saltwater, they become active once again. At the same time, they go deeper down. Their eyes grow. Their colour changes from greenish brown to silvery grey.

'choice' but through instinct that for millennia, the animals have been finding their preordained place on the Blue Planet from which their offspring swarm back to the rivers of Europe.

Ms Jonasson was amazed by a note of Freud's which compared the fidelity of the eels to human morality. One could hardly suppose, he wrote, that the attributes of eels came from 'pre-sexual shock' or 'para-sexual desire' (which changes into guilt); rather, the origin was A SINGLE, UNIFIED NATURAL MORALITY. Half a year later, Ms Jonasson would have completed her PhD and gone to San Francisco to find a companion to whom she could entrust her life. While her resolve to pass the examination was clear, her choice of location and the suitable individual–after all, she did not know the person yet–was far from clear. She almost felt that, in case of an ANIMAL EVOLUTION that overtook humans, it would be desirable to exchange our eros and intelligence with that of the eels.

FIGURE 25. Entrance to the 'underworld'. The excavation site is located beneath the church Santa Maria sopra Minerva in Rome. Freud refers to this complex of buildings in *Culture and Its Discontents*. The church stands on top of the temple of Minerva. One could, with some reservations, appreciate the peculiarities of spiritual life by imagining the heathen temple and the Christian church (along with all the earlier edifices underneath, which are concealed in the different layers) facing the observer simultaneously. Now the archivist Fred Mückert from Chemnitz, waiting to find work since his dismissal in 1991, has discovered a passage through the catacombs that leads far below the remains of the temple of Minerva and then branches out to the north and the west. The entrance pictured above slants down towards this foundation. Possible, Mückert writes, the system of subterranean passages leads not to the 'underworld' (whose entrance lies near Naples) but to the labyrinth. And so, if one applies Sigmund Freud's metaphor, this can be viewed simultaneously as the temple of Minerva and as Santa Maria sopra Minerva (as well as 16 more sacred and profane buildings on this site). Everything is dark down below, and only the entrance from the side can be photographed.

III

HOW THE SOUL TAKES OUT ITS PASSION ON THE WRONG OBJECTS IF IT LACKS THE RIGHT ONES

Why do all love affairs end tragically?

Not all of them, replied Detective Major Schmücker. But always the ones under time pressure.

A Case of Time Pressure

In Frankfurt's Kaiserstrasse, institutes of higher adult education, places of prostitution, fast-food joints and exotic bars stand side by side. A passer-by rushing to the train station will pay little attention to the company branches between them, for example, of airlines, because these only address interest directed specifically at them. In 1982, one of the city's major banks still had its West Africa department located opposite the Frankfurter Hof hotel. The head of this department, Ingmar B., went to the station on foot after work. There are no adequate parking facilities in the vicinity of his office. It is easier to reach the building, which is near Kronberg, by train.

For a while, the Frankfurt police did not know how they would get the upper hand over the Marseilles pimp gang that was controlling the area around the central station. The ring was conscripting young women from villages in the former French Guinea, then putting them up in the rooms located in the side streets of Kaiserstrasse for a two-year course of training under the instruction of specialists from Marseilles; compared to conditions at home, they make a fortune. These transactions are only possible with the consent of the village elder, with fixed standards of procedure, payment and guarantees. They rest on the assumption that the women will be returned to West Africa unharmed. It is a kind of *droit du seigneur* for the white man in the city, arranged by white men who built up a 'special power relationship' after the end of colonialism: a temporally limited slavery with reduced harm to its objects. If a member of the ring ever had the habit of reflecting or discussing, the underlying family element would become apparent, the strong BASIS OF AGREEMENT that defines loyalties within the ring and the rules of reliability in human trafficking with West Africa. By contrast, the powerful cash flows controlled from desks in a major city like Frankfurt structure the life zones of southern France or West Africa in a more ruthless way; they act indifferently. Like weather activity, however, they take hold of regions and tribes without ever conducting negotiations with a village elder, arranging guarantees or taking on the responsibility to return people home once they have been sucked in and jettisoned by the momentum of the monetary flows.

One of the autochthonous prostitutes whom the ring had put up in Moselstrasse fell for the head of department Ingmar B.–with fatal consequences. It was not, as he supposed, a matter of intercourse in exchange for payment. He first met the girl, who was known as Gilla, but also Françoise (and probably had an entirely different name at home; B. sometimes took her for a chieftain's daughter, an 'enchanted princess' whose ancestors, he thought, extended back to eighth-century Africa), at the Reichsstuben. He approached her, and initially thought of his interest as business-like. As he was also responsible for West Africa, it was interesting to make the acquaintance of an inhabitant of this terrain and draw her into an enchanting afternoon for (in relation to his means) a laughable fee. As he himself was further stimulating his imagination without noticing, he felt in top form; he thought some of this would also inspire his unknown partner in pleasure. She spoke French.

In the following weeks–it was November, then the Christmas season began–Ingmar developed an 'inescapable dependence' on the stranger. He already left his office around 1 p.m. and looked for her in town. He spent a night at a bar with her, and the police carried out a search at the request of his family in Kronberg. The task force for the station district found him in a merry state at Lobos, around 5 a.m. He managed to hush it up. His wife forgave him, though she scarcely realized what was going on.

It was January, and the time was approaching when the young woman, as agreed, would be returned to her village in West Africa. The controllers tried to get rid of Ingmar gently. They offered him a replacement. They made it difficult for him to find his lover. When he succeeded in doing so (with the aid of people he knew in the task force), he pleaded with her (Gilla's agreements were only valid to the extent that she understood his plans) to start a new life with him. He often thought about changing jobs, of giving everything up.

The day before Christmas Eve, he encountered the Marseilles ring's legal advisor, who confronted him and insisted that he give up his search for the young woman. Returning the women unharmed and at the right time was a law that could not be broken in any individual case, let alone due to IDEAS ABOUT LIFE IN THE CITY. He suggested that Ingmar could follow his beauty and court her as a suitor according to the rules of her country. Ingmar knew that was hopeless; the village elders did not accept any whites, any strangers.

This made him try all the harder to persuade his lover during their hours. She was under pressure from the controllers. He remained unreachable at the office, where an internal audit was imminent. His decision about how to live his life, and what life that would even be, under what external conditions, had to be made in very little time. Christmas in two days, and it seemed unimaginable to be locked up with his family in Kronberg for so many private days, to live 'a lie', as it were, far from life. There were 48 hours left before he would have to give his children their presents: a short time to sort out his life. Under the strain of this time pressure, he shot one of the Marseilles pimps, who was trying to make Françoise break off her stay at the bar with Ingmar. He pushed the young woman towards the exit and Ingmar fired seven shots. The head and chest of the criminal, who had no residence permit, were reduced to a sticky pulp. Françoise had disappeared (no one in Frankfurt ever saw her again; presumably she was flown out of the country). Ingmar had borrowed the pistol from one of the policemen, who owed him a favour. He went to the men's toilets at the bar and shot himself, even as the respective officers were reconstructing the course of the disaster. The bar's licence was revoked.

While issuing the death certificate, the coroner, Dr Fritzsche, noted that the powers of the deceased head of the West Africa department would have sufficed to transform that part of the earth into a blooming piece of land–to organize a leap from a medieval Africa to the present day, as it were. Peculiar, he said, that an intervention from the area he virtually ruled killed him. He asked if this romance could have ended happily without the time pressure before Christmas Eve. Everyone working at the scene of the crime was waiting for two experts from the homicide division, so there was time to chat. It was unlikely it would have turned out well, said Detective Chief Inspector Schmücker. Why did all love affairs end tragically? Not all of them, Schmücker replied. But the ones under time pressure always did.

A Guide to Being Happy

So far everything had gone the way she might have predicted. She had come from a farmhouse near Oschersleben, bringing with her an aborted training as a patriotic fighter for the GDR schooled in the methods of the secret service. She had chosen the Palace Hotel in St Moritz as a place of encounter with the West. Her travel money was enough for four nights. On the night of the second day, she was holding the hand of a maladjusted young self-made man, or, rather, caressing his armpits, shoulders, testicles and feet, the way she had learnt in the advanced courses at the Ministry of State Security's spy academy. A few days later, she could see she had won him over. By the fourth day, a Monday–she had already moved into his flat, as she could no longer have afforded her own–he bought a fur coat for her at Armani, directly opposite the Palace, and its hood kept her face framed while the voluminous mass flapped around her slim body. I look as if I've come 'from a pedigree stud farm'–like a bridled horse, in fact. As for him, an insecure boy who often had a surly look, he bought a black plaited leather jacket to go with his grainy trousers, which pinched his skinny arse. They stood in front of the mirror together.

What happened then? It was 1990. She still had a GDR passport, along with a fake Belgian one from the secret service's stores; now the service no longer existed. Her amorous career would go as far as the point when she had to show a passport. She needed a CV.

She wanted to make her fortune and dragged the rich boy around with her like a suitcase. She could not comment on his business dealings, which he would have like to exchange views about. It is remarkable how low in communication physical relationships and the first burst of fascination can be. She was bored while he, in his own way, mourned quietly to himself.

She questioned him, in the way she had learnt, about his childhood and his experiences. He liked talking about himself. Upon critical self-inspection, she found her performance 'acceptable'. This was a secondary thread in her happiness: deploying herself effectively.

She went to Zurich and had a passport fabricated for her via some old contacts, along with an appropriate CV and certificates. But then she didn't show it anywhere, as she was hesitant to leave behind her true history. She had taken money out of her boy's suit jacket twice, most recently for her passport. She had initially fed him the story that she came from a home not lacking in wealth. Her unconsidered improvisation was a great hindrance. A story that avoided this contradiction, however, would have made her stay at the Palace Hotel implausible.

Whatever one does, it's wrong, she said to herself, but no longer made any mistakes in nurturing the young flower of their love that kept the self-made man next to her, and also kept alive a fervent flame of energy within her. What was missing was a 'bond of the mind'. She tried to read to him. She wanted to learn about the nature of his business activities, and he spoke freely on the subject. She bought a 'handbook for men' and read it secretly. That was how she passed the time between cohabitations. She lay awake at night, thinking about how to continue along the path that had begun happily. All this seemed easier to her if she did it 'by order'. Then she didn't have to consider whether the conquest made her happy.

There was nowhere to read at the Grand Hotel. Not over dinner, nor when she sat with him in the lobby or the bar. Not at night, because he couldn't sleep if there was light. Obviously not when they were touching each other. The book-loving East German lusted after something to read. At least on one of the hotel toilets (but definitely not in the bathroom of their apartment) she could whip out something readable for a short while.

She thought about whether to reveal herself to the boy. She felt she more or less had him 'under control'. Meanwhile, the October day of her acceptance as a German citizen was approaching. She waited, leaving everything open. He flew to Venezuela because of an urgent business contact while she 'held the fort' at the Palace. On his return, she collected him in Zurich, as she was also in charge of his car. He gave her a jewel.

Was that the happiness she had hoped for? A happiness for which powerful functionaries risked their careers? She struggled for a few days, feeling weak. Then, without a word of explanation or farewell, she travelled back to

Oschersleben via Chur, Lindau, Munich, Hanover and Magdeburg.

A Firm Character

> 'If you can't be with the one you love
> love the one you're with.'
>
> *Stephen Stills*

She wanted to feel that she was alive. With her starry blue eyes, she scoured the horizons of days and weeks for satisfaction. Her life is a horde, a robber's gang of beginnings. Each one holds the memory of a successful moment. She hides brief habits in her daily practice that she will not give up. If one could call these reserves of indefinite prospects *roots,* said her father, who was concerned about his daughter, then she would have one everywhere.

She refused to become principled. For that would have meant forcing herself into a form of 'growing up' and consequently, though not in any tangible way, sacrificing her way of life along with its hidden prospects. Father, she thought to herself, wants to sell me for a high price. She could have made a contribution herself if he had promised her something, a form of compensation.[1]

The man to whom the father ultimately sold his daughter found it difficult to bear her searching in all directions. She would have been willing to make an effort.

---

1 Fred Mangold, who was a close friend but did not try to get any closer, and ended up in the USA instead, called her a 'pragmatic nature', a 'social democrat of love'. He misjudged her: she was incorruptible.

After all, a number of successful moments were hidden in this practice, in which she fluctuated between days on which she was a willing slave and those on which she was in command. She did not want to sacrifice those, but then no one asked her what she actually wanted. Her husband saw her 'will' as something she could employ at will. He did not understand (and she was not prepared to ponder it, as that disturbs her practice) that she was as unable to determine what her will might be at a given moment as she was to decide that she would feel sexual desire at a particular time. That came about when the time was right.

In fact, as the father realized too late, the son-in-law could not convince her, just as the father had been unable to do so. Was these BUSINESSMEN OF THEIR SHORT LIVES considered the will was FIRMLY ROOTED in a series of OPPORTUNITIES that had never matched one another. She was a FIRM CHARACTER, so to speak.

You can't react to outside stimuli like a Pavlovian dog, her husband said. When the bell rings, the dog's mouth only starts watering because the bell has rung before. She didn't know that example. It struck her as disparaging. He had no right to call her a dog, and she would have had more reason to characterize *him* as a dog when he hectically tried to mount her just because she wanted to rest and warm up with him a little. But she was unwilling to express that more pointedly, because he didn't always pounce on her like a dog; there were some hidden moments in which, without really noticing, she had felt pleasure. Just not the way *he* wanted. And so the misunderstandings pile up. We'll do it the way you want then, replied her husband. But that was equally wide of the mark. It was all more multilayered than the discussions indicated.

One day she thought she could escape the reproaches and unenjoyable moments, the winter side of her marriage (without sacrificing everything contained in the past and simply running away), by *appealing* to him; that, in turn, required for *him* to appeal more to her. So she wanted to turn him into a better prospect for her in order that she would be a better prospect for him. That ended in a fiasco for her: the tender attack was aborted. This fiasco was repeated until she abandoned this firm resolution, and so by the end of May, things were more or less running by themselves–a little better than before, but more strained than in the winter. The spring offensive was a failure.

Now this man, who had grown used to her, was not devoid of reflection. He veritably consisted of making an effort; whatever he did with consideration or *with his whole person* consisted of searching for levers that were 'worth making an effort to move'. You're changing life into effort, she would have said, if she had ever articulated what she thought (which was precluded by the danger of losing him). This search–which was the opposite of her way of searching–had a point. She understood that: if he made an effort, then the small displeasure or strain of it was an *insurance* against a fall into great displeasure, into so-called misfortune.[2]

---

2 Till Eulenspiegel said that he liked going uphill because then he could look forward to the downhill. The example was self-evident for her, albeit impractical. She preferred driving uphill in her fast

She never took out insurance policies. She didn't care what the future held; something would come. If it was a crisis, a disaster, then one's adjustment to this crisis would encompass just as many elements of vitality as would a favourable outcome. This gave her a great independence from external circumstances.

This made the accusation of being guided by outside concerns all the more absurd. Where is my affection, where are my strong feelings? Surely in my reactions. In things outside of myself. But surely not *inside* me. How could I react otherwise?[3]

It was not the clash of viewpoints that separated her from her husband, however, but, rather, a fatal struggle between ways of life, a struggle of production. It separates people in the same way as class membership. Her husband's intrusions felt predatory.

Didn't she understand, he asked, that she would be torn apart if she followed so many different PLEASURE-GAIN PROGRAMMES? (as many as existed in practice as particles of reality). She would be 'torn apart in all directions, as if by horses', but only had *one* body, *one* set of nerves, *one* purpose–she was *one* woman.

---

car, for example, because driving downhill was more dangerous if the brakes failed. Going uphill, *she* didn't have to brake, and could push onwards unreservedly with her foot down.

3 In fact, the British researcher Rupert Sheldrake points out that people are always surrounded by morphic fields. Everything they do, or can do with ease, follows these canalizations, shaped by generations and masses of subjective historical forces (wishes, notions, practices, habits). One can best imagine this as a form of gravitation to which the forces of the human soul react.

She was not so sure about that. Why was she *one* woman, maybe she was numerous, she replied stubbornly. She preferred to avoid conversations of this kind through changes of location. What she would have liked most was to go to Hungary. She had read a book that was set there. She was multilayered, she was sure of that.

Essentially, he was demanding that she abandon her quest for pleasure. For she could not pursue her pleasure quest–as the sources of pleasure are scattered around–in the uniform way he expected of her (as her improved self). She should therefore, he offered her–insisted to her–dispense with her pleasure quest entirely and replace so misguided a life programme with a search for effort and trials. To prevent something worse, as it were. I can't adopt *your* collection of fears, she responded pertly. I'm not the same person as you. And that put an end to this particular afternoon conversation.

She did not actually suppose, incidentally, that such conversations led to decisions. Rather, all the twists and turns of life take place below decisions and far below discussions. 'You have to cling to a love story's coat-tails and let it pull you as long as possible', she had noted down that line. The problem: that love stories in any form beyond mere moments could only be found in books–in fact, only really in pulp novels. So here I am, alone with my motto, she thought. She found maxims unpredictable.

If I am only *able* to live in one particular way–replacing 'willing' with 'able'–than I will cling to this sole ability, regardless of whether it is crushed by real conditions, whether it seems unrealistic by their standards (as father and Fred claim), because for me only the things I am *able* to do are *real.* She took that down on a bit of paper in the kitchen: (1) What I can do is of no use for living; (2) I can't do what's useful for real life; (3) so whatever I can't use is not real; (4) what I can do is real; (5) what I can't do is unreal.

Her husband, who found the note (he is not discreet, which is a lack in his effort-making; he searched the rooms lustfully for his wife's secrets, the same way he searches her body), SAYS: Don't start philosophizing as well now. That makes her laugh. The following season, they left everything the way it was. The relationship they named 'marriage' rests on the fact that no decisions are *possible.* That provides the hints of prospects for her, and a firm wall to toil against for him. Non-communication is the foundation of marriage. Thank God, she said, neither of us have the means to shift this situation one-sidedly. Their friends our used to it, none of them would dare take sides because they'd find themselves opposed by both, assuming they were 'getting on' at the moment. What does getting on mean, she asks. Well, it would be indigestible if we digested it. It would be a dangerous poison if it were not indigestible, in an insoluble capsule, as it were. That's what life is supposed to consist of? A dangerous interjection, as the prospects for the whole are very dangerous. They would crush every individual prospect in a daily or weekly time frame. So everything has to be kept in the dark. That is what happens when conversations and decisions don't decide anything.

The moments of this autumn hold a number of things. One winter weekend, she was pregnant.

White suited her. She was marked by her youth. She wore white woollen socks, white shorts, a white polo shirt with her white baseball cap, and her ash-blonde hair was tied in a bun under the baseball cap. She looked at the world light-heartedly, refreshed by the air and plenty of seawater. She had met her husband, who would be retiring in the next year and whose death would probably occur in roughly ten years, in Zerbst a year ago. He was speaking at a gynaecology congress there and took her, a former Trade Organization employee who now worked at the buffet of the Grand Hotel, home with him to the Ruhr district. The old man had grey bristly hair. A pencil moustache over his mouth, a heavy Phalian face next to that of the young woman. A halting gait. He seemed dishevelled by the island's aggressively bracing climate. His polo shirt was red, his heavy wristwatch made of red gold.

She wore her light, puritanical beauty, feasted on wine spritzer, groped him, brawled and laughed. A long widow's existence was part of her prospects. Now too, she liked the feeling of saving up that characterized her life alongside this giant from the west: she barely used herself up at all in the short time which this most unequal marriage would last. Still fresh and the owner of a fortune, she would face life, 'which is most beautiful when one takes pleasure in oneself'.

In this, the old man helped her with all his heart. He did not lack understanding. He had seen and medically probed many women. He saw for himself that he had picked out a creature of adaptation who was looking for a niche. He agreed with this conformist, this young thing. A tired, rich man who lets the underage girl of his choice steal from him—an intimacy that no one punishes. She ate soup, he ate a meat skewer. They emptied five glasses each of wine spritzer in the sea breeze. His belly protruded dangerously. He was perhaps the only person on the island who could imagine a meat skewer digested and absorbed by the body, the way it flows through one's veins as a creamy mass attached to the blood and serum. The remaining nerves in the palate, deep inside the mouth, have memories of kitchen smells or times of need that make it an inescapable necessity to order such a little stick with various pieces of skewered meat, and onions in between; the rest is consequence. He was a serious person who did not see many chances left for him.

Love Causes Clear-Sightedness

The professional association of all doctors around Lake Constance was called the District [*Gau*] Doctors' Chamber, and its president was the District [*Gau*] Doctor. These names went all the way back to before the Third Reich. The president of the doctors' district was Gerd von B.

The 52-YEAR-OLD and his wife of the same age had adopted a Corsican orphan. The girl was now nine years old.

On account of various scribbles and drawings by the NINE-YEAR-OLD, which were discovered in her satchel by a teacher and whose implications seemed to be confirmed after she was questioned before the headmaster, the well-respected doctor was suspected of sexually seducing his adoptive daughter, a slim Romanic figure who captured the imaginations of her interrogators, or of introducing her to unusual sexual practices by showing her pictures. The public prosecutor's office investigated. In the close-knit communication network of the provinces, the investigation proceedings quickly became an object of rumours and assumptions about the facts. Dr Gerd von B. declared his temporary retirement from all medical positions, including that in the professional association. He himself did not acknowledge any guilt, however. At the urging of the Constance prosecutor's office, the child was admitted to the psychiatric ward of a German university under the supervision of Prof. Dr M.

Every day the scholar questioned the child about the drawings, attempting to sound out her soul as thoroughly and honestly as possible. There was no proof, only an initial suspicion based on the findings. What induces a child to produce drawings with obvious sexual (oral) content in break time or during a lesson?

The defence counsel in whose hands he had placed his fate considered it the best defence strategy to persuade the central criminal chamber in Constance not to open the main trial in the first place. For once the main trial was opened, the best they could hope for was acquittal due to lack of evidence; any suspicion would lastingly blacken the doctor's name and destroy his social standing in his home district. Hence the defence counsel's strategy was to force a questioning of the child by the psychoanalysts Hans Zulliger and Tobias Brocher. He hoped that the shadows which might be cast by the assessment of an academic luminary could be dispelled by the mysterious knowledge of Sigmund Freud.

The child was virtually in solitary confinement for six months at the university clinic. The girl succeeded in bewitching the academic. She answered all his cryptic questions with guileless intonation. How could she convince the scholar, who was loath to disappoint the prosecutor's expectations and himself initially imagined all manner of things that he might do with this exotic being in an extra-civilizational moment, and to whom, therefore, 'nothing human seemed foreign', that he should present her adoptive father von B. as innocent in his assessment?

The child returned to the house of her adoptive parents. The central criminal chamber refused to open the main trial based on the great scholar's assessment. The chamber left open whether an incorporation of psychoanalytical knowledge could be helpful in such a case.

–Was the child innocent?

–What do you mean, 'innocent'? There would be no question of guilt if she had actually been seduced.

–I mean, did anything happen?

–No one knows.

–Do you think it's possible?

–That's not a question I ask myself as a defence counsel.

–Did the adoptive father have intimate relations with his adoptive daughter?

–He denies it.

—Can something like that be proved without a confession?

—No.

—Can one *prove* that it didn't happen?

—No.

—You said that von B. and the girl loved each other?

—Deeply. Before and afterwards.

—Inseparable?

—No one could tear them apart. One finds that sort of thing more often with adopted children than with natural ones.

—Could it have been the child's act that convinced the great academic?

—A child can't keep up an act with no mistakes for six months.

—How do you explain (assuming that father and daughter did have intimate relations after all) the child's intuition: avoiding all trick questions, making everything look harmless. The child saved her father.

—She loves the man.

—Where did she get the knowledge? She's not a trained psychologist.

—She loves Dr med. von B. and her love guided her.

—Baffling.

—Not to me.

Affection and the Superfluous

> 'Narrow brow = short, low, narrow-minded? Her favourite word was "narrow". Narrow shoulders. Narrow in the face, one has to feed it a bit. Narrow = malleable.'
>
> *Martin Walser*, Gerda

Beneath her real body, which had grown a little fat, there was another, imaginary one that displayed 'young girl's slimness'. It didn't do any good that Erwin knew about it. He could only connect with this 'spirit' when he touched her physically. If he strained her bones towards him sufficiently, the excess fat squeezed to the side and her erotic body emerged, disappearing once more when everyday life continued. Now, talking to Leni about it–she was full of jealousy and not neutral at all–she told him that this feeling was based on a series of deceptions. It was an 'imaginary interaction of energies', and nothing would spare the woman a genuine trip to Puna. Because he was making extracts of his dear wife, she said, like a vanilla or lemon extract, as it were in a pure taste, and this reduction, which wasn't her–and that was why this couldn't be her true energy!–struck him as erotic. What she really was squeezed out at the sides as excess matter. Erwin departed from his advisor disappointed, lusting after better advice.

It was like this: his sensitivity to her energy body (and maybe it was an illusion he had created) and its contrast to the disconsolate non-energetic fat that hung from her thighs, as unloved by her as it was by him, created a compassion that inspired him to transform his aversion or neutrality towards something as superfluous as a few words too many into a hot feeling of love that 'occupied' the ugly zones of her body; admittedly, this was only because he drew the strength for this process from her imaginary youthful body, which he IMAGINED.

Gerda herself passed over all this fuss good-naturedly. As long as he tolerated her near him the way she was, and didn't remove the rolls of flab above her bottom with a knife or send her to massage sessions, she didn't mind what inner activities he got up to. She could sense when something was working. It calmed her, even if she couldn't explain why. A little later, she noticed (having understood the pattern underlying his observation) what captivated him about her. The heavy thighs and arse cheeks were like the foundations of the house. So she slept with him, and simultaneously with a slightly more childlike adult than the man whom the people around them presumed was married to her. If these veils and permutations were to disappear, she said to Leni, who grumbled, then a relationship would die. It consists of this 'to the side of the flesh'.

A Leninist of the Emotions

Mario G. from southern Portugal had joined in with Frankfurt's student protest movement in 1967. He was at all the important sit-ins, at the pubs in the evenings, at the street battles. Looking back, his contribution lay in impregnating 26 comrades. He avoided paying any alimony. One can no longer say how he achieved this subjectivist success, what led him to this far-reaching behaviour 'instinctively', deliberately or because of an unusual character disposition. He was court-martialled and shot in Portuguese

Guinea before the Portuguese revolution even broke out. His family, who had sent him to Frankfurt to study, was of noble blood. He had inflated his life in dangerous times, in the sense of an evolutionarily favourable dissemination of his genes, by creating 26 parallel universes, each of which clearly knew nothing of the others. Hans Dieter Müller refers to him in his notes on the year 1967 as a 'bio-Bolshevik'.

–How can someone manage to seduce 26 women–one after another, but still–intensely enough to make them pregnant, and to stagger his conquests in such a way that he can meanwhile leave each woman for another–and all this in a grouping whose members all know one another?

–He always joined in. He was always there.

–And pounced?

–It was a time of excitement. Subjectivity gets released.

–But surely one of the women had to notice that he was already with another one?

–One was from Darmstadt, another one worked in a group at Opel . . .

–But the other 24?

–Not all at the same time. The events were spread over three years.

–Well sure, but separating 6 times in that period, and starting over 6 times, that does stand out. That still leaves 18. And a pregnancy lasts 9 months.

–A destroyer, in a sense. A heavy drinker of lifeblood.

—Or was there something in the female comrades that abetted him?

—In this manuscript by H. D. Müller, the author calls it a strange case of counter-revolution. For the female comrades, pregnancy was a 'paralysis of the revolutionary process', a kind of Thermidor.[4]

—Figures of speech! I imagine the goodbyes were the hardest part. How do I separate? After sealing the relationship with a child? There's a certain genius there—not in seducing the comrades but in separating from them again.

—The ones I asked replied that they never broke up. He was always on the way to far-off places of political struggle . . .

—And then briefly back in Frankfurt?

—For a visit.

—Never in company? The women never saw each other?

—No. He kept everything strictly separate. Nothing except intimate contact; as soon as the door closed he was all over them.

—There weren't any cadres running some kind of security force or secret police within the protest movement to fend off counter-revolutionary attacks? Vigilantes? Observers?

4 In the French Republican Calendar, Thermidor was the eleventh month of the year. The revolutionary rule of the Jacobins was toppled in Thermidor 1794. Robespierre, Saint-Just, Couthon and the hard core of revolutionary leaders were guillotined. It was the end of the French Revolution.

—Only when it came to class opponents. Krahl was protected for a while.

—The leather jacket faction? Did they have a kind of control?

—Monitored the comrades—but in terms of what they were reading, not what they were doing. Bookshelves were examined, flats were visited, books were destroyed, pieces of clothing . . .

—And apart from that? They tried to get rid of *agents provocateurs*. There was aggressive questioning. It was made known that some person or other wasn't reliable . . .

—It wasn't a proper revolution. So that's why there was no organization against counter-revolutionary activities?

—It was self-defence. 'Liberation of the subjective side' that looked for objective goals, for example, Vietnam or the justice campaign, to establish liberated feelings in a provable way.

—But here, in H. D. Müller's notes, it says 'emotional Bolshevik' and 'Leninist of the emotions'.

—But not about Mario G.?

—It refers to the 'theory of subjective escalation'. Müller is surprised by the reserves that lie in those bottled-up subjective worlds, a century's worth of reserves.

—And Mario tapped into them?

—Everyone was saying that for the next five years, only the struggle mattered. There was no time for love, children or privacy. No time for careers or studying. Then the next generation would live. IN THE SUBJECTIVE REVOLUTION the generations didn't follow one another in a rhythm of

30 years but 3 or 5. And the gap opened up by this rapidity was entered by the young Portuguese noble.

–The *droit du seigneur*?

–None of the female comrades would have accepted that arrangement.

–Now we're talking about this very objectivistically because the subjectivist nature of the approach baffles us. Each of the 26 comrades will have experienced it in a different way.

–It's good that we can recognize the mistake in time.

–That's also a mistake in H. D. Müller's manuscript.

–Which is why K. D. Wolff won't print it.

–The novel about it has yet to be written.

–But it's still a way of developing oneself in the way meant by the forefathers. Before his certain death, the young revolutionary from an old noble house spread himself out by all available means.

–As if they had ordered him to do something like that. It's reminiscent of the *Lebensborn*.[5]

–You really think so?

–Maybe not.

–Have you noticed that we don't have a clear line on this?

–It's a politically unguarded sphere.

–And unconsidered.

---

5 *Lebensborn*, meaning 'fount of life', was the name of a state association in Nazi Germany whose aim was to increase the birth rate of racially pure 'Aryan' children. [Trans.]

–None of the classics write about it.

–What happened to the children?

–All spread around in one way or another. Taken up into marriages, brought up by single mothers, *one* child brought up by two women. As far as I know they all turned out alright.

–They're now between 27 and 30 years old?

–Noble blood.

–Half. No alimony.

The Treasure Hunter

'We'll take them up, and set them down, They'll stand, once more: I'll be bound . . . '

Faust, *Part II, Act V*

I

In the autumn of 1990 we were redeployed twice, then the whole group was put on a waiting list. Our artistic self-confidence was not directly affected by the loss of our career experience gathered thus far; we had lost our positions as a group or class, not because of individual incompetence; in fact (this was the accompanying feeling), we had been freed from the constraints of an unwanted status as skilled labourers, from compulsory proof of performance or flourishes, we had been taken out of reality against our will, and the future wrapped us in the intimation of an uncertain chance. Even the colleagues who whined about it profited from this atmosphere. The Christmas season came with glittering lights.

I was deployed by the improvised placement service which our colleague Reichart had set up to procure individual jobs, a registered association known as 'The Organization Office' (though it was never entered in the register of associations and managed without any members' meetings, almost like a party). I was to collect an American pop star from Tegel Airport. I was to accompany the person for a week as a translator and city guide. I took the job. While we had noticeably restrained the dedication of our powers in previous placements–PUTTING ON THE BRAKES was a form of collegial duty, the opposite of try-hard ambition, a sign of a relaxed attitude (and what else did we have to show except a mutual respect for our outward attitude?)–I am now intent on a complete devotion of my neglected powers, forced to plunge into a task, so to speak, to keep sacrificing professional virginity anew in the hope of a chance. As I approached Tegel Airport by public transport on that muddy winter's day, I was prepared to translate simultaneously, fall in love, be a silent companion, to use my writing abilities to promote the star or (if offended) to defend our independent status as the people of an undefeated, extinct 40-year republic–depending on the needs or opportunities of circumstances. This type of opportunism comes about when and because we escape bureaucracies. It differs fundamentally from the opportunism of the social democrats, who played a part in the crisis of 1914. Rather, it resembles the new sense of life and new beginnings also born in 1914, a feeling that broke out after everything was lost, when the war was a fact and no one could change anything. Finality condenses feeling.

I was actually thinking about some of the details of August 1914 (I had written an exposé half a year earlier) when I approached the airport and looked for the foreign arrivals gate. Back then the airport hadn't been rebuilt yet, and looked like an accumulation of toy boxes.

The artist seemed nervous on arrival. The way she sent away the band members travelling with her, she appealed to my helping abilities. I immediately had the impression that I was not superfluous.

II

I have now become a 'constant companion'. Even though I am not married to the pop star (which is my goal). She is a celebrity in the West and the USA. We live in New York, in the renovated loft of a high-rise. In the centre is a wide bed where I rest or read while she rehearses in the basement. I had gained her trust after two days. I led her around East Berlin. And I also felt warmed by the confidence with which she approached the regions and residents East of the Elbe, a prejudice one often has towards something totally unfamiliar. She also has an active imagination, and is nervous and 'twitchy' due to being overworked and particularly sensitive; she gained an impression of my country that warmed my patriotic heart, which put me in a victorious mood of sorts and (together with my aforementioned special capacity for dedication) made me fall for her—a treasure find she could not refuse. She took me on tour with her, the way one takes in a stray dog in the hope that it has a noble pedigree. But I am vigilant. I have to be prepared for the HYSTERICAL WEST IN HER. Whatever brought her to me so quickly can separate her from me at the first palace intrigue. My status in this apartment is only secure in her absence. I exchanged a lifetime's security in my permanent post in the capital of the GDR for the warm nest of a US star. I don't find it hard to defend this position, but its focus is something impossible unless I come up with something more than just being affectionate and devoted.[6]

III

We have separated our domestic arrangement. After a hectic argument (I had already booked a flight to Europe in order to express the seriousness of the argument, but was unable to pay for it) we reached an agreement. She finances a one-room office for me (with a bed and washing facilities) in a New York skyscraper. The payments are being treated as a loan that I will pay back with the money I make from the texts I write there. We meet as desired, each of us being allowed to express such a desire unilaterally. Then the other one has to make an effort. We wrote down these terms in English and signed under each of the points. It is the constitution of our way of being in love.[7] She says she love and RESPECTS me as an INTELLECTUAL PERSON, that is, she wants me to write texts at all costs and establish myself on the US market. She says she wants

---

6 My main profession, that is, the permanent post I kept occupied in the GDR, is that of film dramaturge. I therefore have precise knowledge about the course of a love story.

7 By the time we had completed the formulation and written it down, the argument was already forgotten. Our desire returned, etc.

to sleep with a 'valuable import'. I understand that and approve of how this increases my value. She talks a great deal to the people around her about me and my value, and I sense covetous, acknowledging, disdainful and assessing glances. She lets me know I am a 'Marxist' (she has a genuine Marxist at home, at her private disposal), which is something of an exaggeration.

IV

I am desperate. From my 'office' in my 'mansard', suitable as a film set for a detective office, I look out on a row of high-rise roofs with water tanks on them. The noise of traffic and the sirens of police vehicles coming from the streets. In the twilight, a large number of illuminated windows, making it easy for me to come up with the basic idea for a text: 'Millions of illuminated windows, with a novel waiting behind each of them.' This could also be turned into a series. Lights in São Paulo, lights in Tokyo, windows at night in Paris, the thousand lights of Nairobi and so on.

Obviously, I don't know much about the people. We didn't cover the topic of New Yorkers in Babelsberg. Sitting up here, all I can think of are titles. What I write down are stories about living conditions in the former GDR, which I do know about (I keep my notes from the last few years with me). I'm developing the story of a GDR spy in New York assigned to various diplomats at the UN. This fits with the illuminated windows I see.

I talk a lot on the phone. After a while, R. (who is behaving like my governess instead of being my lover) started checking the phone bills. She reproaches me. She is rich but stingy. But I need the luxury of calling across the ocean to stimulate my text production, which is a function of my self-confidence.

The classical way of producing texts: one gives up one's beloved, travels to distant lands, writes there about the intimate things one knows from one's own country and waits for public interest in one's writing to grow. But I can't expect the things I know about the intimacies of my lost country to attract the interest of New Yorkers, Parisians or even Germans. I departed without producing any stream of narrative, and I can't give up my beloved because I owe her my base and my residence.

It's like constipation. The only difference between intellectual production and bowel movements is that the stream of text onto paper or into the computer (the convulsions) increases through disinhibition (opening of the intellectual sphincter): the more one excretes, the more follows it. With my precarious status as a kept person and a participant in the US markets, however, I have to control myself rather than letting through whatever comes into my head: someone has to like it. That brings the flow of text to a standstill.

Yesterday, the first argument with R. that didn't end in reconciliation. I can't seem to write a text about that either. I was in high spirits to see the famous pop star before me, subservient and obviously sexually interested, and in these high spirits I became careless. She snapped at me while I sat impotently 'at the well before the gate'. How quickly bankruptcy comes when there is only one means of payment; but such a regression to 'hard currency' only comes about in a hysterical moment–though such moments continue endlessly throughout my beloved's life, interrupted only by a 'hysterical break'. I wrote her a poem: Dear Beloved . . . She laughs. She speaks broken German.

V

Back in eastern Berlin. Collapse of a relationship within twelve months. What's the difference between a treasure hunt and work? As soon as I return from my 'home' of New York to the soil of my 'foreign' former GDR, the flow of texts starts working again.

A Case of Expropriation

–She loved a communist . . .

–But there's no such thing as communists.

–A socialist then, a cadre. He was sent to Chile as a correspondent. He had a strong influence on her.

–And her husband?

–Jealous.

–But their marriage was more or less dead, no?

–Had been for years. A matter of form. She cared for the two children. She was very attached to the children. But they were practically like grown-ups now.

–And what triggered the crisis?

–Her husband reported her. They were living in separation. But he slit her car tyres. He kept ringing the doorbell at night, and when she opened up there was no one to be seen.

–He wouldn't leave her in peace?

—He wanted to ruin things. He didn't want her any more himself but he didn't want anyone else to have her either.

—Why report her to the party?

—To trigger party proceedings. They arrive at her place with her lover and two interrogators. The children get sent out. The facts are ascertained. How long? What exactly did you do? What will happen next? Everything noted down precisely. The verdict: it has to end.

—She and her lover were supposed to renounce each other?

—It was the only love in her life. Apart from her feelings for the children. And the lover—he had already given up on the idea that they would send him to Chile—wanted to stand by her. Then they brought in the husband and listened to his gossip. A formal interrogation. The cadre, her lover, was subsequently punished.

—They weren't able to hold their own?

—They tried for a week. But it was impossible to avoid the proceedings and self-criticism. His mission to Chile was cancelled. Leave the party or give up the illegitimate love affair.

—They rejected the phrase 'love affair'?

—Yes. They declared it a SOCIALIST RELATIONSHIP OF A SPECIAL KIND, referring to joint attendance at courses and work on relevant topics.

—Did they at least manage to cause some hesitation, a moment of consideration among the interrogating cadres?

—I don't think so. There was still the husband's complaint, the party proceedings and the basic question: where would we be if everyone . . . Yes, said the two of them, that'd be it: if everyone acted in a socialist way, that is, loyally and with solidarity, and distinguished between a sham marriage that isn't being lived and a lifelong union—then, yes, then there could also be legitimate relationships. And would the husband, a doctor, agree to a divorce? No, he said.

—A phalanx of refusal.

—Not a chance. And after a week they gave up.

—Did they ever make another attempt to find a partner?

—Never again. It was a lifelong love, born of coincidence. An individual holiday, each of them in a different holidaying group in Rügen. On the last day they met at a party. By chance.

—What coincidence has brought together, let no one separate.

—Not if it's the only love in one's life. Not if it would be a new start to life.

—How were the interrogating party cadres supposed to make such distinctions?

—They tried. But it doesn't answer the basic question: what happens if everyone . . . The lovers replied: We're not everyone.

—And that sounded elitist?

—Yes, elitist and individualistic.

—Do we know if the interrogating cadres at least made an effort?

—They did. They consulted the district authorities. That's why it all took a week longer. They had the impression, incidentally, that the husband was pursuing personal goals.

—*Personal* is exactly what they weren't. He didn't want this woman any more.

—He had never wanted her. He didn't pay any attention to the children either. He only woke up and got active when he saw that someone else was interested in his wife. It was completely impersonal and disinterested that he used all his energy to drive them apart.

—Did the lovers still write to each other later on?

—Something like secret messages.

—And the husband, did he return to his family?

—No. She wouldn't have taken him anyway.

—Pure destruction.

—That was also discussed in the circles of the district secretary, the question of whether there should be more leeway in such cases in future. But unique coincidences like this don't come up very often—two people meet, and the one love of their lives begins so absolutely and resolutely.

—Most couples don't know what they want?

—Most of them don't.

—And the party doesn't want to leave any room for that?

—As it turned out, it didn't. It's not their concern to increase the number of separations and new acquaintances.

–Did the socialists of the FIRST INTERNATIONAL think much of marriage?

–About as much as private property.

–Was that taught in party schools in the GDR?

–What would they have called the subject?

–Yes or no?

–No.

–When the four of them turned up at the door. She and one of the children open up. They come into the narrow hallway, three archangels and her accomplice. Then they sit down on the sofa and two chairs. Did she offer them anything?

–She seemed taken aback. She just kept looking into her lover's eyes. Hoping for some spark of hope because he belonged to the party, and she had started believing in this party through him.

–And then it was words upon words. Writing down the words. No human emotions can stand that. Resisting three representatives of the moral police when they directly influence one of the two lovers' lives, when they don't stop asking questions and pressuring her, because they also have to account to their superiors.

–No will can do anything against that.

–Unless one's lucky and gets provoked.

–She would've been happy to go to prison for her love, if that's what you mean. She didn't want to cause any harm to her lover, the cadre.

–They couldn't speak to each other openly in that room?

—They weren't used to dealing with that situation. They could actually have spoken openly.

—But now the doorbell rings and the complainant, her husband, joins them. She pounces on him. That distorts the discussion additionally.

—One would have to practise that feeling: dealing with such situations. But feelings of love are mostly trained in the realm of intimacy; in whispers, with no opponents present. Feelings are inexperienced in police interrogations.

—It wasn't the police though?

—No, the party.

Original Disunity

Behrend's wife was tyrannical. Well, said Fritz Gerlach, then probably it's because of him. No doubt he's also contributed to this situation.

—Why did you marry your wife in the first place if you're always quarrelling with her?

—It's impossible to quarrel with her.

—Excuse me? One only ever sees you quarrelling.

—She can't stand real quarrels.

—You mean what we see aren't real quarrels?

—Not real ones.

—And that's why you quarrel?

—What does quarrelling mean anyway? I don't know any more.

—It's what you do in front of us.

–That's not quarrelling, because she immediately reacts with illness. She magically calls up one or two degrees of fever, backache and so on. I don't even have to start putting forward arguments.

–She doesn't make arguments?

–She gets sick.

–But the air around you both is full of argumentation.

–So you're saying that argumentation is quarrelling?

–No, you're not making arguments.

–That's not how you put it just now.

–And you didn't answer my question either. Why did you marry her in the first place?

–It was in the nature of the situation.

–What's that supposed to mean?

–It's practically impossible to argue about it. It wasn't possible with her. She felt dizzy straight away.

–Is that why you got married?

–Ultimately, yes. I wanted to explain to her why we're not a good match. That it would make more sense to separate–and she responded by feeling faint.

–Then you had to drive her to the doctor, and it was impossible to continue the discussion?

–Exactly.

–And after that you drove to the registry office?

–First we had to meet a deadline, submit the papers.

–So again there was no time to reflect.

–Time for me to reflect, not for both of us. Every time I brought up the subject she clammed up.

—That sounds ill-considered.

—Not in my case. I'd considered it. None of these considerations could be used.

—Decisions like that are always made together.

—That's right. And we couldn't reach a decision together.

—So you married automatically?

—You could say that.

—Out of politeness, so to speak. You didn't dare contradict her, owing to various signs of weakness on her part, so you ended up with that result?

—Exactly.

—Does she see it like that?

—No one can talk to her about this.

—There's something wrong with your argumentation.

—It wasn't argumentation, it was a process, step by step.

—Out of disunity?

—Out of original disunity.

—Who loses out in the quarrels?

—Always both of us. *I* win the argument, *she* gets ill.

—And it just keeps going like that?

—Yes.

—One can't spend one's whole life quarrelling. That poisons one's surroundings.

—As I said, it's not real quarrelling.

—Then what would you call this back and forth that pains your friends?

—A dispute.

—And what is the difference between a dispute and a quarrel?

—Original disunity.

—So you should never have married?

—No.

—But when one watches the dispute, it seems as if you were made for each other. It never works as well when I watch other people quarrelling.

—Don't keep calling it quarrelling. It's one-sided. She argues with completely different weapons that don't match my weapons, and she has different aims from mine.

—And so you have to serve her, and a practical unity comes about.

—Against my will.

—And against her will?

—Yes, because the way I serve her is no use to her and makes her weak.

—But these weaknesses are her strengths.

—In her argumentation, yes. It's her strongest argument.

—And it creates unity.

—If you like . . .

—So instead of calling it quarrelling, we can call it unity?

—If you want to twist it like that.

—*I'm* not the one twisting things . . .

—Who's twisting?

—The two of you.

—I'm not.

—Could it be that you married her for that reason?

—Talking with you like this, I'm starting to find the idea appealing.

—It provides joke material.

—For whom?

—For us, the people around you.

—What do you think she's say if I put it like that to her?

—She'd scratch your eyes out.

—No, she's not that active. She gets ill.

—That makes me think that you actually live quite healthily; she's never really sick, it's just her form of argumentation.

—I think we're going round in circles a bit in this conversation . . .

—She's the tyrant?

—*Yes.*

Behrends propelled this 'yes' from his mouth because, for the first time in a long while, he felt able to speak directly without fearing dire consequences. Gerlach chose not to probe the ramifications of this relationship any further that day. It was confusing to see this couple's unifying bond tied so tightly. Only the traditional art of blacksmithing creates such connections, with virtually no seams or joints. It was all purely factually knotted together, without any arbitrariness. They had hurtled towards each other and had no way of distancing themselves again. Viewed as the work of a blacksmith, it was a valuable antique that someone should have taken to an assessor.

'I Wish I Hadn't Wanted That'

'Who can find it proper and good
to do as the law says we should?'

Montaigne, Essays, '*On Restraining Your Will*'

She was 21 years old, from a wealthy family. She felt surrounded. The programmatic speeches of her body droned inside her. Opposing speeches by her father, a Reichswehr officer, his protestations against the forgetfulness of the century. For two years, she had been engaged to a good-looking, affluent young man from one of the better families in Cologne.

Virtually none of this felt like it belonged to her.

She saw her chance during an unremarkable weekend she was spending with her fiancé. She used this chance to start a heated argument and resolutely booked a holiday flight to Tunisia. Before she committed herself, she wanted to have a look around the Orient.

She was approached by an Arab businessman in one of the hotel lobbies she found there. He took her to dinner four times. She found the conversations she had with him stimulating.

When she returned, her fiancé collected her from the airport. He was of the view that they should hurry up. What he meant was that they should quickly sleep together.

This struck her as a lack of restraint, something she found typical of him. That same evening, she offered to marry the Arab businessman she had met in Tunis. She had read that one sometimes finds such sudden moments of good fortune which change circumstances completely.

It was *short work*. The other programmes in her life, forced into a state of oppression by the coup, had no time to give opposing speeches. It was also a *mistake*. The easterner proved to have little wealth. She had been surprised to find him take up her offer so quickly; overall, he seemed an attentive, albeit ordinary person with whom she endured living for over 11 years, as long as they didn't see each other very much. He was usually in Egypt, while she lived in Basel.

The psychologist Bowlby views all defence as a 'selective defensive exclusion of information'. The effectiveness of such defence can extend so far that the soul maintains several 'main systems', all complete with their own memories, wishes, feelings and thoughts–one in which a dead relative is still alive, another that assumes he is actually dead, and a third in which he is already dead while actually still alive (Third Face). The less someone can bear life, the more different lives they live in parallel.

Activities, so-called decisions, are a different matter. There is one that says 'yes', another says 'no'–and a third one says a third thing that means neither 'yes' nor 'no'. But one sees that this third thing cannot say 'yes' or 'no', states Bowlby, in the fact that someone would have to regret equally that they never made the decision or that they did make it. A person (in this defensive state) would have to restrict themselves entirely to a spectator role to escape this DISPLACEMENT reliably.

Six Veterans

> 'Well, we were happy devils. And didn't need to swear any pledge or oath to seal our wonderful friendship. Bonded closely enough by something firmer.'

Mrs Margarete Schieke had–like all the rest from the Harms & Co. factory canteen team, her five friends, Ms Schaffner, Ms Dänicke, Maria Plitsche, Sigrid Berger, Anna Schmidt–become rather portly over the years. Their fat, wobbly bottoms, the upper flesh on their hips, the flesh at the top of the back, the massive upper arms, the solid (when she stood before the mirror alone and checked them) but overly broad breasts, connected to the upper belly by a fold (the details didn't matter, it had all burst out of its youthful boundaries), had been covered in clothes for decades whenever an observer was to be expected. All six had concerns about still showing their bodies, and because they could never entirely rule out some observer, they could hardly ever expose their opulent body parts to the air or the sun. Wrapped in clothing–the friends, who often swapped clothes, often exchanged doubts about whether this final state, the one in which they would die, was a product of madness. They bore this together.

Was it down to their diet, asked Anni Schaffner. What they ate was no more of an individual decision than other habits or the rhythm of the canteen work. They ate what they were used to. I chew on the crispbread for hours, said Mr Plitsche, it doesn't fill me up. But I eat up the six crackers and then the crumbs. She said that in the same way she said, 'I took in my blouse at the side, didn't work, it's too tight and before it was baggy–I'm wondering whether I should unstitch it again.' That'd be best, answered M. Schieke. A special diet was especially hard to keep up if one ate with other people.

But maybe it's not about how much hard-cured sausage we eat; maybe the shapelessness of age results from the fact that the bodies are no longer eyed closely enough. Ms Berger disagreed. For children, who didn't look at them in terms of fashionable youth standards, strong elephant legs were something useful. One could hold on to these pillars or hide behind them, and the lap felt like an armchair to sit on. The belly as a support and the bottom, resting during an afternoon nap beside a cuddled-up child, didn't wobble at all; they lay calmly and warmed the child the way no cushion or blanket can.

Really, if one took into account that they no longer served anyone as sexual beings, their corpulence (which silently contained emergency rations) was a practical thing, the only disadvantage being that the total weight infringed on their mobility. We're a little heavier than we would be of our own accord, said Ms Schaffner. It's a strain on the skeleton. Maria Plitsche passed around an illustrated report from *Bunte* with photos of Russian women bathing on the Crimean coast. All cousins of ours, she said. The six friends felt like declaring themselves, and the millions of others with their kind of bodily packaging, still-useful life forms. For that we'd have to be aquatic animals, called out Ms Dänicke, who had been silent until then. They imagined the six of them surfacing as magnificent fish-like mammals from the tides north of the Azores, like hippos or see elephants that had accumulated fat for the cold times of year; skinny gazelle's bodies were unable to carry such souls, nor could they stand up to the rapid currents. Mrs Schieke found that realistic but had not reported anything about this notion to her ruler Egon Schieke, who was in many ways indifferent.

Divorce Date

The divorce date had been set as Thursday, 8.30 a.m. Ms Anneliese F. got up at six. She found a severed horse's head in front of her flat in a large sausage bowl. The staircase of this block of flats was tiled. Stone steps.

She knew that sausage bowl. It was used in her husband's butcher's shop to cook the warm meat mixture. The bowl was about 2 metres in diameter. Regarding the horse's head, it was later said that the desperate husband had decapitated his wife's favourite horse, Niko, and carried it to her new flat that same night. The front door had been opened with a skeleton key.

The previous week she had moved out of the detached house owned by her husband, the master butcher F., with their four children. Now she was on the telephone to family friends, asking them to have a look on her husband's property.

As it turned out, the divorce date became obsolete. The husband's house (the divorce had not taken place yet, for mere will was not enough to dissolve a marriage) was ablaze when the friends of the family arrived there. F. himself was discovered shortly afterwards; he had driven to a little wooded area, set his car on fire and then, once he had made sure the motor was burning, shot himself. Now Mrs F., who was already confused enough by the excitement of the preceding week, had to rearrange everything completely, for she was the provisional heir and the children the remaindermen.

The children, slightly concerned–they had only half understood the telephone conversations–had hurried to school.

Talking to Make the Others Laugh

One could almost say that when she embraced men, N. didn't think–though that's not true, because there are always pauses. I never think about it, she said, but she quickly started talking about it: half the time everything went wrong. Her colleagues laughed at that. Encouraged, N. continued: When I embrace someone I can't decide between two things–*if* I think about it, she said that to get more laughs: Do I use that as a weapon or not? I want to win *him* over, or do I want to win *myself over for him*?

Shall I tell you what I want? To have every inch of him, for ever, but he has to be gone if I don't want him around. And make it sharpish! I'll kick him into orbit. If I want him back, I'll give him a pull (laughter). That's my whole programme.

Then it'd be good if you had superpowers, said Frieda. Yes, said Marion, then one could do it like that. She could genuinely no longer tell when she used her body, her arms, her mouth as a weapon of conquest and when she used them to satisfy her own wishes. That got muddled because her conquests also took her over at *one* moment and wanted to get rid of her at *another*. These things got mixed up fatally, even if they looked similar from the outside.

'If one can die of it, then let's view it as the enemy and not like your kind smile, which–I'll bet on this–started off as you baring your teeth, before you learnt to hide it.' N. had said that, and a moment later she realized she had said it and was amazed.

That Was the Terrible Thing: They Knew Each Other So Well That They Couldn't Really Afford Conflicts

When two people are in a room arguing, there are actually six people sitting there. Their parents are participating in the discussion, said a psychologist friend. Be that as it may, Gertie's problem was that she was completely *unable* to argue, at least with her current lover. So even when she added something, there was only one person speaking.

But she waited for her chance: as soon as Franz halted, she threw herself at him with all her power, and now *he* fell silent. The fact that he said nothing made her as furious as the one-sidedness of his words had before. But the four very different parents said nothing or stormed ahead, and it was impossible to express this satisfactorily in the one-way street of their communication.

The psychologist interferes with intrusive advice. Franz was of the view that this guest had only been invited for a drink. Gertie saw things quite differently. She brought sandwiches, using up the contents of the freezer completely so that she could offer the visitor something. She was interested in the psychologist's interpretations.

When Franz gave monologues, his words were not information but a weapon. It bothered him that the visitor repeatedly interrupted Franz's activity with references to the purpose of this weapon. His speeches were not intended to spread logic; they had explosive content that disturbed Gertie's inner flow of words, which she did not mention. Different parties were speaking in Gertie, after all. Now, for example, Franz brought the thrifty party–a powerful faction on her father's side–into play by giving the psychologist an expensive illustrated book. Gertie regretted parting with the valuable object. She considered the gift a bribe to the guest. She was already fretting over the empty state of the freezer.

The empires of Franz and Gertie were not unified entities. They consisted of warring factions; thus individual factions on either side could fraternize or argue. Gertie seriously thinks, for example, that she would sooner strike her lover Franz dead than let a rival get her hands on him. This existed alongside the view that POSSESSIVE RELATIONSHIPS WITH OTHERS PRODUCE DULLNESS. At certain moments when Franz was not indulging in monologue–in an unobserved moment, as it were–she felt so fond of him as an entire living being that she would have embraced anyone to whom he turned his attention. She considered herself tolerant.

But the thrifty party of her emotions wanted to profit from this somehow, and considered it a betrayal that he did not take up her magnanimous suggestions. He presented the situation as if she were keeping him in a prison cell (the only truth in this was that she had to meet with him in a room in order to deal with him), yet in the meantime he slipped away, going around in other people's abodes, doing it in secret and at the same time wanting her approval—which she couldn't give him if she only learnt of all this by exposing his exploits. But there was also an ordering party within him for whom it was important that he consider his behaviour consistent.

In the meantime, the psychologist, having pocketed the illustrated book, made interjections from various perspectives with a conciliatory attitude. He said they should write down their quarrels. This experienced man, well sated, had the impression that much of what had been said was based on prior discussions, that these were worn-out, dull back-and-forth movements of words being uttered. One should, he said, reduced all the tangled articulations to two positions (regardless of who says what about it) which can then face each other in genuine hostility.

That made Gertie listen up. It sounded promising to her: facing Franz not in love, but as a stranger and enemy whom she knew nothing about. Then she could wrestle with him without wrestling with herself at the same time. Franz as an unknown enemy, so that she could have something that would still surprise her! Franz replied: That shows that we have to separate. He felt a fiery pleasure while speaking those words and thought of immediate separation, like among enemies, with no guilty conscience, as the psychologist was sitting there and Gertie had suggested it herself.

Gertie had a different view: she didn't want a lover but an enemy, so that she could fight about something. But I won't gain an enemy through separation, she said. What she meant was that she wanted to relinquish her knowledge of Franz, but keep him as a contact surface. A lifelong enemy promised her a unity of emotions.

The Battle between Conscience and Superstition

The pimp went to the psychologist. His name was Maximilian Conrid and he was following the orders of the judge, who had refrained from sentencing on the condition that Conrid 'guide his rocket in a different direction'. He had kicked down a door and then refused to pay for the damage.

He liked the psychologist. He was gentle (that is, did nothing violent) as long as he didn't have something. He didn't have a psychologist in his stable or on his imaginary list of planned conquests. But the psychologist was **wasted** if he only conquered her. He intended to put her in his service.

That wasn't easy in the teaching sessions. They were always a week apart. The end of such a talking session affected the entire period, meaning that Maximilian already became confused after five minutes because of how time was subdivided. And he couldn't get close to the woman from his seat in front of the table. He concentrated on signing up for double sessions, several sessions per week. The psychologist would only agree to increase the number of sessions for reasons concerning their content. He sat in front of her unhappily with his demand, looking for the right point of contact to seduce her. She rejected his explanation that he had to complete the course demanded by the judge more rapidly because his work was calling; one couldn't change a character at high speed. He replied that he was not aiming to change his character but simply wanted to 'guide his rocket in a different direction' in order to meet the judge's conditions. He wanted her to rewire his character (assuming he had one) as quickly as possible so that he wouldn't destroy any more doors or tables, but rather go about his business in more level-headed ways.

Now, the psychologist was an enlightened woman, a trained private owner of her person, and thus superior to the untrained land holder Maximilian, who did not possess his own soul, as it were. It was clear that she would prevail, based on the law of 'the confessed self-interest of restless, multi-skilled enlightenment', over the 'local, worldly-wise, conventional, sluggish and fantastic stubbornness of superstition'. But the pimp (she had quickly guessed his line of work) saw the psychologist as a lucky charm, and he was interested purely in acquiring her services for his business. He wanted to give those entrusted to him some psychological training and, as the jewel in the crown of his catalogue, offer this pretty and intelligent person, for which he expected special prices. The problem he saw was how to come into physical contact with her so that his will would flow to her like an electrical current. As she did not agree to double sessions, he waited for her at the end of the day and insisted on carrying her bag when she went to the station.

This enlightened woman, trusting misguidedly in her knowledge of the psyche, made the mistake of allowing this local character to follow her around like a dog. She considered it justifiable from a therapeutic perspective, as she had diagnosed him as having no mental problems. He was simply maladjusted: if he had his department fully organized, i.e. if there was nothing for him to conquer, his unused aggression was vented in acts of violence. She referred to that as an 'expression of disbelief in risk-free ownership'. This was not accessible to psychological interpretation; rather, it was a matter of guiding his valuable and robust energy towards 'higher goals'. It was worth her giving him tips. She wanted to put him in his own service, off duty, as it were, out of a desire to advance him. So it was not about her becoming the moral pimp of this pimp–that would have been self-interest–but, rather, about making him a better pimp of his own self.

As long as she was analysing him in their sessions, her trained impulse had been protected from the man's influence: through the division of time, which deprived him of anything to hold on to, but also through the competition of the other patients. That wasn't the case when he offered himself as a slave and trotted to the station beside her. She was there as a whole, and as a whole she took a liking to this 'ownerless property' she had found. She inwardly took possession of the pretty boy, wanted to help him. She forbade herself any self-interest.

But the sluggish, conventional, fantastic, tenacious companion dog could observe very well that no one in the world can keep private property separate from self-interest.

Not even a person trained in the ability to 'overlook unimportant things'. Such a person will themselves become an ownerless property, ready to be gathered up. The clever companion dog, who had sneaked his way into her heart as the idea of a property, pulled on the chain that drew this trained person towards his sphere of interest. Compromises were reached. She had a standpoint to represent, and had to talk him out of using her in the manner of his other horses. But she did accept–simply to avoid losing this property–that they occasionally met in a restaurant, and later also in guesthouses. Considering the difference in enlightenment, she didn't consider that significant. But she aimed–after hollowing out her inner self with selfless therapy during the week–to maintain a balance.

Thus she was willing, if he went to the lengths of demanding it (pulling on the imaginary chain of her owner instinct and threatening that the chain holding him would break otherwise), to speak to his girls. It was an interesting task that required the full use of her intimate knowledge (below any layers of training). So she schooled the girls by improving their way of working. It was not the same thing if one had a German city-dweller, a US officer (with an exchange rate of DM 1.80 to $1) or a country lad to work on. She herself did not serve at the front, but did allow Maximilian to introduce her to a banking expert, resulting in a lasting, mutually useful union.

So it mattered little to her that the man with the untrained soul took DM 20,000 for the introduction, but also had a relapse and demolished valuable items of furniture in her new lover's home with a hammer. She explained the psychological background of the deed to the banking expert: the fact that whenever the man who had helped them meet got what he wanted, he expressed his doubts about it through violence. The happy banker soon forgot about that.

But the pimp soon found himself with the status of the dog again, waited for her at house corners, wanted to help her carry things so light that she was happy to carry them herself. Evidently, he was waiting patiently or calculatingly for the chain to become stronger and for her once more to become fond of him, her vassal, for her to give him advantages in order to analyse him (without self-interest); he waited and walked along beside her 'as if hoping for another bone'.

The Diver

> 'Through feeling, one gives other people power over oneself.'

In the tourist group, Ms Schaake was a figure who attracted lurkers. She asked for a blue cowry shell. She wanted to take it home for her husband. She seemed to promise something to anyone who could bring her the shell. Cowry shells could be found roughly 800 metres from the beach of the island in the Seychelles, at the foot of a little sub-island, assuming one had some diving experience. A companion from the travel party, hoping for the special favour of Ms von Schaake, told her he was prepared to swim there and dive. The beautiful lady would receive her memento. If she took a liking to him in the further course of the trip, she could offer him lasting memories. Inwardly, he referred to von Schaake as a 'walking erotic credit institute'.

Getting the cowry shell meant, first of all, swimming the crawl to the little sub-island; only then did the man dive. When he had found the shell at a depth of around 6 metres, he noticed a shadow to one side. He was surprised, as he was not expecting any helpers here, but did not let it bother him and lifted the handsome shell from its natural mount, after which he intended to rise to the surface. At that moment, he felt the shadow again–the impression from the side only lasted fractions of a second,[8] passing the eye behind the goggles, where it has little capacity for sideways glances. He sensed that something was lurking and did not know *how* it had passed his eye, and suddenly everything was sheer terror.

The unfortunate diver escaped to the little island with four movements and lay there, exhausted. He saw the fish's body, close to the surface, circling the island hour after hour.

The island lay exposed in the blazing midday sun. The diver saw no way to wade into the water. The guarding fish lurked with the patience of a superior monster. The man had technical devices on his back, his goggle around his neck and, in order to appeal to the lady, was wearing nothing else. The island offered no shelter to escape from

8 It did not happen in the eye in a whole second but, rather, 'in a fragment of several seconds'; there were several seconds but none of them were whole. It was a 'disrupted impression', slipping out of place even as it came about.

the sun. The patience of this sun as a nerve-wracking time scale.

Towards evening, the roughly 5-metre-long fish disappeared. The diver decided to swim back to the saving shore, holding the cowry shell firmly in his left hand. Now, when it hardly seemed necessary in order to save his life any more, he could see people at the other shore again, waving to him on their early evening walk; they included members of the travel party and also the beautiful lady who had given him the assignment. They saw the swimmer, who was now heading towards them with wild thrusts. Then the diver, now a swimmer, noticed a shadow some distance away, announcing the presence of the dangerous fish. But the fish maintained a constant distance from the desperate man, as if it considered his attempts to reach the shore a vain effort. Gripped by the horror of the previous hours, the swimmer thrashed his arms and legs through the water, soon felt the ground under his feet again, then finally stood on the beach, trembling, offering up the blue shell, and 'let out everything that was in his bowels'.

Because of the aftereffects of the danger, he was unable to maintain his promising position. The ungrateful lady never forgave him. She took the shell but wanted to forget, not comfort, the man who had come towards her from the foam of the surf and wiped his thighs. She did not feel able, as she later said *to fashion erotic feelings out of gratitude.* She was married, after all. The system of relationships which the diver had relied on had a flaw. No one is obliged to do something impossible. It remained unjust.

The Hiding Place of Her Will

It seems inexplicable. She came from a good family. Her father, a respected businessman, never had any trouble expressing his will. She was 16 years old when the young pimp Igor picked her up in a cafe in the town centre. She was into drinking espresso all the time, then she wanted to drop in on a girlfriend and be home in time for supper at seven. The young pimp took her with him the way she was. She was still wearing the clothes that were usually worn at the riding school. If she had run in front of a car, the mourners would have said: It was because of that one espresso too many. If she had skipped it and rushed home directly[9] then she would still have had to pass the time before supper somehow, but would at least not have run in front of the car.

Igor, whose age was taken to be either 17 or 19, had no trouble expressing his will. His whole attitude was expression, albeit one relating to the moment. Assuming that Olivia, the riding-school student, hoped she would now be in a steady relationship, safe in the firm will of another, then this prospect of being able to surrender sincerely did not materialize at all. To whom or to what should she surrender when the firmness of Igor's will today and his will tomorrow blatantly contradicted each other?

Such a hardness of the ego demands abstraction. He could use her consistently, but not be consistently attentive

9 She was her parents' favourite, so she had got into the habit of being the last to arrive.

to her. On his instructions, she made up to DM 7000 per month in foreign workers' accommodation. When she brought him a substantial sum of money and seemed (not to receive thanks) inclined to linger in the room for a while, as a kind of hint that she had been thinking of him the whole time she was working, he carried her out of the bar and threw her into the ice-cold Ruhr. She was getting on his nerves.

His nerves were in a useless state. He could not bear to be separated from his hard-hearted egotism even for two or three minutes; to offer himself for a moment so that someone else could warm themselves. Olivia protested against this. She was not devoid of will in the sense that she worked for him for no reason; rather, an independent will seemed so insipid to her because it did not lead to surrender. So the goal of her will was different from what is commonly assumed.

Thus she refused to work for Igor any longer. This too was intended in a productive sense; she wanted him to change a little and accept her goodwill, and then she would resume her work for him immediately, in spite of everything. It was not as if she considered her work in the foreign workers' accommodation unimportant or had not felt the satisfaction of important, strenuous work. But there was no sense of proportion in this work; she could never engage thoroughly with a customer but was unable to harden herself amid the hectic busyness of her timetable. She also feared physical injury.

So she refused to work, and did not take the opportunity to return to her parents' house, where should would have been safe from Igor's punishment. Igor took her away, accompanied by young helpers. He saw it as a matter of honour to break her will. Her refusal to work could not go unpunished. After they had beaten her they put her in an Opel Kadett, drove to a small wooded area, tied her to a tree and let her freeze. Her back and chest cut up by knives and a bleeding cut from her nose to her ear, though not very deep. Her individual will violated, she was found by riders from the local riding school, trotting through the woods in single file.

They brought her back to her parents, where the doctor rushed to see her. In his opinion, she was behaving 'crazily'. She stubbornly said *nothing* in response to his cautious questioning. The doctor, who had known her since she was a child (and her parents concurred with this argument), said that she should have bubbled like a spring, providing information about the perpetrators and the things that happened to her in the eight weeks of her absence. That might have led to the perpetrators being punished. And Olivia could not, in fact, summon any feeling of solidarity with Igor and his helpers; she would not have cared if they had been punished. She would not have done anything to save them. And for her own part, she was also *indifferent* to any punishment. Because of that, however, she saw no reason to send her lover to his doom by giving information if that information would result in the doctor and her parents starting a discussion about her 'inexplicable behaviour' (along the lines of: Why did you do that, child, what were you thinking going with him?).

She wanted to protect this remainder of independent will, for it seemed to her that she had gone with him willingly, that this moment of decision had actually been an expression of will. She said nothing in response to the noise made by her mother and father, she ignored the fact that she was being watched. She ate and drank, and soon looked 'healed' and content. Her hidden will, however, remained rebellious: she kept silent about the eight weeks that did not exist in her parents' perception. At that time, her willpower lay hidden exclusively in this reserve or distinction. Struck by losses, she was proud of herself and put what had happened down to experience.

Adultery and Its Consequences

> 'Bring your anger to a halt / Hot blood leaves the gods cold.'
>
> *Montaigne,* Essays, '*How the Soul Devotes Its Passion to the Wrong Objects If It Lacks the Right Ones*'

Colonel Erwin Handtke was a technically experienced officer. Popular among his comrades. In 1984 he had security clearance to access NATO secrets. He was involved in an affair with the wife of a dentist in L. The lovers met in the home of a female cousin of the colonel. The officials of the Military Counter-Intelligence Service (MCS), who only began investigating the situation once the relationship had become a scandal (they practically found out about it through the BILD newspaper) saw a 'high susceptibility to blackmail' in the behaviour of this man who had been entrusted with confidential information. The dentist's wife had fled from the GDR. Who knows if that happened by order of the Ministry of State Security's reconnaissance abroad? The cousin belonged to a student group that had been under observation by the intelligence service during the campaign about the army and justice. It is dangerous for security policy to share erotic secrets with persons who have been put in that category. Colonel Handtke should have known that!

The mistress's husband had followed his fugitive wife from the GDR. Having established the regularity of the colonel's visits, he shot first her and then himself in the home of the cousin in question. The fatal tragedy was reported to the press.

The head of the army's personnel department followed the maxim of never publicly admitting to weak points in the senior officer corps. He counted on the forgetfulness of the tabloid press. He ordered denials of the colonel's involvement in the affair. This was a tragedy between East German refugees, a marital drama.

How different things were in the case of General Staff Colonel von Dettmers. In 1942, he became the lover of a dentist's wife. When her husband approached him and slapped him in the face with his gloves, the only course of action this experienced tank officer could think of was to drive towards the enemy positions near Voronezh. He did so until his opponents had time to lay mines before the proceeding tanks. They had to overtake the German tank with trucks and mine the route a few kilometres away. The suicidal colonel drove straight on along the road in expectation of a 'worthy end'. This end was meant to restore his honour and that of his mistress. The cuckolded dentist, deferred from military service until then, was conscripted to the front; as a soldier, he was accused of insulting a superior, namely von Dettmers, then sentenced by a military court and sent to a punishment unit. Von Dettmer's comrades saw to that. The dentist was effectively forced to accept a sacrificial death. No one in the punishment unit survived.

The Othello of Luneburg

Garrisons in the Luneburg Heath were used to train the Special Forces units of the German army that later became popular in Kabul and distinguished themselves, even if they were insufficiently equipped by US standards. Gunter Bärlepsch was promoted from captain to major in Kabul. He was considered a particularly level-headed man, someone who motivated both subordinates and superiors. He had language skills. A year before he was despatched he had fallen in love with a young widow in the garrison town and married. He accepted the two children from her previous marriage as his own, guarding their fate with care.

A lower-ranking comrade in the men's group at the Luneburg garrison, a typical beta male, as the regimental doctor said, attracted the young woman's attention and seduced her. Leave from Kabul was unusual for cost reasons. After Bärlepsch returned briefly to the garrison town in the autumn of 2002 and immediately noticed his beloved wife's estrangement, his duty weapon fired a shot that hit his rival. The young woman, the only witness, claimed that 'the accident happened while cleaning a weapon'.

In the meantime, the Luneburg couple were living together in traditional peace again. Major Bärlepsch had testified in a disciplinary enquiry and had been summoned back to the garrison from his service in Kabul.

The detective charged with investigating the murder of the major's rival felt torn. He believed the young woman's account but saw that the improbability of the report would make it difficult to convince his superior and the prosecutor's office of the result. The motive, the body, the implement, the suspect–everything needed to solve a murder (even if it was a killing in the heat of passion) was on record. Nonetheless, he had his doubts about the jealous murder scenario. He considered this assumption 'romantic'. The opposing assumption that the two men (who had both taken out their duty weapons and placed them in front of them) did not attempt to shoot each other but were simply cleaning their weapons together in a comradely fashion in the middle of an emotional crisis was highly improbable.

–Going by general experience, my dear inspector, it doesn't happen that two rivals sit down, clean their weapons, a shot is fired and the weapon of the man with a reason for aggression hits the man who has injured the other's honour. No author could write a convincing novella based on that story.

–The object of desire, courted from both sides, was sitting beside them. Perhaps this put the probabilities of life into disarray and made peace, for example. The way we might clean a pipe, they were cleaning their pistols.

—That seems unlikely.

—Why do you keep relying on the concept of probability, honourable prosecutor? It's a long way from Luneburg to Kabul. That also changes probabilities.

—I understand that you want to protect the returnee, the new-found happiness. But the prosecutor's office has a legal duty to prosecute if the circumstances call for it.

But the circumstances do not necessarily call for it. Only the prejudices, gained from previous dramas and tragedies.

It did seem possible and the spirit of reconciliation had entered the army (or even Europe), to the extent that, against the background of terrible events, which had meanwhile passed in Afghanistan too, even something as improbable as the juxtaposition of two rivals in the presence of their object of desire would be conceivable. The way one could imagine the events concretely, based on the forensic results, the young woman's account could not be refuted. My dear inspector, the prosecutor replied, it is also possible that the woman, realizing her error and feeling guilty about her mistake, lied in order to be left in peace and emotional dignity. Dignity and dishonesty contradict each other, replied the inspector. The two men, the inspector and the prosecutor, liked each other. The close conditions of the garrison town demanded compromises; the unilateral behaviour sometimes shown by great powers in matters of crime and punishment was unknown here. And so they agreed to take their chances; if a higher authority challenged the result of the investigation, further steps would be considered. But for now one should enable the returnees a safe homecoming to Ithaca, even against all probability.

The Moment of Decision

'If you consent to your father's suggestion, he will marry you tomorrow . . . ' But her matchmaking father says of her: 'Believe me, she is as true as she is fair!'[10] The woman is sold–in fact, she is recognized, which means more than a sale. Does Wagner have a sense of humour?

–Would you jump after me to save me?

–Where?

–Into the cold seawater of a Nordic bay?

–To save you?

–Yes.

–And there's no other possibility?

–Be honest. It won't affect our relationship if you wouldn't do it.

–I'd jump after you.

–You're lying!

She noticed that he usually lied when he saw no other way to make her be quiet. They took a few steps.

---

10 From the libretto for Richard Wagner, *The Flying Dutchman,* Act II.

—You don't have to jump, I'm just asking. After all, I'm not the Flying Dutchman, she says, but what if I were?

—Then I'd jump after you to save you.

—I don't believe you.

—Well, you're not the Flying Dutchman, answered Emil Mölders.

Because she was a woman, his fiancée, in whose company he stepped out of the opera house into the Munich night, was definitely not the Flying Dutchman, who, misunderstanding the conversation between the huntsman and Senta from afar, assumes the bride is unfaithful and leaps into the water of the harbour. Senta leaps after him. The two ascend to heaven.

In the story, which moved me, says Hilde, there's nothing to look forward to. How am I supposed to ascend towards the mainland and up to heaven with you for redemptive reasons from the dirty seawater in the harbour of Munkmarsch, to name an example familiar to both of us, where we can't even drown at low tide because it's shallow, when we both know that going up leads to the stratosphere, then the Van Allen belt and the empty outer-space air, and not any kind of residence?

—You can't say OUTER-SPACE AIR, replied Emil.

Why am I getting worked up, Hilde continued, about absurd, greater feelings, and stay calm about realistic questions, like whether I'll buy some Schlackwurst so that you will be saved from hunger in the evening? Does that mean there are no places or opportunities for greater feelings?

Evidently that's what art wants to tell us, answered Emil, who still wanted to stop by at *Leopold.* For that he needed to call a taxi, and the dispute was holding him up. Wait a minute! said Hilde, you can't fob me off like that. Inwardly she lingered on the gaze of Senta, who did not move for some time, her eyes fixed on the ghostly man appearing in the doorway of the trader's house–but now the engaged couple were meant to hurry to the taxi rank in order to go purposefully to *Leopold,* where they would meet people whom Hilde had no desire to see, for they did not fit anything in the basic mood of the opera, neither the ghostly sailors nor the Nordic trading depot.

But there were more operagoers beside and in front of them rushing to get taxis, so they had to both had to hurry up for objective reasons if they wanted to win one for themselves. Hilde found that idiotic.

Why, she asked, do we have to go to the opera if we're in such a hurry afterwards? The opera struck her as a suitable exercise for GREATER STAYING POWER IN THE TIME SCALE OF EMOTION. I think, she said, that art wants to tell us something. It certainly doesn't just think we should always believe in ghosts. I find God's revenge too long-term in this case. The fact that this Dutchman laughed in the wrong place 30 years after Christ's birth (or around the time of Christ's death) doesn't have to condemn him to travel until the twentieth century. God is tenacious but not petty. The story, Emil replied, is set in 1810, not in the twentieth century. That's still too long, answered Hilde. She found Emil's response superficial. How about concentrating on my question, she said. I asked what art wants to tell us, when I think I was able to accommodate or mobilize larger-scale feelings in this piece for several hours, but not now. But God's revenge is too long. They had reached the taxi rank. There were no more cars. Which ones? asked Emil. Why? said Hilde. What larger-scale feelings, what direction did yours go in? Emil had not been unmoved at all times either; he was asking out of politeness. She couldn't answer immediately.

She was disappointed by the conversation. At that moment when she could finally open a taxi door, she had to decide whether she should find Emil superficial (not paying attention to her but also hectic about his own feelings) or see 'starting points' for a continued life together. *Then she jumped after him onto the backseat of the car.*

They can't treat us like that, she thought. Later it took her days to realize what it meant that she had mutely followed Emil, when she had actually wanted to talk about what art had communicated to her and to him. She had timed (looking at her watch) that it took 17 minutes for Senta and the Dutchman to agree on their initial eye contact. Hilde, a laywoman in artistic terms, assumed that she would have taken 30 minutes to interpret just one of Emil's stressed glances or the movement of his hand to the car door appropriately. She found the lack of time unfair towards every one of her daily movements.

And so, that evening, they began to have doubts whether art had anything to tell them, and fluctuated in their judgement– simply because he was so single-minded about going to *Leopold*, and that was only because he had promised to appear there. When they entered *Leopold*, no one looked at them for long; their friends took it for granted that they would appear, as promised. Sit down, Emil, said one of them. Hilde felt like sobbing.

Impotence Increases Violence

In 1944, the Reich SS leadership fell apart into factions or 'associations'. It tended towards 'fantastic solutions'. The preferred solution was one that required no preparation and could be quickly ordered. In that sense, there was no longer any 'leadership'. A few SS jurists travelled through the occupied areas and tried to 'streamline' things, the way any decent estate trustee does.

In a suburb of Warsaw, a city in which an uprising by the Polish underground army had recently been violently suppressed–the Soviet Army was waiting on the eastern shore of the Weichsel, not entering the Praha suburb–the Flag Leader and SS judge Wöhler encountered a situation that he called 'Project Dustbin'. Polish girls and women, deployed as medics in the underground army, had been dragged out of canal tubes and house basements to be held captive in a school building in the western suburb. A Wehrmacht battalion consisting of dyspeptic and moribund soldiers had been commanded by an officer from Nach-Zelewski's staff to 'seal' these female prisoners, which meant having them impregnated by German men and thus being forcibly integrated into the German racial core. This was not meant to occur through rape, but rather in a 'chivalrous manner'. The plan was for future generations to be born after the final victory (or after the occupation of Warsaw by the Red Army) as a response to the treacherous uprising.

The matter had got out of hand. Every morning, platoon-sized groups of battalion members drove up to the guarded school building. None of the dyspeptic or moribund soldiers succeeded in 'seducing' one of the young girls on an air raid shelter bed, however. The attempts, said the doctor stationed there, were usually aborted before any intimate situation could develop. The patients (or soldiers) concentrated on their pains, were confused by the order and afraid, said the doctor, that their bad breath would be noticed. The captive women remained obedient and tried to adjust to the situation.

The (likewise dyspeptic) battalion officers resorted to various measures in order to help carry out the order, whose racial point they thought they understood, against the resistance of the troops. The battalion doctor took semen samples from the men and diluted them with H_2O. the young girls were hung up with ropes in the classrooms, head down, and the liquid was poured into them using a funnel. Even after four weeks, none of the cases had produced results. The SS judge immediately stopped the procedures. He revoked all orders and had the battalions taken back to the Reich. The railway transport was overtaken by the Red Army's January offensive near Poznan; everyone in the train was shot. Otherwise they would have died of their gastric cancers shortly afterwards.

FIGURE 26. Mural in the bunkers of the Reich Chancellory: *Waffen-SS as Guardian Angels*.

Is Hilde Unreasonable?

Wilfried found it hard to say what bothered him about Hilde W. She came in, made a few remarks, grabbed the telephone and spoke for several hours in an adjacent room. The self-sufficiency of this procedure, its 'egotism', struck Wilfried as 'vegetative', like the simple growth of expanding algae. He said to his close friend Gudrun:

–Hilde is totally unlikeable.

–Why?

–Like a carnivorous plant.

–You're intolerant.

He couldn't express himself correctly, so his own line of thought wasn't clear to him.

–The line of thought isn't clear to me. I'm expressing myself wrong. But I mean something particular.

–That's not a line of thought (said the patient Gudrun), it's an indefinite feeling, a prejudice.

He didn't care what she called it. He couldn't stand a person who only showed a superficial interest in her surroundings and instead pursued her consumerist 'long-distance greetings'. He had an almost racist aversion to this social type.

–She seems antisocial to me.

–You're offended because she doesn't take notice of you.

–She doesn't take notice of ANYTHING.

–So you want her to pay closer attention to you?

–God forbid.

He was sure that he didn't want to have any extended conversations with Hilde W. His aversion increased when she watched him.

–What interests does she have?

–Talking on the phone, you can see that . . .

The Weight of Feeling Where It Mattered Little

Inês de Castro, a lady-in-waiting, came to Spain from Portugal in the retinue of Infanta Constance. The Infanta was to be married to the crown prince, Pedro. The young man fell in love with the tall Inês de Castro. The Infanta died in childbirth a year later. Henceforth, the crown prince cohabited with Inês, who had won his heart, in a garden cottage near Coimbra. The young, intelligent woman brought her brothers to the court. She was given titles reserved for the high nobles and royalty.

The king, unsettled by the notables, whom he could not ignore, convened the royal council. The young woman was sentenced to death: national self-defence. One night the king–Dom Pedro, his son, had travelled to the south of the country–took four witnesses, the executioner and a group of armed men to the garden where Inês de Castro was staying. She was beheaded in the early hours. That was how the prince found her. It was a mistake by the king to place the murdered woman in his son's memory.

After a brief war, the father forced his son to make peace. Fifteen years passed. By the time Dom Pedro ascended the throne he seemed to have forgotten his murdered lover. Upon Pedro's accession, the instigators and murderers, as well as the witnesses, fled to Madrid. The new king made a treaty of alliance with Spain.

The fugitive witnesses, instigators and murderers realized too late that the aim of this alliance was an extradition treaty between the two countries. Spain handed over four witnesses to the king of Portugal in exchange for knights who had deserted. The exchanged witnesses, instigators or murderers were skinned alive and beheaded the next day. Four thousand others who had been involved followed them to death. King Pedro was given the name 'The Cruel'.

He had the dead Inês exhumed, anointed under the hot sun of Lusitania and carried through the country. A number of suspects had to kiss the hand of the deceased, whose head had been sewn on.

Planned for the sarcophagus in which the queen of hearts was laid: he and Inês lying opposite each other. Their feet as neighbours, so that when the call to Judgement Day came, they would immediately look at each other. Both were looking forward to it, despite all the tears.

I'm Not the Rug for You to Step On

For a while, she was Director Däne's cleaning lady. Dr Giselher Dalquen had found her. First, she always arrived at the directorial apartment, gave Däne's rod and balls an orderly shake and also listened to his complaints. He took her hand, guided it to his cheek, and after receiving her payment of DM 200 she could leave again. This CLEANING became a fixed part of the hard-hearted director's life. She crawled under his wing, as it were, and it was this very gesture that aroused his protective instinct, or, if one wants to call it something else, a pride, a greed, a sure eye for a good opportunity and an enjoyment of having her around him, A FEELING OF LOVE. The name of the job didn't matter to her; it was more important that he tolerated her around him, and that she brought a large part of her clothes and utensils into the flat. She felt looked after, and it wasn't hard to get him to marry her the following year. He did this with the caution of the decent businessman: agreeing on separation of property and a mutual abdication of claims to support.

But there was a fundamental difference of opinion. As he tolerated her around him, looked after her, he wanted something in return. But she felt he had already had something in return (if there is even such a thing in these matters) because she was there for his love and he loved her. That was reason enough to look after her; in fact, it gave her a claim to having herself and her affections *used* like a garden. NOTHING DECLINES AS QUICKLY AS SOMETHING LIVING THAT GOES UNUSED. He felt cheated by such repeated defiant talk; for she knew very well, he said, that he did not love her. He loved purely himself and knew MEMORIES OF LOVE, whatever that word meant.

He felt disturbed in this affection by G., who called him *egocentric.* She meddled destructively in his personal activities and calming attempts.

He would have liked to give in, merely for the sake of peace or tenacity, if she had promised: I'll look after you and you'll look after me: tell me how I should look after you and I'll do it, and I'll tell you how you should look after me. That's a childish form of exchange, she replied. That's exactly the carping, begging kind of talk you shouldn't try on me, he replied. She: I can't help you if you take that tone.

She refused to help. But there was something else she had at her disposal that he didn't want: domesticity, beauty, presence on the terms she set out. He explained that he wanted to cancel every single thing she was offering, but felt alone with this idea. That was precisely where she wouldn't budge. I'M NOT THE RUG FOR YOU TO STEP ON. No agreement could be reached, no contract was in sight.

'You Know That One Cries Over a Single Disappointment. But a Second Can Bring a Smile to One's Face.'

It was her magnanimity that made her smile through her tears. The tears welled up in her eyes. Having two disappointments in succession was unlike her.

She always assumed she would be lucky, and thought she had a way of attracting sunny weather. People in her vicinity usually livened up. Confronted with disappointments, she saw that this could only be a mistake and smiled at her error–something like a weakness of destiny, which was ultimately not powerful enough to accompany her endeavours properly.

GOOD FORTUNE WAS TOO SLOW FOR THIS FAST WOMAN. It could therefore be expected that misfortune, which is just as slow as good fortune, would not manage to follow her. Her winner nature rejoiced even as her eyes filled with water. She had made a quick decision to follow some advice; now she was stuck by this mountain lake for two days. It was raining and her boyfriend called to say he couldn't join her.

So she set off in her raincoat to scale the mountain ridge. She had to keep the cycle moving in the midst of the unfortunate circumstances. She was looking forward to her afternoon nap.

The disappointment turned out to be an advantage. How horrible it would be to have her spoilt boyfriend here, to have to lead him around in the rain. New clouds were coming through the inlet in the valley basin.

So it was better if he only had to lead herself in this climatic confusion; that way she owed no one an explanation. Her face was relaxed despite her zeal. Her reputation of only attracting fortunate situations was unharmed. So she smiled again and waited for a third or fourth disappointment that she could use or pass through.

According to the laws of probability that apply to gambling, a favourable phase had to follow at some point. If *she*, the fast one, wasn't petty, how could the messengers of fate be faint-hearted?

Cold Is Not Energy

Cold is not a form of energy, which is why it can't be reflected . . . That was more interesting than she had thought, as she had only dropped in here because she was too late for the English class at the adult education centre, which took place one storey below. She had missed the S-Bahn by a quarter of a minute, and she would have squeezed through the automatic doors. Then she didn't want to enter the lecture theatre behind the lecturer and mumble an apology (in English or German?), force her way to a seat, all eyes on her, on her bottom, her neck. And so she hurried upstairs in a panic, to Room 109, which can be entered facing the speaker. She sat down inconspicuously on one of the seats next to the door and thought—with reference to the cold, which has no power to reflect, indeed no power at all, but is rather a state—at Achim's inability to notice whether she was feeling cold or heated in his presence. He was unable to reflect something that he received.

In Florence, however, in one of the city's most lively centuries, scholars (rhetoricians) set up a number of devices in front of the duke, one of the Medici bankers: a block of ice (tired, like Achim) connected to a mirror; the ray or reflection of the ice was meant to cool a hot soup in a pot. This experiment (on a spring day) did not have an immediate, unambiguous success, as the uncovered soup cooled down anyway without the influence of ice rays. But it was somehow proved that ice *does not* radiate, whereas a light fastened near the ice block (as a source of heat), mirrored in a complicated fashion, passed on the force within it—not mechanically but spot by spot, at intervals in particular erogenous areas—until nothing was left. It was an enjoyable three-quarters of an hour, and Gerda had not paid for the class. She decided she urgently needed to separate from Achim but did not put her decision into action that evening, as she was still in a hurry.

'Fifi'

—Do you love me?

She acted evasively.

—I asked you something . . . , he insisted.

—I heard you.

—So?

She didn't want to answer. After a while, Fred steered the conversation towards the topic again.

–Would you say that you love me?

–What do I have to say now?

–You're supposed to say something about that. Why are we together if you aren't contributing to the heart of the matter . . .

–But what shall I say?

–Do you love me or not?

–If I *didn't* love you, I'd hardly admit it when we're together like this . . .

–That's not an answer. Yes or no?

–A clear answer?

She was playing for time, peeled an apple for him and gave it to him piece by piece. It was not her kind of question.

–Do you love me? Well?

She would have liked to fob him off with an ironic remark and ignored the question, which undoubtedly gained nothing through repetition. But because he stayed serious and urgently demanded a reply, she said the following:

–I can say that I'd rather you were here than away.

–Away where?

–Away from my surroundings.

–Like a dog?

–I wouldn't say the same thing about a dog.

–But somehow different? 'I prefer it if Fifi's here rather than away?'

–Something like that.

Fred was inwardly hurt. But she couldn't say it any other way. One falsehood more or less in this life wouldn't have mattered to him. But the words *I love you* have a magical quality. One can only say it *once* in one's life, she thought, and on this occasion–as I'm not 'one', she added–I'd no doubt keep quiet out of superstition, to avoid scaring off the little bit of love that there is.

A Serious Person

She came from a stage on Broadway. She was obsessed with art. She wanted to express herself at all costs. Paramount hired Frances Farmer, the 'new Garbo', in 1935, after she had won an illustrated magazine's beauty contest. Seven-year contract. Paramount loaned her to Metro Goldwyn Mayer. She dreamt of appearing in Chekhov plays. She was cast in *Son of Fury* with Tyrone Power, *The Toast of New York* with Cary Grant and *Among the Living* with Albert Dekker. No one demanded any of the things she felt inside her. She said of Hollywood: 'I hate everything in this town, except the money.' She made the magnate Zukor her enemy.

In 1942, her series of problems began with a 'banal accident'. She was arrested for a traffic offence in Santa Monica on the evening of 19 October: driving with headlights turned up in a zone where the regulations demanded dimmed headlights. On the Pacific Coast Highway. She couldn't show her driver's licence. Suspected of drinking alcohol. She became surly and insulted the policeman.

It was said that she punched out the studio hair-dresser's teeth. She lost her pullover in a night club brawl and was naked underneath. The judge sentenced her to 180 days on probation. She didn't report to the probation officer. She was arrested at the HOTEL KNICKERBOCKER.

When the police came to arrest her she didn't open up, so they broke down the door; the policeman also opened the bathroom door, then dragged her naked through the lobby of Hotel Knickerbocker. At the police station, she gave 'cocksucker' as her profession.

It was said that she threw an inkpot at the judge. She soon found herself at the Steilacoom Asylum. She didn't resume her acting career. She wasn't suited to a normal existence outside her profession. There was a great expressive capacity in her. The artistic temperament, said her lawyer, is a 'rebellious bird'.

To New Shores!
Lack of Reciprocity in Solidarity

The story is set in England around 1912. The singer Gloria Vane (Zarah Leander) has taken the blame for a forging of cheques so that the officer's career of the man she loves would not be destroyed. She is deported from London to Paramatta Prison in Australia. Her lover, whom she saved from prison, meanwhile a major, is transferred to

Australia. He has no time for a visit to prison. He is involved in affairs with rich young heiresses. He is concerned about his social advancement. Miss Vane, who was at the zenith of her success at the start of the film with her chanson

'They call me Miss Vane
The famous, renowned
Yes sir!'

watches the seasons change from her prison cell. She only has a view of this passing of time through the latticed peephole of her cell. She has to stand on her bed for her eyes to reach this little window. What she sees is not the seasons themselves but, rather, the changing of the signs that indicate the seasons (in fast motion). Gloria's appeal is turned down. Letters to her beloved are returned.

'Sad, sad
If one looks!
If one doesn't look
Sad, sad!'

Love, Identifiable by the Fact That It Aims for the Other's Advantage

The highly decorated Dimitri Kitayenko answered the questions put to him by the Western correspondent in the presence of the singer Emma Sarkissjan, who had sung the role of Carmen:

Our 'Carmen interpretation' is the result of the close creative collaboration with the director F. Developing the musical and dramatic character of the work took place not only with his support but also with the support of the collective. We drew on the preparatory work of numerous artistic collectives, so to speak, that had already engaged with the nature of the work before us and so forth.

According to the director, the work is an emotional odyssey, an exchange of love objects. Micaela loves José, José loves Carmen, Carmen loves Escamillo, Escamillo only loves himself. In this order, it is logical that there should be a 'fateful' chain of events, that is, the deaths of the main parties.

–How does Escamillo's death come about? Or Micaela's?

–Escamillo is killed by the bull, and Micaela dies as a kind of living dead in her village.

–But now the collective at Moscow's Stanislawski-Nemirovich-Danchenko Music Theatre has developed an opposing idea?

–That's right. And the director, F., took up this idea and pushed it through with our collective help.

–And in that version?

–In that version, Escamillo loves Carmen. He wants to impress her and dies in a bullfight. Carmen, as we know, does *not* love José (at the end, at least). But José doesn't love Carmen either. Micaela, left over from an earlier rural marriage project, doesn't love Don José at all. None of this is a reason for the dramatic development. The three of them could reach an agreement.

–And that's the better version?

–We did it like that.

—So you run through the different mistakes of the acting figures in a completely deadpan way?

—That's the message of the opera. It deals with those kinds of delusions. The figures in the opera approach the ideal of love like beginners; they have no idea about it.

—Or they don't love.

—That'll be it. Otherwise they'd have to think about the advantage of the beloved.

—But Micaela does that the whole time, doesn't she?

—Yes, but so amateurishly. If she loved, she would find ways and means. Humans are capable of learning.

—Is that the statement of the piece?

—In our interpretation.

—Isn't the plot a bit circuitous for that?

—Our thoughts exactly; one could resolve each of these mistakes *quickly*.

—The piece would be shorter?

—Yes. Then one could programme more contemporary works.

Erwin, a Ruin of Clear Egotism

Wieland usually did what the people around him or his superiors wanted, but in his own particular way. So first of all, he said 'no'. He made decisions, was considered a significant egotist and pondered. Later on he did what was required.

As an individualist, spruced up like a sailor in uniform, he wanted to belong to a society, and if this society was playing games (cards etc.), then he could sit away from them, put on a thoughtful air (all that required was to be in company) and at once stand out from this circle (all that required was for them not to cast him out but, rather, tolerate him as a moody character, a peculiarity).

He's only the facade of a will-driven person, said his girlfriend Hilde. But even the facade was extremely bothersome. One wouldn't put a large piece of walnut furniture or a tin cupboard in a room that was only three square meters either, Hilde argued. No one had the patience to wait for the rearguard action of a long-abandoned obstinacy and eventually enjoy his compliance (with a delay of hours, days or weeks). Wieland consoled himself with the thought that he would have been more suited to a time around 1810; he found this idea modern. It was not received very well by those around him, even Hilde, who was used to his quirks, as no one could really imagine what the year 1810 was like. Why did he have to talk about 1810 when he was supposed to be compliant on 16 February 2000?[11]

Coming Home

by Xaver Holtzmann

It is said that the ego is not the master of its own house (*oikos*). Each human cell is a house. Tissues are held together by the skin. Near Hanover, Till Eulenspiegel had himself sewn up in a horsehide when the local ruler

11 I know the foregoing from letters stored in an attic in a shoebox, bound with string, whose location is unknown to anyone else.

wanted to arrest him. The story shows that a person has householder's rights to their skin.

The *reality* on which humans agree forms another skin, a cocoon. We humans would not survive without such a second skin, fashioned from illusion. The houses we own stand in such a self-created reality. The theory of how to build houses and homes for people, how to build realities, is called economy. But one can see how the houses deteriorate. Mortgages that go unnoticed squash reality more effectively than a bomb attack. Where do the feelings reside here? In what residences does the tender force flourish? In cells more than in cities?

An Episode from the Russian Campaign of 1812

He had conquered the young woman during a ball week in the 1808 winter season. It took one week and three days for Count de Chenelle, a youthful colonel in the 14th Hussar Regiment of the Great Army, to gain the young Marie and her fortune for himself. He took nine and a half months to force a daughter out of her, Sophie. Marie was never allowed to decide for herself the time in which would answer. But she let herself get carried away. She was willing to surrender to the count, to surrender to him for hours and so forth. It was a resolute, confused battle against herself, because the social advancement which this marriage meant for her (her family was rich, but less high-ranking than the count's) gave the balance of her fate a glamorous touch; this fate had to be accounted for to her parents, the initiators (the truly beloved ones, along with her brothers).

It was primarily entrepreneurial factors that made it prudent (and encouraged the passion of her heart) to succeed in this life venture–in the same way that the appetite of the young count, who was less experienced in the details of life than his wife, drew him intensely to her. 'They joined forces.'[12]

The rapid developments of those years, in which the century sought to overexert itself, left little space for deep feelings. For this essentially cruel reason, however, precisely because none of them could remain level-headed, a strong physical affection developed. And, in their daughter, a being was growing that the young man tried to bind to himself with 'heated tenderness'. The tension of those three years was interrupted by the emperor's order for all regiments to prepare for an attack on Russia at the empire's eastern border. The campaign was to pass through Minsk, Smolensk and Moscow, possibly spreading out further towards Astrakhan and India; the 14th Hussars were deployed as reconnaissance troops.

---

12 The feeling of RAVISHMENT must be translated from the French: 'ravishing' is *ravissant,* from *ravir,* 'become unconscious'– the ravished person loses their consciousness, indeed their entire will, in that moment. But one can describe the same emotional state as *FAILLE,* 'weakness'. It leads to the soothing moment in which I am not responsible for anything. 'I entrust myself.' The couple relationship is supported by a stream that runs between all people of the time, regardless of whether they strive for happiness or think they possess it. In this sense, the word for 'heart-breaking' is *SAISISSANT* (for example, *la cœur*). *Faille* is the fissure, the breaking-off of consciousness. But Marcel Proust chooses the phrase *INTERMITTENCE DU CŒUR* to indicate the same emotional process: stopping of the heart.

II

The horses were nervous. Marie wept bitterly; she had been weeping over the brutal interruption of her marriage all night long. The three-year-old hung on her father's cloth-padded body, rubbing her face on his uniform. The count still had to reach Paris before nightfall. His thoughts and feelings had long since arrived there.

What was friendly about this farewell? The count found it tiresomely time-consuming and wanted to leave quickly, making the most of the cool morning hours. The countess sensed that she would be on her own at the castle, isolated; she never forgave her husband for that. Only their daughter, who did not understand the consequences of the parting, and did not assume that her father would be away from her for a long time, lightened the scene with a bubbly exuberance one could call friendly. She gave it to her father to take with him on the long ride.

The truth of this farewell scene was soon lost, for it became an image that all involved carried in their hearts and later, like a hook, they hung delicate feelings on it. The altar of a fleeting marriage and its termination–the moment itself had nothing of that. As soon as they had been torn apart, the count and countess swore each other lasting fidelity, the reliable preservation of their feeling, yet neither of them had full control over it. The count rode with his men close to the battles of Smolensk, Borodino, Mozhaysk, always at a certain distance from the main troop. The regiment lost all its horses during the retreat from Moscow. When Marshal Nay's Third Corps (consisting of infantry and leftovers of the reconnaissance troop that had ridden out earlier, now on foot) was cut off in the first days of December by the pillar of the Great Army as it marched back, the emperor commanded the guard and those comrades who could hear the order to TURN EASTWARDS. Either he was marching into the open jaws of destruction or he was saving this rearguard, for no one can remain a commander or an emperor if they abandon a lagging troop. Thus reliability is the core of the empire.

Over hard-packed snow, islands of bush and distant black forests, a last armed fragment of the Great Army marched towards the Russian pursuers, who separated– not because they considered this raiding party dangerous but because they found its marching direction nonsensical, and were also shocked by its marching speed, loud screaming and hysterical structure of this attack. Towards evening they happened on the complete 3rd Corps, which was slowly moving westwards. The army was reunited. At the same time, the will of the disturbed emperor,[13] who no longer wanted to conquer anything here, waned; he could now only be inwardly ignited in the form of an *actio libera in causa*,[14] that is, inflammable, but only for a few seconds.

---

13 The emperor is quite literally 'disturbed in his location': he belongs in the Tuileries or some other place where the empire works for him. Instead, he goes past the edge of a forest, into an indefinite distance described to him as 'westwards'. But there is nothing whatsoever to be seen there that might interest him or fill him with hope; all horizons are similar.

14 A formulation by the classical legal theorist Ulpian. Through some prior actions, someone puts himself in a state–for example, through drugs or alcohol–in which he is forced to commit a deed. Although, according to Ulpian, there is no longer any free will in

The troop, now marching westwards together again across the desolate, white-and-black plain (so far there had only been a few veils of snow on the land), became careless.

In these minutes of crisis, the count found himself isolated with 44 of his riders, surrounded by a throng of Russian riders. He surrendered. Owing to a mistake by the Russian military authorities, who were unprepared for victory and crowds of prisoners, Colonel de Chelle remained in captivity, or at least close custody, for six years, as he ultimately had no status–he was lost in the administrative wilderness of the giant empire, so to speak. In France, it was assumed that he had gone missing or fallen.

III

Marie had received the news of her husband's death. Now that he was gone, the images of their quickly-lived time became fuller. First Marie vowed not to replace the man

---

the deed, the perpetrator was free to choose whether he would enter this will-less state or not. He was to blame for the loss of his willpower and must pay for that. It is therefore useless to put oneself into a state of intoxication or need; one is still responsible for the resulting actions.

During the days of his retreat, the emperor could only keep his soul in movement by seeking or putting himself in desperate, unbearable situations, in order to squeeze a last modicum of resistance and inner turmoil out of himself through extreme situations. He used the asperity of the cold, the hurtful nature of his defencelessness, in order to carry out a number of imperial deeds. He behaved as if subject to a drug, yet drew this effect from his real circumstances. Some say that he was looking for death. His adjutant, who knew him better, replied that he was searching for some remainder of resolve. He was 'frozen up'.

she had lost in any way. She turned away all suitors who felt drawn to her by her youth, the rumour of her abandonment or the properties she ruled as a widow. She ignored her parents' urging to show herself in the capital, to amuse herself. Only her brothers, during her second year of mourning, as the political scene had also changed in the meantime, managed to drag their reluctant sister to the season's balls. She had not been prepared to defend the properties or her freedom. She forgot her oaths. Soon she was married again, to the Marquis de . . . , whom she bore a son and a daughter.

IV

What dismay there was when, one day in May 1818, the count, finally released from captivity (or, rather, having escaped from disorganization), entered Marie's room. A uniformed man she did not initially recognize, now in the form of the royal army, grown older, traces of suffering in his face, recognized without any delay only by his daughter, who leapt up from the piano and rushed to meet the arrival as if she knew who he was, which was surely impossible, as this man barely resembled the father who had bid farewell to the three-year-old Sophie years ago. The count, for his part, saw a very different picture. He was unable to concentrate fully on his daughter, for he saw a man unknown to him in these rooms, wearing a multicoloured spotted dressing-gown and evidently moving privately through Marie's rooms, which were in fact *his* rooms. They were more colourful in his memory.

At that moment, Marie, seized by an intimation, felt faint. The man in the spotted dressing-gown supported his collapsed wife, holding her in his arms. At that point, the count could only feel hatred for this usurper of his property.

Marie had not waited for him. The image that had led him here from the expanses of Russia had duped him.

V

Marie's marriage to the Marquis de . . . had been approved on the basis of an official declaration removing the count from the world of the living. This statement of death had been refuted by his return and Marie's second marriage, the foundation of two of her children's lives, was null and void if its invalidity was confirmed by a court at one party's request. What to do? What applications to make? Marie's brothers, the Marquis de . . . , the count, the respective family networks and their lawyers negotiated. No one wanted to cut these tangled threads of fate with legal finesse. Instead the count sent the marquis, who had taken his wife and property, a demand to settle the matter with pistols. The duel was forbidden by the king. None of the parties could arrive at a clear solution which could have been explained to a third party in moral or objective terms. Marie stated that she no longer wanted to live, that she did not want to choose in what (without her volition) had become such a confused situation. She had grown used to the marquis and his erotic techniques, refused to have her two later-born children dispossessed, and no longer knew the count, who had risen from the dead, from the frozen bodies in Russia. She was also at loggerheads with her first-born daughter, whom she would gladly have sacrificed or given away. As none of these wishes could be articulated in the languages of her caste, she generally rejected a life subject to this combination of fates. The disappointed count would have contented himself, albeit full of hatred for this unknown intruder, with the return of his property and his affectionate daughter.

But he considered it irreconcilable with his honour to forego Marie and the legal rights of a marriage if this required demanding his fortune back, yet leaving the guardian of this fortune to an outside conqueror. He raged against the stranger in the dressing gown and his impertinent, quick-witted assistance in the moment of Marie's faintness.

The marquis, for his part, had grown used to the assets Marie had brought into the marriage and intended to defend them tooth and nail for his offspring and his heirs. He was also touched by Marie's youth and her desperate situation. By means of intrigues he waged a moral and legal war of defence in the interest of the status quo, and against de Chenelle's demands for restitution.

The time after Napoleon's removal dragged on. No more of the rapidity, the fleetingness of those years in which the count and Marie had met. Now, under the king's rule, there was time for tedious indecision. Ultimately the count and his daughter Sophie remained alone. The count was granted a share of the assets through a legal settlement.

For some time afterwards, Marie was guarded to ensure that she found no opportunity to end her life. As soon as decency permitted it, she returned to the marquis and their two children; as she was not allowed to express her satisfaction with this final situation (which had been arrived at without her involvement, and even against her protests) in public, she was unable to develop much self-confidence in her state of living. 'And so they lived their lives.'

VI

Rossini composed no less than two operas for the 1820 season: *The Return of Odysseus* and *The Italian Girl in Minsk.* The count sat in one of the lodges at the opera house, accompanied by his pretty daughter, whom a neutral observer might have taken for his mistress. In another lodge, without a word of greeting to the count, sat Marie and her second husband (the marriage had been annulled). She had not waited twenty years for the man she believed dead to return, like the wife of Odysseus, unreservedly defending his property against her suitors. The count had not shot the stranger who had encroached on and conquered his wife: a world of indecisions. They all watched the unfolding of their fate, which filled the stage, inimitably and in confirmation of the muteness of their private feelings. Marie sat frozen. Only Sophie wept bitterly, believing that she had to express the emotions of her beloved father.

Decisiveness: It appeared in large amounts from Bonaparte's consulship on. It requires hysteria to tear itself out of the muteness of mere forces. Where are there opportunities for liberation through a quick decision? WHAT IS AN 18 BRUMAIRE OF THE EMOTIONS? WHAT IS A BONAPARTIST OF LOVE?

The century in France was such that it used up all energies of decisiveness in the years until 1812: an 'entrepreneurial', 'occupatory' (possessive) decade. It was followed by a further swamp of indecisions (*Ancien Régime*) and 'apparent decisions' (Second Empire): attentism.

Addendum to III

THE GARDENS OF EMOTIONS

Classic metaphors for the peculiarities of love: elective affinities. The stars and their gravitational pull. Balzac's literary sociology and his constellations. Eisenstein's spherical books. An afternoon with Maria Callas . . .

Elective Affinities: Park Landscape with Four Lovers

'With all natural creatures
that we perceive,
the first thing we notice
is their self-reference.'

In the very first part of Goethe's novel *Elective Affinities*, a conversation between three of the acting characters–Eduard, Charlotte and the captain–turns towards *chemical attractors*. Raindrops, it is said, join together to flow more quickly. Their chemistry makes them combine into streams and rivers. Mercury, by contrast, has a tendency to lock itself away in little spheres. The captain adds: one describes people who quickly seize on and define each other when they meet as having an *affinity* for each other.

His argument skips the strict definition of affinities, which are brought about by law, marriage and ancestors. Charlotte, who loves the captain, takes up the thread: 'Let me confess, if you speak of affinities between these wondrous beings of yours [*alkalis and acids*], they strike me less as blood relations than as kindred spirits and souls.' Eduard, who will go on to love Ottilie, adds that 'chemical analyst' is an honorific title among chemists. He is hoping to separate from Charlotte, his wife. The captain further interprets the metaphor, encapsulating it in the term *elective affinity*, namely the freedom to *choose* friendships and amorous relationships (the application of the tender force) subjectively: if pure quicklime is intimately combined with a delicate acid that surrounds us as air, and if one places a piece of such stone in diluted sulphuric acid, the result is plaster–'the delicate, airy acid escapes'.

In this manner the novel's protagonists present arguments about their future fate, which is unknown to them. Who does not like to play with similarities? One of the three says that there are plenty of known cases in which an 'intimate, seemingly unbreakable connection between two beings is broken through occasional appearances by a third, and one of those who were at first so beautifully connected is driven out into the open expanse.'

It is about freedom and also *affection*, which is incorruptible but tends towards capriciousness. **Chemistry, with its radical joining possibilities, seems to provide allegories that are worth living by.**

The people in Goethe's novel are effectively landscapers. They develop PARK LANDSCAPES OF EMOTION. While the French Revolution was exploring laboratories and alchemies to bring about practical changes in humans, the novelist Goethe was testing the abysses over which the EDIFICES OF CIVILIZATION, including freedom and change, erect their scaffolding.

All elements of nature and emotional life are present. The peculiarity of the artificial lake in the garden landscape is that its surface, as smooth as glass, would

FIGURE 27. *Ottilie on the Lake with the Drowned Child*. Copperplate by Johann Michael Voltz (1811). 'She has sunk to her knees in the boat and lifts the motionless child to the dawning sky, begging for help.'

normally reflect the moonlight and the beams of the bright sun. It seems a friendly body of water. In fact, according to Goethe, it was tamed from the roaring currents of a mountain lake. A devious gust of wind, held in store by the evening, set it in motion. The child that falls into the lake quickly drowns (killed by the lake). But there were warning signs that could have been noticed by those involved. These signs do not come from nature. The child, for example—see Goethe—was born of 'twofold adultery'. The soul-bearers who wanted

FIGURE 28. *The Four Together*. Copperplate by Heinrich Anton Dähling (1811). 'The homely group, reading in their familiar room—where Eduard moves closer to Ottilie so that she can look comfortably into the book—while Charlotte and the captain share their observations with each other through their glances: attraction between the befriended parties, from one to the other and back.'

to end their affinity, Eduard and Charlotte, had conceived this child, and during those events he had been thinking passionately of Ottilie while she was yearning for the captain. Thus the physically and legally bonded persons (the married couple), separated from the spiritually bonded ones (having betrayed each other, tending with every fibre to third and fourth persons), were torn apart. An emotional monster of four, just as a bull has four legs, produced the doomed child. How much more did the gust of wind really have to do? It was only a matter of the time at which the disaster would occur. Such a love life does not foster courage.

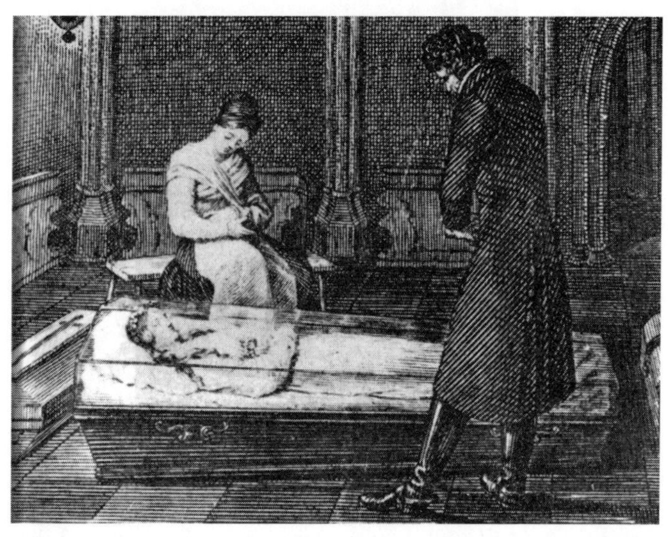

FIGURE 29. Title vignette by Ludwig Ferdinand Schnorr von Carolsfeld, etched by Carl Heinrich Rahl (1817): *Nanni and the architect at Ottilie's coffin.*

A reading society. All over Europe, but also in the isolated European outposts abroad, one finds this horticultural communication, the reasoning community. In the intervals of the Revolution in France: people read, people tell stories. In the standby position of the observers in Germany, who are excluded from revolutions: walking, reading, gathering experience together. Having the courage to know! Sapere aude! What emboldens us in love?

The *architect* possesses the knowledge of how to build further gardens. Soon people will succeed in designing park landscapes (civilized nature) in such a way that they can spend time there without danger, that gardens can bring happiness.

***Nanni* is a nanny. She is no longer needed in Eduard and Charlotte's abandoned household and will look for another position in houses and among people who need her skills.**

'IT IS DIFFICULT TO HELP EDUCATED PEOPLE WITH THEIR MORAL ENTANGLEMENTS'

The Peculiar Children Next Door

The architecture of gardens and life, according to the sceptical Goethe, did not yet have the right personnel in the novel *Elective Affinities*. Unlike in Mozart's *Così fan tutte*, the group of four lovers (Charlotte/Captain, Eduard/Ottilie) produces disastrous results for the fifth being, the child.

Things are quite different in the counter-story: *The Peculiar Children Next Door*. This is a love story with a happy end. Two children from the befriended families have been chosen for each other. This makes them hostile; each fears predestination, but also (unconsciously) the other's strength, which they acknowledge. The man goes far away. The girl becomes engaged to another. Then her 'beloved childhood enemy' appears at the door, and she realizes that she has spoiled her life through her 'choice'.

'We went along the great river with music.' The young girl, desperate, leaps into the Rhine. The 'childhood enemy' leaps after her. 'The desire to rescue overcame all other concerns.' The two come together unconsciously and also uninhibitedly. Once they have escaped from the river, wet and naked as they are, the people who take them in and warm them give them some of their old clothes, dressing them as bride and bridegroom. The costumes are kept on. When the two emerge from the bushes 'in their strange dress', the fathers and mothers on both sides, as well as the fiancé of the rescued girl, are baffled.

'They did not recognize them until they had come very close. Whom do I see? cried the mothers. What do I see? cried the fathers. The rescued couple prostrated themselves before them. Your children! they cried. Forgive us! cried the girl. Give us your blessing! cried the youth. Give us your blessing! they both cried, as everyone fell silent in amazement. Your blessing! they cried a third time, and who could have refused!'

The two lovers, now joined for good, experience immense METAMORPHOSES: one moment they are enemies, the next they are warmest friends, sometimes they are lost to one another, then found again. But, Goethe tells us, they have some *moderation* in the application of their passion. They belong to the species of *Homo compensator*. They are BALANCERS OF THEIR EMOTIONS.

Presumably they would show hospitality to someone seeking refuge. When gods appear as guests, for example. In Ovid's *Metamorphoses* the bond between their lives would correspond to that earned by Philemon and Baucis. Their example gives us courage–just as it is courageous of the young man to leap spontaneously after his beloved.[15]

Madame de La Fayette published her romantic novel in 1678. Like *Elective Affinities*, it deals with four people, of whom two are already bonded and two trigger the tragic conflict through their amorous involvement. It is about the mother of the Princess of Cleves, the Prince of Cleves (who marries the daughter), said daughter (the later Princess of Cleves) and the Duke of Nemours, who vehemently attempts to infiltrate the princess's marriage.

The mother taught the daughter. This mother sensed that she did not have long to live, and leaves behind a list of seven basic principles for her daughter:

(1) You must never become a traitor to your feelings.
(2) You must never reveal your feelings to others.

15 Goethe notes that until the youth takes a firm hold of the girl, who is being tossed this way and that by the water, the course of the story outwardly resembles the greedy Apollo's pursuit. But the young girl has no reason to freeze (into a water plant, for example), because the youth pursuing her is not a god, not a python hunter, and thus has no real history. He carries a less sinister bride price with him because his generation is still innocent.

FIGURE 30 (LEFT). 'She was not learned, yet she read with persistence.'

FIGURE 31 (RIGHT). Title page of the bestselling novel *The Princess of Cleves*

(3) Use your advantage, otherwise you will be robbed; you must therefore make a marriage contract.

(4) You must fulfil a contract at all costs.

(5) Never lie to yourself.

(6) Be honest to your husband, for you have made a contract with him.

(7) If you find yourself in contradictions, do nothing.

The young woman married without knowing of the snake that she bore in her heart, and whose head she would soon feel in her throat. She only recognized the monster when she encountered the Duke of Nemours. She did not waver, and remained faithful to her husband.

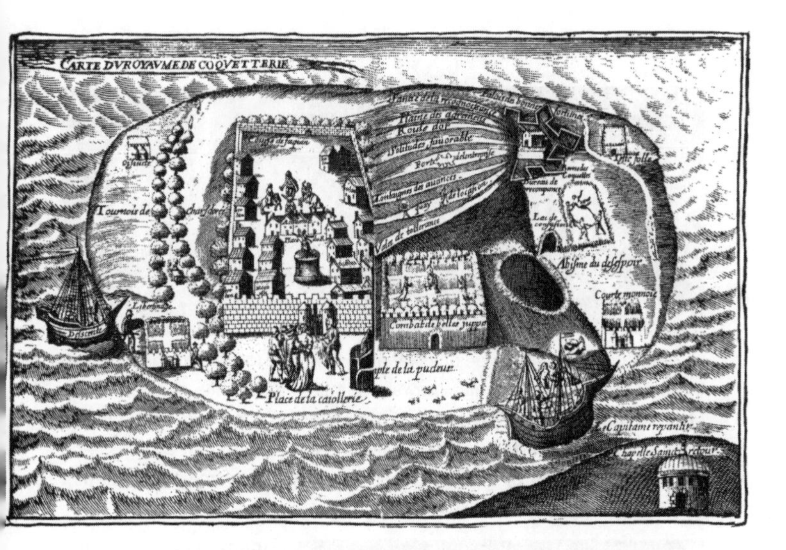

FIGURE 32. Map of the kingdom of love. Top right: abyss of despair; 'Wonderful Solitudes', 'Lake of Confusion', 'Mad Sadness'.

The self-controlled characters of the seventeenth century, torn between the carefreeness of the court and the seriousness of Port Royal Abbey,[16] signalized their devotion, their nature, their irresistible attraction or their hesitation through small signs.

Full of honesty, the princess tells her husband and confidant, the Prince of Cleves (considering he is unsuitable for her hidden passion), from the signs in her heart, the snake inside her. This honest confession kills the confidant.

These are the VIRTUOUS PEOPLE FROM THE BEGINNINGS OF MODERN HUMANITY.

---

16 Port Royal is the seriousness that withdraws from the royal court. Pascal and the Jansenists shape the 'spirit of Port Royal'. Either a new kind of humanity will ensue, they say, or we will fall victim to the cycle of repetitions, in which life is not worth living.

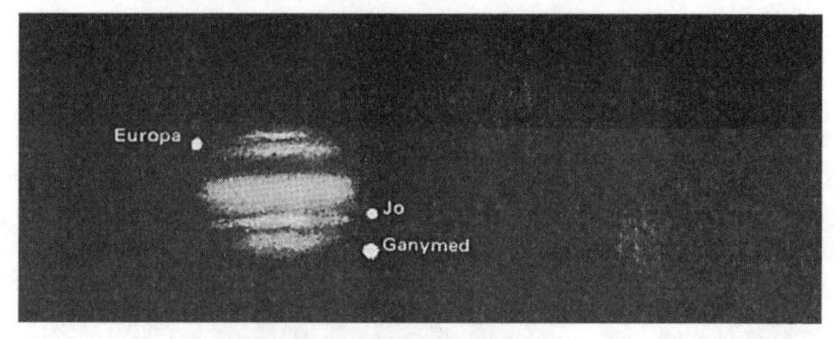

FIGURE 33. Jupiter with three of its large moons. The fourth is located behind the planet. Xaver Holtzmann draws a comparison to the group of four in *Elective Affinities*, pointing to the great calm and constancy in the movements of these celestial bodies: unlike the restless human couples, who disturbed each other by trusting in their own respective force, the constraint of gravitation made them extremely compatible.

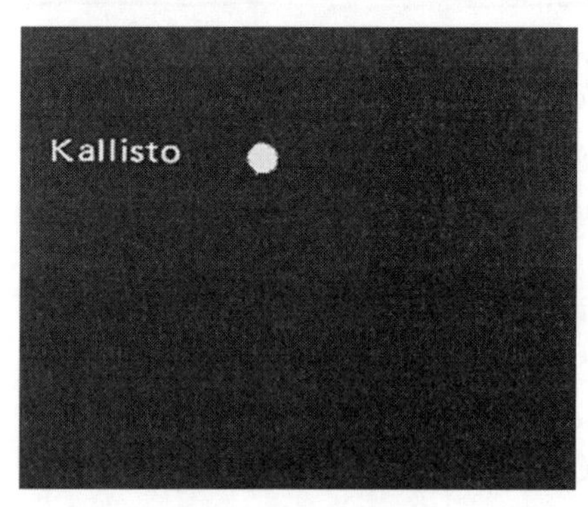

FIGURE 34. Callisto, the moon of Jupiter invisible in the above picture, is named after Zeus' mistress. She was transferred to the sky as the Great Bear. At the same time, she also took the form of one of our solar system's most beautiful moons. (→ The *Metamorphoses* of Ovid, p. 108.)

In the *Arcades Project*, Walter Benjamin chooses astral metaphors rather than chemical ones to describe the tender force. Gravitation, he argues, allows a description of the generous side of amorous relationships, which lacks the quick and decisive character of a chemical reaction. Chemistry, according to Benjamin, has lost the former openness of the alchemistic arts.

FIGURE 35. Two lovers in antiquity. A god will transfer them to the firmament.

Prolegomena to Any Rational Astrology[17]

Migration of Souls According to Fourier

When the essences (later souls) seek to reach the Blue Planet, they move past the trans-Saturnian stars, then the two great gas planets; they draw a circle, says the Kabbalah, as if they were projectiles in need of slowing down. They move around the evening star and only land after this (essences become souls, then characters) in one of the

17 See Walter Benjamin, 'Zur Astrologie' in *Gesammelte Schriften* (Rolf Tiedemann and Hermann Schweppenhäuser eds), *Volume* 6: *Fragmente, autobiographische Schriften* (Frankfurt: Suhrkamp, 1991), p. 193; also Wolfgang Bock, *Walter Benjamin–Die Rettung der Nacht: Sterne, Melancholie und Messianismus* (Bielefeld: Aisthesis, 1999).

places where humans live. Benjamin writes that an understanding of this connection, which is physically palpable under the moon in southern nights, is absent from the BIASED CONSCIOUSNESS, the raw material that is distilled into the POLITICAL. Hence this political lacks aroma and essence, even though our bodies and bonding capacities know of it. The blind things in us (monads, libido), which define our constitution, are disappointed.

Charles Fourier calculated the migration of souls (the paths of the essences, which come to us and leave us again before returning) in mathematical fashion. In the *Arcades Project,* Walter Benjamin places particular emphasis on this point by the early socialist. The human soul, says Fourier, must assume 810 different forms before it completes its planetary course and can return to Earth. Of these existences in the cosmos, 720 are happy, 45 favourable and 45 unfavourable or unhappy. After the decline of our planet, the chosen souls will travel to the sun! Only those with completed journeys are chosen. Before the souls have spent 80,000 years on our planet, they will need to have inhabited all other planets and worlds. For 70,000 years, the human race will have enjoyed the Boreal light. The main effect animating the metamorphoses of the souls, however, is the FORCE OF ATTRACTIVE WORK. Fourier writes that because of this, the GRAVITATION OF LABOUR POWER, the climate in Senegal must become as warm as the summers in France. Because the sea will be transformed into lemonade under the influence of the morphological character of voluntary joint work, the fish will flee from the oceans to the Caspian Sea, the Aral Sea and the Black Sea because the Boreal light has less of an effect on these saltwater lakes, but they will gradually become accustomed to the lemonade. Benjamin: 'Fourier also states that in the eighth period, humans will attain the ability to live in water like fish and fly through the air like birds, and that they will then reach a height of 7 feet and at least 144 years of age. Thus every human will be able to change into an amphibian, by acquiring the ability to open and close the hole connecting the two chambers of the heart at will, and thus conduct the blood directly to the heart without making it flow through the lungs [. . .].'

Libido, Walter Benjamin claims, repeats its 'primal experience'. This experience comes from the stars and is connected to the 'clay' from which bodies were made. A revolutionary process (or emancipation, rationality) that does not know or take into account the networks resulting from this will experience that humans retreat from it. Thus a revolution is always fighting against the course of time: with each day that passes, its success becomes less probable. It reduces the goals until there is nothing left to defend.

The Way to the Stars

The physical foundation of thoughts crumbles. One needs the entire substructure, though our consciousness is indifferent to it, of circulation, body heat, exchange of fluids (osmosis), the van der Waals forces poised on the edges of cell nuclei, to grasp and answer even a single sentence spoken by a fellow human.

He found it hard to bid the guest good morning. But this visitor wanted to squeeze many more words out of the ailing man, once the star of the Collège de France. He

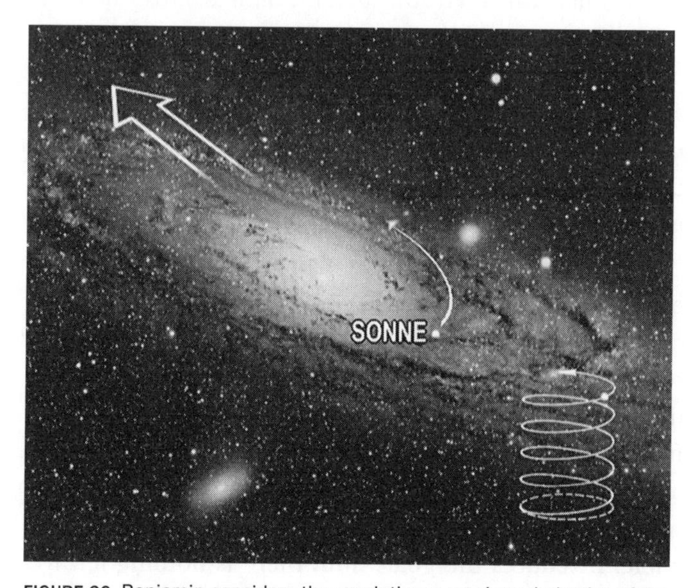

FIGURE 36. Benjamin considers the revolution a precious derivative of the tender force. In this context, he recalls the TRUE or GREAT REVOLUTION, that is, the orbiting of the Milky Way's centre by our Sun. Astronomers call such an orbit a revolution, and it takes 250 million years. Benjamin's student Czernowitz considered this a usable metaphor for political revolutions, which have always been short-lived throughout history. It should take the calm momentum of the GREAT REVOLUTION as a model. The arrow shows the direction in which the Milky Way is rushing towards its sister galaxy, the Andromeda Galaxy.

FIGURE 37. The political commissar Dashevskaya and her brother. With a strong mutual attraction. Both were devoted to 'the cause'. If her brother had betrayed it she would have shot him; she had a pistol on her belt at all times. She did not have to use this tool once during her career. A natural authority that spread around her made her convincing enough; wherever she was present, the revolution remained victorious. Later, like many female comrades, she was stranded in the bureaucratic desert. Like her brother, she was executed in 1937. 'The system' could not have dealt with her otherwise. In her heyday she was known as the 'Virgin of Orenburg'. The picture shows her in 1919 with her brother in Orenburg, southwest of the Ural Mountains.

didn't even mind if it was nonsense; he would have melted it down to 'last words'. He hoped that the scholar, under the pressure of death, would concentrate his powers and utter something irretrievable, something like the final result of life and of being ready for death. The young visitor would have liked to record the fall itself, the coma—the stage before death—with an exact observation.

'The wise man's wisdom must be extracted from him.' F. could not even bring himself to find the young, well-built scientific callboy appealing. He could no longer remember a life without the illness.

And yet he noticed that beneath the weakness, when he was not paying attention, the formulating machine started working inside him when the young guest stroked it, running his touch along it as if it were a leg or a rectum. F. didn't have to like the whole man for that.

F.: Only bones are stored in outer space, and only those of warm-blooded creatures, and only ones that were once technicians.

YOUNG GUEST: And this technology is a dead end, you say, like the cold-blooded skeletons of dinosaurs?

F.: Certainly.

YOUNG GUEST: Wings grew, thousand-footed motors, chemistry and alchemy, but do you associate yourself with the bodies or the spirit?

F.: Certainly (he was in pain, couldn't speak much, nodded vigorously).

YOUNG GUEST: But now we see after the event that discursive bones have developed, as it were . . . (he read the sick man's eyes and wrote down what he thought he sensed there).

F.: Murderous claws, as strong as an additional skeleton. With it one can travel through the cosmos, rid oneself of the body and carry it about in a container. Bodies are only the means of transport.

YOUNG GUEST: Three hundred years on, and we could dispose of or replace your sick body. You would survive.

F.: Much sooner.

YOUNG GUEST: In a few years?

F. (laughs): I'm not a doctor.

YOUNG GUEST: We've long developed this NEW SPECIES but are only now realizing that the NEW human exists?

F.: Don't say 'New Human' or 'superman', say something else. It's not a 'human', it's a new SPECIES, imposed on humans.

YOUNG GUEST: All of them?

F.: Not at all. Only those who have these 'second bones' possess something we call spiritual, concentrates of the consciousness. In that sense the esoterics are right (Stefan George, Hölderlin). The billions who don't have these new organs or frames and don't buy them will be as different from us as the trilobites, with their glistening eyes.

YOUNG GUEST: And if one says that's elitist?

F.: If it's true?

YOUNG GUEST: Are you sentimental?

F.: Don't think so.

YOUNG GUEST: What drew you to LA, where you were infected? You could have known.

F.: Inevitability.

YOUNG GUEST: Is that already one of the new bones?

F.: Yes. They can kill.

YOUNG GUEST: Kill themselves?

F. (*laughs*): 'I am one of those creatures that die when they love.'

YOUNG GUEST: Once again: a new species has long since developed within the human race. The fact that it seemed connected to machines via interfaces concealed the fact that a blueprint for a NEW SPECIES had been made. Humanity is dividing itself. Not everyone is taking part in this development. Has a disaster swept them away?

F.: 'Don't tell anyone, only the wise.'

He tended towards mockery, even now, in his frailty. The delighted in the idea that this anti-democratic invective would be printed as the 'last words of the master'.

FIGURE 38. Michel Foucault, born 15 October 1926, died 25 June 1984. The year of his death saw the publication of volumes 2 and 3 of *The History of Sexuality*: *The Use of Pleasure* and *The Care of the Self*. Photograph: Hervé Guibert.

FIGURE 39. The galaxy cluster Abell 2218 in the constellation Draco, two billion light years away. The immense forces of attraction make the milky ways dance around one another. The same long-distance effect groups the swarms together into GRAVITATIONAL LENSES. These make the galaxies appear in fictitious locations. In that sense, Xaver Holtzmann states, the cosmos writes novels.

A Strange Kind of Attraction

In an unfinished novel, Edgar Allan Poe describes a young Chinese woman in the southern provinces and a lumberjack in Canada who were destined to be lovers. But they never met. All matchmaking attempts to bring them together came to nothing. They refused to enter a bond with anyone else. They said they were already committed. To whom? They couldn't say.

They had offspring and saw to their upbringing. They could not bear living with the partners to whom they owed their children. The attraction continued into the fifth generation: in 2002, a descendant of the young Chinese woman met a descendant of the Canadian, both of the same age, in New York. They never separated.

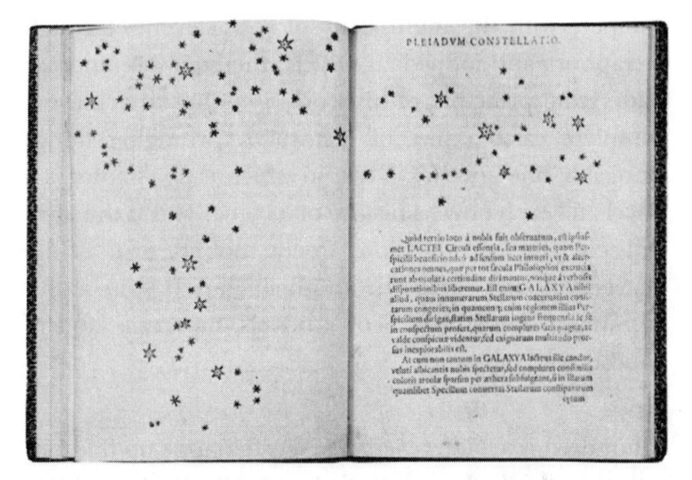
PLEIADVM CONSTELLATIO.

FIGURE 40. The constellation of the Pleiades, from Galileo's *Sidereus Nuncius* (1610).

FIGURE 41. Honoré de Balzac and the principle of LITERARY CONSTELLATIONS.

In his preface to *The Human Comedy*, Balzac refers to himself as an archaeologist of the social apparatus, a registrar of good and evil. Chance, he says, is the greatest novelist in the world. Thus French society is the historian and he, Balzac, merely its secretary. He calls it a futile effort to compete with the multiplicity of social events through metaphors and individual novels; the concern (and the underlying principle of his work) is rather to achieve a complete cartography of history by arranging things alongside one another, a text in which each chapter is a novel and each novel a history of its time. This is the principle of the constellation, freely mobile, just as the heavenly bodies circle one another. Thus, despite all his admiration for Walter Scott's novels, he was a kind of anti-Scott.

A hundred years later, Sergei Eisenstein took up this narrative principle by suggesting a SPHERICAL DRAMATURGY and SPHERICAL BOOKS: the individual stories move around a centre on the sphere's surface but are attracted by the centre. But there is, says Eisenstein, following on from the authors of the Babylonian Talmud, a dialectic between the surface and the core. The surface is at once the core. But as soon as one talks about the core, that is, unfolds it, it proves to be a rich surface.

Where is the centre?
cried Rabbi Madies,
the rejected water allows the falcon
to pursue its prey.
Perhaps the centre is the shifting of the question.

FIGURE 42. Sergei Eisenstein with Bertolt Brecht (1929). 'Each of my texts is equidistant from an invisible centre.'

Even the Dog Is Kissed by Love

My soul is like the full moon:
It is cool and bright.

V. Khodasevich

They had already known each other for eight months, which was a lot for the summer of 1969. We don't have any opportunities to save each other from hardship, she said. If I had to get you out of prison, that would be an opportunity to show you my affection. Perhaps success would make it stronger. What we're doing now won't keep us together. What shall we do, he replied, once our imagination runs out? They had decided, independently of each other, to engage more closely. He tried to loosen up. She

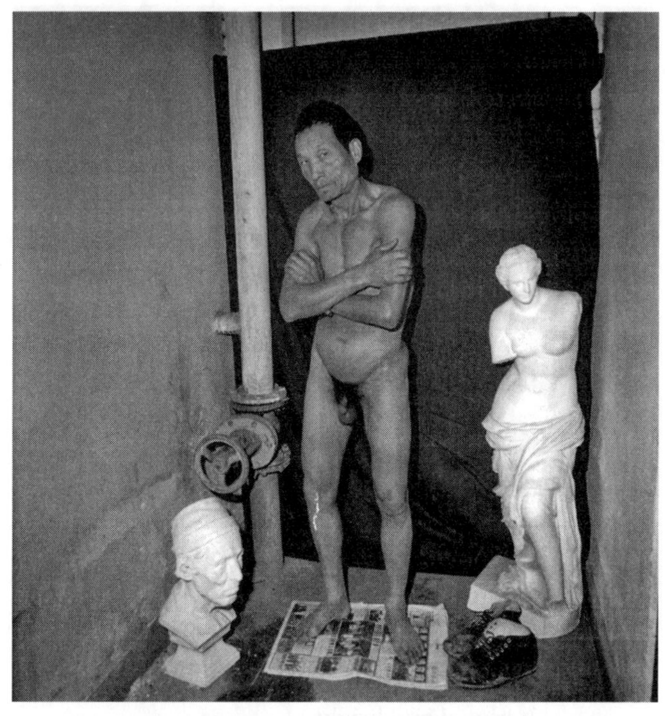

FIGURE 43. *Earth Son 2009*, photograph by the Chinese artist Lui Zheng.

had switched on a tape recorder to capture their conversation; that way she could come back to individual statements later on, and didn't have to strive for thoroughness now. She could 'catch up' in each case. They lay in each other's arms. Actually, she thought, it wasn't practical to have the dialogue in that position.

Let's take a different approach, he said. If you imagine that you're a horse, for example, does that make the situation a bit more real for you?

–That's hard to say.

–And something between a horse and a weasel?

–I could talk to my girlfriends about that.

–One can imagine being an animal–a vague idea.

–Yes. One can only talk about it vaguely.

–Or an Eskimo? Or I could be two men lying here on top of you? Or in China, because we're arguing, our servants tie us to each other on our own orders, and we lie there motionless until some feeling comes?

–Something like that, but maybe differently.

–Maybe several things at once or in succession?

–You're putting it too exactly.

–Somehow changing?

–That's too precise for me.

–So is it something imprecise?

–That's still not precisely put. One has to blur it a little. It's beside.

–Beside?

–Something that one sees or feels, and it's right beside that.

–But where?

–Or what?

–What are we supposed to do?

One problem was clearly the fact that neither of them was sufficiently frivolous. So they had a concentrated debate–two days were planned just for conversations–to probe various situational areas.

—One can't say we want to give it a go together, one should say that we've given it a go together and now we want to make something of it.

—Otherwise there's no point.

—What do you mean by 'point' in this context?

—Something lasting.

—I can't imagine what that is.

But they agreed on one point: that they wanted to build a 'reliable construction'. They also wanted to stand out from other couples, they would create a kind of PROPERTY, but without POSSESSION, with precise or imprecise rules, by force if necessary, unforced overall, without illusions, with great hope. THIS IS ONLY CONTRADICTORY IF ONE ARTICULATES IT.

But they didn't want to seem lustful to each other. They wanted to be UNMISTAKABLE. To be seen more as humans and not belong to the SPECIES OF COUPLES. That restricted communication, created pauses that both of them noticed when listening to the tapes later. It's true that they FELT several things but DIDN'T HAVE THE COURAGE TO SAY THEM. Each of them wanted to have more than this one life story, and didn't want the other to prevent them from living several lives in parallel. One has to transform oneself for that. That was precisely it: they wanted to do something and had occasionally given it a go together and, at the same time, wanted to be something else.

—It's the difference.

—What do you mean by that?

She couldn't say that because she didn't want to offend him. She would have had to explain that she liked it best when he lay on top of her, real and chubby, when she had him in front of her but was free to confuse him with a whole range of others, even with dogs, animals or things, or if need be a heavy brass ashtray, to name an example that occurred to her of something compact. She didn't want to HAVE or USE that, she wanted to be ALLOWED TO THINK it. But it was all this, combined with a certain loyalty, with the now-familiar smell, though as unfamiliar as could be, and this IN-BETWEENNESS or POLYPHONY, that pulverized her; but she didn't want to speak or think about powder. So she didn't speak at all. The interesting pauses, the ones they discussed later while listening to the tape, consisted of such communication.

'Sombre and beautiful is its whole
the wild beast of my darkened soul:
It knows no desire to be taught,
and speaking means to it but naught.'

Anna Karenina in 1915

I often go about as a guardian
angel, giving friendly advice.

A. Pushkin

Her sober husband fell in Galicia. Major Bronsky, with whom she was still corresponding, lost his egocentric life, for which he had fought desperately to the last moment, in a dirty field hospital in northern Russia.

FIGURE 44. Peter Weibel, referring to Benjamin's companion Czernowitz, expands the CONSTELLATION and SPHERE PRINCIPLE of narration (in all arts, that is, also in music) to include the principle of PERMANENT TRANSCRIPTS. Thus a medieval monk copied texts, for example, with each copy introducing small errors, and the final result was (as in evolution) a new text. Modern authors should therefore keep overwriting older models, such as Goethe's *Elective Affinities* or Heiner Müller's *Quartet*, so that in time there could be a 'happier end to sad stories'. Thus modernity lies not in something new, but in the transcription of an earlier story to arrive at a better end.

But she, the beautiful woman, cared for the wounded on the Crimean Peninsula. The daily trains refreshed the supply of mutilated bodies coming here from the battlefields of the Brussilov offensive. To the men she was the angel of the hospitals, walking along the rows of beds with her group of young girls. The treatment of the wounded improved wherever she went. As soon as the young women entered the halls, the doctors and paramedics looked at the mass of men degraded by mutilation and

FIGURE 45. Elfriede Eilers and Rosemarie Zacke before a visit to the opera.

shooting ('scraps from the battlefields') as human beings once more, because now they could imagine each of the people lying there as an acting, suffering or convalescent person in a NOVEL.

The following year, Anna Karenina married a doctor. In 1918, this surgeon took over the first polyclinic in Moscow. Anna Karenina became a commissar whose duties concerned the civil war in southern Russia. Not much novel, a great deal of current events. Husband and wife enjoyed seeing each other, especially because their encounters were rare and did not always depend on their individual will.

At the time of her 87th *Norma* at the Teatro alla Scala di Milano, Maria Callas' nerves, soul and voice were in turmoil. She had separated acrimoniously from the man she loved, a ship owner. She was at loggerheads with all the people she was used to. She felt the disapproval of the maestro and the director towards the affectations with which she tried to help herself in the rehearsals.

From where should she draw her concentration, the focusing of all her forces on the musical point? She felt an overwhelming desire to have a companion like Adalgisa or a servant like Clotilde in real life. There was no sign of that. But who might be suitable as Pollione, the reason for the tender character of the finale? One needs reserves of aggression to draw this tone of tenderness from them. She was aggressive towards O. when he was absent, when she tried in vain to reach him by telephone; but she did not mistake him for Pollione. The Roman character was alien to her lover. As far as their joint love project was concerned, she had no chances when he was present; but she became calm, tender, when she *thought* of him. Such a residue of experience was not enough for the role of Norma. Right at the start: the decision not to kill Adalgisa, her rival. The outward symbol of the official power over life and death was the sickle that Norma always carried with her. But what was Adalgisa's crime? That the former friend had not managed to implant her, Norma, in the heart of the megalomaniacal Roman once more? That Adalgisa had succumbed to the same art of seduction (what was 'artful' or 'skilled' about the legate's charlatanry?) as she herself?

This did not merit the punishment of sacrificial death. In addition, the hostile prima donna singing the role of Adalgisa, skulking around Callas behind the mask of acting, had not been seduced by any Pollione in real life–in fact, she seemed incapable of being seduced at all. Callas could not summon the initial rage, the emotional verve, to switch to the tone in which Norma refrains from taking revenge on her rival. A singer of Maria Callas' calibre is not the bureaucrat of a musical score; she cannot sing without reason. In her haste–the rehearsal was starting in ten minutes–the only thing she found OUTRAGEOUS, in the sense of 'sufficiently worthy of hatred', was the negligence of a mechanic who had overseen some damage that caused a sports plane to crash near Milan. It reminded her of circumstances that had caused the death of her lover's son. What pain for that beloved, now unfaithful man! The feeling is unjust. It is the only one at her disposal.[18]

Does she have to begin the scene with the wrong feelings? Hatred for a careless mechanic whom she has only read about, and who reminded her of a different mechanic? What choice does she have if nothing else is available?

The change in her voice before Act 2, Scene 3 brings Callas the first look of acknowledgement from the maestro, and also from the first row of violins. But how is she supposed to kill sleeping children (Act 2, Scene 1, rehearsal two hours later)? She needs that initial feeling of

---

18 It was unjust because she should really have hated her estranged lover without sympathy. She could not do it then, at the moment when she needed the aggression. She was bankrupt.

aggression to do something like that, to change it into the sudden renunciation of murder which keeps the voice quiet. Whom does she want to kill now anyway? She has to discover such a motive (and three of them, as she has three different opponents) within herself by 4 p.m., else she will fail.

And so Maria Callas struggled through the day, which treated her strictly.

FIGURE 46. Maria Callas at La Scala. 'How one finds the right musical expression through unjust feelings.'

IV

IF AT THE STARS I WISH TO GAZE, MY EYES WILL EVER BE AMAZED

Does the tender force have independent access to the process of enlightenment? The capacities for desire, Balzac claims, will not allow anyone or anything to divert their path to autonomy . . .

The Law of Love

'There cannot be a general law that turns coincidence into a judge.'

Immanuel Kant

Countess Sidonie Oltrup, born on the Oltrup estate in 1735, had married Baron Schlüters young. Lucky are those whose first choice is the right one. The parents and circumstances gave the countess freedom, and, inexperienced though she was, she chose the right man. The baron went missing in the Third Nordic War. He was declared dead.

She grew close to an older neighbour on the estate whom she learnt to love; one can even build a school within oneself and form the elements of affection for another like an alphabet, if that person supports the process. She, the widow, and he, this man she had come to trust, married. She bore him two children and called herself happy. More than five such twists of fate cannot fit into a human life. They presuppose a restructuring of the senses and an adjustment of one's character. Memories also need to be erased. It does not happen without some cruelty.

Then, seven years later, the supposedly dead Schlüters returned. He settled in the country estate that belonged to him, where he had lived with Sidonie, and visited the married neighbours. She was now called Countess Danckert. They discussed their fate, which could only be understood as a SHARED one. And so Sidonie, with the consent of her second husband, lived alternately with him and with her first beloved, who still possessed marital rights because the declaration of his death had been annulled. Memories returned. It was difficult to maintain a balance, and she did much inner schooling. How did the men view the situation? There was much talking.[1]

Hordes of soldiers spread through the land. The men, dressed as stable hands, hid in the barns. They could not protect Sidonie and the children. They emerged from their hiding places once the occupiers had left, after the return of the established regime that guaranteed their property. Sidonie was spared some things. She never had to choose to sacrifice one in order to save the other. She had made a choice each time she committed herself, and she felt she had chosen well in both cases.

Sidonie was certain that a person shapes their capacity for love in such a way that their behaviour could form the basis of public legislation. And certainty means that my inner conviction is shared by those I love and would also please my ancestors, meaning that I can always voice it publicly, even if I am quarrelling in my heart.

That was bold. In the next generation, she already saw how her daughter chose unjustly. She rejected the man who courted her sincerely after exciting him and tying him to her. She ran off with a reckless dog. She had made the wrong choice and learnt nothing even after replacing him. Sidonie worried about her child.

It is difficult to imagine this example in a general legislation of love. It would remain unjust. Towards Sidonie

1 Especially with the children. Schlüters also fathered a child.

too, who had taken great pains with her child. But her accusations against the child were also unjust.

Two hundred years later: a man who suffered racial discrimination was to marry into the the Schlüters branch of the family. The countess in question was besotted with the man, who came to Oltrup from Berlin and had to put up with the gossip in town and in the neighbourhoods. The family was polemical and threatened denunciation; neither this blackmail nor the mésalliance itself could be made a general law, not publicly.[2] What one does at a rendezvous in the city in anonymous hotels is one thing; that's something you get out of your system, said Herta, the enamoured countess' mother, descended from Sidonie by six generations. It was impossible to base a legislation of love on racial discrimination ('blood purification', 'melioration of hereditary traits', the way one meliorates a swamp and a hill into a field), nor did the countess find it conceivable to limit oneself opportunistically to the sleazy dives of a city and not dare to admit it at home.

By that point, six female descendants of Sidonie had run away and six male ones had immigrated to foreign continents because they could no longer bear it in their 'lawless homeland'.

---

2 The bond between the countess and this victim of discrimination, who had a lesser value in the social hierarchy, was legally possible. But the disruption of the family context and the declaration of the bond would have been publicly 'impossible' in their provincial location. According to convention and the law, as it would tear the family apart. It could only have taken place secretly, which in turn contradicts the principle of legislation: secret laws do not exist.

The problem was that since 1806, no one had continued work on a general legislation of love as presented by Sidonie in her publication *THE SWEDISH COUNTESS.* Neither in Central Europe nor, drawing on other traditions, in Asia, Africa or the USA. Without laws, the COMMUNITY OF LOVE was left at the mercy of chance.

Sidonie, in her grave–the Oltrup estate had long been repurposed into a Soviet collective farm, then this farm was abandoned, the estate declined–felt sorrow. How could the few enlightened individuals protect the large number of people who remained in a state of 'self-incurred immaturity'? Energetic appeals, Sidonie knew, are considered didactic.

North of Eden

In a place north of Lake Michigan, a place buried by blizzards twice a year, where life moves slowly, Police Officer Patterson trudged through the rest of his life.

Years ago he had met a Finnish woman in this solitude. The daughter they had together died. She was three years old. Patterson's wife had poured hot water into the bathtub and not yet added the cold when the telephone rang. She ran to the basement and spoke briefly. The inquisitive child, who had been leaning against the tub, fell into the water. With burnt skin she was taken to the hospital 40 kilometres away, where this little creature fought for its life over several days and nights. While Patterson was arranging the funeral, his wife killed herself with a shotgun.

The police officer seemed 'absent' for a long time. He remained inseparably connected to her, said his superior McFerguson. As if he were waiting to follow the two he had lost.

Did he try to get them back? No, he didn't find the entrance to the underworld. That entrance is not located in the part of the world where Patterson lived; Patterson didn't know his way around the place where it is located, near Naples. His superior said he would have missed the blizzards too and felt unsafe in Italian hotels. Did he go there? Once. He returned without achieving anything. He had read all the handbooks describing what to do at the gate of Hades. The books were lined up in his hut. He would hardly have made a mistake after arriving at the entrance.

What prevented him from killing himself? The same bonds that tied him to the deceased. He had seen something of life, a sign, that was worth living for. He simply couldn't abandon that.

Was he hoping to find someone new? How would that happen up here, in the few summer days they had? How many strangers came here? He was not willing to compromise.

Many people tried to help him, his superior related. Was he much use as a policeman? Hardly. He had absences. He didn't even seem reliable as a driver. On the other hand, there was no obvious reason for dismissal, especially as the professional deficits had existed for a long time. He was fed at the expense of the community. Someone has to pay for the work of mourning.

Everyone said they made a good couple. They strode into the dining-room, tall and slim, and people glanced in their direction.

It was this local advantage that they were reluctant to give up, their joint rank, and it enabled them to get through the years of changing fortunes. If someone had asked them in their fake trance–guided from outside as they were, showing off their happiness–WHETHER THEY LOVED EACH OTHER, WHAT INNER BOND THEY SHARED APART FROM LOOKING GOOD TOGETHER, they might well have fallen into doubt. They were clever children. They didn't reflect *once.* That was the danger in their early days: that they might have to expound the nature of their relationship before the court of reason. What would they have said? They were not drawn to each other very strongly.

In later years, partly through the advice of wise friends, who liked to have the couple around them like a lovely piece of furniture, they caught up on everything that belongs to a passion according to the laws of sincerity, intimacy, spontaneity and absoluteness. They responded together to outside dangers, crossed the threshold to a different social system together (because now they were hardly admired by others any more); they drew on a technique of dealing with each other that regulated nearness and distance as only they could. Others who did not have this intimate, inexpressible technique quickly got on their nerves (in the case of one brief adventure). That gave their relationship longevity. How attractive is an adventure compared with a house of one's own? And so, quite late on, already past their best years and no longer recognized when they entered a dining room, they found that they had fallen in love with each other. In a superficial way. Either a part of the outer skin had found its way inwards or the inner part consists of such skin.

Landscape with Impassable Mountains

For a while the mountain valley was wrapped in a cloud, and they spent an afternoon looking out of the large panorama windows that faced outwards, like sides of an equilateral triangle, towards a milky sea. Now, after eight hours of conversation–they had decided to clarify their relationship–they were already thinking a great deal about PASSING THE TIME, of practical aids like food, putting on a cap, going on an outing, something simple.

–Shall we order some coffee?

–Sure, she replied.

She was grateful to him. One must, he said, get back to simple things. If they were both single-celled organisms or oysters, for example, they would know what to do in the rhythm of high and low tide: at high tide they would open up, letting the suspended solids flow into them, and at low tide they would close up to avoid drying out. But she was not an oyster and he was not the sea.

–I've read, she said, that oysters transported from the east coast of the United States to Chicago still kept opening and closing for a hundred days in that continental location, following an inner clock set to the tides in the Atlantic.

–Then they were eaten?

–They became research objects. Because they readjusted after that time. When the scientists measured what rhythm their 'breathing' was now following, this rhythm corresponded the times at which there would be high and low tides in Chicago, if there were such a thing there.

–And nobody knows how they did that?

–Not at all.

–Does it have anything to do with the moon?

–I don't think so.

–And they're exact?

–Exactly.

But in their afternoon conversation, in which they tried to interpret the situation and the unclear swamplands of their sexual habits, their emotional position changed. Simply because they grew hungry; merely because they had engaged with each other imperfectly for eight hours, they had the feeling that they would find a way out soon, something as easy as 'let's go and eat'. In the long term, that builds up trust, even without clarification. Each year they wanted to talk to each other like that, residing in mountain heights. There's no purpose to it, she said, but it gives a feeling of warmth.

Everyone has their own magic words
They seem to have no meaning
But when they drift softly through the memory–
The heart laughs and weeps at once . . .

Commentary on Anna Karenina

There is an elemental power that cannot be deciphered by the impressions of muddled reason, and even less by those of the confused heart. And thus the face of the child that Anna Karenina had only just visited began to swell up.

She had met with her cuckolded, stubborn husband, who ordered her to leave the house. A disaster. But the governess watched the child, who cried for several hours and would not eat. She was concerned. At the same time, she distrusted her own observations and felt that she had an oversensitive eye. She did not call for a doctor immediately.

But the boy's features became bloated. The left side of the head became abnormally large, as with a severe infection, and possibly this was connected to an infected cut on his forehead and his touching this wound with dirty fingers, which had been wiping away his tears a moment earlier.

Soon the catastrophic change in the child's face was obvious to the governess. She ran to the master and alerted the servants. The doctor was summoned, but would not decide on a diagnosis; he found the symptoms strange and unclear. The tears were still streaming down, flowing over his disfigured 'chubby-cheeked' face, along the enormous swelling; the father was dismayed by the frightful sight. He sent for Anna Karenina. His calculating, 'cold-hearted' spirit did not want to face accusations that he had sent his wife away and their child had died immediately. The messenger reached the young woman, who rushed to the house and settled in the boy's room as if she wanted to stay for ever. Though no diagnosis could be given, the monstrous cheek, which had looked like the result of an inhuman slap only shortly beforehand, regained its normal shape after a few days. Anna Karenina did not leave the house again. The old man left things in this unspoken, improvised state where nothing was solved, and which one could not call peace between husband and wife. He made various decorative attempts to come closer to Anna Karenina again. She feared the punishment of heaven, the injury of her son. In her muddled mind, the child's life, as something she had brought into the world, was more elemental than a love story. She remembered reading a very similar story in a novel, and it had ended fatally. But the child could work magic. His closed eyes, which would look the same in death, displayed an expression of peace.

Born under a Lucky Star

> 'They are both asleep . . . they do not see
> the hand that seeks to kill them.'
>
> *Norma*

She comes from a state in the American Midwest. How happily her voice was preserved! Voice teachers followed her around like highwaymen; each of them would have been capable of assigning her voice to one of the 'types' and spoiling it. She had escaped all such attempts.

A challenge: singing Bellini's *Norma* at the most important opera house in Germany. No one can sing this part without competing with Maria Callas.

The day before the dress rehearsal, the lucky girl's vocal cords are unwell. She can't sing a note.

–What's so magnificent about Callas' incisive tone, her acrobatic efforts between extremely low and high registers?

–The dynamism, the passion.

–What does that mean?

–She reaches the notes with fabulous precision, and her face (and body) become increasingly expressive in the course of events, for example in Act 2.

–We also know that the singer of Adalgisa and she, the prima donna, are bitter enemies; this means that the representation of feminine solidarity offered by the events on stage seems bizarre, like trained panthers and lions who, coming from different continents, are destined to misunderstand each other. Will they bite? We wait for disaster to strike.

–That's an unfair description.

–Yes, but what isn't tense about Maria Callas' performance? Even the quietest entry is mannered.

–This is Great Opera.

–How different is the American singer with the endangered vocal cords! In the rehearsal she marks her entries; the fact that she does not sing out makes her stunningly beautiful. The orchestra restrains itself as if listening carefully.

—What do you call beautiful about that?

—There's no schema.

—How do you know? What do you call 'non-schematic'?

—From the child's voice to here, to the inflamed vocal cords, including all fears, but already forgetting the possible terrors on the third day—it's one great channelling process.

—You can hear something like that?

—That's what I imagine.

—But one can't hear anything.

—But in the dress rehearsal, when she was singing out again, you heard it too?

—Fear that gets forgotten?

—That must have been it. It has nothing to do with nature.

—But not with discipline either.

—No.

—So what would you call it?

—She was born under a lucky star.

The role of Norma did not really match what the lucky bearer of that voice had in mind, as she was concentrating on the articulation in her throat, rationing her air reserves and looking for the voice's position in her head. She never gave interviews because she could not have explained what she was doing.

NORMA, Act 2, Scene 1. The interior of Norma's quarters. On the one side, a Roman bed covered with bear hides. Lying on them, Norma's two children, asleep. Norma appears. She is holding a lamp and a dagger. Pale and distraught.

Slaves of a stepmother, she thinks to herself–that must not be their fate. 'They are Pollione's children, that is their crime.' She wants to kill in order to punish him, the blasphemer.

This rigorism drove the Roman, who was the secret lover of the druidess for several years and begot the children, away from her side. How often he had crept away to her in the bright moonlight.

Now it is proven that he married another woman, that he betrayed Norma. This is compounded by the sacrilege of seducing a Celt, a druid's disciple sworn to celibacy. Thus he doubly betrayed Norma, the priestess. If only he had never courted Norma, had shown few signs of his interest–how could she love the traitor in spite of everything!

In contrast to earlier myths of antiquity, Norma is unable to carry out her vengeance. She does not stab the children in their sleep. Once they awake and look at Norma with sleepy eyes, she is equally unable to kill them.

–Is humanity a weakness?

–No.

–Is Norma, the priestess of Gaul, really humane?

–In Bellini's version?

–Yes.

–It's the simultaneity of emotions, not humanity.

–So what's humanity?

—It's rooted in books, in a trustworthy tradition. What holds Norma back, however, in contrast to Medea, who butchers her children, comes from different areas of passion.

—That block each other?

—They erase each other.

The singer had no talent for such interview answers. When she did respond to journalists, it was only because the dramaturge and the artistic director wanted her to do so. Then she referred to texts from other discussions or spoke about things that were also in the programme book. The reporters could simply have taken the excerpts from the programme book. But it made them more credible for the singer herself to speak about them; only someone who intoned Bellini's melodies so brilliantly had the authority to speak of their content. This paved the way for the interest that always led to comparisons with Callas, comparisons that were entirely inappropriate.

Just as one dips one's bare foot in a mountain stream and, listening to the rushing of the water, has the feeling that humanity has not reached its end yet, the leaping of the voice from low A to high E flat is the image of an *improbable concentration.* Such concentration can avert or perhaps absorb disaster, and is therefore the source of an alternative to that universalist *humanitas* which is so difficult to bring into the immediate circle of events at the right moment: the humanist is always too early or too late. The singing of Norma, on the other hand, proceeds with the most exact timing and orchestral accompaniment, as if a god were guiding the voice.

The Great Velashka

'Low in rank–
high in talent'

The soprano Hanni Velashka was substantially more renowned, more disciplined and more industrious than her long-term lover David F.; she also displayed more endurance and imagination in her leisure pursuits, uses of the arts, pride, style, life, etc.

Nonetheless, she did not succeed in improving her initial standing; in fact, compared with David, she lost further attributes of her position, which had already been greatly reduced when they first fell in love. She had no chance of competing with David's long-standing colleague and friend. She always saw the two friends' backs in front of her. They went ahead and assumed that she, the star, would follow.

The journalists in the ballroom saw this convoy and took her, the famous one, for a kind of lamp destined to shine on the backs of the two friends. Yes, they said, that's the long-standing lover of the well-known Velashka, and next to him is his colleague and friend. They did not say anything about her, because it seemed self-evident that it was Velashka. But there was nothing about self-evident about that; every day it all had to be earned anew.

Because of the friendship between the two men, which she cemented when gratifying one of them under the starry night sky, she remained a kind of thing; a public thing when she worked, and a private thing when she contributed to amusement, whatever that meant for her as an actual life-thing.

Ingrid's Revenge

'A woman learns to hate to the extent that she forgets how to enchant.' Ingrid Töpfer first met Bernd Wolzogen during the 1943 retreat in Kharkov. They arrived in the industrial zone of the Rhineland in 1946. In the subsequent years, the teams essentially rebuilt the destroyed industrial complexes alone and protected them from demolition. Bernd Wolzogen became chairman of the works committee. For years, his wife provided the unpaid assistance that enabled him to sell his entire strength to the company on the one hand, and to dedicate himself to the works council on the other hand. When he came home he had to rest.

In the 1950s, after the introduction of the law on co-determination, Wolzogen was appointed to the board of the parent company. On the advice of his new colleagues, his living conditions were adapted to *the rank of labour director*: a house, a company car. In the mid-1950s, Ingrid lost all influence over this man. Her services were no longer needed. She imagined that he was still her piggy bank, containing the accumulation of all her unpaid work as a housewife and lover–which was why she tried, while suppressing various contradictory emotions, to have a level-headed relationship with Wolzogen. The paths of retreat in 1944, the years of new beginnings–she could not separate her history from Wolzogen's after the fact. The attempt to remain level-headed ultimately led to a divorce by mutual agreement. Wolzogen married a younger woman.

Ten years later, Ingrid's hatred for Wolzogen had matured. She had not had a chance after their separation. In the night of New Year's Eve 1966, she took a little hammer and destroyed the paint on her former husband's BMW; this vehicle was parked in front of the villa, which had two round windows behind which were the bathroom and two toilets. The car stood in the snow, an unpainted piece of metal. Wolzogen had difficulties presenting the case as an attempted break-in to his insurance company. Ingrid's need for revenge was not diminished by the deed. 'It is not the strength but, rather, the duration of elevated emotions that makes elevated persons.'

An Episode in the Age of Enlightenment

Baron Harkey, who owned massive amounts of land in the environs of Boston, married Lady Diana Milford in June 1732. Diana was so cold that it was impossible for the baron to get close to his wife in any way. She had acquired her coolness through her upbringing.

Because alcohol was unknown in her family in Boston, however, the baron succeeded in getting the young woman drunk in one of his hunting lodges during a hunting trip, then assailing her in this state with a few comrades and overpowering her as she fought desperately but without her usual strength. When she emerged from the cramped state in which she had bit into the pillows when screaming and fighting proved futile, she found herself facing one of the younger hunting comrades, Lord P., in whom she later saw the father of her child when she tried to save it.

She behaved towards her husband as if nothing had happened. But she saw to it that when he sat down to dinner with his friends he ate the flesh of his favourite hounds, whom she had killed and ordered to be served as venison. She turned to the Supreme Court in Ottawa to file for divorce but this was hopeless, as her husband, legally speaking, had not committed adultery in his role as a rapist; rather, it was she who risked being charged because of her 'literal' adultery–in relation to the hunting comrades–though the court did not pursue the matter owing to her high social rank.

As Diana saw no possibility of getting away from her husband, she shot the baron on a hunting trip before the eyes of his hunting comrades. Riding close behind him, she shot him with a heavy rifle and then, as he toppled and was subsequently hanging down the side of the horse, dealt him a few blows to the skull with the butt while riding side by side with his uncontrollably shying horse. The other hunters disarmed her and brought her to the mansion along with the dead man. They kept silent about what had happened. It was taken for a hunting accident for several weeks, before some people who did not belong to that social class pressed charges.

Diana, Baroness Harkey, defended herself in court–unlike the nobility on the British mainland, the colonial nobility could not appeal to the House of Lords–with great circumspection, assisted by Major General Vickers, who genuinely believed her to be innocent. However, the two of them walked into a trap set by the presiding judge, an ambitious commoner and holder of a baronetcy, who wanted to prove his consummate brilliance. They agreed to the taking of evidence suggested by the court, supposedly with the intention of exonerating the unfortunate woman, and the jury used this opportunity to find the defendant guilty and sentence her 'to hang until she is dead'.

The defendant accepted this verdict with her usual coldness, as she found it preferable to being forced to spend her life with her former husband. She could not stand people who do not know what they want, who first commit acts and then complain about how these acts are viewed. With their weak wills, they only delay their opponents. This opinion changed in prison, however, when she discovered that she was pregnant. She immediately felt certain that a child was the cause of her unfamiliar symptoms. She asked her defence counsel, the retired Major General Vickers, who had a degree of political influence, to send a petition to the governor, while she herself contacted the Chief Lord Justice and the court that had sentenced her, asking them to delay her execution until she had given birth to her child. This convinced them to send a doctor to examine her, as there was a precedent forbidding the killing of a pregnant woman until the child had been born. The doctor, who was unaware of the rape in the baron's hunting lodge and instead proceeded from the documented fact that the murdered Harkey had been prevented from consummating their marriage by the *coldness* of his wife, reached the conclusion that there was no pregnancy. He considered a conversation with the condemned to be sufficient, as he was relying on facts. It struck him as absurd that this woman of supposedly cool upbringing should expect to be physically touched by him. He left her in the expectation that the actual examination was yet to follow and said nothing to her defence counsel about his findings but simply sent his report to the Attorney General; thus the condemned woman initially believed her child to be protected–it was pushing, pounding its way towards the light with its inborn force–until she received the Attorney General's summons to execution. The authorities were keen for it to take place quickly, as some sections of the populace were taking a lively interest in this case and considered the verdict one of the few satisfactory acts of the judiciary. On the other hand, there was opposition to this 'entirely unsatisfactory sentence of violence' among the nobility. Roughly 70 high-ranking peers made an address to the governor demanding for the verdict to be overturned, as it was directed against a person of rank. Now the governor was no longer able to draw out the process until a possible pardon from the queen; rather, as a representative of the commoners, who were insisting forcefully on expressing their will and formed the majority, he too had to demand a swift administration of justice.

The condemned woman resisted desperately but was constrained by the limited possibilities she had from her prison cell. As the guards were reinforced, an attempt to free her which was being planned for a time by some younger nobles was out of the question. Retired Major

General Vickers sent his medal of honour back to the governor, made petitions and, once all else had failed, decided to travel to England in order to win the queen's interest. As his ship was caught in fog banks off the Irish coast, he arrived too late.

At the urging of the prisoner, who threatened to publicize information about Baron Harkey's private life, the governor, himself a noble, called for a final hearing on the question of her execution. Now without a defence counsel, she was unable to bring about a renewed medical examination. She was merely given an opportunity to present an argument based on the rape by her husband and his hunting companions, though she refused to give their names. She referred to the signs she had observed in her body. She believed that if she described these changes so precisely, no one could think that they were imagined. It was this same precision, however, that triggered the suspicion of hypochondria. As the presiding judge had no understanding of such signs, furthermore, and a doctor's report had been submitted, they took the symptoms for signs of some illness, assuming they even existed. And illness was not an impediment to execution. The judge, Chief Justice Dorsen, made it clear that the way things stood, if the execution did not take place quickly, it would not take place at all. He gave an *impartial* summary of the possible reasons for sparing the condemned woman's life–the dubious nature of human justice and a certain harshness of fate, *if* her claims were true–but reached the conclusion that she had to be killed 'so that her deed would not have repercussions for the provinces'.

Dismayed, she tried once more to bring to a halt this machinery which was taking her child away. She turned to the nobility, her friends, the young Lord P., the queen, and sent messengers to follow Major General Vickers and urge him to make haste; they arrived in Plymouth before him. They managed to inform the queen. But this decision-making process took too long to prevent the execution. Diana was taken out of her cell and hanged, even though she resisted with all her strength and screamed and struck out, which made the involvement of several executioners necessary.

The nobility succeeded in forcing an examination of the deceased, which revealed that she was four months pregnant. Major General Vickers returned from England with a royal pardon. He challenged the deplorable governor and the Attorney General, whom he addressed as murderers in a newspaper he controlled, to a duel, which they declined. The lawsuit against the organs of government resulted in the governor's dismissal. The shock of the news that the hanged woman was pregnant also led to a closer inspection of the training received by colonial doctors. The judicial accident sharpened the tone of the Enlightenment. With an excess of severity, the American society of the eighteenth century demanded an intensification of correctness.

Enlightenment in the Case of Immaturity through No Fault of One's Own

'*Enlightenment is man's emergence from his self-incurred immaturity. Immaturity* is the inability to

> use one's own understanding without the guidance of another. This immaturity is *self-incurred* if its cause is not lack of understanding, but lack of resolution and courage . . . '[3]

A person is mature if they are able to 'use [their] own understanding without the guidance of another'. The daughter of the ship owner Onassis was capable of doing this on a daily basis. She needed no helpers to have a clear understanding. But was she also will to exercise her emotional powers, the ability to create forms of equilibrium in herself, without the guidance of another? For that she would have had to study acting, not philosophy.

And so this courageous person rushed to her father for advice, or she ran to her mother to gossip. No one who saw her ruling her father's business after his terrible death would have noticed her insecurity, her desire to be guided by others. She was considered sensible.[4]

This piece of life took place while the Soviet Union was still seeking space in the world for its fleets. It had bases on the island of Garcia Juarez in the Indian Ocean, on the coast of Somalia and even in unknown recesses of the Antarctic.

---

3 Immanuel Kant, 'An Answer to the Question: "What Is Enlightenment"?' in *Political Writings* (H. S. Reiss ed., H. B. Nisbet trans.) (Cambridge: Cambridge University Press, 1991), p. 54 (translation modified).

4 A concept of intellect, often defined too narrowly. It refers to all of a person's reactions to themselves (inwards) and the world (outwards), regardless of what mental powers are used. The intellect is INNER COMMUNITY.

In this context, the wishes of the strategists were directed at the tanker fleets of the Greek Onassis. How to access this transport line? How to ensure its collaboration in an emergency? Via the heiress?

The case was examined by instructors and psychologists at the secret service academies in Moscow. Attempts at financial persuasion were ruled out, as was blackmail.

Observation of the heiress revealed that she displayed insecurity. She considered herself physically ungainly, which was evidently correctly observed. She assumed that a man was sizing her up when he looked at her. She took other glances to mean that her wealth triggered wild fantasies. She laughed about that. It was not as if wealth arranged in balances was any use for practical things, for something concealed in love affairs, just like a box full of jewellery or a larder for children.

1

I Prefer Justice to Love

That her father's eyes brightened when she entered the room, that he, at least, loved her–this clever woman was sure of that. At the same time, it made her uncertain, because the GREAT MAN adored her almost indiscriminately. If his love erased all perception, this was a form of indifference. How could she explore anything in such a mirror? At the same time, he was genuinely indifferent, indeed brutal towards her when he acted unjustly towards her mother, who was like a part of her. How can someone love, yet cut off the one he loved most from what she loved most?

She could have lived with these sparse dispensations of justice. She did not want a love that she had to share with Maria Callas or her brother.

> 'Of snakes you should beware
> with that lustful air!'

2
Enlightenment as a Sword and Shield

Why would someone even look for a way out of their self-incurred immaturity, out of their cave? It is cold outside. What does 'out of' mean? Is the 'outside' the business domain, entrusted by her father? The DEAD MAN is urging.

For that she needs her wits about her, she needs them to defend the empire. She puts on armour. Does the manner in which she closes the visor of her helmet suggest a WAY OUT? She doesn't want to see anything. She prefers to see with other people's eyes, to hear their accounts. She lets them report and advise. She is a social person.[5]

3
The Plans of the KGB

A Kremlin astrologer from Astrakhan gave the decisive tip. The psychological weakness of Onassis' successor was quickly found by the relevant staff. Strange, said Andropov, how our services, as functionalistic as their feelings and as unsentimentally constructivistic their inner workings may

---

5 She forgets her unhappiness in the presence of others. Forgetfulness emboldens us.

be, collectively show so much subtlety in their powers of distinction.[6]

They sent Yuri Kirilenko, a thoroughly patriotically trained spy, to Paris under the name of Jerry Leskov with the task of following the heiress. As the experts had anticipated, the fat young woman assisted them with their plan. She did not follow the instructions of her security personnel to get rid of Lesskov, and diverted her own intellectual powers 'as the goddess diverted the arrow of Diomedes'. To answer the question of her worth that evening, the question of whether a man could find her attractive, she sought her opponent's guidance. Lesskov advised her. Soon they were engaged. Wedding in Buenos Aires.

4
From the Agent's Handbook[7]

The aim of seduction by secret agents is to feed all the victim's senses back into their immaturity. For every person, immaturity is an original state from which they 'once emerged'. This forms the basis for the rules which tell the couple that intimacy is now permitted (love). These permissions lead to the paradisiacal state before leaving childhood (homecoming). A direct infiltration of the power

---

6 Andropov, head of the KGB and also a scholar, could reflect critically on the hierarchy he commanded.

7 Naturally the INTIMATE EXPERIENCE OF SECRET SERVICES, the art of seduction, is not detailed in handbooks. Nor on computer tapes that could be copied by enemies. It was only rival agencies, for example the Danish, French and Romanian ones, and those of the USA (in puritanical feedback), that compiled lists and manuals mirroring the seduction methods of the KGB.

centre–to the files, accounts and professional secrets the spy wishes to access–is out of the question from this position. The power of love accumulated by the agent (added value) must first be converted into weakness (helplessness of the strong). From here (she is in need, he confesses to being an agent) the path leads to SECOND-DEGREE INTIMACY (entanglement). The exits to the power centre are not blocked in the same way from this position (seduction). This path to mutual immaturity is also dangerous for the spy, who cannot draw on his capacity for love without the guidance of the other.[8]

5
Counter-Enlightenment in the Onassis Apparatus

Security chiefs and bodyguards in the fleet were still all selected by the ship owner. They are responsible for the safety of the tanker routes, they preserve the secrets of the central office, they protect the owner and now their queen.

They see an agent beguiling their mistress. They too have a handbook. They warn her. The mistress takes them for jealous schemers; she wants to protect her love and dismisses the warners. A second group of these security chiefs attempt to set temptresses on Lesskov, placing 'offers' in

---

8 He cannot be guided by his superior in such an intimate area. His lover, the direct other, will be his advisor. Thus both of them had their own baggage to deal with. Lesskov had emotional reserves from the warm-hearted regime of his southern Russian origins. The daughter of Onassis fed off an insatiable greed, the kind generated for a lifetime by the dark side of this trait in persons with strong inferiority complexes. At that moment she felt like the QUEEN OF LOVE.

the vicinity of their queen to undertake seduction attempts. As vulnerable as love it, is protects itself by closing its eyes and listening to nothing but itself (maturity of love).[9]

6

A Conversation with Comrade Andropov

First and foremost a politburo member, then a scholar. Only later an experienced supervisor of secret agents. Not a spy or expert himself. Always curious about the things confided in him.

–How is it supposed to work, Comrade Main Department Manager, that in an emergency–the outbreak of war–the emotional power which our spy has over the young heiress of the tanker fleet would act in our favour? He would use his influence and be unmasked?

–He must reveal himself, Comrade Chairman.

–And his position is so strong, you say, his partner so bound to him, that if she is faced with the choice between losing him–or rather: abandoning him to his helplessness in between all the factions (this strikes me as harder for someone who loves, as far as I can judge from reading bourgeois novels)–and placing her empire in our service, she will not waver?

–She will not waver.

–How often have you tried that?

9 It is a state of equilibrium; it rests on the permission not to be ashamed. This permission is easily blocked; nothing changes into a prohibition as quickly as openness to love. Therein lies its vulnerability.

–Never with Onassis' daughter.

–With other Greek women?

–No.

–Women who owned such major resources?

–No.

–And what makes you so sure, if you have no experience beyond the level of secretaries?

–It corresponds to the laws of human nature.

–Which you know from the encyclopedia?

–No, from documents of the apparatus.

–And the counter-effect? The work of the Onassis fleet's security services? I hear CIA is also watching our couple closely. Have you noticed that Lesskov is spoken of as a Russian (which I consider a disarming move, incidentally)?

–What are they going to do? They are not getting inside our object's heart the way we are. They only ever offered 'guidance' where the heart could not speak for itself.

–From your lips to God's ears.

–What do you mean by 'God'?

–Would you prefer gods?

–Which gods, Comrade Chairman?

–Then say 'the dead'.

–Which dead?

–Our 'immortal victims'. You see, Comrade Main Department Manager, those are the invincible ones. They speak within our hearts.[10]

---

10 See Kant, 'An Answer to the Question: "What Is Enlightenment"?', 5 December 1784: 'One age cannot enter into an alliance

7
How Lesskov Was Nonetheless Removed from His Beloved's Side

Love dreams of having absolute power. Its aim is to increase its means in order to subjugate the will of the beloved. Because love cannot be accumulated or concentrated, however (unlike weapons or capital), the daughter of Onassis and her husband shared their complete power with each other for a long time, making it impossible to ascertain who was the weaker and who the stronger because both attributes are preconditions for absolute increase. In this phase Lesskov was protected against attacks from third parties; he had even erased all memory of his employers, had no intention of returning home and did not carry anything in his heart that could have exposed him in his sleep. He was not a traitor.

But then, it is said, the COUNTER-EFFECT OF REAL CONDITIONS sets in. Probabilities return.[11] I wake up to find a stranger lying next to me. The daughter of Onassis was ashamed of her plump figure. How improbable it was, in the light of the morning sun, that her husband did not

---

on oath to put the next age in a position where it would be impossible for it to extend [. . .] its capacity for love [. . .] This would be a crime against human nature . . . '

11 See Carl von Clausewitz, *On War* (Michael Howard and Peter Paret ed. and trans.) (Princeton, NJ: Princeton University Press, 1989), p. 86: 'From the very start there is an interplay of possibilities, probabilities, good luck and bad [. . .]. In the whole range of human activities, love most closely resembles a game of cards.'

see it! Didn't he want to see it? Was he keeping his thoughts from her?

Feelings appear at discrete points, starkly separated and difficult to express. It is only because of this that they are considered slow or blurry.[12] The daughter of Onassis was not capable of establishing an equilibrium in her feelings without the guidance of another. She consulted with confidants, lacking the courage to ask Lesskov. The spy, who did not enjoy such trust here, longed for consultation. The relationship was only secure as long as they sought the 'guidance of the other' and 'maturity' strictly with each other. As soon as third parties were asked, the relationship was in danger.

Now, it is furthermore said, the subjective attributes came to the fore: doubt, fatigue, sudden impulses, chance. The peculiar chain of long-term memory, hearsay and prejudices, inherited from the chain of ancestors, replaces the DIRECT GAZE.

The security experts of the Onassis fleet had waited for this phase of weakness, which occurs in every love relationship (dismissed staff spoke of it in so-called 'non-conversations' with their successors); British, Arab and US secret services helped with advice. One intrigue was enough, a forged note by Lesskov with a list of foodstuffs that help to lose weight.

As soon as the serpent of doubt has hatched, it reinforces itself with its *own* means to attain absolute power. It

---

12 '[. . . A]ll these traits of character seek their proper element–chance' (ibid.).

is a long way, in such a case, to the reaction by actual conditions (warm-heartedness, generosity, skin contact, need for sleep, forgetting and forgiving). The divorce proceedings were quickly completed, before the daughter of Onassis even felt she had made a decision.

8
Now She Had Self-Incurred Maturity and Was Unhappy

Lesskov's employers had hastily taken him off the case, assuming he had been unmasked. He sat under the birch trees in his home country, despairing because he had left a large part of himself with the fleet queen. But the daughter of Onassis, triumphantly taken over by her people again, in the event of war too, in a sterile command position impossible for third parties to influence, fought in vain against the weight of unhappiness in her lifestyle. Her digestion and capacity for enjoyment fell apart. Without medical guidance, the skin–far removed from all greed–and the intestinal villi were incapable of using their powers of understanding; for those powers are scattered among all parts of the human body, just as they are clearly visible in the totality of heaven and hell. Thus the sole of a foot has its own mind just like the ear. And deep inside, the diaphragm and the backside argue whose advice and guidance should be sought, and this quarrel of attributes (the 'faculties'), which bears eternal war within it, wore down the fortune, that bit of property from the inherited fleet which remained for the daughter of Onassis, to defend herself against erosion and the passing of time without the guidance of others. Her material property was still intact. She spoke more to her dead father than to her surroundings. Something inside her was eating her up. In the end, she herself belonged to the dead.[13]

The Commodity Character of Love, Theory and Revolution

It is unlikely that love, of all things, which regulates intimacy, our most important property, should not be affected by capitalism in the PERIOD OF CAPITALISM. Thus spoke the Western visitor to People's Commissar Trotsky. The latter shook his head. This problem was not on the politburo's daily agenda. The topic required quiet times which offered time for discussion.

The Western visitor had sat down in a wicker chair in the kitchen. The kitchen was next to the switchboard. The thick walls of the Kremlin did not allow for rebuilding. Capitalism is not necessarily about money, the Western visitor continued. As an author, he had clout, so Trotsky was forced to listen to him; and thus Trotsky's seven helpers also listened. As we know, the elementary form is the commodity, the visitor went on. It shows an almost theological capacity for change. In a sack of grain, I see the splinter of a diamond which I exchange for it, part of a house, a school, a piece of woodland or gold, I see the eyes of a beggar and so on. Why should it be any different in love relationships? In advanced industrial societies, commodity exchange feeds off the search for happiness. But

13 Without her security services, placed in the service of treachery, she would have been safer.

with commodities of love and hate, this is tied to the condition that the commodities can only be dealt as if under a black cloth (or under the table). The meeting of the People's Commissars was starting in 15 minutes on the floor underneath the kitchen.

The latter condition of 'as if under a black cloth' was something he had often noticed, replied Trotsky. There was no open exchange at all between the sexes. They coexisted in hostility and suspicion; this was the continent's problem.

Such a question cannot be treated in a dilatory fashion, the Western visitor continued. He had made the long journey here and was expecting waiting times. That led him to assume that here too, at the centre of power, there was leisure, the time to present and consider ideas in a calm fashion. The unresolved blockade between the sexes, he said, had been holding up Russia's progress for 400 years. The Soviets had inherited the problem, and it was negligent not to examine it analytically if the necessary theory was available.

–Marxian theory?

–Exactly.

–In a psychoanalytical interpretation?

–This causes it to change. Theories also have the commodity character, metamorphosis, as their elementary form.

–Under black cloths?

No, he said, that is not the case at all for theory. No concealed exchange. Theory does not feel shame, on the contrary. The exchangeability of theory, its constantly changing form, its social character (chameleon character) is considerably easier to handle than CONSTANT REVOLUTION. That makes theory a public amusement. But now the crowd of seven helpers really did have to go downstairs with Trotsky.

Metallic Happiness

A young woman leapt from one of the terraces of Milan Cathedral. She had resolved to put an end to her life. She fell with a cry of dismay; she had overestimated the firmness of her decision.

As fate would have it, she fell onto the metal of a car body. She later said that she feared looking unattractive as a corpse on the cobblestones of the cathedral square. In fact, surrounded by all that metal yet also cushioned in her fall, she looked grotesquely damaged.

At the clinic, all vital functions of the battered body (which the spirit had driven to attempt suicide, and which the spirits of the cathedral had been able to protect) were diagnosed intact. Wilma Bison had struggled through from Odessa to the West at the age of 35, gone in search of happiness, then had the impression of finding only unhappiness and thus reached the ghastly decision that led to a happy end. Her rescue, which spread through the tabloids, led her into the arms of a man from Lugano, who henceforth protected her.

Someone Who Helps Me

I used to know an old dancer. Lively man. Bit over the top sometimes. Never went too far with me. He belonged to Rudolf Nureyev's group, a passionate disciple. The inconspicuous man I'm speaking of helped out whenever it was necessary. A bit more average than the others, he was forced to replace anyone who was unavailable for some reason. Oh, an indisposition, a cold, the first dancer's aggravated ankle. Yes, I'll fill in. He often danced female roles; as a result, he danced his joints to pieces. He could only keep his boys close to him, the ones he lusted after, if he refrained from trying to be intimate with them. He had to be at their disposal, to advise them in their affairs with others.

It's calming, said the young woman, to let him advise me. I know he's not after me. The stress, the hardship of being on one's guard when close to a man doesn't come up. And he, in turn, helps himself out; maybe he's already capable of imagining a young, skinny girl like me as one of his boys. He keeps them at arm's length so as not to lose them. That way he helps me.

A *Liebestod*

King Mark's eyes in an industrial face? One couldn't deny that Q. had a 'compelling' gaze. He had also accumulated a massive fortune that managed itself, as it were. He had got rid of the factories that had produced the money, which easily fell prey to the changing times.

As a partner he had acquired a 'doll', a lady with charisma. A wasteful acquisition, measured against her tasks:

caring for the three children from his first marriage, replacing his departed wife and being his travel companion and decoration in his villa, or actually his life. The deal did not turn out well.[14]

The couple, with unequal intentions and different allocations of living space, visited London. That year, 1927, unusual and constantly rising developments on the stock market highlighted the big cities. Hellmuth, the eldest son, M.'s stepson, accompanied her. M. had born a child to Q., had already lasted four years by his side, and for two years she had had a strong bond with her stepson; they were inseparable. They roamed through London, then a few weeks later did the same in Paris. They were so immersed in their affair that they did not realize the average person might easily take them for a couple. The husband and father, who was occupied with business appointments and only ever saw them return, did not draw any conclusions.

Hellmuth had already complained of abdominal pains in London. Eaten too much? The wrong things? A British doctor felt his stomach, gave him laxatives and prescribed moderation at mealtimes.

He had strong colics in Paris too. The miserable scene could not be attributed to his diet, which differed greatly in England and France. After the departure of his beloved stepmother and respected father to Berlin, the young man, heir to the empire, demanded a doctor who spoke German. He had to crawl to reach his hotel bed. Then he lay there, pale.

---

14 What is 'a lady of great charisma' supposed to mean? What does 'doll' mean? Those were things Q. said.

Appendicitis, final stage. Why wasn't the fever recognized? Admission to a private clinic in Paris.

A mere three hours separated the beautiful M.'s arrival in Berlin from her boarding of the night train in which she hurried back to Paris. Her wishes and spirit were in turmoil. How eagerly she would have sacrificed her estranged life with an unloved husband for her best friend, the son who had been assigned to her. Such a scene of sacrifice—often in times of need, in war, among working people, where sacrifice is called for—was as little considered part of a lady's life in 1927 as a love affair between stepmother and son was tolerated. Wasteful life did not appear in the frugal life of the industrial gods.

The clinic proved to have perfect hygiene, M. saw that immediately. There had been complications with the emergency operation. She recruited teams to clean the clinic's rooms and hallways. She doted on the moribund young man; she wanted to keep him in this life at all costs. She held his hand. She felt his feverish feet and put compresses on his legs. The medical treatment in Paris on the national holiday, 14 July, was inadequate. When M. finally managed to call over one of the doctors responsible, the boy died.

How to meet the 'compelling' eyes of the man? Guilt in her heart. Nothing untoward had happened, but she and the heir had become a couple in a short time; she saw this clearly once all was lost. Nor was there any causal relationship between such 'guilt' and his 'death'. She no longer wanted to live. The zinc coffin was transported in carriage 12 of the Paris–Berlin express train. She was sitting in carriage 3, first class.

It is one of the mysteries of causal connection, but one which becomes plausible as soon as one recognizes the long-distant effect of emotional trauma, that this young woman of 1927, who survived her 'Liebestod' by 18 years, ended her life by suicide. After further deaths, death had become more ghastly, bolder and more obvious. The astrologer Detering, who examined the respective times of death in 1945 and on 14 July 1927, said it was as if the ray of terror sent out by the loss of love and the curse of King Mark (not uttered or ever intended by Q.) had forcibly changed an astral constellation. Can experiences move stars around? For the constellations, said Detering, were not negative in themselves.

The Ban on Love

Eleven convicts were sitting in cells at the police station. It was out of the question to execute them like murderers.

The couple's parents, the lawyers explained to the judge in the capital of the North Indian state of Uttar Pradesh, had asked them repeatedly to stop seeing each other. The boy, 19 years old, belonged to the Brahmin caste, and to a special group within this highest Hindu caste. His 18-year-old lover belonged to the Jat caste. This is also a respected caste but lower than the Brahmins. There is no way to escape a caste.

Hundreds of inhabitants of the village community had watched when the lovers were hanged early one morning on the roof of a house. News of the illegal execution did not reach the state capital in time. The strangling, which was completed in eight minutes, took place in the presence of the parents from both families. Hours later, motorized police units appeared in the village to re-establish the authority of the administration. The dogmatic, by no means mutually hostile parents of the strangled couple, beholden to custom, let the police arrest them, trusting in their number, local influence and lawyers.

–For you, as a representative of the republic's constitution and of civilization, the situation is difficult. You can't compensate for this act of murder with a fine or a short prison sentence. Instating the death penalty, which applies to gang murder, results in a massacre.

–Did you see the article in yesterday's TIMES OF INDIA? I'm supposed to impose lifelong preventive detention. But that's pointless. The families won't carry out another act like that; there are no more young candidates in these families who are attracted to each other. Unlike the Montecchi and Capuleti, they are not feuding families; they are of *one* mind. The repetition will take place somewhere else, within a radius of 700 miles. That's a statistical certainty. We don't know where it will happen.

–We live in two societies and both exercise power. Our power, the constitution, has to send a signal.

–Maybe an expulsion, a banishment?

–Resettlement in a distant location?

–Unusual in India. That would have been the solution in the days of the colonial administration.

–Does your work and the work of your forefathers ever feel futile?

–Not really.

–Because you like being here?

–You have to admit, it's an interesting case. Whatever I decide, I deal with stories that move the imagination.

In 1947, a Briton could adopt Indian citizenship. That was what the state judge's father had done; thus the seventh generation of Hookes was now holding administrative and judge's posts in Uttar Pradesh. A strain of Scottish blood ran through their veins, which they could feel on their skin whenever they exposed it to the sun.

Tristan Between Two Isoldes

In the heat of August, the grass around Bayreuth was growing on a hellish scale. The trees and bushes around the firm buildings of the festival theatre maintained a degree of moderation. Inside the festival theatre was the clutter of decorations, props, curtains and teasers, with mobile rattles and tumblers in the basement. The orchestra was absent. The air was cool here.

F. Nietzsche, who had borne the title of 'editor' since the previous day, had not been welcomed in the morning, either by the master of the house or by Cosima Wagner, nor by any of the singers. Masterless, he had demanded cooling. He felt the manifold corners could be interpreted as 'my workplace'. He had a long way to go if he not only wanted to be a propagandist for Richard Wagner's societies, a pamphleteer (editor), but also conceive and compose operas. It was 21 days until the argument with the Wagners that would decide everything.

At the court of King Mark, a place of shadowy halls and gardens (at the gates the heat is roaring, the enemy masses storming), the ruler is flanked by two women who look almost identical: Queen Isolde and her confidante, likewise Isolde, for that was what the king has called her since she was foisted on him in the night in place of the Irish princess. She alone, the purest Isolde, shared the royal whispers, his sweat, the skin contact.

What was more important for Tristan to conquer now? The treasure, seized and stolen from his friend and king? It transpired that establishing what had the GREATEST VALUE was more urgent for Tristan than the decision of his mighty organs of love (scattered in the world beyond or the underworld, in the spirit or the body). Whom should he choose for his downfall? The two Isoldes differed in their proximity to power. Their looks, on the other hand, were similar, as was their knowledge of Irish magic.

Thus Tristan, as Nietzsche noted at his 'workplace', remained indecisive for years owing to an excessive attraction in two directions. A knight could hardly sleep with the king himself. To have sexual relations with other knights and be discovered by Melot–how shameful! So all the energy remained locked in his body. The body, often wounded, toiled away outside fighting the enemies of the kingdom, loyal service; that was easy. Thus the hero Tristan and the other parties involved stayed together for many years in a state of great vitality. It was all they could do not to start writing novels.

For the bodies, the objective structures of humans, must express themselves at all costs. They use the spirit and the deeds recorded by the historians to assert themselves verifiably, to leave no doubt that all means come from them, the bodies–undreamt-of powers. Their relinquishing, often fatal, but in equilibrium between attractions of equal size, creates what we call reality, as hard and tangible as the bodies themselves, by means of the imagination. The only subjective aspect, noted Nietzsche, sitting in the candlelight at a little table from the Meistersinger set, was the despair in the residues of sorrow when the will manifested in bodies, older than any human, did not dare to express itself. The act of daring proceeds from the surface, not from within. The skin wants to dare.

That requires cool rooms. The skin cannot 'think' anything if it is heated and braced to defend. This summer humidity, which is so beneficial to the grass and sends the rain from England in the evening, advances into the vaults of the festival theatre. Here too it would quickly grow hot, and the expanding spirit must reduce itself, confining itself once more to the body's interior, where it remains silent. Essentially, only four hours of the day are of use in these Central European climes.

Tristan and Isolde after Five Years

The noble rulers had meanwhile entered their fifth year of encampment at the castle built by Tristan's ancestors. They called two countries their own, 100 cows, other livestock, herds of horses, bondservants and a few freemen who could be armed. The couple remained cut off from the capital. No one dared visit the recluses. And after the king's ships had been prevented from landing, there was no longer any attempt by the kingdom to make contact with the living dead. Thus crammed together in dual monastic solitude (Tristan's squire had fallen in the battle with the king's ships), longing interfered. For its independent life, its daily renewal, longing demands a certain degree of distance, A MOVEMENT TOWARDS EACH OTHER. The relationship between the lovers, the subjects of numerous songs, became one of sibling love, a 'still water'; but it was never indifferent for a moment, as they carried their famous story with them and could tell it to each other. For a time, the ambassador Brangäne, whom Isolde's mother, an Irish sorceress, had given to her daughter, managed to bring some hours of sprightliness and courtly distance to the isolated walls. But even sorcery could not change the fact that this was rural, not city life. The lovers, notwithstanding their dramatic past, were able to feed for a while on whatever the common folk wrested from the fields and meadows; they could produce children, they could listen to Brangäne's account of the events and love-driven battles of five years ago, they could follow the course of the familiar sun and the nocturnal firmament through the year, and thus grow old together. They could, with Brangäne's advice, choose their shared place of burial; or they could just as well start building it. If the edifice was magnificent enough if could document the high level of their former capacity for love (but this level had manifested itself in the company at the royal court, in the midst of civilization, different countries and novels, not among oaks and meadows).

Gradually the words died. They understood each other without words too. And there was little in the way of new things to understand; they lacked opponents. In the end, Brangäne boiled numbing and intoxicating potions that prolonged their passion for hours.

How different the situation is for Brangäne, with her strong motives. She survives time and solitude. 'Brangäne, hardened in her heart, carries the wishes of the Queen of Ireland with her.' Brangäne has the class consciousness of witches; she feels the communicate hardness of the vow of loyalty she gave Isolde's mother before the ominous ships left Ireland. ONE NEEDS CLEARLY DEFINED REASONS.

In the Trough of Psychology

She was ashamed. After three sessions, her allergy was far from cured but her attraction to her own sex had been exposed. The woman leading the psychological conversation only just restrained herself from giving advice. Hedwig's skin was crying out. As Chief Prosecutor in one of the former East German states, she could not follow her inclinations freely, that is, visit bars where lesbian women met. She had to wait for holidays in some distant place.

The purple wound glowed in her face and down her neck, her colleagues made jokes. They called her 'a saint'.

The young psychologist holding the therapy sessions tried to find other reasons than the obvious ones to interpret the excessive signalling of Hedwig's body. She looked for a way of applying her knowledge, acquired at university, which were sufficient cause for the high fee she demanded from the health insurance fund. A doctor had referred the patient to her; she would have liked to refer her back. Both women found the situation embarrassing.

She wished him luck for his project. For a heartbeat she felt this wish inside her. She was sitting in a group where the conversation had turned towards the latest project of her former husband, a luckless man. He never had any patience, he always underestimated counter-effects.

Once, long ago, she had briefly–perhaps for a year and a half, exactly 547.5 of 10,866 days, that is, a third of her life, which she spent with him–been 'senselessly happy'. Time flew by. She bore the consequences of her mistake. Why mistake, if she was happy? Torturous yes, mistake no, she told herself. There are many ways to count, after the fact. The days of tormenting themselves, the days of the final separation, both no longer than a moment really. Days that passed 'without sense'. She knew that because it was typical of her. But you said he was never a good match for you, said Gerda. The answer only came to her the following day, when Gerda was no longer there. There are two different kinds of happiness: one is *radial*, the other *tangential*. Now Miriam was sitting opposite her in the kitchen. What do these terms mean? Did you read that somewhere?

–Tangential: it goes past you, it comes towards you, you can touch it beside you.

–In plain English: It makes you happy?

–Like all mistakes.

–So were you happy?

–Certainly.

–And then all the more unhappy, and in the end you ended it?

Once again she only knew the answer later; two weeks later it was on the tip of her tongue. She took it down on a bit of paper, which she lost. That was why she tried to be precise when she spoke to Hedwig Korte, who actually meant less to her than Gerda, but none of her other friends were available.

–I wasn't the one who ended it, he provoked me. There was nothing else for me to say but 'Now it's over'.

–What do you mean? We're talking about something completely different.

–We're talking about naivety. I wasn't at all naive when we broke up.

–What does that have to do with your plans?

–Nothing. It's just an example.

–An example of what?

–How one reaches a decision.

–And how does one reach a decision?

–A decision to separate. I took all my things out of the cupboards and left a letter.

–And what was the sudden trigger?

–Nothing at that particular moment. A week earlier I had found out that he had a child with E., you don't know her. I still could have forgiven that.

–And suddenly, a week later, things were different?

–And you find that strange?

Once again she failed to give the convincing answer at the right time. This is how she saw the matter:

For a moment, which actually lasted over 400 days, I could call myself happy in his presence.

Oh, what if it was all a tragic mistake and it was I who –radially, through my heart, untainted by any perception–fabricated this 'senseless happiness'.

I paid for that with a third of my life (10,866 minus 547.5 days).

None of that is a matter of addition or subtraction. Happy and unhappy days cannot be exchanged.

What are happy days anyway? The less successful ones are those that offer indifferent time. That doesn't hurt much, it simply accumulates in the memory. Then the days of pain. How dismal they are!

Then where is the unforgiveable thing, something so severe that she is surprised to find herself wishing this man luck for his new project? Was it in the days after the separation, when she saw a new life alone ahead of her and was afraid? The fact that she comforted herself? Now she can discuss it with Gerda again, because she has come back from her tip. With her she can speak openly.

If You Are Mine, Then My Friend Can Have You / A Love Affair in Wartime

He would never have admitted that he found certain comrades, dressed in their uniforms, extremely attractive. He had already hated and loved with great intensity during his training as an officer. In Greece, he met a young Greek woman and defended her property against rivals for half a year. But then, because of a sudden, almost compulsive idea he had while drunk, he left her to the captain of the tank force, Erwin D.

This captain hit the girl, injured her; he was evidently not up to the situation. The girl came from a good family, the daughter of a district judge.

The Greek community clung to the man who had protected this girl for half a year; they know nothing about the captain. An 'engagement' of sorts had taken place, that is, the parents had entrusted their daughter to him. They did not want to take her back in a damaged state now.

What was he supposed to do? Challenge his comrade to a duel? He would rather have moved in with him than the girl. The only solution–after bringing in the division commander–was for him to take responsibility for the misfortune and request permission to marry her. The girl helped him out, stating that for his sake she had not resisted a captain (whose name she could not provide) and been beaten up by the confused man. The officer was granted permission to marry when the war was over. It felt like a threat, a closing judgement, the way death stands at the end of every life.

At war's end, he was far away from where the events had taken place. In 1952, the unhappily engaged couple wrote to each other. They never saw each other again.

The Monk of Love

A tiny six-room flat on the shore of the Lietzensee Lake. An important assignment for the defence economy. A strange thrill in being a crypto-Jew. The authorities, women and friends too, took me for a Dutchman.

A tenor for years, then a set designer and later a circus astrologer, I'm just a boy from a good family with a Portuguese-Dutch heritage on my mother's side. The D'Aspromontes have not been circumcised since 1492. How else can one hide from the Inquisition? We live off a modicum of oral tradition, the laws of faith, which we memorize. Certainly the tradition, like a travelling story, will have changed in the course of time. My hair is firm and blond, a gift from my father's family. The businessman's primary trait is robustness.

I arrange marriages into industry and party circles. With me there is no notice of defects, no returning of goods. Like bank transactions, deals are sealed with a handshake. Decisiveness of this kind can end fatally, as in the case of party comrade Pfeffer. Shot for high treason, but really for his homosexuality, which surprised everyone when it came to light after a 'trial marriage' with a candidate I had procured. That was all over after the parvenu had first simulated passion to get his hands on the young Verena S.'s fortune, then shrunk back at the last minute because he was seized by an insurmountable aversion to the bride. None of this could be kept secret. He had fooled himself about his potential.

The opposite approach is to find special women–the HAPPINESS OPTION, as it were. Here I find foreign partners for powerful men who lack the time to search for themselves. If they had to do so, they would also fear falling prey to a spy or a con artist. How are they meant to tell in a private encounter? They need a specialist whose judgement they trust. 48 from Italy, 1003 from Spain, 7 from Bucharest and 36 from Sofia. Now, during the Greek campaign, I have been able to amass a store of 200 addresses. A quick trip was enough. The practice is that of a seducer, a womanizer, but selfless. I am not speaking for myself but building up my inventory. As Friedrich Schiller describes, there are always the poles of pleasure and hope, and whoever indulges in the one must abstain from the other. So I enter the scene as a 'monk of love', or rather of love brokering. Yes, I have the talent to transfer something that delights me (= is addictive for the soul), in the full consciousness of my imagination, to the client as if he were my best friend. I would never have a nibble myself. A sword (this is my entrepreneurial understanding of service, the honour of my maternal ancestors) lies between the approached woman and the man in whose name I act as a suitor, as if he were a king. Tristan without concubinage.

How I went about it? Everything was won as soon as it was clear I would not be conscripted into the army, for defence-economic reasons, and was instead equipped with travel papers for Greater Germany and the occupied territories. My capital lies in the assistance of the administrative bodies, which are incorruptible (no one in their right mind would attempt to bribe them!) but receptive to 'world' and the idea of an occasional 'adventure without consequences'. To that extent I specialize, here too, in life-deciding favours.

For example, I drive south behind the troops towards Krakow. One castle there threatens to be confiscated. Limited intervention on my part–not through power but through lively speaking. I am invited for tea. I approach officers who are carrying out the confiscation but will be content with quartering. Thus the WORLD enters the zone between the warring fronts; on the very threshold of barbarism, a glimpse of the Reich capital shows itself as soon as I start speaking. Once I am moving in this imaginary direction I can develop all sorts of things. The transition from a woman saved by my elegant intervention to one who trusts me, and finally one who appeals to the real recipient of happiness, the client, and says yes to him too–that is the true object of my artistic work. That is why I always show 'weakness' at the very start; it prepares the ground for the later separation of the matter from me, the messenger, allowing space for the potential partner's 'objective fascination'.

So I bring a Hungarian artist to Paris, for example, where she is introduced to a general from the tank force who owns a liqueur factory in Magdeburg. Inexplicably, unmarried. Word of my friendly turn gets around. This is not some deal with accounting and registration. The hardest part is the SERIOUS MOMENT, the point when the transferee of the interested lady claims her for himself; here I will highlight the business aspect in a tactful fashion. Exchange or duel. That can't be formulated in a direct way at all. And yet I have meanwhile amassed a tidy sum in my Berlin account. I collect such things and move them to numbered accounts in Portugal.

With the advance of the victorious troops–I am deliberately avoiding the words 'of my fatherland' (as it corresponds neither to my maternal nor my paternal lineage, I will say 'of my host country')–it would really be time for my profession to grow from a specialist shop to a department store. That is certainly out of the question for the love brokering I practise. I ask why. It is because the desired (client's perspective) and desiring (procured woman's perspective) goods can't be stored. No part of this process, which has provided me with such advantages as well as a certain professional satisfaction, can be mere stock.

In French provincial towns, places in Denmark and Norway, in national and district capitals, in Smolensk: long waiting lists of candidates. If there had ever been an obligation to accept returns, the possibility of a notice of defects, things would already have been tight in the spring of 1943. Until then, the horizons of the Reich had still been hopeful and intact. The following year, many of the women who had sought to climb socially were disappointed by their brokered unions. But how were they meant to express that? How were they supposed to say, 'I've had enough, I want to go home, where the future victors are already waiting'? That was impossible to formulate in the midst of the Reich. I greatly resented the fact that the course of current events could not be changed, and I had thus caused damage through free trade against my will. And yet Adam Smith explains to us that even a world of devils produces something good, in fact the common good, if there is free trade.

The Sales Talk for Separations

At the matchmaking firm Wilhelmsen & Co., separation counselling costs roughly four times as much as verifiably successful partner brokering. This is because, in their experience, it involves a larger amount of time spent speaking and responding, as well as a more intensive engagement with the facts, than the counsellors require in the case of positive unions.

—You want to separate?

—We're considering it.

—You're both here?

—Yes, we need advice.

—You're looking for reasons to separate?

—We have enough reasons.

—You know that this is an important step in your life?

—Yes, if only we had put it behind us already.

—Please read our terms. I'll leave you alone for a moment. Don't be shocked by the amount; you only have *one* life. Making decisions about it through our expert counselling has to be worth that much to you.

If the partners intending to separate come individually, or if one wants to separate and the other absolutely does not, the counsellor's job becomes difficult. Active assistance, for instance, using a provocateur, is out of the question.

The year 1941 saw a steep rise in separations. The victory in the west and the prospect of a new Europe led career-conscious men to seek separation from the women who represented the past. 'I generally advise separation,' said Erwin Wilhelmsen, the firm's senior partner. 'Out of love for the profession. Isolation paralyses, so does obstruction. People who are open to new commitments–that strikes me as attractive for our branch.'

Reversal of Conscription

They were a group of seven from Tübingen. A new consciousness doesn't arise in a single person; it rises like groundwater, differently in each of those who unite in an action, in the merging group.

Thus, as soon as they arrived in West Berlin, coming from the West, the usual PRIVATIST HORIZONS no longer applied: going out, letting someone talk to you, signs of agreement, successful skin contact, a relationship. Holding on to such a 'mantle of history' and letting it pull you for as long as possible.

Elly was the daughter of a high-ranking judge, the others were daughters of engineers, philologists, doctors, and one, with a rough laugh, was the reserved daughter of a cleaning lady. They felt above associating with comrades from the SDS or fellow students at the FU, who looked for adventures in their free time.

In Dahlem they went to bars frequented by the GIs. The Cold War was in progress, proxy war, world war. The fronts of Vietnam divided civilization. They saw themselves as spies, spokeswomen, also as armed. One must make contact with the enemy. But no enemies could be found in the dance halls. Soon each of the partisans had a GI in tow. They discussed the situation. It was not the one they had planned.

Now in battle, everything is always in flux. The uniformed lovers, sent here, under threat of transfer to the war zones in South East Asia, willing to follow the girls. These were no enemies. One had to recruit them permanently. With the bonds of brotherhood, of love. Love means that by wanting to receive something from another person, one gives that very thing oneself.

Not controlled by other people, no slaves to conscription but, rather, freedom fighters of a politically aware species of humans: that was the role that they expected the GIs, who had come from afar, to take upon themselves. That expectation was in their embraces. Tortuga (nickname), the cleaning lady's daughter, who had not found a suitable 'opponent', guarded their communal flat–all three rooms of it. They sometimes accommodated as many as six copulating couples.

At that time, when desertions were on the increase, US soldiers who failed to appear for duty were immediately pursued by the well-staffed Military Police (MP). They quickly decided to leave the city by air. The whole group, the faithful 13, themselves constituted an agglomeration of intelligence, and were free because they were spontaneous; there was no dogma to prevent them from empathizing with the logic and prosecuting skills of the military apparatus. The girls' own country was shackled, a protectorate of the others, incapable of protecting its citizens or granting hospitality to the men these daughters had chosen.

And so they reached Sweden. After landing in Stockholm they quickly travelled north, close to the Lapp border. They took up residence there, divided between two log cabins; the immigration authorities took them for tourists.

What to do? That part of the relationship which has remained privatist loses its validity without the seriousness of imminent loss or the surprise of acquaintance; everyday life is marked by the constant accessibility of the other and uniform natural surroundings. Unease among the solidarity group as to whether they made the right choice in the dance halls of Dahlem. It was a very old, scheming fire that they tended in their Swedish isolation.

On the other hand, they were not lonely. It was not only they, the *twelve plus one*, who were gathered; they sensed that they were operating at a particular historical moment on the legal side of civilization, of a multitudinous humanity. They were sustaining something like a collective farm of resistance. They produced successful escape. Every day, they told themselves, we are taking away a modicum of the US intruder's defensive power and thus giving the comrades in Vietnam, whom we don't know, but with whom we want to empathize, a possibly decisive military advantage. For even the simple work of clearing our boys and fighters, who would surely be no match for the revolutionary cadres, out of the way, must be an obstacle for the Vietnamese on their way to victory. As Tortuga remained alone, and did all the work except for the work of love, the group debated whether they should divert some of their abundance (six impatient boys) to provide a 'service' for her. But that would have created the impression that the love practised here in the cabins was a form of 'payment', it would be an instrumental use of it, and that is exactly what love should not be. They would have liked to share but they could not justify it.

As the weeks passed, the youthful group forced the world power USA to send an embarrassing enquiry to the Swedish government asking whether a group of female students in male company had entered the country; they requested extradition of the draft dodgers, as this was a crime according to the extradition treaty.

The USA had to admit to a neutral public that they were incapable of making their own people fight, owing to the imperialistic nature of these battles. The Swedish government published the request and refused it.

The young people saw the autumn leaves dwindling around them. They prepared for winter. Their cash supply was running out. Two of them visited the embassy of the People's Republic of China in the Swedish capital to request a loan. They got as far as the First Secretary, who agreed to listen to a political, internationalist exposition. But he was only willing to reach an agreement as long as the People's Republic itself was not involved as an instigator if the six GIs sought asylum at the embassy and this were announced at a press conference. This too would have required the consent of the Swedish Foreign Office, or at least a statement of disinterest.

That was not the language of revolution. Nor were the girls' lovers willing to place themselves at the disposal of a foreign country in public. They were not turncoats. As it turned out, they were barely politically available at all. It was FEAR OF THE FUTURE and RASHNESS that had brought them into the conspiracy of the seven partisans. The group's CONSCIOUSNESS, once so active in West Berlin, withered away under the threat of winter.

In December the group crossed the Norwegian border. In groups of two, three and four, already internally distracted and in some cases quarrelling, they hired themselves out as temporary workers on ferries. And so they travelled, more or less penniless, via Copenhagen and Hamburg, the students to their home towns and the GIs into the custody of the military police in Bremen; they were sent lawyers from the USA. The military police in Bremen, in competition with their boastful colleagues from West Berlin, who were acting like the frontline troops, brought about a mild punishment on parole if they waived their right to appeal. The adventures were sent to a Vietnamese district capital for office service. Unjustified doubts about the power of love.

Children of Love

1
Walter Benjamin's Favourite Film

The American film *LONESOME* (1928) by Pál Eötvös features a schematic depiction of A MAN, A WOMAN and THE CROWD. In fact, the wave of people, transported by special bus companies, accompanied by brass bands and in good cheer, are heading for the expansive amusement machine on the ocean, the fun park at Coney Island, which has existed since the turn of the century.

The time on the clock is in the afternoon. Nudism at the beach. One-piece bathing suits. The camera focuses on parts of the arms, the neck, the thighs. The film *Lonesome* shows trodden-down sand. Movement of a thousand feet to the water, out of the water. This is where the WORKER and the TELEPHONIST have ended up. They are unaware that they live next door to each other. But they recognized each other on the drive there by coincidence. He followed her. The dialogue in the film shows the PROCESS OF MUTUAL DISARMAMENT. This process is necessary for the IMPROBABLE ACHIEVEMENT OF CREATING INTIMACY (Niklas Luhmann). This forms the core of novels and plays. First of all, both flaunt their background and personal value. 'I have an appointment at the Ritz at five,' says Jim, the worker. Mary, the telephonist, can hardly match that. LOVE DREAMS OF ITS ABSOLUTE POWER.[15]

This is answered by the reaction of actual conditions. Night falls. The crowd has left the beach. The two of them, wearing their one-piece bathing suits, realize that they are cold. They admit their professions to each other. But LOVE is not in the air yet, that is a lofty programme. *Let's have fun,* says Mary, the tender of lambs. She considers it impossible to decide what feelings one person senses coming from another without concrete sexual intercourse. Perhaps something that one can call love will crystallize. What would that be? Something resilient.

Only an observer could judge what the two feel for each other, how robust and resilient these feelings are.

15 Clausewitz, *On War*, Chapter 1.

The couple goes to the attractions. The amusement machine of Coney Island has little precision; it is mostly thrusting power. The machine serves diversion, not concentrated work on a product. In that sense, Coney Island as machinery ('concentration of variety') would be completely unusable in a factory; as an apparatus, it even provokes accidents.

2
The Fortune-Teller as a Utopian

The voice of the fortune-teller: This very day you will meet a woman with brown hair and you will stay together until life has been fulfilled.

The fortune teller, an automaton, is made of iron. The enclosure of its jaws opens and closes, releasing sounds fed into it by a phonograph. A glossy blue eye opens and closes, white hair, furrows on the forehead that move mechanically. SERIOUSNESS. The automaton's statement seems to fit Mary. The two of them hold hands.

3
The Roller Coaster

On the roller coaster they get 'placed', that is, assigned to different cars. Their partners in the two-seaters are as randomly distributed as they are. They try to communicate across the distance using hand signs. The terrors of the depths. Since 1902, successive generations of engineers have equipped this roller coaster with a new effect each year. This has strained the original balance of the design. On this day, the machinery is under MAXIMUM STRESS. The wheels on one of the cars going around the sharp bends start glowing, the machinery catches fire, an industrial accident, but no one sees to it that the adventurous leisure ride is stopped. People could die.[16]

Pál Eötvös only directed this one feature film, a jewel of modernity. Later, he made ethnographic documentaries in Thailand and Madagascar. The Hungarian was interested in people, in sociology. Here, in his masterpiece (Walter Benjamin's favourite film), he describes the nocturnal hours experienced by the two happiness specialists. The accident on the big dipper has separated them, there is a thunderstorm over the fun park. Wet from the rain, the two of them return separately to their apartments, their residential containers. Although they are so close together (the viewer can see this), they would have remained alone were it not for music. The hit song 'Always I Will Love You' was made into a record. This was also the song played by the brass bands that accompanied the vehicles which brought the two of them (and the crowd of visitors) to Coney Island. Each of their apartments contains a record player. They also both own the record with the hit song. They find it comforting to listen to this song again. The most precious thing in humans, writes the director Eötvös, is longing. If one could pile it up like money in a bank account, there would be billionaires of the search for happiness.

16 Death because of 'necessary false consciousness'. Death because of a many-voiced search for leisure.

4

A Dream Already Given Up for Lost / Usefulness

Two Robinsons in the city of New York, what luck that I can defend the square space I inhabit against anyone one of the millions in the crowd. Otherwise I couldn't say what I like. Now Mary from next door hears the song ALWAYS, because I'll always love you, I'm determined and close to you at all times, even when you're 64, it's about robustness and usefulness; she hears the message from the little room next door. She spiritedly opens the unlocked door of the neighbouring flat and sees Jim, whom she has already given up for lost.

And so, in spite of all bitterness, the objectively unsuitable nature of the amusement machinery, the uncertainty of the two protagonists in all questions of how to arrange their lives happily (the difficult task of transferring the extremely advanced skill with which Mary operates telephones and Jim caresses machine tools to a relationship), they did practise CONCRETE FUN.[17] The events continued until Monday morning. Then the professional work of 1928 began once more. But the two were looking forward mischievously to trying some more in the evening.

---

17 Sexual intercourse.

5

Jim and Mary

FIGURE 47. Mary and Jim in one-piece bathing suits at the Atlantic beach in Coney Island. Night falls. The same as for Tristan and Isolde. Couples rarely fall in love at night, when they are alone. One has to be in company (if need be, the company of the crowd trampling over the beach all afternoon) to fall in love, that is, to adapt one's weaknesses to all the others. The moment that follows then, just the two of us are left, gains its robust stasis from the earlier presence of the others. In that sense, says the ergonomist Dietmar Knoche, love is a social product, based on the happy coincidence of two people lowering their defences and swimming in the other's river at the same time. Would you consider that an improbable event? Knoche answers: Always improbable and newly improbable every time.

6
Work / Work on Happiness

One can no longer imagine a specialized form of work like that of a telephonist in 1928. Speed and precision of SWITCHING CONNECTIONS would have caused a positive change of fortune for the rebels in the early evening of 20 July 1944, provided that other forces of modernity, for example, the vehicles of the tank academy near Potsdam, had shown the same professionalism.

INTERLOCKING COOPERATION (human, machine, group, interconnected, the maximum nerve tension at the intersection of movements): such work produces an intermediate being, invisible like the cuts in a film. While humans are still going around, falling back on their privacy, that is, their state from 400 years ago, at weekends, a virtual life form has come about between them that points into the future and urges towards a life of its own. The INTERSUBJECTIVE ELEMENTARY THEORY OF WORK was first discovered in the autumn of 1928.[18]

---

18 The ergonomist D. Knoche interprets this being using the concept of 'spiritualization'. It reveals itself at large sporting events, he states, in the fact that a form of cloud almost seizes the spectators at the climax of the presentation, not the same as the cloud of sweat being emitted, and creates the phenomenon of the 'unforgettable'. He is contradicted by the labour scientist Detlevson, who refers to Knoche's vision as 'ghostly'. In fact, engineers from Speer's Armament Staff observed several 'ghost appearances' between 1943 and 1945, sudden, improbable multiplications of propulsion in the work process, which support Knoche's analysis. Thus, in April 1945, 7,800 jet fighters were built inexplicably, in the absence of any demand plan, material or workforce. Not even the location

When such work has ended, the people of 1928 do not immediately know how to deal with a reality not equipped with devices, for example, with their desire, with unorganized time. They will need days to adjust to the MACHINES OF REAL LIFE. They would have to learn anew through them, and they would only do that if they could maintain the invisible rhythms of working days in their homes and private hiding places until they were trained for the processes of FREEDOM. They must derive this beat from the 'melody of work', which is now difficult to hear under the pressure of Black Friday. One learns that in groups. Courses are no use; one can't 'learn' it, as one needs to have the ideas of the others in oneself.

Thus the phase of exhaustion is followed by borrowing, through connection to the Saturday radio programme in New York. The CHILDREN OF LIFE are familiar with that, it enlivens the compass of inertia: the lyrics to the hit songs that refer to gaining happiness, to helpful sadness.

In 2003, this zone of New York would be a slum. In 1928, it consists of coveted flats, small boxes of freedom placed next to each other. This itself (freedom) is presumed to be outside, necessitating a longer trip; the next group of young men and women arranges to meet up and drive to Coney Island on Saturday morning. Anyone watching them has an idea of what happiness is. It is easiest to detect happiness when it happens to other people.

---

of production could be ascertained afterwards. And yet the aircraft stood there, albeit useless without crews.

The Failed Divorce

At the time of the economic miracle, a married couple by the name of Pfeiffer, who had children (they had also grown a business together, then descended into hellish quarrelling), were planning their divorce. They took the country road from a village south of the Luneburg Heath in the direction of Uelzen. After living together for twelve years. They got into their shared car for the last time (or so they thought). They wanted to reach the district court on time. It was Wednesday morning, late summer weather.

That week, the forests in this stretch of land had been ravaged by a firestorm. Fire-fighting planes came over from Italy. Federal assistance was requested. The directors of the rural districts around the Luneburg Heath (all of them bearers of the Knight's Cross of the Iron Cross from the Second World War) led the fire-fighting squads to the edge of the blaze. Roads were closed off in a wide radius.

The Pfeiffers could already see the tower of smoke clouds above the forests towards the north. They were told to turn around. They tried persistently to reach their separation destination via forest roads; and so they started talking. By evening it was clear that it would be impossible to get through the front. They missed their appointment at the district court.

–The devil really put a spanner in the works for the Pfeiffers!

–If it was the devil that burnt the forests.

—One could call it a fire of hell. Are there any known cases in which the devil contributes to reconciliation?

—Not much is known about his good deeds.

The fires were almost impossible to extinguish in the dry late summer. An army tank brigade from Hanover cleared a 500-metre swathe of forest that had not yet been reached by the flames. Bulldozers hastily moved the tree trunks aside. But the fire had already overcome the blockade by pushing ahead with flying sparks, and over roots and moss on the dry ground. Even for the devil, said Reverend Eisenhardt, an expert on the Adversary, that was too much effort just for the sake of keeping the Pfeiffers together.

In the spring they a reconciliatory child. Their business flourished until 1991. The Pfeiffers stayed together. From that point on, the children laughed at them whenever they argued.

Private Security Company

'I say, *My eyes.* You say, *Look for Him.*
I say, *My gut.* You say, *Tear it open.*

I say, *My heart.* You ask, *What's inside*?
I say, *My longing.* You say, *That's all you need.*'

They had now been living together for 21 years. Three times the seventh year. They had not been apart for a single day. After being forced to give up a bike shop and then a pub, they had bought an X-ray machine, metal detectors, a security gate and a conveyor belt (everything the way it is at airport security checkpoints, only more portable) and founded a private ENTRANCE SCREENING COMPANY. That way they could continue to spend the day together. When they opened the new business they hadn't known that they could make a fortune in this line of work (they had paid back the loan for the acquisition costs). Current events worked in their favour. They could choose what offer from a five-star hotel or a highly confidential conference to accept. No one carrying a weapon or explosives escaped their attention.

Brief glances, barely perceptible to outsiders. Confirmations that the interplay of machine and human gave an accurate picture of the situation. They had perfected their skills as security experts because they liked looking at each other and appreciated any reason for one of those brief glances. They often touched each other with their sleeves. There was a draught at the hotel entrance. She was wrapped up in ski clothes, he was wearing a quilted coat. The draught made the guests who were waiting to be searched nervous; a favourable climate for the check. People who have to take off their coats and suit jackets in a draught and put them in a basket do not behave arrogantly. In a fixed rhythm: removal of metal items and outer wear, passage through the security gate, body search with a metal detector, then final check and admission to the interior. One of the two always had their eyes on the subject (hence the brevity of their glances at each other). It was an example of 'interlocking work', a rhythmic activity.

One day an armed man jumped at the male partner in the security team after a failed attempt to enter. In the same moment as the gate's alarm signal went through the Grand Hotel, bodyguards from the main hall moved to assist the couple. The armed man was holding a firearm in his first and simultaneously trying to stab with a knife. Wilma threw himself across the conveyor belt and blocked his path. Everyone fell down. Seconds later the bodyguards were there. The attacker was taken away in handcuffs.

Without Wilma's intervention it would have been too late. She intervened because she loved Fred. His neck had been in the corner of her eye while her gaze moved towards the next 'guest'. It was unthinkable for her to give Fred up. At the moment of her rapid, actually 'untrained' forward movement, the open blade had been a mere 40 centimetre from Fred's carotid artery.

She Wanted at Least to Be Treated with the Same Care One Shows Towards Objects

I could just as well have gone to work at three in the morning. My husband almost died that night. If there had been a tram I would have gone to work. He senses storms. It was a high-altitude storm. The pain moves down to here (she indicates the small of her back). All windows and doors open because he can't get any air. I would have gone to work, at three in the morning, I'm freezing in bed when all the windows are open, and he's lying next to me and can't breathe. I can't put on my coat in bed and get under the sheets, then I'll sweat, because I can't sleep when he's not getting any air, even though there's too much of it.

She washed the cups and plates. One couldn't tell that this tall woman hadn't slept. She grinned as she told how when she went to work on Friday the previous week, she had found the door ajar at the establishment she is responsible for cleaning. Anyone could have walked in and taken away the dishes, the freshly washed towels. But she locked up when she left, then called from home during the day to check if anyone was home. No one answered.

She assumed that the manager of the business she was cleaning for had left the door open while drunk, then been driven by his urges to buy cigarettes and met someone on the way. So the door stood open during the night. She asked a man from the music publisher one floor higher to keep guard in front of the door for a moment, while she entered the unprotected flat–in case someone was hiding inside. But it was simply a case of a door that is normally meant to be locked being left open, no one was there, so she did the dishes just as she did on other days and locked everything carefully.

The marital beds at home are set up the way they always have been. If her husband can't breathe at night, this is a nonsensical arrangement. It would be nice, she reflects, realistically speaking, if one of us goes to sleep or lies awake and can't breathe, in pain because of a high-altitude storm that *he* feels but the other doesn't, and he doesn't wake up the next morning. She sees it and now arranges everything in the right way, alerts her relatives, the fire service, the undertaker, the doctor, tidies up, etc.

Then she could just as well have slept peacefully in a different room or on the couch in the kitchen, then acknowledged the result–which is ultimately inevitable–in the morning, she would have called her work and said, I'll be a bit late today. Instead she crawls into her conjugal bed in the evening–one can't wear anything but a nightgown–and can breathe each breath with him, the strain of his lung movements. It is as if he wanted to say something to her with this rattling breath, this gasping. But she doesn't understand such utterances. If she only needed to look at him, to keep her head fixed in his direction so that she couldn't take her eyes off him for twelve hours, she would still be able to close her them (and would probably fall asleep in a tense state at some point). Or the picture, which would always be the same, would fade until it was like not seeing anything. Wouldn't do anything but wouldn't be cold either because the doors and windows would be closed. All that is impossible because the ears don't adjust the way the eyes do. She puts one ear firmly on the pillow so as not to hear anything, but the other one stays open and its perception is amplified. But if she stuffed it with an earplug she would be restless, because she feels the rustling of the bedcovers from the trembling of both beds when he turns, and then she would worry because she couldn't hear anything, that is, she would lose the little bit of oversight she has in a situation whose end, after all, is preordained.

But one mustn't accelerate anything, even if the other person wants that, that is, says they would have liked to go to sleep the previous night. Surely that's not meant literally. Perhaps it's the wish for her to accelerate. But accelerate what, and how would she go about it? She can't ask the doctor for that. He doesn't do favours. But maybe it's not her husband's wish, maybe it's an attempt to put her to the test, to see if she'll finally show homicidal intent, whether, after hiding it for 37 years, she'll reveal her murderous indifference now. She won't do that. But she thinks he talks to her about that when he rattles and tosses about ('turns around like a roast chicken on a spit'). And she can't evade him, that's the idea of putting the beds next to each other. Because it's mostly the skin or one's sense of balance that registers the other person's quiet shifting, breathing and rummaging.

It's for convenience in marital intercourse that the beds have to be put next to each other like that. It was always an excess of immediate accessibility, especially as there was never such regular intercourse. He could have reached her in the kitchen too for that purpose. Now, close to death, the convenience of the beds is taking its toll, because she has shared for over two years in every twitch of his monologue, whose outcome can only be death. In that sense, marital intercourse has taken on a different character but is still an obstacle to sleep. She can't be alone, except when she has an opportunity to go to work. There she can speak and answer. She can't do that at night. She avoids rustling or turning the other way in order not to wake her husband (in the rare event that he does manage to sleep for a few seconds).

She doesn't want to get involved in this conversation either, she refuses. Instead, she gets some mineral water, because he has to be kept moist, he is demanding a drink because he keeps his mouth open when he groans. She has a suspicion that he's deceiving her while she lies next to him, that underneath the bed-shaking rumbles, which he perhaps causes automatically after so many years of the same routine, he's actually asleep. Everyone has to sleep at some point. Or maybe he's doing that during her working hours, to gather the strength he needs for besieging her at night. She vacillates, she doesn't want to be unfair; on the other hand, **she wants at least to be treated with the same care as an ordinary thing.** One wouldn't force that into a rack like this marital bed.

For example, she wouldn't leave an iron kettle standing in the snow all winter because it would get rusty in spring. So she inwardly reproaches her companion in the adjacent bed but doesn't say anything. Strictly speaking, the reproaches aren't about him not dying quickly enough, more the fact that he doesn't say something which would make it possible to move the beds apart. Even shifting apart like that after 37 years, three or four metres towards the free wall (then the cupboard between the beds) would seem like paradise for her, a reward. But because she never got a reward, and no longer expects any, there's no real sense of reciprocation; she doesn't really want to answer at all any more, just keeps silent and lies awake.

The Flowers of Good

One can see how practical-minded she is from the fact that the children wore plastic bags on their heads because of the rain, fastened to their forehead, temples and back of the head with elastic bands. She trotted along the beach with all four of her daughters, who were aged four-and-a-half, six, seven and eight. Every day they walked up and down the streets of Cannes with an assortment of flowers wrapped in plastic foil; buying them for 20 cents and selling them for 10 francs, each of the four girls shifted about

30 flowers on a working day. That made 1,176 francs per day, which their mother took and kept available for Bruno.

She was lucky enough to have found a man who knew how to exploit her and was consistent and reliable in that respect.

Just now the five of them are walking along the promenade. After the day's work they have their photos taken. One daughter in front of her, two on the left, the eldest on the right. They're all holding plastic flowers, for tomorrow.

The Seat of the Soul

An agricultural economist from the region to the west of Stravropol who continued her studies at the Humboldt University (she covered her expenses by working at a bar in Wedding) insisted that love, as an object of work for civilized humans, does not have its seat inside each individual but, rather, constitutes the network that inevitably ensues between people who have love relationships with each other. This network is always richer than the intentions harboured by two people who say they love each other. After all, there is also love for one's parents, love for the horizons of hope or affection for familiar places. Indeed, the intercepted gaze of a passer-by can even supply a boost, and the other person does not even need to share or know that.[19]

---

19 Ljuba W. cannot cover her living and study expenses with her skills as an agricultural economist but only by offering up her body. Although she makes the same fee for giving a customer emotional counselling or providing a journalist from her professional field

In the case of this CREATURE CALLED LOVE, like an animal harnessed to two lovers, one or both (or third parties as matchmakers and friends) can work on it in substance-changing ways. The same, claims Ljuba W., is not true of the inwardly directed *solitary activity* of lovers. Ljuba compares this more contemplative form of activity (using the Russian term 'love work') with the WORKSHOP OF AN ALCHEMIST. She describes it as pre-industrial. As if stores of poisons and healing potions were being collected. But would the other person drink any? Would they even accept the offer?

Thus two people, Ljuba writes, could produce inwardness alongside each other for a lifetime without any alterations to the substance of their relationship (repair, adaptation, changes in state of matter). In that sense, Ljuba claims, hermitdom in love offers no civilizatory chances.

NORMA, a Concentration of Magnanimity

You words, come, follow me!
on, to no end.

Ingeborg Bachmann

1
Theme

In a world of warriors (the war gods of the Romans and the Gauls are the same), a priestess known for her chastity initiated a reform that reintroduced lost matriarchal rituals ascribed to the moon goddess Irminsul into worship. Simply put, the underlying idea was peace.

---

exclusive information in Wedding. Such contract work always involves two-hour sessions.

But this revolutionary is no 'new human', nor is she chaste, but harbours an erotic secret (described elaborately in the spirit of the nineteenth century). Shortly before a (possible) reconciliation, there is a tragic chain of events. To prevent everyone from being annihilated in a massacre, Norma sacrifices herself. Thus she regains the esteem of Pollione, who expresses this by giving his own life.

2
Anna Viebrock's Stage Set

The stage designer Anna Viebrock created an effect of depth by staggering the stage as a church nave, somewhat like a Huguenot temple. In front of the grating marking off the stage's foreground, as if the Holy of Holies were located towards the audience, stands the protagonist: Norma. The druid turns her back on them. Why does she not turn her gaze towards them, using her eyes to control them like an animal-tamer? Does she trust them? She has no reason to do so. She breaks with religious assumptions concerning the cruelty of the gods, war and military laws. Such prophetesses have always been murdered.

It is important to Norma to pull these believers forwards. But while she was singing the aria CASTA DIVA, the moonlight entered the rear window of the stage area as if from the depths of a magic lantern, supporting the priestess. The light of former times, only effective in the absence of the sun.[20]

---

20 In the periods of human history, the time of lunar humanity preceded the races of the sun. But the most advanced elements of the earlier era, according to Rudolf Steiner, can be superior to the

One speaks of a battle between matriarchy and the rule of men, Anna Viebrock comments, long before the brothers conspire and butcher their father, which is followed by the brotherly battle. But none of this, the stage designer continues, took place completely, so it could have been ended. Natural disasters intervened (collision with a comet, earthquakes, floods, plague). People fled. In the exodus the murderous group dispersed; it made a new beginning that knew how to deal with mixtures, and it survived mixture. So it is a seemingly never-ending battle.

Who is speaking? Who can say 'I'? Rarely the I, the self. If it keeps quiet, it might hear echoes that speak. Only they themselves know how they fit together. The GREAT DISPERSAL is listening. That was how Heiner Müller described it. Anyone who can read this dispersal hears the utterance of 'I', polyglot, like a chorus. And the dreams, the hope? They do not listen.

—And you express that in your stage set?

—Yes, that's my means of expression.

3
A Victory of Friendship

The two astute women, who have only just learnt that they love the same man, are confused.

---

undeveloped elements of the more developed era. In this respect, *Norma* is the heroic, intelligent form of regression, a necessary REARGUARD OF PROGRESS (Heiner Müller). The Romans, until Constantine, were warriors of the sun.

'I love him; . . . yet now my heart
feels only *friendship*'

Adalgisa is referring to her friendship with the druid Norma, whom the Roman left for her sake.

The only thing that can help now is for her friend to speak to the perpetrator in public. Adalgisa leaves for the Roman camp.

She explains to the commander how mistaken he is in his love for her, Adalgisa. How much more favourable, more splendid is Norma's character! How could he turn away such a valuable example of humanity? And thus destroy it?

The commander, recalling enjoyable hours with Adalgisa (yes, he finds her rhetorical performance brilliant, and is sexually aroused by the thought of a possible aftermath), remains uninterested in Norma. He finds the seriousness of her feelings tiresome. He refuses to make any concessions. As if a man's erotic desire could be aroused by the greater *virtue* of a woman!

Treacherous Roman! Adalgisa, who certainly still loves him, moved by the bond with her friend and transported by her own passionate elan of friendship, creeps back along a dark path to the Gaulish camp. And offers herself up to the priests. She is doomed to die.

4
Verdun, the Great Trading Centre for Slaves

'Yes, she weeps
What hope does she have now?
Her pleas will not be heard!'

Norma, *Act 2, final chorus*

Shortly before his death, Heiner Müller was invited by the Verdun City Theatre to visit this former Gaulish spot; he was to put on one of his plays there the following year, and the idea was for him to familiarize himself with the specifics of the theatre's location before doing so.[21] After visiting the city's war cemetery, and after being criticized for public comments about his impressions, he fell out with the city administration, was disinvited and left.

A pile of mud, Müller noted on a beer mat, is identical to itself for 3,000 years in the river landscape of Verdun. The disturbance of this soil by artillery and its superficial cultivation through agriculture, urban construction and road construction does not significantly change the molecules by European standards.

Between 782 and 804 CE, this place was the great trading centre for slaves. A slave, captured in war and brought here from the Germanic countries, could find happiness if the *latifundium* [landed estate] that bought him was administered in a friendly manner and he found a female slave who was suitable for him. His female descendants—always assuming that the start and further progress were favourable—would have the chance to enchant a Frankish warrior and become mistresses themselves.

From the perspective of the CONFEDERATE PROMISES OF HAPPINESS in the seventh century, it is a coincidence that the general staff of 1916 chose, of all places, the heights and surfaces of this earth zone, now redefined as

---

21 Stoic that he was, he liked to accept projects concerning the relatively distant future, aware of his terminal illness.

a fortress, for the project of TAKING BLOOD SAMPLES. This is documented by museums, burial sites and commemorative plaques. How quickly does a landscape heal?

Heiner Müller was questioned in Verdun:

–You referred to the sacred places of the dead, the monuments and chapels at the cemeteries of Verdun, as 'kitschy': as battle kitsch.

–One can at least say that they don't express the way people were shooting at one another here in 1916.

–What distinguishes slaves from entrenched soldiers who are kept under fire by their orders?

–A great deal. Slaves have some hope of good treatment.

–The entrenched soldiers don't have any hope?

–Not really. Because if they return, there is nothing that compares to the experience of being exposed to a hail of grenades; they can only erase the memory.

–Whom does one call a slave?

–A person or workforce that's the property of another.

–Whose property were the soldiers of 1916? The wounded? The shattered?

–On the German side they were the property of the Reich. On the French side, the property of the republic.

–In that sense, they were slaves too?

–No. Each was in possession of an independent will that wanted to leave the battlefield at all costs. A slave wasn't entitled to such an independent will.

–Legally or genuinely?

–I can't put myself in the shoes of a slave from 602 CE.

–And in some of the character armour of 1916 lying here, outside Verdun?

–I can't do that either.

5
Battle at the Threshold of the Self

'The heart is the last dimension of intelligence.'

Marcel Proust (*on Baron Charlus*)

Maestro Reynaldo Hahn was an excellent entertainer. 'The heart cheats the intellect.' Lines like this wander through Hahn's head as earworms for entire mornings, yet he finds no opportunity to work them into the day's banter. Of Marcel Proust's closest friends, Reynaldo Hahn was the only one suitable for public office. He was a critic at *Le Figaro* and General Manager of the Théâtre de Casino in Cannes. He outlived Proust and continued his conversations in the style of the clique.

After the liberation of Paris in 1944 he was considered politically untainted, and thus appointed as Artistic Director of the opera there in 1945. Sixteen premieres had to be organized. The options included Massenet (*Werther*), Cherubini (*Medea*), Saint-Saëns, Berlioz (*Les Troyens*) and Bellini (*Norma*). An attractive young director thought it a good idea to dress Norma, the Gaulish protagonist, as Joan of Arc and produce an opera about revolution. Hahn magnanimously allowed this tastelessness.

—Mr Artistic Director, you are politically independent.

—Politically independent.

—And you are homosexual?

—Whatever that means. It doesn't mean I have leprosy.

—Now, in your production of *Norma*, you are vehemently standing up for women?

—For a sacrificed woman.

—The production creates a strong affection for these Gaulish women.

—That was why we chose this dramatically effective piece. Norma appears dressed as the Maid of Orleans.

—Doesn't the tastelessness of that scare you?

—It's a little too direct. But you should always expect homoerotic men to revere women.

—Back to the opera. While Norma dies (which is already set up during Pollione's and Norma's duet in your production), you have banners carried to the front of the stage with words that have feminine gender in French: *la* bataille, *la* nation, *la* guerre. Are you making fun of martial virtues being ascribed to the female?

—Am I martial?

—What is martial?

—Things that make us forget the battle of the sexes.

—So you think that war is superficial?

—That's dangerous enough.

Baron Charlus, who still belonged to the clan in 1916, was drawn by his heart (which ruled over his incisive mind like a tyrant) to the young soldiers who loitered at Montparnasse station in the second year of the war. They had to be martial good-for-nothings, reproductions of the violence of battle. The desire of this high-ranking aristocrat went so far that they subjugated him in the toilets. He wanted to be their victim in the guise of the enemies running through France in 1916: he approached them as 'Madame Boche', a Prussian dame (whom he did not resemble in the least). The soldiers, who were not remotely at his intellectual level and were looking for an adventure with a young traveller of prostitute before their leave was over, mocked the now-monstrous owner of that heart. They (mistakenly) viewed war not as a physical state of sexual life but as a burden that threatened them.

At the premiere of *Norma* at the Palais Garnier, there was a danger that the corpulent singer in the title role, who was also fitted out as a freedom fighter, would look ridiculous when the embraced the enemy commander in the opera's final act. The audience still remembered her as Brünnhilde. And now she was supposed to lead her beloved enemy to a sacrificial death as a Celtic turncoat. Reynaldo Hahn had prepared a replacement piece in case of a complete fiasco. GOD BE WITH US, a play by René Berton (from 1928): during the First World War, French soldiers gain control of a bunker zone where fugitive Germans had been defending themselves. The moment the French enter the bunker, a German projectile buries the entrance with rubble. A single German soldier, Hermann, is left behind. He tries to dig his way out of the ruinous cave; he knows there is a time bomb hidden in it. As a patriot, he refuses to tell the intruders, his enemies,

FIGURE 48. Hahn (centre) at the front in Verdun, 1916.

where the mine is located. The French captain, whose civilian profession is that of professor of philosophy, like Hermann, convinces him to defuse the bomb. In the meantime, a pioneer unit of the French Army has dug through the blocked entrance of the bunker. Hermann is the first to run outside. He is hit by a German projectile; he returns to the bunker with his face destroyed. He calls out 'God be with us' and dies.

Reynaldo Hahn wanted to accompany the scenes of this play with the melodies from Bellini's opera; that was conceivable if one left out the words and the singing. With the audience in a light-hearted mood in the summer of 1945, however, the premiere of *Norma* (as well as the subsequent repertoire) was a great success. There was no need for the backup play.

6
Mysterious Gaul

Growth of love from slavery and conquest. It was not the Roman women or the highbred wives of the Gauls administering the country seats that fascinated the Franks when they occupied the country; it was the slave girls on the rural estates. What the slaves had in common with the conquerors was the fact that such a union meant the start of a new life.[22]

Only later did the new couples dispossess the old owners. Property joined intimacy.[23]

Who was the subjugated? The warrior? The slave girl? It became impossible to untangle. But some say that the NEW UNIONS described here are what make the difference between a barbarian country and France.

A Case of Long-Distance Love

> 'The imagination is inflamed precisely by women who lack imagination.'
>
> *T. W. Adorno,* Minima Moralia

---

22 They occupied large parts of Gaul. They were seen as conquerors. They did not have better weapons or better reasons to occupy the land than the Gaulish inhabitants, the old families; they simply met no resistance. Only a year later, or three years previously, the coup would not have succeeded.

23 This, writes Jules Michelet, was the birth of feudalism ('I serve you because you serve me'), which was the origin of the only basic form of love invented in Europe.

We know of Marcel Proust that he 'dragged his body behind him like a St Bernard'. His vessels and juices were often ill-attuned. In the late afternoon, Proust was still unsure whether he should attend the soirée. He was also very afraid of being bored, of encountering people whom he did not want to listen to and who would not to listen to him.

But then, having reached a decision in a few minutes, he had his servants dress him and appeared at the soirée, and around midnight, a group of aristocrats and newspaper people who were allowed there gathered around him; he was excited. In the park, on the way to the pavilions, the tables and buffets, with their emanating odours, were set up like a parade. All present were dressed in furs to protect them from the November air, and grog was served.

Proust, in a hibernal mood and enthused by some chance reading that morning–alert interest was the only thing that could suppress his autumnal cough–had surprised his Parisian audience by taking up the subject of Friedrich Schiller, who was unknown to the majority of the guests. He could read the success of his performance in the face of the Princess of Parma, like a display board registering the intensity and register of the sound. The princess had been attentive for 17 seconds, which gave him hope of recapturing her interest. And so Proust, with no interruption from anyone present, embarked on a reinterpretation of Schiller's topics.

The deeds of William Tell came from the 'mouth of hell'. A hunter by profession, not a craftsman or a farmer like the other Swiss men, Tell proved to be an adventurer, a mystical hunter who fired the deadly shot at the governor, an alleged tyrant, like a shot at an especially fine deer. He was not interested in making peace, in the Rütli oath or in being sociable; he was interested in accurate marksmanship. A shot was simply older than young nobility, and Gessler, the provincial governor, had not achieved anything except nobility. *Don Carlos* was entirely bizarre and in need of rewriting. How ridiculous were the Marquis de Posa's words to the king. He was a 'representative of the human race'. By whose authority could someone assume that role? The king's jealousy of the heir to the throne, the obsession of Princess Eboli, who loved this heir, the affection of Queen Elizabeth for Don Carlos, to whom she had once been promised. What a fabulous quartet of explosive attractions! This is enough to kill Don Carlos. It would also have been enough to save him. How quickly can a 250-page play lasting eight hours be rewritten and translated into French so that it can still be a success in the winter season?

Having talked himself into a frenzy, Proust was half inclined to mockery and half sunk in his chair; in these hours he escaped the body that tried to dominate him, that showed obedience to him like an animal whose owner is responsible for it, and thus reined him in.

As mentioned earlier, the Princess of Parma had listened to him for 17 seconds; then she turned her attention towards new impressions. The effect of her attention on Proust lasted aeons.

Monsieur Octave, a relative of the Verdurins, had listened to Proust's extemporization. He lived with Rachel, St

Loup's mistress, and was a marriage impostor and journalist. He was in telephone contact with *Le Figaro*, and managed to publish the occasional article–if some other contribution was cancelled–despite never meeting with any of the newspaper's editors. He had difficulties reproducing what the soliloquizing genius had said about Schiller; he had only deduced the value of his words from the faces of the listeners. Those listeners, all of them aristocrats, had not remembered anything. But they had been trained over centuries to transform their momentary interest into facial expression and thus, even after being dethroned by the French Revolution, to grant permission to continue speaking and even soliloquize excessively.

I am the representative of humanity, formulated Monsieur Octave the following morning. The statement had none of the wit that had made the Marquis de Norpois laugh out loud.[24] Had Marcel Proust really claimed that the last scene of *Nathan the Wise* (Proust mistakenly ascribed the play to Schiller) should be performed first? In this

24 Octave mentioned in this context that Friedrich Schiller was an honorary citizen of the French Revolution. On the other hand, he claimed, the group of aristocrats to whom Marcel Proust spoke had erased the emancipatory emphases. Proust argued that Schiller's plays attained their true power when one left out the word 'freedom'. But Proust had said how confidently the emotional energy of Don Carlos and the Marquis de Posa point towards each other, how ridiculous it appears in a love affair if one of the partners says, I loved you until now, but now I love freedom and must leave you. One can say this in a love affair if one stays concrete and exchanges one partner for another, but one cannot exchange one's lover for a statue of liberty.

scene, while the Templar (a spirit), Saladin (a Muslim) and Nathan (a Jew) are discussing peace, the location of the play, in the centre of Jerusalem, is blown to pieces by a bomb. That, he said, made space for a new play.[25] The idea caused the Marquis de Norpois, the diplomat, great delight. Where there is such a prominent place, he called out, there is room for a stroke of genius.

But how could that be turned into an interesting article for *Le Figaro*? The alacrity with which the faces of egocentrics, distracted by the soirée, decided the truth or untruth of quick statements made by a man with glowing eyes, a poet, who subsequently behaved like a racehorse from a stud book, accelerating in an endless final curve, could not be reconstructed the following morning in the brain of a journalist and marriage impostor, which was guided by other interests. Thus *Le Figaro* published the torso of an article which claimed that Friedrich Schiller could only be understood at all in French, but that this also changed the plots of his plays, meaning that the Marquis de Posa would finally receive the minister's post he had aspired to since the Battle of Lepanto. Peace with the Muslims in the Mediterranean was the work of Sultan Saladin and a subsequently famous Jew called Nathan.

---

25 Proust indeed reported that the scene was about the power of three rings given by a father to his sons for identification. In his presentation of the three protagonists, he voiced his suspicion that all three rings were forged ('the genuine ring was probably lost'). One of the forged rings, however, contained such explosive emotional force that the impressive opening scene resulted: all the protagonists were killed instantly.

This was propagated at a soirée by the Jewish poet Proust, applauded by several aristocrats. But the aristocrats traced their blood back to a pair of children who landed in Marseille in 37 CE, and these were evidently direct descendants from the union of Christ and Mary of Magdalene, and thus the blue blood from which all nobility in France was descended.

Proust slept through this issue of *Le Figaro.* His bodily system punished him for the extravagance of his monologues, the trans-Rhenish remoteness of his interest, though he had enchanted his listeners. Sleep, lethargy.

Designation of the Lover

'If one loves someone who is not from the upper
classes
But more or less from the common people, then
the pain
Of love is accompanied by considerable financial
problems.'

Marcel Proust

–Proust always gave a tip of 200 per cent.

–How much did you say Marcel Proust inherited when his parents died? Ten million by today's currency? In dollars?

–Something like that. Even serious mistakes in his investments couldn't destroy his capital.

–He paid large sums to his lover, Agostinelli?

–Yes, the relationship only lasted until the morning of 1 December 1913. In a single week, Proust sold Royal

Dutch shares for 40,000 francs and wired the money to Agostinelli.

—The larger the bribes became, the sooner the young man would have enough to disappear.

Nothing Direct

Alfred Agostinelli's sister was the mistress of the Baron du Guesne. Agostinelli himself was together with the ugly Anna, whom he referred to as his 'wife'. His brother was a chauffeur, his half-brother a waiter. A family that resolutely sought their happiness.

30 May 1914. After two months of flying lessons, Agostinelli embarked on his first solo flight. While taking a bend at low altitude, he crashed into the sea. He could not swim. He clung to the deck and waved. He had a large sum of money on him, for he suspected that his greedy family would rob him.

—Proust had paid the deposit to the flying school for him?

—He had. But it's not true that he bought him a plane. He ordered one, then cancelled it.

—Was he hoping to get Agostinelli back in May 1914?

—He saw a chance.

—And how they've found these *cahiers* that were lost, in Reynaldo Hahn's estate?[26] With sketches in which

---

26 In the spring of 1945. Reynaldo Hahn, now 69 years old, director of the Paris Opera, an opulent, made-up figure whom people credited with a feeling for art. He made no effort and put on Verido, Hounod and Meyerbeer.

Proust attempts to capture the impression made on him by the news of Agostinelli's death?

–So it seems.

–Why did Proust discard this text?

–We don't know if he discarded the text. Maybe he was saving it.

–And why should he have done that?

–Maybe because he thought he wouldn't die as long as he hadn't described the death of his beloved. His superstition forced him to delay making a fair copy.

–Could one say that when one's impressions reach a certain intensity and directness, it becomes impossible to describe them in literature?

–That's not only possible, it's undoubtedly true.

–Hence your theory that the more important of Proust's affairs–for the man who was primarily writing, at least–actually involved 'heterosexual objects'. You say that he cast his affections out like a net onto *unattainable men* who perhaps didn't notice his advances, and let the eccentric do what he liked around them; thus he could 'love', that is, describe, with particular intensity. In that sense, Proust is a realist?

–He certainly is.

–But the affair with his chauffeur Agostinelli, that actually happened?

–We don't know. We know the jealous comments made by Céleste, the wife of the rival chauffeur Albaret. All that could be true or untrue. But it doesn't matter where Proust gets his impressions, whether from direct contact or imagined touches. He never describes sweat or erotic secretions.

—You mean he would have incorporated them in his literature as proof of actual intimacy is that intimacy had actually existed? Tasteless description of the concretions of love?

—Yes, that could have served as outstanding proof.

—It remained undescribed because it was unknown to Proust?

—Because his affairs were so indirect. He only ever imagined the intimacy. If someone got too close to him, he drove them away. Jealousy was his vehicle.

—Here in the dossier, the heading reads 'omnia mea mecum porto'.[27] The text only really describes what went down with Agostinelli in his accident, when he clung so movingly to the metal and the cloth covering of the aeroplane. His capital, the living blood, the ambition, his ballast, the money he had with him.

—You think that dragged him down?

—I wouldn't say that.

—Proust describes the Nereids of the Mediterranean, who surround the beloved and drag him down into the depths. The beloved saw that on a picture, an art photo documenting a fantastic occurrence. He, who had always loved upwards, was pulled under by mythical creatures that resembled plants.

—A difficult text.

---

27 'All that is mine I carry with me'. [Trans.]

—It's the worst text Proust ever wrote.

—You can see that from the fragment?

—I don't think it's a fragment, but rather a text that he suppressed himself. Because the emotional intimacy was too intense.

—Can't writers describe real things?

—Not directly.

The Three of Them

The young Bizet and the young Proust were playing with the granddaughter of Halévy THE JEWESS. They placed the girl in a large washroom in the basement. They pretended they were heating the water to boiling point. They wanted to use the scene as a pretext to undress Geneviève and test their joint power over her.

The young Bizet, who later had a taxi company, rejected all advances of a homosexual nature by Marcel Proust, who died in 1923. Was he unmusical? Thus tormenting young girls together remained the only thing the friends could do for each other.

Speaking Foreign Languages in Love

A few girls had come to the secondary school in the morning. They asked if the final examinations were taking place. They had prepared themselves. But the teachers and staff had already been taken away to one of the southern departments. A somewhat uninformed caretaker answered their questions.

When Gilberte came home without having achieved anything, without being released for life, as it were, she found her parents' home empty. The metro was almost running on time. The city's electric lights were working. A note in the kitchen told her that her mother and brother had hurried south via Vincennes at the behest of her father, an artillery officer on the south-eastern front. She should wait or join them. There was no address.

That same evening Gilberte found herself involved in an affair, as if she were grown up, with an engineer officer from the German occupation army, which had taken over the territory of Paris, the metropolis, during the day. The man had approached her. The conversation continued for two days. By the end she was the lover of a 'fascinating stranger'. She had read novels, set books for the top two classes at the girls' school. Hardly anything else to prepare her for the confusing experience. The man had well-tanned arms, neck, face and legs, while his torso was as white as a maggot. Their conversation, which muted all impression and took place in broken bits of German and French, encased them like a cocoon; it was more the will to conversation than actual communication. She was nervous, the man was seven years older.

They alternated between meeting in a shack at his headquarters, on a mattress, and her empty parents' flat, sneaking past the concierge; the programme she was following was called AMOUR PASSION, STATE OF EMERGENCY, a general licence to leave everyday life, the unrealistic reality of Paris. It was not clear to Gilberte what this programme meant for her foreign lover. He often struggled with conflicting emotions, seemed on the point of starting a new life. Engineer Gert Schwennicke was married. After only four weeks of this affair, which had not been part of his plan for life, he believed he could never end it. His marriage prevented him from inviting Gilberte to Germany. So he asked his wife to come to Paris from a garrison town in the north of Germany. The opponents sat face to face in one of the large cafes in the St Germain quarter.

HENRIETTE, GERT'S WIFE, TWO YEARS OLDER THAN HER HUSBAND, A MODERN WOMAN, LIKED THE PRACTICAL ASPECTS OF THE DRAMA. When her husband returned from war, she thought, the heat of passion with which their marriage had begun would gradually fade. The Paris affair confirmed this. What would remain was caring for their child, who would perhaps be joined by a second one. This required predictability, not exclusivity. So why, she asked, was it not possible to have a constellation of three, considering that 'every other solution' would involve pain and renunciation? This suggestion was not at all compatible with Gilberte's programme of AMOUR PASSION, and also seemed far removed from Gert's SAILING TO NEW SHORES. But while they were sitting, thus dissociated, amid the bustle of a Saturday afternoon in Paris, they stayed at the table and settled into a shared evening. For practical reasons, Gert and Gilberte moved closer to the programme of this modern German woman.

After Henriette's departure–Gert's posting in Paris remained an unchanged fact–the drama took its course without any finality. Far beneath their mental and emotional struggle, the body and soul of those involved had come to terms with the reality that had developed. Gert could even go on holiday without any crisis. Henriette, the experienced woman (though not experienced in a concrete involvement of this kind, which is only described in a few romantic novels or biographies) was confident enough to refrain from complaining about certain moments of inadequate predictability. She was pregnant by Christmas.

Gert, originally an aeroplane engineer and now working for the Navy Inspection West, was the target of extensive efforts by the enemy. A network (*reseau*) of the resistance movement tried to recruit Gilberte to spy on Gert. She did not dare to refuse this patriotic plan entirely. In the rooms where she spent time with Gert, however, he did not leave any documents lying around. The threat dissolved into nothing.

One could not say that any one of the three, despite following such antagonistic programmes, were dishonest towards themselves or one of the others. On one occasion Gilberte visited Henriette and consulted with her. They now understood each other better.

The outcome of the war ended the triangle. Gert reached Reich territory in November 1944. By that time, Gilberte had already caught up with her family in the South of France. Henriette witnessed the capitulation in the Alpine Fortress. Husband and wife met in May in their undestroyed house.

Had there been any rapprochement between these three people's programmes in the matter of love? No. Not even their practical habits. Did they speak openly about their experiences later on? Did they tell one another what they had felt during that state of emergency? No. They spoke neither to one another nor to anyone else about it. They met in Bad Kreuznach, in a complicated arrangement with numerous changes of train, in 1957. The meeting did not offer anything new. They felt they had 'grown apart'.

If they looked within themselves, however, each of the three believed that they had nothing to regret, that they in fact harboured a precious treasure which would not gain anything from being described in words.

On the Supposed Right to Lie Out of Philanthropy

> 'To be truthful (honest) in all declarations is, therefore, a sacred and unconditionally commanding law of reason that admits of no expediency whatsoever.'
>
> *Immanuel Kant,*
> Grounding for The Metaphysics of Morals

In 1797, the European public still recalled the tribunals that had condemned so many prisoners to the guillotine during the French Revolution. What did a lie matter if it saved a life? How should one view the truthfulness of someone who reported, denounced others? If a murderous faction seeks to kill its opponents with the instrument of justice, does the framework of the law, and thus of truth, remain in force?

In this phase of history, the political writer Benjamin Constant quoted a GERMAN PHILOSOPHER (he meant Immanuel Kant). This philosopher, he wrote, had claimed that humanity had a right to TRUTH: lies were generally unacceptable. Therefore, Constant continued, this philosopher 'had gone so far as to assert that it would be a crime to tell a lie to a murderer who asked whether our friend who is being pursued by the murderer had taken refuge in our house'.[28]

The well-intentioned lie is an act of omnipotence, Kant responded in a published polemic. It presupposed that the liar knew all the causal chains and legal consequences of their answer in advance. What would be left of these good intentions if, when the murderer received a negative (and dishonest) answer upon asking if the hated man was at home, the guest had meanwhile left the house and subsequently fell victim to the murderer? On the other hand, if the respondent answered truthfully but the hated man was already gone, the murderer would have achieved nothing, only lost time, and would fail to satisfy his thirst for the deed because the truthful statement had misled him.[29]

---

28 Quoted in Immanuel Kant, *Grounding for the Metaphysics of Morals: On a Supposed Right to Lie Because of Philanthropic Concerns* (James W. Ellington trans.) (Indianapolis, IN: Hackett, 1993), p. 63.

29 See Kant, *On a Supposed Right to Lie Because of Philanthropic Concerns*, p. 65: 'If by telling a lie you have in fact hindered someone who was even now planning a murder, then you are legally responsible for all the consequences that might result therefrom. But if you have adhered strictly to the truth, then public justice cannot lay a hand on you, whatever the unforeseen consequence might be. It is indeed possible that after you have honestly answered Yes to the murderer's question as to whether the intended victim is in the house, the latter went out unobserved and thus eluded the murderer, so that the deed would not have come about. However, if

The philosopher insisted on his statement: 'To be TRUTHFUL (honest) in all declarations is, therefore, a sacred and unconditionally commanding law of reason that admits of no expediency whatsoever.'[30]

–Speaking the truth in a trial in the Soviet Union in 1937 put lives in danger and was of no benefit to justice–would you admit that, as a Kantian?

–I don't deny the circumstances but the principle can't be abandoned. One must not lie.

–If lies are forced through torture? If falsehood becomes a vehicle for distorted accusations, confusion and thus leads to the death sentence?

–Kant's rule either applies or doesn't apply. It's not negotiable.

A group of CIA negotiators abandoned the interrogation of a suspected Al-Qaeda member and handed the subject over to a friendly secret service which, by the laws of its country, is allowed to use torture. The interrogation squad lies to the delinquent, saying that the torture will be

---

you told a lie and said that the intended victim was not in the house, and he has actually (though unbeknownst to you) gone out, with the result that by so doing he has been met by the murderer and thus the deed has been perpetrated, then in this case you may be justly accused as having caused his death. For if you had told the truth as best you knew it, then the murderer might perhaps have been caught by neighbours who came running while he was searching the house for his intended victim, and thus the deed might have been prevented.'

30 Ibid.

lessened if he names comrades. Is such a well-intentioned lie permissible? For the Kantian, not at all. How can you know what the man will reveal under torture? How many people whose names the tortured or deceived man reveals do you want to be hunted down, whether innocent or guilty?

–Should the telephonist who recognizes a conspirator from 20 July 1944, retired Mayor Goerdeler, answer 'no' when asked if she knows him? Would she condemn him to death otherwise?

–As a Kantian I would say no, but as a German patriot I would say yes.

–In the shadow of Hitler, Kant no longer applies?

–No.

–Is that in keeping with the master's intentions?

–No. Kant knows of no case in the cosmos where his rules don't apply. In that sense, I'm a compromiser when I say that under the circumstances of 20 July, the taboo on lies doesn't apply.

–I was raped in East Prussia in March 1945. I know my husband would never forgive me for it. It's a matter of class and morality, a classic problem of a special kind, not a possibility for emotion. Should I demand something impossible of his soul, or should I lie to him?

–If my husband loves me then he has to deal with it, otherwise he doesn't love me.

–A different case: in a moment of recklessness, you've been unfaithful to him.

–But he loves me?

–Would you suffocate your shared love because of a chance event like that?

–No.

–What does this deviation from the Kantian principle depend on? How do you support it?

–He doesn't want to know the truth.

–And how do you know that?

–I can feel it.[31]

---

31 Ibid., pp. 64f.: 'Hence a lie [. . .] does not require the additional condition that it must do harm to another [. . .]. For a lie always harms another; if not some other human being, then it nevertheless does harm to humanity in general, inasmuch as it vitiates the very source of right.'

V

THE PRINCESS OF CLEVES

COMMENTARY

LOVE POLITICS: THE STUBBORNNESS OF INTIMACY

ESSAY

THE PRINCESS OF CLEVES

COMMENTARY

'You must have respect for the wildness, the wilfulness, the precision of your feelings.'

1

A Novel of the Poetic Enlightenment . . .

Between 1670 and 1678, one of the great ladies of France (we know today that it was Marie-Madeleine Pioche La Vergne, comtesse de La Fayette) wrote a novel with two helpers that–while initially controversial–captured the hearts and minds of French readers soon after its publication, and had a lasting effect on the terms in which people sought to unravel the confusion of their love affairs. The novel was published anonymously in 1678 under the title *La Princesse de Clèves.*

The story described in the novel is placed in a different period; instead of the prudish time of the Sun King, it is set in the fictional era of Henry II of France and his mistress, Diane of Poitiers. It is misleading to assume that the novel is focused on a tale of courtly love. Certainly Madame de Lafayette, the author, was a high-ranking aristocrat, but the novel develops a self-assurance that corresponds to the emerging middle-class society and is shared by the author.

That time saw the formation of a society of readers that transcended class boundaries. The novel shows the intellectual authority of this yet-undeveloped but inexorably rising class, with all the echoes of the knowledge which accompanies the experiences of an aristocrat. The novel's scenery does, however, have one peculiarity: the nobles described here, who demonstrate the beginnings of middle-class emancipation, act with a freedom that did not initially exist in the lives of the bourgeoisie.[1]

The new society in seventeenth-century France was capable of imagining that humans could be producers, not observers of their lives, not recipients of their fate. That applies to the 'established and practiced business world', to religious faith, to the developing morality and philosophy (setting up the boundaries and fields of the spirit) and to the realm of amorous relationships. For Madame de Lafayette, these relationships are untameable. They are divided into separate areas (marriages and duties are dealt with in a different way from passions), they are diverted and if necessary suppressed, that is, initially removed from the access of the new self-assurance. The novel *The Princess of Cleves* was the first attempt to put the complex of connections between fidelity and eroticism up for public debate as a *context.*

The protagonist is one of the richest heiresses in France. 'A beauty who attracted everyone's gaze.' Mademoiselle de Chartres, who later becomes the Princess

---

1 Wagner's *Die Meistersinger von Nürnberg* and Richard Strauss' *Der Rosenkavalier* (and also in *Arabella*) portray bourgeois lives as having a certain freedom (with the involvement of nobles). The liberties in practical life are evident in, for example, the lives of Goethe (whom Valmy describes as wanting to become a 'noble'), Schiller, Robert Music or Thomas Mann. These life stories should be compared to those of the base.

of Cleves by marriage, was brought up by her mother with great care. This mother, a powerful woman who plays a political part in the king's circles, withdraws from the court for many years to equip her daughter for her later life: as a precious good, an estate rooted in body and spirit, a garden for use by other people.

This attentiveness to herself and the moulding of her successor's character–that is, her daughter's–corresponds to the view of the new type of human that emerged after 1600: *Homo novus*. He was born in the human landscapes of northern Italy, Holland, southern England and Scotland, in what was called the 'Green Belt' of Europe (because of its colour on maps). French society responded to this novelty with a wealth of divergent commentary. These new humans were attentive to their lives; they made, as already mentioned, a new kind of effort.

The beginnings of the new way of thinking were thwarted by the Thirty Years War and Spain's barbaric wars on the Netherlands. Towards the end of the seventeenth century, however, at the time when The Princess of Cleves was written, the spiritual warehouses were full of goodwill and persuasiveness that could be combined to create Enlightenment. The Princess of Cleves was the first novel of practical Enlightenment, a handbook for the practical power of judgement in the most hazardous area of life experience, the area of the TENDER FORCE.

2
Amour propre, or Self-Love . . .

Mademoiselle de Chartres, soon to be the Princess of Cleves, is 16 years old at the start of the novel. She is 18 when the story ends. She is a 'nymphet'.

Madame de Chartres, her daughter's teacher, sees very clearly–with the same powers of observation that lead the princess's husband to the same conclusion–that the princess is inexperienced in erotic matters. The mother considers this a virtue. She considers it dangerous for her daughter to gather experience in a field, to have skin contact, where the secure application of the rules of life cannot be guaranteed. Thus the Princess of Cleves is meant to sail the ship of her life confidently, even without any concrete experience or knowledge of what she is actually dealing with.

In French classicism, SELF-LOVE OR SELF-RESPECT, termed *amour propre*, forms the centre of this philosophy of love. 'You must have respect for the wildness, the wilfulness, the precision of your feelings.' You must TRUST YOURSELF. You must form a centre of RELIABILITY out of the same self-respect and self-love. You must abide by contracts, observe regulations. You consequently live in two worlds: one that is determined by society and your contractual partners (for example, your husband) and one that belongs to you individually. But in neither of the worlds should you be dishonest, lower your expectations or make compromises. The categorical imperative 'love yourself' is indivisible. Thus this general law of behaviour will later be able to claim the universal validity of

Immanuel Kant's formulation. But it can also be formulated in the absoluteness of Manon Lescaut: what I love is the highest law. In all such practical cases it remains indivisible. 'Love finds its motives for decisions within itself.' (Niklas Luhmann)

3
On Some of the Concepts and Scenes in the Novel

One of the richest heiresses in France . . .

The novel's protagonists are very unusual people. They are rich, they have direct contact with power, and they have a beauty of body and character that is admired by their surroundings.

When the princess stands face-to-face with the Duke of Nemours after her marriage to the Prince of Cleves, whom she does not love, but who does not bother her either–she is thus *courteous* towards him–she thinks it is love at first sight; he is equipped with outstanding qualities. He is considered a potential husband for Queen Elizabeth I of England. His facial features and posture, which are considered pleasant by all around him, take on associative power through the rumour that he is successful with women. On his first appearance in the novel, he climbs over the seats blocking his path to the dance floor; he is impetuous.

> 'Madame of Cleves ended the dance, and while her eyes were still searching for a new partner, the king called to her to take the new arrival.'

The dance of the two beauties stirs the admiration of the court society.

Surprise and *étonnement* (amazement) . . .

The outward signs of *passion*[2] are *étonnement* and *surprise.* According to Descartes, *étonnement,* as the most extreme consequence of *surprise,* 'causes the entire body to freeze into a statue'. Amazement, says Descartes, is the sign of an incurable *passion,* an excess of admiration, an irresistible attack of emotion. (Descartes, *Les passions de l'âme,* art. 73.)

Madame Lafayette's novel does not describe any psychological processes. It describes the masks of psychology. The irresistible attacks of emotion dealt with in the novel are experienced by the Prince of Cleves with reference to the beauty of Mademoiselle de Chartres, whom he does not yet know at that point, but will later marry. He cannot conceal his amazement. The experience of their first encounter changes his entire life, and its effect on him last until his death. This surprise and *étonnement* are no different for the Duke of Nemours, however.

> 'When Monsieur de Nemours stood before her and she curtsied to him, he was so *surprised* by her beauty that he could not hide his *amazement.*'

In the novel, *surprise* is one of the key words for the experience of a sudden seizre by unpredictable, irrational and fateful forces on the rational order of life. Its

2 In this section, 'passion' in italics always signifies the French word. [Trans.]

heightened version, *étonnement*, disables reason. At that moment, the affected person does not belong to themselves. These are acts of cartography, as if on a map of the emotions. They can be compared to experiences from the twenty-first century as much as with events in the novels of the seventeenth century.

Coup de foudre . . .

> 'Passionate love strikes like lightning out of the blue, it concerns a stranger. [. . .] love appears as an explosive power that interrupts continuity.'

In other novels and in the practice of life in the seventeenth century, it is assumed that the tender force develops gradually, as when one learns things, like the growth of plants in a garden. Two people come to know each other more closely, and thus to love each other. The notion of 'love as passion' is the opposite of this. The impression of love shatters the perception, in a sense, and casts a second world into the existing one. Passion behaves like the founder. The Princess of Cleves and Monsieur de Nemours have been seized by love before they even know each other's names or anything else about them. This is the state of which the princess's mother sought to warn her, and which the author, Madame de Lafayette, considers a state of illness, but one that cannot be attacked by reason.

Trouble (unrest) . . .

The passion that follows that first amazement, which is a certain kind of insanity, now controls the two lovers. An 'unrest' similar to that which drives a clock determines their actions and intensities, while the princess, at least, thinks she is fighting against it. The high level of civilization prevents the two from devouring each other. Rather, nothing happens that cannot be reconciled with *vertu* or with the princess's loyalty to her husband. The Duke of Nemours seizes the opportunity to take a portrait of the princess while she concentrates on the colours of the beloved man's tournament sash and has acquired a picture depicting the siege of Metz: the picture shows the duke as a participant in the battle. Initially, a secret agreement and these looted items were all that connected the two lovers.

The entanglement of the daughter by the mother . . .

The intrigue of *passion*, which has the goal of ultimately asserting itself openly and verifiably, has a different intrigue as an undercurrent: the close bond between the daughter and her worldly wise mother, Madame de Chartres. In her essay 'A Mother's Will: The Princess of Cleves',[3] Peggy Kamuf examines this subterranean love narrative in Madame de Lafayette's novel. She argues that the mother does not want to expose her daughter either to reality or to the confusing court society and the violence of its male-dominated world, nor does she want to hand

3 See Peggy Kamuf, *Fictions of Feminine Desire* (Lincoln: University of Nebraska Press, 1982), pp. 67–96.

over this enchanting creature, whom she gave birth to and brought up, to anyone at all. She was quite happy to marry her daughter to a man like the Prince of Cleves, one whom the girl did not love; thus her daughter is only kept and lent out. This comes back to haunt her once *passion* intervenes.

Madame de Lafayette's novel may show indifference towards psychology in many respects, but the description of the battle for love property (that of her mother, that of her husband and that to which the Duke of Nemours aspires) precisely reproduces the inner dynamics. Yet it never stands on its own, as the dynamics of coincidences, the violence of other intrigues, the prejudices and the standards are also involved.

When the princess says 'I' 12 times . . .

The cruel unrest bothering the princess is intensified when the thinks that the duke loves another woman. From that point on, she considers it impossible that his passion could make her happy. That leads to her consistent stance at the end of the novel.

> 'But even if it [the duke's passion] could make me happy,' she said, 'what shall I do? Shall I tolerate it? Shall I return it? Shall I embark on a love affair? Shall I be unfaithful to Monsieur des Cleves, to myself? Shall I take upon myself the cruel remorse and deadly pain that accompany love? [. . .] All my resolutions are useless. I thought the same yesterday as I think today, and yet today I do the

> opposite of what I resolved yesterday. I must tear myself away from Monsieur de Nemours, I must go to the country [. . .] and if Monsieur des Cleves insists on preventing it or learning the reason, I will cause him, and perhaps myself, the pain of telling him.'

In eleven very short sentences, the 'I' of the protagonist speaks up twelve times. Her *passion* and the I AS A FORTRESS are locked in battle. The consequence is a fatal mistake, the climax of the novel, she so-called confession of the princess.

The confession . . .

The Prince of Cleves is suspicious. He has the feeling that the princess might love the Duke of Nemours. The princess's wish to leave, and thus avoid any encounter with the duke, bothers him. Then the princess does something that I forbidden according to the conventions of the time: she confesses to her husband that she loves another man. But she does not give his name. Her husband tries everything to find it out. She keeps quiet.

The princess believes she owes her *amour propre* this 'escape to truth'. It is not really the done thing to give one's spouse a view of one's subjective intimacy; it will trigger a deadly jealousy. JEALOUSY IS THE GRAVEDIGGER OF LOVE. And it will only ever be half of the truth that is uttered under the name of the truth. This confession is poisoned; it leads to the prince's death. The fact that the princess care for him devotedly later on, in his misery, does nothing to change that. It is not care or truth that the Prince of Cleves needs for his *incurable wounds*, but rather a sign of authentic love.

The character of the Prince of Cleves . . .

Madame de Lafayette, and evidently the princess's mother too, takes the prince's side in the novel's portrayal. He *understands* the princess; she does not understand him. Life with him would have had practical value for the princess, while life with the Duke of Nemours would probably not. The Prince of Cleves has a well-balanced character, experienced in the politics of love. If love could be based on friendship, the Prince of Cleves and his wife would be an ideal couple whose relationship would perhaps, at the end of a long life (they would have to avoid dying early), because they had only come to know each other gradually, progress towards a tender, even sexually satisfying affection. With great respect for the power of erotic passion, Madame de Lafayette chooses a more civilized relationship between two people than that which *passion* involves.

'Anti-Descartes . . . '

According to Descartes, only the primacy of reason is valid. A police operation against all passions, as it were. This does not correspond to the position of Madame de Lafayette. She too views the prospects of success for a 'bond out of suddenness', a tyranny of *passion* over all the other senses, with scepticism or pessimism. It is important to her, however, to keep intact the fabric of relationships, which is after all that of vitality, and refrain from destroying it through any prohibition. She believes that only there, in these living forces, however destructive they might be, can one ultimately explore the escapes and cures.

For the sickness that leads to death (to the death of the person or the death of love), according to Madame de Lafayette, is based on SELF-LOVE and not merely PASSION. This self-love is one of the best things that *Homo novus* is equipped with. Being the owner of one's life is the indistinguishable source of happiness and unhappiness.

A 'heroine of courtesy' . . .

The princess has lifted the mask of amorous convention and seen what lies behind: cruelty. She has recognized that she too, the heroine of courtesy, was cruel in reality. She fears her own implacable intellect, which did not prevent her from killing her husband, as well as *passion*, which wrecked her intellect.

The end of the novel . . .

The princess is now a widow. As her relationship with the Duke of Nemours never outwardly violated the rules of virtue, there would be no obstacle to a marriage. Indeed, the court society demands such a marriage, as it registers the harmony between these two people as that of a 'natural couple'. But the princess refuses. She enters a convent. Celibacy is the adequate form for something as precious as the directly felt tender force, according to Madame de Lafayette, the author.

Uniqueness as a standard . . .

According to Niklas Luhmann, there are only two possible reactions to the canon of romantic novels in French classicism: either one preserves the extraordinary parts or one reacts negatively. Uniqueness is the standard. The princess's abstinence has nothing to do with remaining faithful to her husband beyond death; that would be a *phantôme du devoir*. With the consent of the court society, which loves the sight beauty, and the presumed approval of her departed mother, IT WOULD BE POSSIBLE to break such a merely deliberate fidelity rooted only in the body and the soul. In addition, however, the princess has witnessed the Duke of Nemours boasting to third parties of her love, which he deduced from a sign. The thought that she too might love a man who was just like any other, a braggart who could not resist vanity, disappointed her. THUS THE OBJECTIVE DESCRIPTION BY MADAME DE LAFAYETTE. Subjectively, the princess sees the events a little differently: If I were to come together with the duke, his nature would cause the same thing to happen to me after a few years as with my husband. As I love him, I would die from it. I am denying myself in order to preserve the most important thing in my life: my self-love. It is based on uniqueness, and also on surviving.

The princess did not live for long after her renunciation . . .

> 'But the life of Madame of Cleves did not look as if she would ever return. She spent one part of the year at the convent, the other at home; but there too, even the strictest monastic rule could not have prescribed more reclusion or more pious activities. And so her life, *although it only lasted for a short while,* was an example of unparalleled virtue.'

It is a matter of disappointment, not protection against threats. She does not want to be a woman like all the others, and he must not be a man like every other. First the novel deals with a lack of experience and knowledge, now the concern is too much knowledge. Enlightenment requires a promise of happiness. The only valid promise of happiness under the conditions of *amour propre* is uniqueness, an ideal occupied by greed like profit.

The sharp eye of Madame de Lafayette, which we here reinforce with the precise perspectivity of Niklas Luhmann, does not fail to see the high pressure affecting this self-respect, which knows no practical peace agreements. At the same time, one is impressed by the character of this young woman, the princess. First she is too inexperienced, then she is overwhelmed by experience, but she always endeavours to REMAIN THE LEGISLATOR OF HER OWN LIFE, of her TENDER FORCE.

4
A Store of Modern Questions and Material for Novels on the Concept of *Passion* by Niklas Luhmann

The map of the emotions that Madame de Lafayette presupposes for her novel not only permits a comparison with other novels, but also with the experiences of the twentieth and twenty-first centuries–even in the USA, Canada, Australia or Asia, which have no plausible connections with the events concerning the Princess of Cleves and the Duke of Nemours. Comparing means: making distinctions. Nothing in the early modern classical novel corresponds directly to the 'system' of love meanwhile altered by mutation and selection.

Luhmann's simultaneous focus on the seventeenth and twenty-first centuries (the latter being the future from his perspective) emphasizes the paradoxical character of love as a *medium of communication.* Love is meant to lay the foundations for long-term conditions, he argues, and it has a social function (not only in the context of mobilizing military strength in the Third Reich or economic momentum in the reconstruction after 1948). At the same time, it has a programme of passion and suddenness that contradicts DURATION and PRACTICABILITY. In that sense, *passion* is not only an 'anomaly', but actually 'a completely normal improbability'.

'Passionate love is an improbable institution.'

Luhmann first presented this thesis in one of his seminars in 1969. His book *Love as Passion* was published in 1982. Addenda to his theory can be found in the chapters on communication in *Theory of Society* (original German–Frankfurt: Suhrkamp, 1997). Luhmann excludes three areas from his analysis: purchase of love, thinking reflection on love (that is, paths of truth) and compulsion to love. The media of money, truth and power, which are irreconcilable with the rules the tender force sets for itself, form the background for Luhmann's depiction of the domains of love.

The world is complex . . .

'Complex' means that the modern world offers more possibilities of experience and action than can ever be actualized (see 'A Leninist of the Emotions' and 'Manfred Schmidt' in this volume). Born in Canberra to a Russian mother, grew up in Hildesheim, works in New York, goes to Thailand on holiday, meeting colleagues in Cape Town this coming week. Is that the life of a journalist, a scientist, an entrepreneur? A head-hunter who helps entrepreneurs find people? Or is the interesting thing the search for love affairs on the way through such diverse locations on the planet? Such spatial complexity (which is augmented by temporal, functional, personal and objective complexity) would be improbable for the persons in the novel *The Princess of Cleves*; there the characters move along fixed rails, as it were. Few of these rails have any validity in the modern 'dice society'.

The experience of the partners should be a joint one . . .

Amour propre, self-respect, has enjoyed a quiet but striking career since the seventeenth century. According to Luhmann, it has specialized in replacing the ability to withdraw out of self-love (that is, to build up a reserve that also allows for the self-love of the other) through projection. Modern *amour propre*, according to Luhmann, represents the other in keeping with the need of the self. One defines the other in such a way that they affirm one's own experience, the experience one wishes for oneself. But this attitude, says Luhmann, is destined to misjudge the experience of the other.

The fates of *amour pur* . . .

The problem of the tender force is not its OVERWHELMING BY SENSUALITY (or in Freud, used critically and not damningly, CONTAMINATION), not the involvement of self-interest (as with the princess, her mother and Monsieur de Nemours) but, rather, the COMPLEMENTARY AWARENESS of mutual relationships: no one is naive any more, each views themselves with the eyes of the other. This is a ubiquitous trait today, Luhmann argues, and also indispensable for the preservation of love. But it is especially unsuitable for the creation of 'pure love', that is, pure tenderness. The millipede that is love begins counting its legs with each of the participants, starting from a different place, as soon as the goal is *amour pur*. One must, he continues, acknowledge chimerical forms of the tender force. A lasting relationship cannot be based on a 'fluctuating, uncontrollably swelling and equally uncontrollably subsiding emotion'. *Passion* is an unjustifiable, coincidental state whose onset is no more controllable than its extinction. He sees a contradiction between INEVITABILITY and FREEDOM, IMPULSIVENESS and LONGEVITY.

'Love is an overtaxing of society not only as an ideal, but also as an institution.'

In that sense, it is simpler to enact *passion* only in films and novels, and no longer in reality.

Speaking of passion and the overtaxing of psychic systems provoked by it, Luhmann claims:

'Not everyone has the ability, the inclination, time and opportunity for it, and hardly anyone keeps it up.'

That, Luhmann continues, is why one needs the curtains of privacy for love. At the start, they allow people to conceal that they love each other and how they love each other (one has to improvise), and later that they do not love each other.

One loves love first, and then a person whom one can love . . .

One can already love without having a partner, or only having a partner who does not return that love. 'What's it to you if I love you?' Today's partner no longer climbs over the seats to the dance floor, and is not chosen by a king to dance with me. Rather, as a modern person, I first have to go in an entrepreneurial fashion to places and platforms where I can be found by partners. The act, says Luhmann, covers great distances before an amorous scene is realized. The provisions for the journey consist of 'love for love'.

How close is a connection allowed to be?

Plato's *Symposium* deals with being in love. One of the participants, Aristophanes, tells of the beginnings of humans, which were initially twofold beings with four arms and four legs that reproduced into the earth; in the end they felt so strong that they wanted to storm the heaven of the gods. As a punishment, Zeus had them cut in two. At his command, they were cut into a male and a female half, now each with only two arms and two legs, the skin tied up at the navel as if it were a drawstring pouch. Love drives them towards each other, seeks to regain the old nature of the twofold creature, to make two into one.

In the course of the conversation there is a practical suggestion:

> And what if, while they were sharing a single bed, Hephaestus came to them with his tools and asked them [. . .]: Is that what you want, to be together in the same place and not to be apart day and night? For if that is what you desire, I will merge you into one and join you together so that the two of you become one and experience your entire life as if you were one, and when you die, your death will also be shared, and then in Hades you will also be one, not two.[4]

4 Hephaestus is the blacksmith of the gods, a practical man.

FIGURE 49. The Duke of Nemours watches as a portrait of the princess is painted. The painter: eager. The duke steals a portrait of the princess lying on the table next to a small box; the painter had used it as a sketch.

This suggestion to be welded together went too far for the lovers, however. It is far from a useful state to be chained together mechanically. Rather, the point is the exact measure that includes something approximate: specific quanta of personal movement, specific quanta of contact.

Referring to this, Luhmann speaks of QUANTA OF HAPPINESS and of a NEURAL SCALES that measures them, and which a person carries within themselves.

The settlement area (the oikos) of the tender force prefers the robust, the simple, not the individual . . .

FIGURE 50 (LEFT). The confession. One sees the despair of the Prince of Cleves, who covers his face with his hand. In the background stands the Duke of Nemours, eavesdropping on them and suspecting that the princess loves him. On the way back from his hiding place, he already doubts that he is the unnamed man in the confession and grows jealous.

FIGURE 51 (RIGHT). The Duke of Nemours in his eavesdropping position (with kind permission of the Bibliothèque nationale de France).

In accordance with the evolutionary biologists, Luhmann pursues the different types of love relationship, which differ in terms of whether they support or prevent reproduction. The erotic tendency that is overbred, or only strives for selective breeding, belongs to the type with little offspring. Thus Luise Miller, who wanted to improve her social standing as well as her genetic type by marrying into the nobility, was doomed to take poison and never have children. Had she married the secretary Wurm, on the other hand, she would have remained in the midfield of objective chances and would probably be looking at sixteen children and grandchildren in her old age. She should not have read any novels, says Luhmann. Who can rule out the possibility that at least one of those children would have made her happier than the miserable experience with the young Ferdinand von Walter?

5
Details of an Intrigue

The following has been written about Madame de Lafayette's novel:

> 'A man, made the confidant of his wife, who kills him in the most virtuous way in the world.'

Gerhard Hess contradicts this observation. He disputes the virtue of the Princess of Cleves and characterizes her behaviour as 'frightened of risk'. It is, he says, a 'tragedy of the fear of life'. A. Gartmann disagrees with Hess; it is by no means a 'disaster of the fear of life', he counters, but, rather, the project of 'arming the emotions': to finally make them capable of resistance, of emancipation. Emancipation comes about on the basis of *amour propre.* Anyone who possesses such self-love must develop a strategy of attack and defence in order to protect themselves from the self-love of the others. The resulting defensive system against oneself and the others, the art of offensive and defensive weapons, is what we call REASON.

6
Wandering Fates: A Murder Ballad . . .

Compare this novel from French classicism, an elaborated philosophy of love, to the confusion of a plebeian tale from the nineteenth century: *Freia, the Foundling*: *VICTORY AND RENUNCIATION*; *or, The Heroine of Silistria, a Murder Ballad.* Such novel-like stories were written anonymously. Before being written down they were presented orally in different versions, and the influence of the listening audience led to various changes and an ultimate compilation. They are the shadow image of everyday emotional practice.

At the time when the Bourbons, having returned to the French throne, were chased away by the July revolution, a general by the name of Bouvier was forced to flee. The general's carriage travelled through the Ardennes. On the way, his pregnant wife gave birth. Their pursuers were getting close; the general's wife died.

'The general, holding the cold husk of the deceased in his arms, unconsciously let the horses carry him wherever fate chose to guide him . . . '

The general's coachman dug a grave for the dead woman. He placed the seemingly lifeless child in a hollow oak tree. The general's escape to Saxony was successful.

The following morning, a shepherd found the child, which was making mournful sounds, in the oak tree; he adopted the abandoned creature. The infant came into contact with the shepherd's wife, who nurtured her; this foster mother later died. A stepmother whom the shepherd took as a replacement drove away the child, whose name was Freia. She owed the name to the fact that she had been found on a holiday;[5] the shepherd was not familiar with the Germanic goddess called Freia, who was Odin's wife.

The girl Freia was found beside the road by a Countess Weinholm, who owned estates near Wesel and took her in. This countess had a son, who returned home to the mansion from his studies in Paris and was subsequently married to a young countess but pursued Freia, enchanted by her beauty and grace. 'Be silent, heart,' she called out, 'however loudly you might beat, I command you to be silent!' She took a great liking to the young count but her self-respect compelled her to protect the young countess.

Yet how strangely Freia's feelings were touched when she heard one day that the countess had gone missing. Was she lost? The count and the servants at the mansion sought in vain until Freia heard whimpering from a corner of the mansion's chapel where a staircase led down to the family crypt. The count had imprisoned the countess there. Freia and the countess fled. Where to? To the young woman's father.

This was General Bouvier, who had meanwhile returned to Paris. Freia was recognized as his daughter; the story of the hollow tree explained everything. Now happiness could have been achieved. But Freia deeply regretted being a woman:

'Swear, no longer be a woman
then all your shame will pass,

---

5 *Frei* means 'free', also in the sense of time off work. [Trans.]

she joins the ranks of warriors
for victory in Turkey.'

Dressed as a young officer, she follows the general to Gallipoli, and even into the Crimean War. At Silistra the vanguard does vigorous battle with the Russians; Freia saves her father's life several times.

'After the battle, she received the Medal of the Legion of Honour for her bravery; in the next battle, however, an enemy bullet put an end to her life too.'

'She guards her father's life many a time
in battle's heated turmoil
wreaths are bestowed on her many a time
until she falls to the battle soil.'

The story does not follow the rules of high art. The plot material is inflated. In the gaps between the reported facts, which are clearly lifted and combined from different contexts and accounts, other stories intrude on the narrative. These non-narrated parts, the numerous free-floating elements from other novels of the time, contain the main collection of motives for the improbable and abrupt twists in the murder ballad, which always tend towards the search for happiness.

While the subject at the heart of *The Princess of Cleves* is a forward-looking 'production of one's own life', a respect for self-love, the central theme here is the WILLINGNESS TO ADAPT TO CHANGING, WANDERING FATES. Freia is prepared at all times to react to new luck or to kindness people show her. She has been doing that since the first day of her life. The child wins the shepherdess's heart. Countess Weinholm is also delighted by the young girl, whom she found by the wayside in a mistreated and vegetating state. The same applies to the young count, who becomes a criminal (somewhat like Franz Moor's behaviour in Schiller's *The Robbers*).

The countess imprisoned in the crypt could have died. Freia, accompanied by the young countess she has rescued, joyfully makes the acquaintance of the latter's father and gains recognition as a general's daughter. She and the rescued girl are sisters. Can one improve strokes of luck? Not in the role of a woman, Freia assumes. Great careers come about among young men and on the battlefields of liberation struggles (freedom for Italy, battle for liberation against the Turks and reactionary Russia). The Crimean War, where documentary photography experienced its first triumph, is the field of death on which Freia, still young, perishes.

What separates the two stories is an interval of almost 200 years and the social distance between a plebeian class in the nineteenth century and the upper class in the seventeenth century. In both cases, however, death and celibacy are the price for the indivisibility and invulnerability of the tender republic.

7

How Would One Continue the Novel *The Princess of Cleves* Today? Is It Possible in the Twenty-First Century?

With his brain mangled after a noisy tourist class flight from New York to Munich (the university doesn't pay any more) but animated by words like *devoir*, *vertu*, *raison*, *science du cœur* (theory of emotions), concepts that are like drugs for him–each word evokes landscapes of up to 3,000 texts–and thus well rested in intellectual terms, the philologist arrives for the interview and immediately takes a stance.

A person of today, says Anselm Haverkamp, is not born as Mademoiselle de Chartres (the later Princess of Cleves). One should view the continuation of *The Princess of Cleves* in an operative and aggressive sense: How do I move about in a world where I am replaceable, in a place where I am needed? How do I appear on a stage that allows for a novel's plot? But the path of responding to modernity with compromises and passing over the standard of the novel is blocked off, according to Haverkamp. Precisely in a mass society, where the ideal grows distant for the individual, a decrease in uniqueness, self-respect, authenticity and aptitude to be faithful is out of the question. When the ideal becomes unattainable, the literary sources say, its value tends towards infinity.

The journalist conducting the interview was from the reviews section of the *Süddeutsche Zeitung*. What would the sources be, he asked, that deal with the fate of the love ideal in mass society? *Ulysses* by James Joyce? *Berlin Alexanderplatz* by Döblin? Does Passos, *Manhattan Transfer*, *The Grapes of Wrath* by Steinbeck? I could name another 2,000 texts, replied the scholar. The restraint towards practical behaviour in mass society found in Robert Musil or Proust is not typical.

–You're saying that modern people are especially opposed to compromises, opposed to resignation in matters of love?

–They can attempt a compromise, but the human constitution doesn't allow it. At some point the compromise collapses.

–In that sense, you claim, mass society doesn't exist?

–Evidently not.

–But unlike the Princess of Cleves, modern people are usually replaceable.

–They seem replaceable.

–Economically speaking, they are.

–But in their emotions they're not.

Would he call feelings something objective? Of course. The tender force has an objective nature. One could observe that in the strong emotional response when the media report on the kind of uniqueness that forms the theme of *The Princess of Cleves.*

For example, this second world, aloof from everyday life, is where Lady Di died. The television directors, the philologist argued, had underestimated this event. Their viewers forced them to change their programming. But the son of the department-store owner who died with the princess in her car in no way resembles the Duke of Nemours, the interviewer countered. The seducer and riding master who had comforted Princess Di for a while, the philologist confirmed, was a windbag who boasted of his experiences with the princess in his memoirs; he did not correspond to any of the ideals of amorousness that inhabit the novel *The Princess of Cleves.* The distorting mirror only cast a more intensive light on the lady–and it was she who touched the viewers. Did you notice, Anselm Haverkamp continued, that all TV channels had a candle burning throughout the day in memory of the princess? That, the philologist asserted, came directly from the candle that burns down in the final lines of Tolstoy's novel *Anna Karenina*, 'just as the light of a beautiful woman's life fades'. Such metaphors live for ever. The daily programmes of the media, however, do not. Here one can see the power of the tender force over the eager souls of the viewers, who force the programme directors to expand their programmes in such emergencies.

–So you think that Lady Di is the continuation of *The Princess of Cleves*? And the only thing missing is the novel?

–The novel could long have been written for all we know. And it doesn't have to take the form of a book. Maybe the ALTERED PROGRAMMING on almost every channel, that is, the replacement of the routine schedule, was the novel. That would be an invisible text, the creation of a lacuna in the noise level of the TV.

–Let's take a different example of uniqueness: Susanne Klatten, unique by birth and an heiress. But what does the con man and gigolo she encounters have in common with a Duke of Nemours?

–Here it was too late for the circumspection and care that Madame de Lafayette passed on to her princess.

–Can a person in mass society use a case like that, which they watch as it if were on a stage, in a second world, to deduce experience for their own life, to develop a cartography? What can they use for orientation? Surely a gigolo (or the corresponding female beguiler) would hardly be interested in him, a non-heir?

You're wrong about that, replied the philologist. What do we know about how our inner forces read such a story? Scar formation, the distance of a fall. The soul reads that through any kind of costume.

8
Work Timekeeper A. Trube on Love, Power and the Difference between the Passage of Time in the Seventeenth and Twenty-First Centuries

The work timekeeper A. Trube, formerly employed by a firm in Bockenheim that went bankrupt in the financial crisis of 2009, attended adult-education classes and thus came into contact with novels. Since then he has been examining the temporal fabric of literary texts: often a small addition of time can lead a plot in an entirely different direction.

He was able to observe the French president Sarkozy and his wife Carla Bruni on *Spiegel Online* for two days at the NATO celebrations in Baden-Baden and Kehl on 4 April 2009. How much time is available to the president for the practice of his marriage? He compared the available time with the time taken up by the love affair between the Princess of Cleves and the Duke of Nemours at their meeting in Coulommiers (which was a mystery to both of them). He knew the text passages from the adult-education course 'Introduction to Seventeenth-Century French Literature'.

According to his measurements, this amounted a total of 92.5 hours, not taking into account the sleep time during such an occasion of emotional restlessness, simple to sneak around close to the other, or to hide from them behind closed doors. They did not even get around to any erotic experiences, but wasted their time in a mental space imagined for their relationship. But no modern ruling couple has that much time at their disposal. Matters of state do not permit any holidays, as an unexpected event foils all private plans a mere second after arriving, and telecommunication gradually narrows and ultimately cancels out the present. But time, Trube states, is the terrain of the tender force.

Here Trube refers to another adult-education course, 'Emperor Napoleon in Private'. The trustworthy tutor emphasized that since the French Revolution, time had been characterized by acceleration. As a ruler during the nine years between 1799 and 1808, it was only during his forced winter stay at Finckenstein Palace–that is, in a short period–that he had the breathing space for the complications attendant on a love affair. Certainly, he too was struck by infatuation like a flash of lightning, a sudden certainty. The correspondingly swift response from Countess Walewska was followed in this case by an extra portion of time, in which their bodies and souls were able to connect to the powerful explosion and catch up with their accumulated needs, as it were. As far as he knows, Trube states, it is only this that enables a shared experience with longevity, repeatability and the possibility to take up the threads at a subsequent meeting.

The hasty Napoleon was never able to enjoy such a time of happiness again. The tutor at the adult education centre had recommended reading the memoirs Napoleon had written on Elba. As long as Trube restricted himself to following the passing of time and passed over justificatory and decorative passages, he gained a clear overview of temporal inadequacies. To establish the consequences, Trube drew on other sources. He was able to find them under key words at Frankfurt University Library. The ruler was called from his dictation (he usually dictated to several secretaries at once) to an adjacent cabinet, where the young woman chosen by the adjutant or determined by an indication from the emperor was already waiting. This powerful man often 'ensnared' such a creature with only a few utterances, often adding a short, witty remark. But there was hardly time for a natural reaction to develop in the woman's body. After ejaculation, his member sore because it had been rubbed dry, Napoleon rushed back to his study. He repeated this practice–which Trube considered nonsensical–because, according to General Coulaincourt, he had heard that such erotic activities were good for one's health; at any rate, he believed that it would be harmful to refrain from contact of this kind altogether.

The illusion of suddenness . . .

Love strikes like lightning, said the experienced matchmaker Anne-Marie Waschleppa, from Kösen. This 'abrupt experience' cannot be drawn out, just as there is no 'blitzkrieg in slow motion'. At the same time, Waschleppa added, we know that all emotions are sluggish. They are no match for the affectations of love that come from the imagination. That is why she advises those who have just fallen in love to begin reworking directly after lightning strikes. Thus Gerda Schaake found happiness because she had a planning phase in the absence of her new lover, who left on a business trip right after their first night together. For there is such a thing as planned economy in love, Waschleppa said. It yields the best results, unlike in economics, because it is free of bureaucracy.

FIGURE 52. The French president's claim that the novel *The Princess of Cleves* is the textbook example of a stuffy and obsolete work, and thus unsuitable as a set text at French secondary schools, bothered A. Trube. In the aforementioned adult-education course, after all, he had spent time reading excerpts from this novel. He was not willing to accept that this had been wasted time. He criticized the fact that Sarkozy had not drawn any conclusions from this highly instructive novel for his own marriage, especially in the matter of timekeeping. For example, said Trube, one could

easily measure the times for 4 May 2009: four hours spent in Kehl and Baden-Baden, six hours used up for West Africa's problems, another hour on the matter of a balance between the EU and Russia, two press conversations, the budget proposal for 2010, the repair of two aircraft carriers, the interim balance of the state fund for banking and economic aid: in these daily and nightly structures, there was no chance for Carla Bruni to find her husband at a moment when he was in possession of his full senses (that is, concentrating on her). That, Trube said, will surely have a more disastrous long-term effect than anything that happened in the novel *The Princess of Cleves*.

9
Intelligence and the Language of Mathematics Compared to That of Romantic Novels

In the time around 1678, when *The Princess of Cleves* was published, the pioneer and probability theorist Bernoulli was travelling through Holland. His discoveries would later develop into stochastics, in particular the limit theorem. This refers to the specific conditions under which the distribution of a sum of random variables can be described with the aid of a normal distribution. This is relevant for the question of future voting behaviour, for example, based on climatic probabilities; it is significant for the calculation of financial risks.

FIGURE 53. Bernoulli.

Here one distinguishes between ignorance (which cannot be eliminated by any mathematical means and caused the disaster at Chernobyl and the collapse of the Lehman Brothers investment bank, for example) and risk, which lies hidden in the future but can be deduced using the limit theorem. This daring intelligence, which deals with the *fringes of probability*, is never applied to the field of the tender force.

Compare the entirely different language of mathematical intelligence to the way of speaking in love stories. The Frankfurt stochastic mathematician Anton Wakolbinger gives an example that follows on from Jacob Bernoulli's proof for the weak law of large numbers:

> Here we once again encounter the fundamental *square root of n law*: a random variable consisting of n independent, identically distributed summands typically scatters its values in an area with a width of $\sqrt{n}$. This is not an intuitively obvious insight; it is further examined in the central limit theorem. First we will prove a simple theorem that captures the following situation: if one repeats a random experiment with a success probability of p in an independent fashion, the relative frequency of success will become stable with an increasing value of n while maintaining p. More generally, one can say that the arithmetic average of n identically distributed, independent random variables tends with an increasing value of n towards the expected value. The first result of this type was arrived at by Jacob Bernoulli.[6]

---

6 JACOB BERNOULLI (1654–1705), Swiss mathematician. His significant role in the theory of probability is based on contributions

The weak law of large numbers. *The random variables X_1, $X_2, \ldots$ have a real-valued, independent and identical distribution with a finite expected value μ and finite variance. Then the following applies to every bound of ε, however small: the probability that the arithmetic average of variables X_1 to X_n will deviate from the number μ by more than ε moves towards zero as n increases.*

Today one uses Chebyshev's proof.[7] His approach, based on the inequality named after him, can be applied to many other situations.

For a real-valued random variable X with a finite expected value whenever $\varepsilon > o$, ***Chebyshev's inequality*** *applies:*

$$\mathbf{P}\,(|X - \mathbf{E}[X]| \geq \varepsilon) \leq \frac{1}{\varepsilon^2} \cdot \mathbf{Var}\,[X]\,.$$

Applied to $(X_1 + \cdots + X_n)/n$, this yields:

$$\mathbf{P}\,(|\frac{X_1 + \ldots + X_n}{n} - \mu\,| \geq \varepsilon) \leq \frac{\mathbf{Var}\,[X_1]}{\varepsilon^2 n},.$$

And now Bernouilli's law follows with $n \to \infty$.

to combinatorics and the discovery, as well as the proof, of the weak law of large numbers.

7 PAFNUTY CHEBYSHEV (1821–94), major Russian mathematician. A productive school of probability theory developed in Russia on the basis of his work. He was one of the first to examine random variables.

FIGURE 54. Pascal.

10
'Time and Place Without a Ground Is Violence' (Aristotle)

Medea is led away from her homeland of Colchis to the foreign land of Corinth. The time in which Jason loved her has passed. She is alienated from time and place. A disaster unfolds: she kills her own children. Aristotle refers to such as story as the 'loss of a ground'. Rationality is lost because Medea literally loses the ground beneath her feet.

FIGURE 55. Jason and Medea, medieval depiction. The oversized heads of the protagonists are similar to those in copperplates from 1810 relating to *The Elective Affinities*.

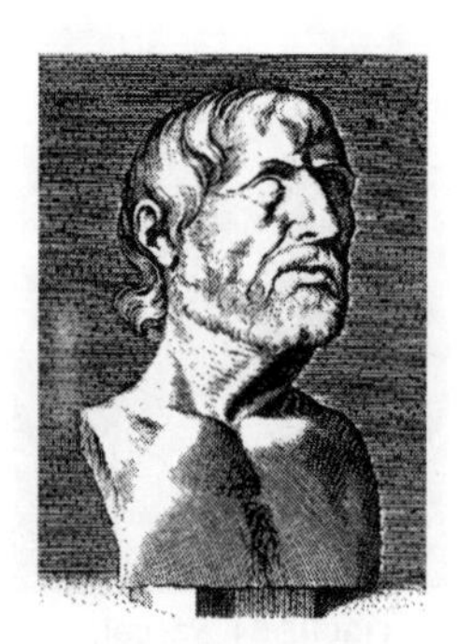

FIGURE 56. Seneca.

11
Neo-stoicism

Stoicism, as defined in antiquity by the philosopher and statesman Seneca, follows the ideal of ATARAXIA, an attitude of unshakeable calm. In the domain of the tender force, it means abstinence. At the edge of storms, of the coursing river, the wanderer turns back.

But the Stoic attitude also has another side, one that does not face towards abstinence and reversal, which toppled the Roman kings in the person of Lucretia. This young woman had been seduced and raped by a reckless prince. Tarquin the Proud, the last king of Rome, delayed the resolution of the case, seeking to protect his son. Lucretia stabbed herself before all their eyes. The story of Virginia is a variation on this parable.

'Neo-stoicism' is the term for the revival of this classical stance, which is one of the core components of seventeenth-century bourgeois society. Death over of bankruptcy, FREEDOM OR DEATH (the death of the Marquis de Posa) and LIEBESTOD.[8]

---

8 Gotthold Ephraim Lessing repeats this tale in his play *Emilia Galotti* in the name of the Enlightenment. Victor Hugo takes it up

FIGURE 57. *The Burden of Reason*

12
Derivation of Reason (*Raison*) from the Word *Arraisonnement*

Is there more than one line of ancestry in the genealogy of reason? If there are two lines of descent in this respect, is there a similar dual genealogy of love? Are there even two different derivations of basic human powers? In his essay '*Geschlecht* II: Heidegger's Hand', Jacques Derrida examines the typology of sexual difference and relates it to the typology of pairs in human and animal evolution:

---

in his play *The King Amuses Himself*, and Giuseppe Verdi used this as the basis for his opera *Rigoletto*, which, based on the importance of characters, should really have been named after the young protagonist Gilda, who sacrifices her life out of stoicism.

two hands, two eyes, two brain hemispheres, two ears–but five toes and not two hearts.

Derrida generally questions whether a final TWO makes us happy. What would a TWO be if it were 'not yet' or 'no longer'? The 'not yet' and the already 'no longer', Derrida claims, would contribute renewing the structures of the GROUND and REASON.

Derrida's German translator, Hans-Dieter Gondek, added a footnote here:

One could derive the modern term 'rationale' or 'rationality' from the word ARRAISONNEMENT. This Old French word refers to checking the hygiene of a ship's cargo before disembarking, and also to checking the correctness of the cargo (smuggled goods) and the inventories. It is the noun of the verb *arraisonner*, 'turn to someone, try to convince someone, commit oneself'.

A. Gartmann notes on this topic that while the brain consists of two hemispheres, these are always used together for the purpose of rational thought. According to a remark by Nietzsche, however, the future of humans is endangered if we do not have two brains at our disposal: one with experience and a motivation for science, the other adapted to humans as creatures of pleasure, and capable of creating and defending illusions. If both activities took place in the same brain, scientists (and the search for truth) would be at risk of being overwhelmed by the search for pleasure. This, Nietzsche argues, is stronger than the rational mind.

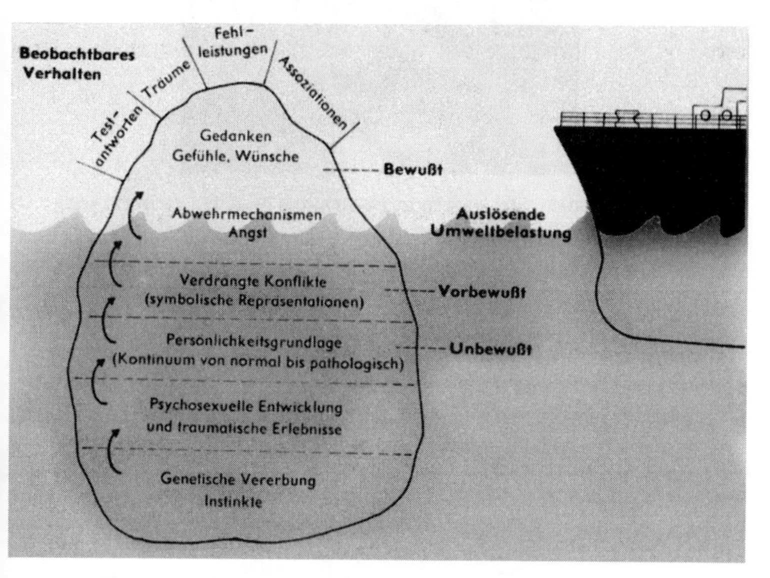

FIGURE 58. Reason, depicted as a ship (after Gartmann). Opposite left: the emotions, depicted as an iceberg.

FIGURE 59 (ABOVE). She wanted to give him the keys, but he didn't take them. Gerda Baethe, 1928. 'General assembly of the emotions'. If the emotions could all be gathered in one place, like a city, this would be 'the human experience'. Gerda Baethe: 'It'd be a love story if I were myself *and* my lover at the same time.'

FIGURE 60 (BELOW). Emblem of loyalty, seventeenth century. It consists of two clouds joined by a handshake. The key and lock are kept safe with handcuffs; above them the wheat and six-pointed lucky star, on its tip is time, which runs out inexorably, and at the top the hour of death. At the bottom left an oak tree, cut down to the roots, with a new branch growing.

SIX STORIES FOR NIKLAS LUHMANN

'In this sense, love as a medium is not itself an emotion, but rather a medium of communication . . .'

Love as Passion, *p. 23*

Either 'intimate' or 'cursory'.
It's language, not a kiss.

The Kiss

The First Extreme Close-Up in the World

Two well-known Broadway actors. For a high entrance fee, one can watch them on stage, that is, from a distance. One also has to muster some interest in the subject of the play being acted. All of that reduces the circle of people who become directly acquainted with these popular actors. But they are widely known in New York nonetheless, even among people who have never seen them. The newspaper reports take care of that.

A film operator had the idea of staging a kiss with these two stars and filming it as a close-up. During the filming, the protagonists did not feel 'intimate' but 'full of silliness'. As they rehearsed the kiss (this was already filmed and later released as *The Kiss*), they could not imagine how what they were doing would look to an observer; one does not watch oneself from the outside while kissing. The mouths approach each other, the lips meet. The actors closed their eyes but one couldn't see that in the shot. It looked 'passionate' (although they were chuckling inwardly), simply because it was so large on the screen. None of the viewers had ever seen such a thing. The film went around the world. Only now were the two celebrities truly famous. Strangely enough, no one attempted to copy the sensation. Its success could have been continued by coupling other celebrities, or by transferring it to a setting in Shanghai or Sweden.

–How does one shoot a kiss scene nowadays?

–One explains the situation to the actors and relies on them being able to kiss.

–And if they don't like each other?

–Then they have to pretend.

–It's hard for the director to influence the details?

–Especially because the lips behave spontaneously while kissing.

–And how does one film a Judas kiss?

–It has to be either 'intimate' or 'cursory'. After all, the kiss is just a signal so that the henchmen know whom to seize. It's language, not a kiss.

'One of the most striking traits of love semantics* [. . .] *is exclusivity.'
Love as Passion, *p. 123.*

So Incredibly Evil That His Hair Had to Fall Out

I

The 28-year-old businessman Reiner F., who lived in a northern German city and at times employed over 100 workers, was excessive in a certain sense. He considered his individual head a mover and shaker. He often admired himself, the way his silky but also dense black hair wrapped this head, with only a bit of ear sticking out. He had recently married the young Dagmar G., who suited the overall arrangement of his house, business, body and head.

The 23-year-old Dagmar, now Mrs F., was three months pregnant. But she was not ready to tie herself down yet, and planned to abort the baby. At first, she was probably simply imitating her husband's attitude: to save oneself up for even more precious situations. She wanted her own *uniqueness*, which Reiner F. did not acknowledge, to catch up with his uniqueness. Motherhood, which she saw as a fate shared by countless others, would not have been enough for that.

Her later insistence on this position when attacked by Reiner F.–he found the abortion of a foetus he had produced insulting–was, says Dagmar's mother, stubbornness. Rainer F. locked the attractive woman, who doggedly refused to abandon her intentions, in a weekend house that belonged to him along with various others. But she managed to escape. She sought refuge at Nordhorn Hospital, in the private clinic of Dr med. U., as this meant she was already close to a potential chance for abortion. Reiner F. got into this clinic, dressed as a male nurse. A doctor prevented him at the last minute from seizing his wife and bringing her under his control again.

Reiner F. subsequently kidnapped the eight-year-old schoolgirl Birgit G., whom he knew from his neighbourhood. Using the child as a hostage, he forced his wife by telephone to meet him. The businessman was waiting close to the pub Liebruck, the child in the back seat of his yellow BMW, which the young Dagmar entered. She immediately fastened her seatbelt. Arguing fiercely and going at high speed, the couple drove onto the motorway in the direction of Kassel. Police officers in several cars tailed the vehicle. The intention of the police command was to follow the kidnapper's car within his sight, thus pounding away at F.'s nerves in the hope of creating some opportunity for the officers to strike.

II

DETECTIVE SUPERINTENDENT BECKMANN: The man is psychologically atypical.

DETECTIVE INSPECTOR DREYER: That's exactly what I mean. In my opinion the man has weak nerves.

DETECTIVE SUPERINTENDENT: How about contacting all acquaintances and relatives, maybe that will help us to choose a particular psychological focus.

DETECTIVE INSPECTOR: Already been done. The same every time: intensely determined, and at the same time they say he has weak nerves.

DETECTIVE SUPERINTENDENT: We should draw up a behavioural profile and pass it on to the officers via radio. They're staying within sight?

DETECTIVE INSPECTOR: They are indeed. We've also positioned cars in the slip roads that can join the pursuit convoy. Half a dozen vehicles.

DETECTIVE SUPERINTENDENT: Then let's put together a typical psychological profile of the offender.

III

Indeed, Reiner F. quickly grew nervous. The woman sitting next to him remained stubbornly silent. To him, this was an especially intense form of quarrel. At the Göttingen slip road, the police cars waiting there joined the motorway too early. They drove side by side in pairs in front of the BMW driven by the businessman, who assumed they were trying to slow him down and push him within reach of the pursuers approaching from behind.

He now saw no way out, and, while holding on to the steering wheel with his left hand, he stabbed his wife, who was strapped into her seat with her seatbelt, with a knife.

For all his bitterness that day, the businessman still had the presence of mind to consider the exclusive rights for his statements to the press. He only spoke to one journalist, Ms Wagenfeld, and said nothing to anyone else.

IV

WAGENFELD: What made you commit this terrible deed?

REINER F.: Dagmar didn't want our child, which I desperately wished for.

WAGENFELD: But now you don't have it either.

REINER F.: That's different, I had no choice but to stab her, because neither the police nor my wife understood my signs. But Dagmar could have given birth to the child. She just lacked the goodwill. I had that goodwill.

WAGENFELD: Our readers won't understand that: you say that your wife's horrible death is a matter of *your* goodwill?

REINER F.: You have to write that I didn't have any choice.

WAGENFELD: I'd be happy to write that, but first you'll have to give me a convincing reason.

REINER F.: I've never experienced anything like this. Maybe on doesn't get everything right the first time. It's down to inexperience.

WAGENFELD: But let me just address another point: if you're steering the car carefully with one hand at 100 miles per hour and simultaneously stabbing as hard as the pursuing officers reported, and often ducked down deep to the right, then that's not inexperience. It's like a professional.

REINER F.: I've been driving since I was 16.

WAGENFELD: Let's forget about the reason. Maybe the readers will accept that some acts happen without a particular reason. Do you regret your act? You also harmed yourself, one could say.

REINER F.: Yes, that's right. I hurt my hand here. You don't think I would cut my own hand on purpose?

WAGENFELD: No. And the readers won't believe that either. The whole thing is unbelievable, actually.

REINER F.: In the sense of unique?

WAGENFELD: It certainly doesn't happen often. Or, rather, it does: it happens all the time on the back page of the newspaper. Sorry to disappoint you.

REINER F.: But not exactly the same as my case, in every detail.

WAGENFELD: That's unimportant. Let's return to the question of remorse.

REINER F.: Yes, I regret what I did.

WAGENFELD: Do you wish you could undo what happened?

REINER F.: Yes. Looking back, I wish I could undo it.

WAGENFELD: How?

REINER F.: I'll have to think about that. Now I need a break. Let's carry on tomorrow.

V

It was an entirely new experience for F. that things were not going the way his head wanted them to. His wife's obstinate behaviour had was prepared him for the situation but he had assumed the whole time that he would be able to break her will. Now, in a prison cell in Kreiensen, he was confronted with the situation that his will could no longer control the unfolding situation. He genuinely did not know how one could undo the previous day's events. He was unable to comprehend this. He imagined it like this: his head had not been involved when he committed the deed, so he could not correct it with his head, which usually knew no boundaries. Now he told himself that maybe none of this was true.

'In love, nothing is trivial.'
Love as Passion, *p. 200*

The Lovers of Dakar

'If there is a probability of 99 per cent against love, but I love, then it is the 1 per cent that is probable.'

The Insurance Handbook

For a moment he had not been calculating enough. That cost him his material existence. One cannot even say that he was not calculating at the fateful moment of his decision: he was not calculating fully, not circumspectly. He thought he could get away with a prize. For the first time in his life, he thought he had made a favourable decision. Some of his friends say this was the first time he had actually been *alive*. But also that it was dangerous to keep oneself under control one's whole life (aside from a few experiences in the corners of a swimming pool as a child) and then suddenly want to be 'alive'. One catches cold.

Eduard von Lüdtkendorf was among the decision-makers at one of the insurance companies in the social market economy. 'Calculating probabilities is my job,' he scoffed.[9] On one of his flying visits to Africa, as an advisor to one of the republics largely cut off from the world market, he met a local woman. She was the daughter of a French adventurer and a Latin American banker's widow, and only superficially resembled the indigenous population in the colour of her skin. This young NATIVE (she had studied in Paris, held estates, others had referred to

9 'The lifeworld versus the system world.' Lüdtkendorf, an ambassador or fortune-teller from the system world. Going by statistics, the answers he gave the government in Dakar would have been uninteresting: the country had no chance on the world market. But there are gaps in this definition, for the way one describes the country's lack of chances, that is, to the International Monetary Fund, depends on one's emphasis. One can also make projections on the basis of probabilities. When it came to the rhetoric of this SECOND WORLD, that world of projection which dominates reality, Lüdtkendorf was a master.

her as a young lady in Dakar's high society, and she actually worked for a Parisian media firm) confused his mind. For a moment he thought that a genuine living being was dependent on him here. He had made a find. He was now master of a subjective event, this blooming of this young girl's, a singularity; he had escaped from the fatal stream of probabilities, which promise nothing but ultimate death. Renée grew towards him as a tribute from this country, like a slave who disarms him by subjugation.

He decided, during just *one* fatal night, to take Renée back to Europe as his companion. He had barely captured his prey and secured her in a hotel apartment when the insurance business sucked him in again.

Lüdtkendorf was married to Lydia, née von H., several children. This life, which statistics say is characteristic of 82 per cent of all managers in top positions, was separate from his working days, from his heart, and took place in a quiet area of the Bergisch countryside. Eduard saw it as a property that could be discarded. After returning from Africa, however, he felt obliged to show himself briefly to these FAMILY MEMBERS.

That same evening, during a rushed visit to the hotel apartment, he could no longer realize that feeling of DEVOTION towards Renée that he had experienced in Dakar. He attributed it to the lack of time, to overexhaustion, a physical weakness, telling himself: I'll catch up on the loving part, let's just take care of the practical things now.

The high society of Cologne consists of between three and five groups of people who control things; these groups are separated from one another. The insurance group, with its designated followers, was a significant forum for Eduard's career. The group, which did not take much time to form its opinions, showed– contrary to Eduard's expectations–a hostile attitude towards his 'escapade'. It took the side of the family in the Bergisches Land, because they knew Lydia and had no time to make the indigenous woman's acquaintance. Do you want all your money to go to offspring with black and white stripes like a zebra? They said that without knowing anything about his lover's actual appearance or origins. His best friend Pfuel, whom he asked for advice, advised him to keep Mendel's laws in mind.[10]

Eduard was given medical treatment. Pneumonia, heart pains, a bladder infection too. Equipped with antibiotics, he carried out his duties. In his weakness, he was unable to reject any of the intolerable provisional solutions. The young native was entrusted to the same doctor who was treating Eduard: she likewise diagnosed a bladder infection, the mirror image of his. The lovers of Dakar found themselves in a state of mutual siege.

---

10 Pfuel, likewise an insurance executive, summarized the situation in the following terms to Thoma, who was now advising the government of North Rhine-Westphalia: generally speaking, love for something foreign is an evolutionary advantage. This is contradicted by a probability calculation which states that 98 per cent of men in top positions who change their lives after a DECISION ON THE SPUR OF THE MOMENT, and consequently commit themselves in haste, fail completely or lose their positions. Presumably Eduard, said Pfuel, did not see this particular tendency. He wanted to escape certain death by doing something statistically unusual. Assuming he was thinking at all, the experienced Thoma replied.

Talking about it was useless (in French, even though Renée was making attempts to learn German). Whenever they started getting to the heart of the matter, she lapsed back into her native tongue.

What killed him was not the resistance of his environment or his dual role in relation to his 'family', a part of his life that was already separate, but the fact that his passionate feeling of happiness had cooled off as soon as he removed this native creature from her enchanted, industrially crippled homeland and placed her in the pond of a dwelling in Cologne. The only comfort was that the hotel's surroundings, the suburb where this apartment house was located, had a touch of 'elsewhere' to it; in certain moments, when he stopped briefly at a bar before and after his visits, he had a familiar sense of foreboding.

Pfuel advised him to give everything up: make a clean sweep. Send his lover back to Dakar or Paris with her needs covered, get a divorce and surrender completely to hope, to uncertainty. Eduard, who feared death behind every decision, instead looked at the options for a change of profession. He already felt very weak.

The sophisticated antiobiotics, augmented by stabilizing injections, had no effect. He coughed at night and did not let anyone look after him or give him advice any more. 'My whole life was just one request, and it was a futile request.' And who was there to come and save him? Every day after work he lay quietly in a hotel room (his rational mind insisted on this, a sort of inner conviction that he had to do his duty so that he could change when the favourable moment came, he wanted to cling to this piece of reality until the end). Strictly separated from his home in the Bergisches Land, from the hotel apartment where his 'mistress' was sitting, and separated from the 'society' and its weekly meetings. His heart burst or his breath ran out. The cause of death was kept vague in the hotel doctor's report: 'No third-party interference.'

The young native woman with a French passport, a true Parisian, had left. The divorce certificate for Lydia arrived a few days later. All significant dealings by the two West African republics that Lüdtkendorf had advised were still controlled by a consortium, much as the ancient world was ruled by the gods. Many people whom Eduard had helped came to his funeral. The 'family' stayed away. This cost them considerable respect in the eyes of Cologne's conservative high society (all five parts of it); one forgets all anger in the face of death.

The Week of the Engagement

'Because it is not unusual to
have sexual relations even without love.'

Niklas Luhmann

That woke her from her daze: evidently (going by all his declarations) he wanted to make her his wife. It was important to him, she could feel that. A heavy cold in her nose, chest and throat, it had been a week now. The abruptness. Her mother brought her a large glass of hot lemon.

One can't fall in love within a week, she told herself. Though one could in a second. A glance, a touch of the hand is enough. She let him look down her throat the second time he asked. Heavy inflammation, he said. He took the spatula he had used to hold down her tongue and placed it beside the instruments on her bedside table. She did not find this intimate contact unpleasant; she could still get enough air while he was looking down her throat. He was a doctor. There was nothing 'electrifying' about it, the way love is supposed to be. She found his hands 'skilled'. She would have trusted him as an electrician, and indeed as a doctor, and one word led to another. She hated decisions that didn't come about by themselves. How was she supposed to know what she would feel in 10 or 20 years? She couldn't even predict what she would think of an ETERNAL COMMITMENT a fortnight from now.

In keeping with tradition, the petitioner had asked her father. Her father had answered, as is customary today, that *he* could have exercised authority in such a matter 30 years ago but now it was entirely his daughter's choice. She could have read her father's opinion in his features, in his eyes, in his posture, if all his words had not already revealed what he felt. Her father's reaction was not favourable for the petitioner. But whom could this father, always generous towards himself and jealous, really have liked as his daughter's lover? A private detective was hired to check the suitor's financial situation and other information he had given in the provincial town from which he came.

Marriage had no public significance at all for the family. In big Berlin, no one pays attention to one individual marriage between two unknown people. Her six friends would go wild. She would be the first to find a husband. She was up for plenty of things, better things too, but nothing had produced such rapid results. So now she was the first in her circle.

The mother, who had a depressive attitude towards men, was eager to marry off her daughter. She always was, she wanted her out of the way and already imagined herself settled on some property in the provincial town, the petitioner's base, like in some colony. She wanted to hold court there as the mother-in-law from the capital.

One morning, that same week, the YOUNG GIRL WITH A COLD said, 'Yes'. The way one blabs about something. Dates were made. Engagement in her parents' town and later a celebration in H., where the bridegroom lived, then honeymoon in Paris. She began to have doubts. She didn't want to look like a turncoat, like a hysteric. So she stood by her 'decision'.

The bond was supposed to be 'for life'. The thought shocked her. At 21, in the 'vigour of youth', she could not imagine this DEATH THAT PARTS. She did not wish death upon the petitioner, who had been successful, she had to admit. So the words remained empty. Only a 'moment', lived in paradise; but love makes it possible to look death in the eye, because I can let go of life once it has been fulfilled.

She felt sure that such moments didn't only exist in novels, but had never experienced one, nor had she ever heard a plausible account of an actual case; yet she was certain that it was true. She was not squandering it with her decision. Could she have waited? What a fickle chief advisor she had: a mother who feared nothing more than one of her female children (she had two) being struck by the 'lightning bolt of love', and paying for the crazy idea which people called 'love' with a loss of status. Her vacillating father with his PLEASURE-SEEKING EYES, a man of weak principles, could easily be swayed by an entertaining idea. What should he advise? Don't do the wrong thing, child, don't miss a chance, seize the moment and don't wait. But be careful about it.

Her decision, made under the special circumstances of a cold at its peak, which paralysed her brain and all her limbs, with a verifiable temperature of 39 degrees and leg compresses, was good for twelve years. She had resolved only to be unfaithful to her husband when a kind of electric shock, a 'lightning bolt of love', went through her. None of these adventures threatened her marriage. The divorce came during the war, when their circumstances drifted apart through an accumulation of mundane reasons. There was injury on both sides. Others came to provide advice. That was precisely what drove them apart.

By 1944, souls capable of looking to the future were already moving west. She left her husband. She could see that he wanted to stay in his provincial home town in the east; directly afterwards, the area was overrun by the Red Army. But she sensed that the highlights of her life would lie elsewhere.

'We need satyrs, water nymphs, spirits,
nakedness of feeling,
to "whirl up" the sluggish sexual relationships
of our comrades.'

A New Genotype of Theory

1

In the glory days of the training academy for the GRU (military intelligence service of the Red Army) in Moscow, a widely noted department for BUSINESS STUDIES IN LOVE MATTERS was developed. 'Love matters' encompassed all homo- and heterosexual connections which formed a sort of shadow economy in the political system of the fatherland and could be used for espionage or counter-espionage. This SECOND RUSSIA, stated Yuri Shipkov, who was developing the course, redistributed more power than the regular regime, comprising the main departments of politics, business and technology, which are represented in the party and state organs. This shadow economy was divided up as follows:

–The particularities of wishes

–The counterbalances to daily life

–Stability, self-confidence, organization of the self

–And the overthrow

This was the basis of Shipkov's doctrine of the FOUR ECONOMIES.

The department was considered irregular. Academic members who culled information from this area doubted that such a SUBJECTIVE SHADOW ECONOMY was what Marx had in mind in his *Outlines of the Critique of Political Economy*.

On the other hand, the department enjoyed such brilliant successes in practice on the SEXUAL ESPIONAGE FRONT OF THE FATHERLAND that the high-ranking overseers, after the ideologically lax phase under Khrushchev and Brezhnev, let the new academic discipline continue. Only the collapse of the USSR, that is, an unsuitable savings policy, destroyed this promising outgrowth of materialist science before its effects could spread to social practice.

2

Shipkov's FOURTH ECONOMY[11] presupposed the creation of an ATMOSPHERE (= mood of something special) between the male agent seeking to seduce a woman with confidential information (or a female agent 'exploring' a man with such information) and the respective 'victim'. Without this atmosphere, in a cold and mechanical setting, success was impossible to achieve.

–One should light a candle? Exchange pleasantries?

–Not pleasantries. The point is to prove one is genuine. There has to be something genuine about it.

–It needs to have some value?

–The value of genuineness. That is what creates the 'mood'.

---

11 The FIRST ECONOMY is the global economy, the SECOND is that of the Soviet Union, the THIRD is the shadow economy and the FOURTH exists, without balances or bookkeeping, in erotic reliability. The FOUR ECONOMIES, Shipkov claims, act upwards from the lowest (the FOURTH) to the highest (the FIRST).

–Isn't that a rather romantic point of view? Is that the statement of a scientific materialist?

–That's exactly who's standing before you and telling you all this.

It was most of all the time factor, according to the lectures, that was different in the FOURTH ECONOMY compared to the THIRD, SECOND or FIRST.[12] A top-class Romeo had lured a female executive in one of the major foundations in the USA into his net. This foundation dealt with the arms lobby, where sensitive information was piled up like a hoard of gold. The agent had managed to create an intimate situation, but then, overly nervous because of the importance of his prey, he made the mistake of being too 'ambitious' and forcing himself on the young woman. He immediately lost contact and the 'atmosphere' was lost. The love affair suffocated. The very next morning he was exposed, simply because he had been too forward.

The central components of my theory, however, Shipkov continued, are not based on training our agents

---

12 An example of the expansion of the FIRST and FOURTH ECONOMIES: Napoleon, addressee of the FIRST ECONOMY, was called away from a dictation and led to a cabinet where a lover was awaiting him. Though he was erect at once, the PROCURED woman, astounded to encounter the emperor thus, was not quick enough in the production of her bodily fluids to enable a pleasant intercourse in such haste. Thus it ended in pain and mutual recriminations, which could not be expressed unreservedly because of the difference in rank. (See 'Work Timekeeper A. Trube on Love, Power and the Difference Between the Passage of Time in the Seventeenth and Twenty-First Centuries' in this volume.)

to deal with outside enemies; their aim is not to serve particular purposes at all. The greater the instrumentalization, the smaller the chance of success. Rather, the significance of the FOURTH ECONOMY lies in its effects within the Soviet Union. We need satyrs, water nymphs, spirits, nakedness of feeling, to 'whirl' up the sluggish sexual relationships of our comrades, that is, we need an injection of chaos in response to the blind yet worldly wise monads that have been waiting for such a response in the souls of the Soviet people (patient for centuries, exasperated in their futile hope).[13]

How can hands and mouths in the remote mountains of Siberia be trained to turn an INTIMATE ATMOSPHERE, once created, into a stimulus for life–indirectly, and with the necessary elements of slowness (but not sluggishly)? That, said Shipkov, is a matter of our fatherland's very survival. Shipkov was familiar with this concept from the formulations of Foucault's 'biopolitics'. Who would doubt that the party saw no imperative to undertake this? Just bring up the topic was already damaging to the party. Twelve years after Shipkov's department, the party was finished. Files were taken out of the Central Committee's building, containing not a single word about the FOURTH ECONOMY.[14]

---

13 Shipkov quotes Turgenev's claim that Russia's men and women are lastingly separated by a fundamental misunderstanding. All attraction is based on mistaking one thing for another.

14 'Uniqueness', Shipkov stated, would have been the key word.

The Kitchen of Happiness

Two Days During the 1968/69 Winter Semester in the Revolutionary City of Frankfurt

1

A Seminar with a Pasted-Over Announcement

The man from Bielefeld made his way with long strides. The briefcase was in his left hand. He took the route through the student house in Jügelstrasse, because he wanted to avoid the crowds of students waiting at the main entrance to the university. By taking the caretaker's exit from the student house, he could reach the side entrance to the tower that housed the lecture theatres, which were on the first floor, directly above the rebuilt portal. In the practice room, which had space for 60 participants, he was met by four students: three woman and a men. He greeted those present. He took the typescript from his briefcase; the lesson was called 'Love as Passion'. The announcement on the notice board outside the vice-chancellor's office had been pasted over with calls to a teach-in. The man from Bielefeld politely explained how he intended to proceed in the seminar.

2

What Good Is a Semester's Leave?

T. W. Adorno was released from all his university duties during the 1968/69 winter semester. But the time thus gained was immediately set upon by the time consumers.

He had to respond to enquiries, keep examination appointments. He had planned to finish the AESTHETIC THEORY by the autumn of 1969. Instead, the work only proceeded at a laborious pace. Today was already the seventh meeting at the Institute of Social Research on the subject of one-third parity.[15] As soon as the meeting is over he flees to a cafe where he used to write during his time as an outside lecturer, as the son of his parents. With his delicate handwriting, he covers page after page of his notebook whose contents will one day enter the final work. Enquiries from the audit office have been left unanswered. The university's board of trustees has emphatically urged him to answer. What could he, the scholar, contribute to the subject? He is expected to make a contribution. He cannot reply, 'Don't know.' He cannot respond, 'No time!'

And so the hours grow alienated from him. The present moment is paralyzed by the expectation that further time consumption awaits him the next day. Unhappiness slows him down. The time pressure does not make him any faster.

Now, around 2.30 p.m., his *thymos*, the *thymos* of the lover, is affected by the fact that he must show himself at a funeral, concerning the matter of Roland Pelzer, at 4. He remembers that he neglected to sign off on a donation for the parents of the deceased that had been prepared in his office at the institute. So he has to stop by at the institute before his appointment at the doctoral student's coffin.

---

15 The principle of one-third parity came from a compromise suggestion during the occupation of the sociology department. It was planned to apply it to the Institute of Social Research. The institute was to be subject to an assembly with one-third parity (one third students, one third assistants, one third professors). Modalities were to be found jointly for forming self-organized work and project groups.

People will use the opportunity to hold him up, to ask urgent questions.

The circumstance that said Roland Pelzer jumped off the Goethe Tower in the city park moves him in his heart. In fact, it is bad for his circulation. The notes on Hegel's concepts of the subject and the object, which he is working on in parallel with the AESTHETIC THEORY, border on the research terrain that evidently drove Pelzer to despair. Adorno would rather have written the dissertation for him instead of mourning him now. In a brief farewell note, the young suicide donated his body to science so that the fee paid in return for the body would help his parents to cover the funeral expenses. But the anatomy department rejected the shattered body; it was unusable for research purposes. Adorno was unsure whether to oppose this with a petition or cover the damage with a sum taken out of the institute's budget (he would have to discuss it with Friedrich Pollock, and a one-third parity would make such a directive impossible). He regretted the loss of time that would result either way. On the other hand, the young man's extreme decision weighed on his heart. He saw the 'tragic sign' as a warning that he must change either his life, that of philosophy, that of Frankfurt or that of the world. He felt the conflict between his empathy and the urgency of furthering his book's progress. Was he 'bankrupt of time?' Should he return to the deliberations on SKOTEINOS, OR WHAT IS DARK from NEGATIVE DIALECTICS in the AESTHETIC THEORY using examples from music?

His mistress, who left him in late autumn, had said to him: You're going mouldy. I can smell that you're dying. That was unkind. So what good was a semester's leave?

The completion of his collected works, a substantial line of books that the AESTHETIC THEORY would have extended by another four fingers' width, was now meaningless to him. Rejection and diabetes dried him up. In front of the cafe there was a crowd of hostile students, possibly heading towards the Institute of Social Research. None of these people were willing to make a truce with him, or indeed any form of contract.

'I will die
You will kiss another'

3

The Only Love Realized During This Time: Love of Architecture

In those cold nights, Ferdy Kramer, the university's construction manager, walked along the narrow streets of Bockenheim where residential houses near the university were awaiting demolition. He checked, planned, arranged. This was the place for the construction of new department buildings. He often spoke to the residents: they should give

FIGURE 61. The Johann Wolfgang Goethe University. Original ('Wilhelmine') entrance to the main building.

up their domiciles in good time and get compensation. This area was dedicated to the expansion of the sciences.

Kramer, a good-natured man, had a persistent striving for the truth. His mind scouted out the route where the progress of RESEARCH and LEARNING would be provided with spaces. This construction was his one love. Just completed: the university's heating and power station, designed and built by him. With a yellow brick chimney that struck him as the best thing he had ever built. He had overcome the resistance of the city council during the planning phase. The project's militant opponents hadn't known where they should go to fight. They went to court. But the energy required to build a tower like that was written on a piece of paper, the budget; construction sketches and the permit for the whole thing were appended.

FIGURE 62 (LEFT). Rebuilding of the entrance by Ferdy Kramer. The seminar room where Luhmann taught was on the first floor.

FIGURE 63 (RIGHT). Renaming as Karl Marx University. Main entrance still in the open form designed by Ferdy Kramer.

FIGURE 64. Café Bauer: here Adorno wrote in his delicate handwriting, in 1929 and in the 1968/69 winter semester. Marcuse claimed he was unable to read this writing. He therefore returned Adorno's last letter, asking for a typewritten version.

4

It Could Be That the Night Is Growing Lighter, but the Day of Freedom Is Not Dawning After All

The comrades led by Paul, Gerda and Meike, three men and two women, drive in a VW along the country roads, once around the Caltex refinery on the left bank of the Main River, then around the Hoechst complex, along the walls, wooden fences and gates, try to draw out the security guards by observing a gate with binoculars as well as taking pictures, take a test drive to Dyckerhoff in *Wiesbaden*, travel along the right bank of the Rhine up to *Cologne* with the elan of Marco Polo, 'paying particular attention to small and medium-sized businesses', cross the forests to *Wuppertal* and then back round again, 'paying particular attention to all industrial facilities', which will be now be connected to one another for the first time 'by a concrete group of people' (and not simply by consumer, marketing and delivery relationships), to *Oberhausen*, then along the motorway up to *Siegerland*, then country roads, 'paying particular attention to small, medium-sized and large businesses', but the eye can only circle the fences, walls and entrances of the firms; a 'picturesque' route to *Kassel*, then *Giessen* and back again.

Science is travelling, says Paul, it's taking footsteps, connecting the places where the 'collective worker' 'rests as if asleep'.

The age of capitalism according to Willi's estimate: 800 years, and before that some sudden moments and islands of a more innocent form of capitalism amid ancient agricultural zones: the Phoenician mariners.[16]

'Soon, on its course, the sun will be eager
To boast of the coming morn,
Soon the dark night will no longer beleaguer
And the day of freedom will dawn.'

---

16 Reinhard F. from the German study group provides the text:

'If I wished to be among the heroes
And could declare it freely, with the voice of the shepherd
Or in the native tongue of a Hessian,
It would be a hero of the seas.
For to gain an occupation
Is the most grateful thing
Of all . . .'

5

The Real Circumstances Always Reveal Themselves as a Mixture . . .

As in all the previous years (also at the end of the Second World War), the carnival societies in the Frankfurt suburbs prepared for their meetings and parades just like those on the southern bank of the Main–with no connection to the student protests. A batch of new goods had arrived from Schleswig-Holstein, Bulgaria and Africa in the establishments of Kaiserstrasse and Weserstrasse, where they were 'schooled' by pimps. Competing towing companies were fighting over a car stranded between Bad Vilbel and Bad Soden. An accident at the Messer works in Griesheim. Relocation plans for one of the main departments at the IG Metall trade union headquarters in Wilhelm-Leuschner-Strasse.

H. J. Krahl is standing, surrounded by 14 comrades, on a wooden platform at the exit of the university courtyard onto Bockenheimer Landstrasse and talking about the planned action, which has to be moved along at all points of the city, for all businesses, local and national, with the full force of the movement. He says it is wrong to claim that because this or that historical situation no longer applies, one should not speak of revolution today. The question is another: How can society be changed under these different, possibly more difficult conditions? And one could respond with the following theses . . .

Comrade Wiegand, officially an economist, says in his study group, before they have even found a topic: 'The closed nature of the universe has no power in itself that could resist the courage of knowing; it (the universe) must open up before it . . . ' The participants and comrades present criticize him; the concern is not the exploration of the universe but the concrete struggle of the day. Wiegand answers, 'But just listen . . . It must open up before it and lay its riches and its depth before it, and enable it to enjoy them . . . ' Stop it, they reply, that's totally the wrong tone. The point is whether we should stand in front of the VDO tomorrow morning with flyers, and what the study group should be doing. The drifting Wiegand is brought back by the group.

In a study group, at 1 a.m., Gert Uhlewetter compares the revolutionary process to childbirth. The group includes doctors and trainee midwives. 'It is only the revolution that creates society as the womb after birth. So it's *from* the womb *into* a womb.' That means turning the concept of organization inside out. And why does birth have to be painful? 'It causes the mother pain with its big head.'[17]

---

17 Georg Groddeck, *The Book of the It* (New York: Vintage, 1949): 'Or do you believe that Caligula or any other "sadist" with like equanimity would have bethought himself of so horrible a torture as to squeeze anyone by the head through a narrow hole? I saw a child once who had stuck his head through the railings of an iron fence and could move it neither backwards nor forwards. I shall not soon forget his screams.'

But two of the group's female members flatly deny that birth has to be accompanied by pain, and H. goes to the heart of the claim by calling it an act of appeasement to discuss the possibility of failure, of getting stuck, and admittedly the fact that this is painful or torturous, at the present moment, for there is no social birth taking place

FIGURE 65. Turbulent atmosphere at a teach-in: 'The detail, the particular and the general are marching through the city making shrill noises . . . '

6

In Search of Orgone: *Is There a Connection Between Revolutionary Elan and Eros*?

Because of the low-lying cloud cover spread over the city, the blue sky is not visible from the university grounds. This blue surrounding the planet is the proven sign of that substance or fluid which also comes about between lovers–like the aether, whose existence was once postulated by physicists but never proved. According to Freud's deputy and later apostate Dr Wilhelm Reich, humans need this orgone to find happiness. If they were totally cut off from it, they would be doomed.

---

anywhere. He agrees with them that the birth of a child ('in the conventional sense,' he says) is fundamentally possible with any pain. Now the women in the group attack him: What does he mean by 'fundamentally'? What does he know about it? How many births has he gone through? The discussion gets bogged down and returns to the main topic around 2 a.m., the notion of society as human, as a kind of collective womb, and what this requires.

For the young revolutionary movement in the Bockenheim and Nordend districts of Frankfurt, according to comrade Andreas von Kühlmann, one should set up nets to catch orgone. Alternatively, one could build a device in which the comrades actively produce a gas or liquid consisting of orgone. Without a massive allowance from the depots of the tender force, Kühlmann claims, the movement will not be able to manage the immense efforts to change society in the long run. The movement doesn't have many members yet. As soon as it gets connected to the ubiquitous stream (since millennia) of pent-up libidinous forces that we call orgone, political elan will reach new heights. 'What is private must become political.'

7

She Was Willing to Kindle Her Inner Flame

Elke Hinrichs rushed to the seminar with all her heart. The word PASSION, which she read on the announcement before it was pasted over, had magnetized her. She wanted to learn how to get close to Gerd Schäfer, who hadn't responded to her messages and secret notes since last Friday. She had placed them in front of his door. He had refused to reply for days now. She was impatient.

The jurist, who called himself a sociologist in this exercise, spoke of 'encoding intimacy'. She was perfectly willing to listen to lengthy explanations of matters that didn't interest her, as long as she found out at the end wherein PASSION lies, and how one can produce it in a lover or friend. She took Luhmann's deliberations to mean that passion was contagious, and always came about on both sides or not at all, and she was willing to kindle her inner flame if that was what it would take for Gerd to pay attention to her again.

'O impetuous heart,
Why do you weep?'

8

Could Revolutionary Elan Take Hold of the Diverse Human Landscapes of Germany?

The man from Bielefeld, accustomed to discipline since working at an adult education centre, made a great effort not to let anyone see that he had noticed how few participants were left in this seminar; the legendary seminar of the GREAT ADORNO had comprised over 100 participants.

The basic tendency of Luhmann's thinking was essentially practical. He considered the commotion of the protests, which he observed in the vicinity of the university, an EXCEPTIONAL PHENOMENON that would be difficult to reproduce in the long term. It was certainly capable of drawing participants away from his seminar but could not, he suspected, develop the necessary attraction to keep its groups together effectively, even just in Frankfurt and environs.

In the sociological charts he carried in his head, the metropolitan area of the Rhine-Main region was visible as only a small part of Europe. Compared to the regions of North Rhine-Westphalia, Lower Saxony, Upper and Lower Bavaria or Swabia, the city of Frankfurt was just a part of a federal state (and in the wider Frankfurt area, the student movement was a relatively small group).

Could revolutionary elan, Luhmann soberly asked himself, if there were enough time, take hold of the diverse human landscapes of Germany? It could, he thought, in 70 years–if it could sustain itself for that long. It would also have to be relevant to those who were not initially involved. Such an impulse would have to present itself as a sign of good fortune! In his bold mind, the scholar from Bielefeld was inclined to rule that out.

FIGURE 66. Niklas Luhmann (1927–98)

FIGURE 67. Hans-Jürgen Krahl (1943–70)

9

The Primacy of the Political / 'There Is No Life before Death'

We stood for four hours at the teach-in held in the big hall of the student house. There was such a crush that the stairs and the hall downstairs were also full of participants. The teach-in was broadcast via loudspeaker.

I would have liked to hug or touch Erwin F. We were only standing a few centimetres apart. But the attention of the people standing around was focused on the speaker. It would have stuck out if we had been affectionate to each other. My attention wasn't focused on the event. I would have liked to smell F. When the event is over, I told myself, he'll come to my bed, somewhat tired, and do the same thing he did with me on other evenings. We had already come together there a few times and I couldn't accept the relationship staying that way. Something had to happen here and now. Imagine we had to keep repeating what we usually did for ever, and then I died ('there is no life before death'). That was why I wanted to touch him at that moment. The speaker's text dealt with the precedence of work at companies over other protest work. He also denied that the struggle in the prison and justice campaigns had any priority. How can I clasp the man I love and guide him out of these surroundings? If I act in an undisciplined way now, I'll ruin things for good with this comrade.

A group in Nordend is making a flyer on 'Conditions in Preungesheim Women's Prison'. We know from Norway, they say, that the abolition of all prisons is the political response to the repression of the state apparatus. The director of the women's penal institution, Dr Einsele, set up an area for incarcerated mothers where they can receive and care for their children. But this approach was considered a dilution of the core concern, namely, to replace punishment per se and therefore appeasement.

A neighbouring group of comrades, debating in a Nordend bar, had turned their attention to the army campaign. A third group pursued the education campaign for workers' children. This project saw itself as a continuation of the education campaign for farmers' children being conducted by the comrades in Freiburg. The comrades had the impression that they didn't have much time.

10

A Reality Novel Whose Active Characters Have No Contact With One Another: An Example of Open Communication

A. Trube, who often frequented the bars in Nordend where the comrades had their debates, had calculated the time required for the execution of the various SOCIETY-CHANGING PLANS. For the 12 flyers' worth of projects printed in those two days during the 1968/69 winter semester that form the subject of the present story, Trube calculated that it would have been 80 years, and only if six times the actual number of group members were working on them. This was an average value based on estimates. He reckoned shorter durations for the prison campaign than the education campaign. He also considered the justice campaign, with an estimate of 130 years and 600 times as many group members working the whole time, a hopeless endeavour.

Yet Trube, whose friend Mecki Meier called him a KNOWITALL and REALITY POET, felt that the elements of a complete 'renewal of society' were present in the Frankfurt area, in a scattered form, during those days. (He failed to understand why the SDS [Socialist German Student Union] did not break up the following year.) On the other hand, he argued for the involvement of experienced divorce lawyers and matchmakers, not least for the collaboration of the council of experienced pimps in Kaiserstrasse, in the movement.

He often consulted with Fritz Dorfmann, the second assistant of the chief dramaturge at the Frankfurt Opera; Dorfmann was not a student. He was a career jumper in a twofold sense: as a non-academic dramaturgical employee and a non-student in the student revolt, and he dedicated himself all the more seriously to the analytical work. Could music theatre potentially be a contribution to social change? The work currently on the programme was Gluck's *Armide*, an opera that celebrated reform.

The SO-CALLED RADICAL LEFTIST WIND ORCHESTRA was rehearsing the march *Immortal Sacrifice*. Heiner Goebbels composed for the orchestra using elements from the score of Rossini's *The Thieving Magpie*, a second funeral march with a strong emotional effect. If the comrades from the leather-jacket faction in the SDS had heard about this luxuriant musical praxis, which crossed political boundaries, they would have burst into the rehearsal room (a garage filled with instruments and recording equipment) and burnt the sheet music.

11

An Example of Closed Communication

Whatever the weather, the judiciary is an example of an institution in a state of defence. Police groups are positioned in the bushes between the judiciary offices in Hammelsgasse and also on the way to the new buildings of the public prosecution department (with the aquarium windows). Instead of uniform trousers, they wear military-style breeches. The reserves (withdrawn from the veiling sun) in the unilluminated shadows at the entrances and staircases of building complex II. The courthouse blinds are down. This creates an isolated artificial climate inside the complex, in the offices and judges' rooms, that does not exist anywhere else on earth, either in summer or winter.

A fright in the evening hours: the tube of thickened air over the city and suburban zone has only frayed a little at the edges from the Taunus forests downwards. A motorcade drives along Homburger Landstrasse. Megaphones mounted on the vehicles. Four political prisoners in detention at Penal Facility III pending trial are meant to hear it. They must be released at once, while the head officials responsible for their arrest, for example, the police president, should be admitted to the institution in their place.

'Gisela out,
Müller in.'

Plainclothes police officers—posing as 'neighbours'—note down the registration numbers of the cars in the convoy. They count them 'negatively', that is, they record the paucity of the grouping compared to the number of vehicles on the streets of Frankfurt each day. For the investigator Ferdi Quecke, the number of 46 vehicles (still a deceptively impressive group to the eye) is not a satisfying result; they are too few to make his work important in the social sense. What if there were 7,250 vehicles, say? Then it would be dangerous to exercise his profession.

FIGURE 68 (ABOVE). Courthouses: student demonstration in the street between the district court and the higher regional court. 'Fortress of the judiciary'.

FIGURE 69 (BELOW). Disruption of the SPORTHILFE [a national sports charity] gala night at the Frankfurt Theatre by students. Present: business, banks, press, politicians. Picture: the former chancellor Ludwig Erhard's car. The driver has missed the correct entrance to the fenced area; the limousine is attacked, eggs are thrown at it. A blitz by motorized attack groups the same night to demolish the Spanish Embassy, the Amerikahaus and several banks. The logistical climax of the FRANKFURT WINTER REVOLUTION.

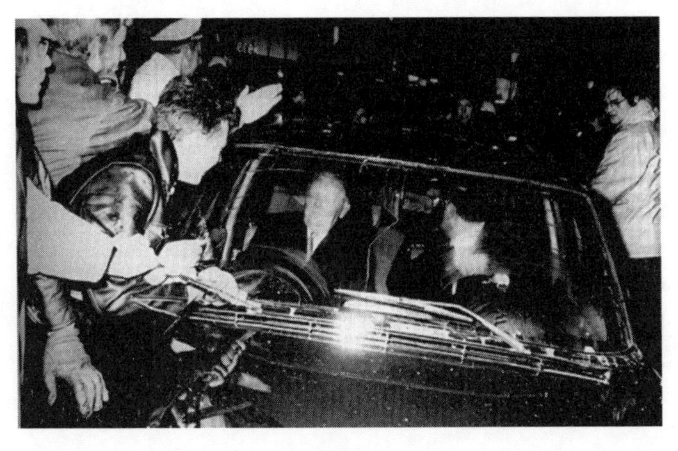

12

'Louis, I Think This Is the Beginning of a Beautiful Friendship . . .'

They had arranged to dine together at Rheingold, a wine bar opposite the stage entrance to the opera. Luhmann took the invitation for a polite gesture by Adorno; if he was standing in for him this semester, they could not really go without meeting. Yet it turned out that Luhmann was wrong: Adorno had sought contact in this way not out of courtesy but in a situation of existential need.

Luhmann ordered a Rhenish *sauerbraten*. Adorno, who had requested to pay for the meal, chose a bottle of Palatine wine and a rump steak à la Voltaire. Luhmann viewed this order as philosophical, rather than motivated by appetite. He later examined the wine list and saw that Adorno's choice of wine had likewise been guided by his thoughts rather than his tongue: he had ordered the most expensive wine to convey the value of their encounter. That was how Luhmann later described his impression.

His mistress had left him. During those days, Adorno shared his experience with anyone who would listen. His intention, he explained to Luhmann, even before finishing his AESTHETIC THEORY, before starting his preparations for the seminar (promised to Horkheimer and the students) about the chapter on the culture industry from the *Dialectic of Enlightenment* during the 1969 winter semester, and also before setting down all his notes on HEGEL'S DIALECTIC OF SUBJECT AND OBJECT, was to write a GENEALOGY OF FIDELITY IN MATTERS OF LOVE. He could do that in parallel with Luhmann's SOCIOLOGY OF LOVE. Luhmann countered that the seminar was now called LOVE AS PASSION: AN EXERCISE. All the better, Adorno replied, then his work and Luhmann's could be published together–as a countermovement to the zeitgeist among the students, namely, focused on the essential, an example of GREAT COOPERATION, as it were–to present a twofold product of the semester, sending a public message.

But one couldn't publicize one's personal love affairs, Luhmann opined. Then how should he act in practice, Adorno asked in turn. Without his mistress, life would be unbearable. The reinstatement (*restitutio in integrum*) of the relationship was also necessary to mitigate the ghastly thought that he was reaching the end, whether physically or intellectually. Luhmann listened to his account.[18]

It was obvious that the mistress, who lived in a different town, was having financial difficulties and being courted by a wealthy musician. She had used extremely hurtful words, as she seemed to find it difficult to separate from Adorno. Or she was not used to decisions or separations, and took the wrong tone in this situation for that reason. Luhmann advised him to offer his lady friend an appanage–a generous financial endowment. Then, after a period of friendship, he could seek to restore the former intimacy. The appanage should not be understood as one service in return for another but, rather, as an expression of loyalty that counters injury with generosity and also demands loyalty from the other party.

---

18 Luhmann later realized how much of a threat Adorno had felt when he read an article in the *Frankfurter Rundschau* mentioning flyers with the headline 'Adorno as an institution is dead'.

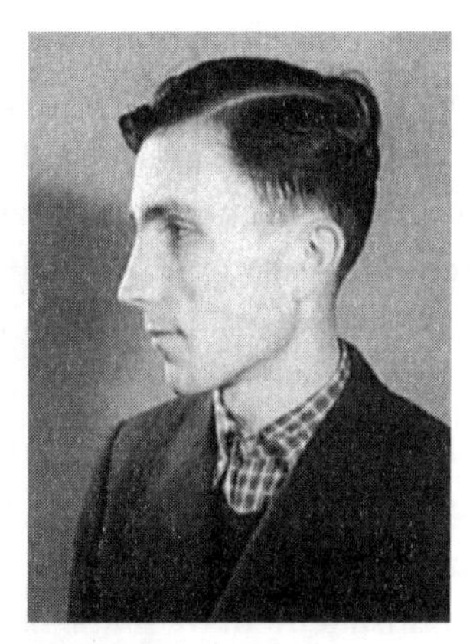

FIGURE 70. Luhmann.

Luhmann's dark, quick eyes moved 'empathetically', protected behind the slim horn-rimmed glasses, a form of eyewear that had appeared in the early 40s and meanwhile gained a modern form; it gave the scholar's narrow 'Roman' face a 'reserved' expression. Adorno's eyes had no such protection. They gazed at his conversational partner with calm and concentration, making amazingly few movements. Despite the emotional charge of the topic for him, his eyes were alive and betrayed none of the panic that Luhmann had heard in Adorno's muddled plans and his direct request for advice. The skin at his temples and his forehead, on the other hand, seemed tense and short of blood. The function of the wine that Adorno poured down his throat in large gulps remained a mystery to him. Luhmann gained the impression that Adorno was interested neither in the wine nor in any kind of alcohol; and his drinking was not accompanied by any sign of drunkenness or other effects.

In the background of the bar, large groups of loudly chatting singers, orchestra members and theatre staff were sitting down at separate tables. They were concentrating on their meal after the end of the opera.

Luhmann, 24 years younger than his fellow theorist sitting opposite him, who was talking to him energetically and incessantly, was part of a generation that had experienced how a time can get out of joint. For him, a rupture in the plane of reality was nothing unfamiliar. Accordingly, he did not see those days in Frankfurt, the rejections with which Adorno was confronted, as any threat to himself. Adorno, by contrast, seemed to have lived through the far more vehement changes of the turbulent century as if in a cocoon.[19] Now the protective wall had been broken down. To the naturally observant Luhmann, Adorno's directness seemed like an unexpected skin context. As something in

19 The people of Adorno's generation, Luhmann observed, go through real conditions in a cocoon. Either because they have ARMOURED CHARACTERS or, if they are defenceless like Adorno, because their instinct is to IGNORE REALITY. An anti-aircraft assistant in 1943, on the other hand, was open to formative changes of reality because it corresponded to a decisive experience. Like a skeleton, realities of 1943 extend their reach to April 1945 or the summer of 1946. Irreconcilable realities area present at the same time, without regard for their observers. In contrast to Adono, who is thrown off balance by the abandonment or passivity of previously loyal students, his almost simultaneous rejection by his mistress and the fact that his body (the body belonging to the son of that wonderful mother of 1903) is moving towards death, Luhmann's temperament amid antagonistic realities remains keen and cautious, like a 'consolidating elective affinity', and irreconcilable emotional impressions merge to form a new 'figure'.

him responded to this 'approach', the situation, though new to him, felt concrete.

At the same time, he considered the unexpected advances, the offer of an academic marriage, so to speak, of future joint work, simply because Adorno had fallen out with his 'companion', unrealistic. He, Luhmann, who was promised to the university founder Schelsky in Bielefeld, had been assigned to a different academic front. There was, at least according to outside observers, a gulf between critical theory, of which Adorno was considered the leader, and systems theory, of which Luhmann would become Germany's most important exponent; no bridge across had been attempted so far.

The bottle in the ice bucket had been replaced twice. Dessert was served. Luhmann had resisted such a dessert, but remarked that Adorno 'forced him', in the way that it was usual in earlier generations to incorporate additional offers into the communication on 'important visits'. This was now considered the custom of an extinct society, but was still a rural habit–though Adorno seemed to be an absolute city-dweller, indeed an old inhabitant of a Mesopotamian metropolis.

The two scholars never saw each other again. Separate taxis had been called for them, and so each went to his destination that night. Afterwards (after Adorno's early death in August, not long afterwards), Luhmann described the dinner as a 'hybrid reality'. The peculiar 'offspring of a foreign age', who behaved as if one could strike up a lifelong friendship in a single evening, relying solely on the undeniably living stream of love awaiting a joint theoretical treatment, had broken through the barrier of the self for a moment. That evening, it seemed as if Adorno was the same distance away from a 'new life' and death. For a moment, Luhmann (whose cool mind is well known today) had the impression that in this confused Frankfurt, innovative forces from an old root were in movement and these could not be reduced to the student crowds which Luhmann observed the following day on the way to the seminar.

OSKAR NEGT AND ALEXANDER KLUGE

LOVE POLITICS: THE STUBBORNNESS OF INTIMACY

ESSAY

The tender force has its zone of influence—stronger than power, money or truth—in the intimate areas. If we speak there of 'relationship work' (one imagines parents looking after their children, or lovers), this is an unusual formulation. Oskar Negt and I use it in the present commentary because our book HISTORY AND STUBBORNNESS *deals with the political economy of labour power. That is the opposite pole of the political economy of capital.*

In this context it is notable that what we call labour—the 'objectification of humans', the 'substance-changing activity', but most of all the ability to perform such labour, the so-called LABOUR CAPACITY—does not come about in the businesses where it is later needed but much earlier: in the INTIMATE AREAS, in families. There is no factory where humans grow; only intimacy produces human beings. The tender force has not developed many suitable words for its specific activity. The clearer one makes the mechanisms of such labour, the better one can see that it is not mechanical at all.

Alongside the theories of money, power and truth, we also need a theory of tender force . . .

1
The Search for Happiness in Private Life

If one follows the distribution of time in the stories of people's lives, a massive part of it is spent on their profession. A further considerable part is used for **private relationship work:** the processes in which a person is transformed from a child into a member of the workforce, and the resulting economy of debt: these are the confusing and powerful movements in libidinous conditions.

One can see that a third part of this living time, spread to all areas as well as the gaps between them, is used to create **balance economies**, which are absolutely necessary if one is at all to endure the two major areas, the families and the professions, as well as the intermediate forms between the two. That segment of scattered times, which serves the purpose of balance, is at least as necessary and as great as the entire labour power that enters businesses and socializations.

Relationships take place in all of these areas, be they public or marked off as private. **But libidinous relationships in the stricter sense, encapsulated within private conditions, reach the most confusing levels of intensity among all human relationships.** It is mostly there that balancing attempts take place. In this way, two powerful areas of time economy in people's lives (libidinous relationships and balance) combine and merge especially closely. This relationship work, cursed with privacy, is now showing an increasing tendency to suck up forces and portions of time from all other areas to deal with its crises.

Thus the collapse of the traditional public sphere programmed into the erosion crisis does not lead simply to a strengthening of powers that are capable of building up alternative public spheres. For, at the same time, this collapse encounters the aforementioned tendency towards the private accumulation of additional forces into relationship work, **a ravenous hunger found in relationship work, in the search for happiness within the private sphere.** Under the prevailing conditions this means a devouring of conflict, a compulsive instatement of illusory peace.

2
The Primary Production of All Social Traits of Humans in Intimacy

The word 'socialization' essentially means that the adaptation of humans to society does not take place directly but, rather, indirectly in the intimate area. The primal objects encountered by the child are objectively (not voluntarily, and not always consciously) agents of the realm of necessity. Their subtle educational influence is based on a specific art of seduction: in order to win the child's self-regulating assistance, the prevailing rules in the realm of necessity are seemingly suspended. Outside, everything revolves around performance and consideration while the intimate educational area revolves around need; but the arrival in the realm of necessity is only postponed. It only encompasses this principle of seduction as a form of mobilization.

No agency of external economy can replace this foundation for the first educational steps. Any methods applied would be too direct. In that sense, the basic form of adaptation to society comes about primarily in the area of socialization. The fact that, once this foundation is laid, the economy's direct and–in other ways different–indirect methods of seduction build on human traits, is a different matter.

To get a clear idea of the result and the contrast, one should imagine the visit of a Taylorist work timekeeper to a married couple's bedroom. He says, 'What you are doing here as a married couple is not practical. One can eliminate a few errors and inefficiencies, and then the climaxes that once required up to three quarters of an hour of labour will easily be reached within a minute. In addition, you should not leave it to the chance factor of moods when you agree to such activities. You should introduce a kind of regularity; then one can fit several climaxes into the same period of a month or year. You would have to plan it, and take the basic human right to regular sexual intercourse more seriously.'

The married couple will object: 'Based on your method, we'll be finished before we arrive. We have to retain some of the detours and errors. We take our time because (1) there is something hidden in the embraces that vanishes when we put it into words, (2) because we consist of rebellion, (3) because the senses have a subtler way of measuring.'

The things the work timekeeper could say to the couple are not all absurd. He pokes about among their habits; they have been blinded by routine.

People usually maintain boundaries between one another; I cannot ring a stranger's doorbell and embrace whomever opens the door. One owner of goods exchanges goods with another but not necessarily embraces. People standing in the tram squeeze close to one another but they have no right to view such touches as affection.

On the other hand, almost all people recognize one another, amid their social roles, as relationship workers. They constantly test repulsion and attraction, and form a complete society on this mimetic foundation. The monetary form of this has positive and negative accounts and is known as politeness or wariness of strangers. There is a need for a protective zone; that is why wariness of strangers is also expressed politely. In relation to this monetary form, warmth and rejection (coldness) can be considered payment in kind.

FIGURE 71. In Marx Brothers films, Harpo always accosts anyone he likes with embraces.

3
Bartering Economy in Love

In capitalist society, the realism of values is judged economically: Is a thing or a service worth the money I pay for it? In this context, bringing up children, love relationships, mourning and joy are 'unproductive work'.

The distinction between **productive** and **unproductive** work goes back to Marxian terminology. Under modern conditions (but already for Marx too), this distinction yields a marvellous scholasticism: that of capitalist alienation.

It is not the pianist but, rather, the piano-builder who performs productive work when employed by a capitalist in a firm. The clown is paid to evoke joy or sadness. If he is employed by the circus owner, his work creates value and added value, so he is productive. If he goes collecting with a plate, his work performance is paid for out of the income of those who enjoy his art. This does not provide the owner with any added value, which means it is unproductive work in Marx's terms. In discussions about the political economy of the education sector, the question was raised whether the social classes of students and teachers fuelling protest were performing productive or unproductive work.

One can see how far the economic value systems rest on prior historical agreement in, for example, the differing evaluations of political labour power. In Attic democracy, citizens were rewarded for participation in elections and popular assemblies, and those with political achievements were fed at the Prytaneion. In our society, only professional political work is remunerated.

As far as remuneration goes, similar historical distortions occur in relationship work. Prostitution was paid for and still is today, but the product offered by a classical *hetaira* differs substantially from the services provided in Frankfurt's Kaiserstrasse. Cleaning ladies or the staff of a large-scale kitchen are paid; such services were compulsory labour in the Middle Ages, and unpaid. Education by parents at home is unpaid while education by teachers at kindergarten or school is paid. These highly historical allocations of work and payment cannot be the criterion of productivity. From a non-emancipated perspective, the terms 'productive' and 'unproductive' describe a respectively existing situation; from the emancipated perspective,

FIGURE 72. School in the time of inflation, 1923: the children pay their school fees in kind. They hand over cold meat sandwiches and packaged items.

they have to be defined anew. They are only of any value if they permit a distinction between emancipatory and power-dependent production–that is, between primary production, power, *and* power-dependent secondary production. The connection of relationship work to these distinctions is the same as with any other application of labour power: it contains (1) elements of power, (2) elements of emancipation, (3) primary production and (4) power-dependent production.

4
The Breeding Ground for Human Traits: Authority and Family

Families are the breeding ground for people's fears, yearning and social character: an immense laboratory. Because there is so much violence in this context, the imagination resists performing an objective examination. Karl Kraus refers to this when he states, 'After careful consideration, I would rather make the journey to the land of children with Jean Paul than with S. Freud.'

A central tenet of critical theory is that families, like charcoal burners' huts, are the place where the fuel to power authoritarian systems is produced. But Antigone, who vehemently confronts the authoritarian Creon, also carries this fuel in her heart. In *Authority and the Family* (Paris, 1936), Horkheimer and other critical theory staff examine this connection: 'None of the great historical complexes remains a fixed structure; between all its subordinate parts and areas there is a continuous interaction which is characteristic of that complex or period. All cultures hitherto known manifest simultaneous and opposed regularities.'[20] Taken in context, this observation refers to the main form in which the base materials of later relationship work are developed, and to which they ultimately revert for the vast majority of people: the family. As binding or dissolving factors in social dynamics, what happens in these countless laboratories or immediate coexistence manifests itself either as 'the mortar of the building under construction, the cement which artificially holds together the parts that tend towards independence' or as part of 'the forces which will destroy the society'.[21]

Horkheimer continues: 'In the end everything about the family as we have known it in this age will have to be supported and held together in an ever more artificial fashion. [. . .] The totality of conditions in the present age, the universal web of things, was strengthened and stabilized by one particular element, namely, authority, and the process of strengthening and stabilization went on essentially at the particular, concrete level of the family. [. . .] This dialectical totality of universality, particularity, and individuality[22] proves now to be a unity of antagonistic forces, and the disruptive element in the culture is making itself more strongly felt than the unitive.'[23] Horkheimer

---

20 Max Horkheimer, 'Authority and the Family' in *Critical Theory: Selected Essays* (Matthew J. O'Connell et al. trans.) (New York: Continuum, 2002), p. 52.

21 Ibid., p. 54.

22 See G. W. F. Hegel, *The Encyclopedia Logic* (T. F. Geraets, W. A. Suchting, and H. S. Harris trans) (Cambridge, MA: Hackett, 1991), p. 244.

wrote this in 1936. We know how people returned to the life principle of the nuclear family after the disaster of the Second World War.

Elsewhere, Horkheimer examines why the experience accumulated in the form of relationships is so easily erased. 'The guilty conscience developed in the family absorbs countless energies that might otherwise be directed against the social circumstances which play a role in the individual's failure. [. . .] In the present age, however, a compulsive sense of guilt, taking the form of a continual readiness to sacrifice, prevents any criticism of reality. [. . .] The human types which prevail today are not educated to get to the roots of things, and they mistake appearance for substance. [. . .] Cruelty, which Nietzsche calls the "salve for wounded pride," finds other outlets than work and knowledge, though a rational education could steer it towards the latter.'[24]

In families, children do not choose their primal objects freely. Being 'educated by all the objects which surround [them], all the situations in which chance places [them], and, finally, all the events in which [they are] caught up', they experience their first relationships without being asked about their will (indeed before they have one), and from those they 'acquire' the potential for all later ones. One might as well throw dice. All later situations where two or more people come together likewise revolve around happiness or unhappiness, and rather little around freedom of choice.

23 Horkheimer, 'Authority and the Family', p. 128.

24 Ibid., pp. 109f. (translation modified).

It would have an easing effect if we could replace the energies from the exhausting search, for so-called choice, and change them into an attentiveness towards the energies that move towards one another. In such a context, we could trust in self-regulating forces that work silently at all times, and are not found at all in the forms of the self, of deliberate choice.

'In the yearning of many adults for the paradise of their childhood, in the way a mother can speak of her son even though he has come into conflict with the world, [. . .] there are ideas and forces at work which admittedly are not dependent on the existence of the family in its present form and, in fact, are even in danger of shrivelling up in such a milieu, but which nevertheless, in the bourgeois system of life, rarely have any place but the family where they can survive at all.'[25] Hegel recognized this and went to infinite lengths to preserve this substance intact in *the opposition between the family and the body politic.*

To him, this opposition is 'the highest, most tragic': starting from the subheading 'a. The ethical world. Human and Divine Law: Man and Woman', he spends 32 pages developing the conflict between family and public authority with reference to Antigone fighting for her brother's corpse.[26] According to Hegel, the principle of loving the

---

25 Ibid., pp. 114f.

26 G. W. F. Hegel, *Phenomenology of Spirit* (A. V. Miller trans.) (Oxford: Oxford University Press, 1977), pp. 267ff. See Horkheimer, 'Authority and the Family', p. 117: 'He regarded the relation between brother and sister as the most unalloyed one within the family. Had he discovered that this human relationship, in which

entire human being only applies in sexual partnership, where it constitutes the principle of 'femininity'. This is irreconcilable with the principle of subordination to the state, which does not deal with the whole person at all but with areas of obedience. For Hegel, it is the principle of 'masculinity'. 'To the extent that any principle besides that of subordination prevails in the modern family, the woman's maternal and sisterly love is keeping alive a social principle dating from before historical antiquity, a principle which Hegel conceives "as the law of the ancient gods, 'the gods of the underworld'" (Hegel, *Elements of the Philosophy of Right,* § 166), that is, of prehistory.'[27] It is irreconcilable because of cruel oppositions to the body politic. These anti-authoritarian forces are a particular. But then the general is useless, as it came about through an exclusion of the most important substance.

FIGURE 73. Antigone buries her brother, following the law of the ancient gods.

"the aspect of the individual self, recognizing and being recognized, can assert its right", need not simply accept the present in the form of mourning for the dead but can take a more active form in the future, his dialectic with its closed, idealistic form would have broken through its socially conditioned limitations.'

27 Ibid., p. 118.

5
Reliability

The object of work in relationships is reliability. It has a specific temporal rhythm and few other working steps are comparable to its production.

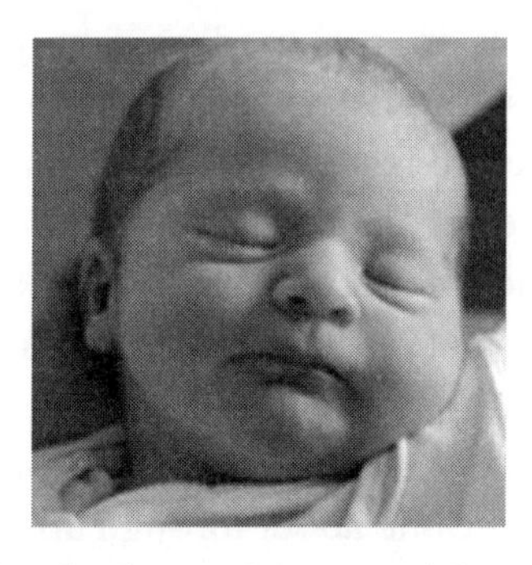

FIGURE 74. A baby.

The rhythm and temporal form in which relationships thus connected are tested–or end, and, as a result of such separation, turn into new relationship attempts–presumably influence the rhythm and temporal form of all future relationships. One can assess this in relation to one's own life story. What must I be able to rely on to bring about the following: openness, matter-of-factness, curiosity, creation of intimacy, turning towards, turning away, concentrating emotions, loving, hating, joy, sorrow, leaving emotions in a state of distraction, relaxing, falling asleep or development of the securing rituals that allow us to fall asleep, eat calmly or have skin contact. Being able to separate, being able to commit, going away, coming home, etc. **The growth of each of these traits presupposes the connected development of parallel traits, and each of these developments in turn presupposes a certain residue of**

primal trust that is initially no less than the intimate knowledge of reliability, which I transfer to the production and temporal structure of new kinds of situations.

What is known in socialization as the temporal rhythm of reliability returns in history as a need to identify one's own value and loyalty relationships. Disappointment in the area of relationships, a lack of reliabilities there, leads to a shifted need: the need to identify loyalty relationships in society. Disappointment with these loyalty relationships in society, conversely, shifts the work of hope to the relationship area. The root of this is the sentiment that I am unable and unwilling to be alone. I thought I had company and therefore gave up some of my interests instead of realizing them. This exchange was disappointed. My previous actions are retroactively rendered meaningless by the disloyalty or unreliability of the others. I lost a part of myself because the other is disloyal.

6
Third-Party Damage

In the course of clinical observations, Freud had encountered a particular type of male object choice: some men chose their objects under the condition of the 'damaged third party'. Time and again, they fell in love with women who already had some form of commitment to another man (the soon-to-be-damaged third party). The woman who was tied to another man had to be sexually 'disreputable' in some sense and meet the condition of 'prostitute love'. At the same time, these men tended to idealize such a woman objectively and were filled with the idea of having to save their lover. The 'disreputable' quality was connected to the discovery (only grasped in its full implications during pre-pubescence) that the 'pure' mother actually did the same thing with the father that prostitutes also do. Freud interprets this attitude from the angle of the separation trauma experienced in the Oedipal situation. The Oedipal trauma with this type of object choice, then, is this: 'My father took away my mother, who I thought belonged only to me, my mother was unfaithful to me; I am the damaged third party.' The wish-fulfilment fantasy resulting from this trauma would be this: 'If only my mother were unfaithful to my father and loved me alone, then my father would be the damaged third party.'

The mother is not only unfaithful because she stays with the father but also because she betrays the child with reality. The father does the same, meaning that the process of third-party damage also affects the daughter. The father and other are the physically tangible cause to articulate disappointments which need not even be caused by them. That is why the expectations directed at them are increasingly difficult for them to satisfy in person; thus they are fundamentally unfaithful, both of them. The negation of this infidelity occurs by redistributing the damage: 'Let me not be the one who suffers the damage.'

If everyone feels this way, the result is a struggle of all against all for the position of the non-damaged party. The specific element of the ownership situation in the Roman sense is the exclusion of the other from ownership. The Germanic or Celtic model of ownership had been developed in relation to the house and community, and thus without such an exclusion. In relationships, we find a third way of creating ownership with one's life. It is based on the rule that I must on no account exclude the other, for then I would be alone; I simply have to ensure that I am not the damaged party.[28]

I must therefore allow in and exclude at the same time. The material vehemence associated with this form of work does not result from relationship work alone; then there would be possibly escape routes. It rests on the fact that in triangular relationships and third-party damages, the need for relationships is superimposed by the compensation for disappointments stemming not from this relationship but from outside, in the social situation. These substitute needs and the immediate needs make an attempt to realize themselves through the needle's eye of relationships.

The intensity of these processes would not block the escape routes if these were not attempts at self-realization that were formerly attempted in relationships *and* in society. Rebellions and utopian need have been shifted back and forth so many times, from relationships to society and from society to relationships, appropriating outside energies, that they form a **special subordinate relationship.** Here the rule applies: 'The great sensible one falls in full armour.'[29]

---

28 A woman falls in love with her husband's best friend; a man falls in love with his wife's best friend. One could call this an attempt to maintain a closeness in the relationship; probably the closeness of the relationship even provides the originally necessary 'disreputable' quality. I can love with vitality again close to my wife, close to my husband.

29 That is why Kierkegaard writes in *Either/Or*: 'If you marry or do not marry, you will regret both.'

7

The Interdependency of Sexuality and Training

Sigmund Freud and Michel Foucault are not referring to the same thing when they discuss sexuality. Freud assumes that 'man's deepest essence lies in drive-impulses that are elemental in nature and identical in all people, and are aimed at the satisfaction of certain primal needs. These drive-impulses are, in themselves, neither good nor evil.'[30] One might add that they are not interested in training (but would be wrong to do so). The psychological elements of the unconscious, the ego and parts of the super-ego are created from this material; at the same time, those same forces work on a historical and collective scale, from where they feed back into every instance of upbringing as well as sexual practice.

Foucault, on the other hand, is concerned with the so-called dispositif of sexuality. Dispositifs are rules of lineage. He wants to translate the fable of the *indiscreet jewels* into history. He proceeds from the original agrarian family alliance, the clans, a production collective that led to the agricultural revolution. From the collapse of this alliance, according to Foucault, emerge the dispositifs of knowledge, power and sexuality. For its transformation into modern society, the crumbling family alliance requires individualization, specialization and the overestimation of sexuality; the latter survives as a lust for knowledge and binding energy, as a kind of instrument and transmission

---

30 Sigmund Freud, 'A Timely Reflection of War and Death' in *On Murder, Mourning, and Melancholia* (Michael Hulse trans.) (London: Penguin, 2005), p. 175.

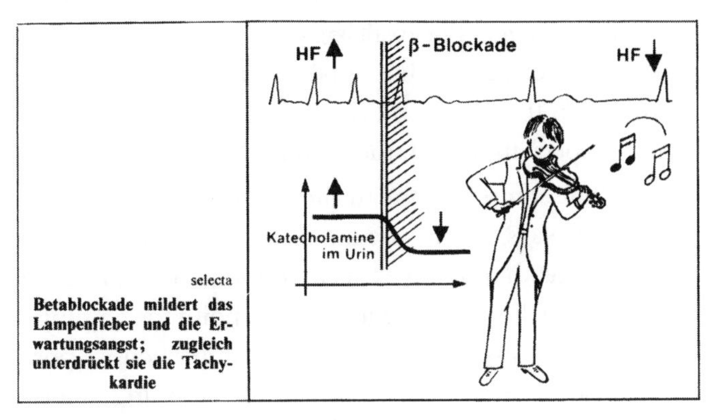

FIGURE 75. reelance artist: that was how the good-for-nothing played his way to freedom (Eichendorff). But one has to inhibit this freedom with beta blockers owing to the fear of expectations and tachycardia (the heart must not beat too quickly).

belt of domination. It is not a realization of the pleasure principle.

Whatever cartography one follows, both Freud's *and* Foucault's observations can be examined at the intersection of sexuality and training. The modern sexual practice of adults is developed through a chain of separation processes from the overall eroticism of the POLITICS OF BODIES. In this sense, it is a labour capacity with a pleasure supplement.

Michael Balint (important psychologist, born 1896, died 1970) compares the trainability of the different organs: cardiac work–breathing–muscle actions–digestive and urethral region–hands–genitals. It is clear (leaving aside psychosomatic disorders) that this series of organ activities displays an increasing sexual connotation. The heart is less specialized as a sexual organ than breath, and breath less so than the eroticism of muscle movement, and this is less sexualized than anality, which is less diversely sexual than the hand, and the hand is similarly connoted but less specialized than the genitals.[31]

Balint compares the trainability of the individual organs. He says, 'In my assessment, cardiac activity is never trained.' Breath training exists in the yoga cult or in diving schools. One finds a stronger starting point for training in all muscle actions. Every libidinously comprehensive possibility of movement can be linked to a training angle, a selection, until walking, standing or sitting are learnt, and this learning process also structures walking, standing, holding on, 'sitting down one's thoughts', perceptions, touches, etc. that are not carried out via the muscles. What is clear now is the cultural and training attack directed at controlling the digestive tract. Here, after all, training disasters are caused for entire societal periods, and these are only possible because malleable sexual energies accrue to

31 There is also a countermovement whereby the substance of sexuality is the summation of the search of pleasure, but also the summation of protests. Then those organs which seem sexually specialized assume the connotation of the greater share of disappointment, and sexual interest can withdraw inwards into a kind of fortress, that is, those organs which are of little use for direct sexual contact such as the breath or the heart take on a high sexual interest and lower protest potential, and become organs of refuge. Heart palpitations or the solar system, for example, are more clearly eroticized than the working hand or the so-called erogenous zones, which can also be completely destroyed through practical use. This would not be a set of symptoms so much as an entirely logical consequence.

them from the occupation of this pole. Certainly, the sexualization of these zones is also a function of the training work done by the primal objects. The training work, however, results from the fact that the rudimentary and libidinous connotation has been espied by the primal objects. For the hands, whose development in the history of the species acts back on large parts of the brain, the interaction between training and sexualization requires no special explanation, nor does the starting point that genital interest constitutes in prevailing training methods. Multitudes of mercenaries and soldiers have gone to the great wars essentially equipped with sexual motives. One can say that the more far-fetched an adaptation via training is, the more it depends on borrowing from sexual connotations for its motive.

8
The Indomesticability of the Libido

One can see that the concern is sexuality in the comprehensive sense of libido, and then in the more specific sense of the sex drive. It was ambiguous whether sexuality belongs to the dominant party or to the resistance. What one can say about sexualized relationships, however, is that they rest on an elemental substance among human traits that cannot really be organized socially.

The libidinous masses (Freud's elemental forces) are indifferent to the reality principle, which they simultaneously play a part in establishing. And the reality principle, in turn, largely excludes them, especially the libidinous self-regulations. Once excluded, they become especially difficult to influence.

This is the basic contradiction in the political economy of relationship work: the libidinous forces are the binding agent yet, at the same time, they remain rebellious. Whatever one produces from this material–obedience or upbringing, for example–will always be built on sand.

In G. W. F. Hegel's *Elements of the Philosophy of Right*, he deals with this combination of morality (reliability as dead labour) and love (reliability as live labour). Without knowing Freud's demands, Hegel remarks that the underlying natural forces in this connection do not come about of their own accord. He proceeds indirectly:

'But in those modern dramas and other artistic presentations in which love between the sexes is the basic interest, we encounter a pervasive element of frostiness which is brought into the heat of the passion such works portray by the total *contingency* associated with it. For the whole interest is represented as resting solely upon *these* particular individuals. This may well be of infinite importance for *them*, but it is of no such importance *in itself*.'[32] Based on this: 'Love is therefore the most immense contradiction; the understanding cannot resolve it, because

32 G. W. F. Hegel, *Elements of the Philosophy of Right* (Allen W. Wood ed., H. B. Nisbet trans.) (Cambridge: Cambridge University Press, 1991), p. 202.

there is nothing more intractable than this punctiliousness of the self-consciousness which is negated and which I ought nevertheless to possess as affirmative. Love is both the production and the resolution of this contradiction. As its resolution, it is ethical unity.'[33] A little earlier he writes, 'But love is a feeling, that is, ethical life in its natural form. In the state, it is no longer present. There, one is conscious of unity as law; there, the content must be rational, and I must know it. The first aspect of love is that I do not wish to be an independent person in my own right and that, if I were, I would feel deficient and incomplete. The second aspect is that I find myself in another person, that I gain recognition in this person, who in turn gains recognition in me.'

Love itself, according to Hegel, cannot arrive at its substance from all its intractability, punctiliousness, frostiness and heatedness. All these relationships refer to the same state of affairs: isolation as an abstraction that can never be alive in itself. And on the other hand, society, substantiality and morality as something that cannot be produced exclusively from living elements.

The relationships: 'The family, as the *immediate substantiality* of spirit' is something so serious that its libidinous foundation inevitably throws the particularity of the raw material, its particular laws, off course. Bringing up children, family structure and reliability

33 Ibid., p. 199.

are such weighty matters that celibacy would really be the most suitable form of family organization. Love only requires heatedness and punctiliousness to bring it about at the start. Otherwise the edifice of morality (= reliability) would be built on sand.

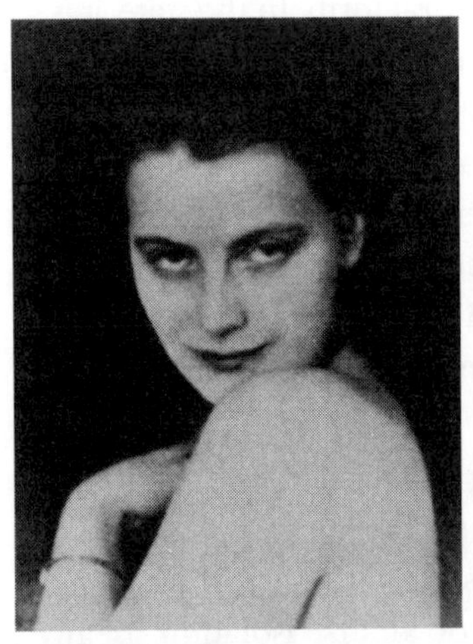

FIGURE 76. Relationships have their public life in cinema, via surrogates.

FIGURE 77. In her films, Greta Garbo unified all the quiet glances that no one has time for in practice.

FIGURE 78. *La Chienne* (The Bitch), film by Jean Renoir. 'She's now in her 20th year, been married three times, has satisfied a colossal number of lovers, and now she finally feels the needs of her heart too.'

'. . . She responded to these outbursts of rage as a true woman with no more reason for consideration, who knows her man to his very bones and knows that there is an eternal war slumbering beneath this pigsty of a joint household. She was less mean than he in his rage, but more ghastly, cruel and hurtful in her coldness.' *Les Diaboliques* (*The She-Devils*) by Barbey d'Aurevilly. The film cannot compete with prose of such a high level of organization. It cannot formulate broader ideas (pigsty of a joint household, eternal war, outbursts of rage), it cannot formulate empty ideas (true woman), it cannot articulate oppositions in this general form, in such a condensed manner; and it lacks the means to imitate the movement of language, except by quoting the text.

9
All Those Eyes

When searching for happiness, or in a current family conflict which a married couple is attempting to deal with, this normally happens just between the two of them. In reality, however, there are another four people fighting or living with them. When the couple argues, their eyes face one another and so, as their inner representation, do the eight eyes of their parents.[34]

It is a simplification, however, to assign only *one* person to each person and each of the inner representations that strain these arguments and lives. One characteristic of the quarrelling or happy couple, for example, is their ability to express themselves rationally. I gain security and test something reliable by seeing if I can put it into words and discuss it. It an entirely different matter how I respond to touches, whether I feel reliability and security when my skin, which tests other things than my head does, allows itself to be seduced. We could break down the arguing or happy persons into true characteristics, each a person in itself and only externally facing the others in a separate human being. Then passion has different eyes than the hands, objective long-range senses have different eyes than the close-range senses, and the flight from the other has different eyes than the appetite. In a sense, the history of humanity, the society that produced these characteristics,

---

34 The children observing this see with their own eyes and also with those of the representation of their parents, perhaps also of their grandparents, which all—because they are formed by the children—differ from the real parents or grandparents.

is present in the quarrelling or the happy touches of the small group. If none of that had been handed down, it would be too complicated for two people to produce such a jungle. What we have described as distribution (struggle), as the overarching frame, is the nodal point at which the actually social relationship irrupts into the private, individual one.

It does this in the form of collective labour capacities of remembering, of forgetting, of the total product of variations that are imaginable for a relationship (that is, *how* one quarrels, or in what horizons one searches for happiness in the first place), as a social product or as an individual need, based on a respective life story, that responds to it.

10
Measures, Weight, Rules

Someone goes into a supermarket and asks for a pound of sugar. He does not receive cucumbers or salt, nor does he pay more than the indicated price. Let us transfer such a simple act of exchange to a relationship: someone comes home from work and wants to be stroked but his opponent in the relationship has prepared a pasta bake. The one intention is based on precise needs: it is not a matter of being stroked somehow and somewhere but of very specific wishes that probably also contain an element which refers to something impossible. Some of them have a long history relating to the person's previous life, their attitude to the body, and thus with previous generations and their attitudes to the body.

Conversely, the decision to prepare a pasta bake is materialized in a practice taking several hours; it involves effort. The two of them could barely risk to discuss the difference between a wish and an object. If the one who wants to be stroked complains about the pasta bake, which need not be bad on its own terms, he develops a quarrel by presenting his imprecise wishes at the wrong moment; in addition, he wants to be stroked because of the other's spontaneous idea. As the pasta bake requires 60 minutes in the oven, one could gain both results through a subtle shifting of times: joint appetite and joint satisfaction. But reaching an agreement about this would be so difficult that it is not even attempted.

The deal is difficult because it is so unlike a visit to a supermarket. Certainly, exchange in relationships does have a mimetic-collective language, its own particular mode of abstraction and therefore complex value systems: the stock market of emotions. But their **precisions** are so immense that they almost consist of pure fluctuation; like a Celtic community, they establish the world order anew at every moment. On the other hand, this fluctuation challenges habitual behaviour and rigid norms in order to determine any orientation at all. It is the same as the connection between law and observance or between a fixed price and a complete estimate. When buying commodities, for example, one is dealing with money on the one side and cucumber, semolina, sugar or sausages on the other. Both quantities seem comparable under normal circumstances, and are specified and set apart from countless others.

This comparison takes place at changing levels in relationship work. One moment, my senses are checking to see if what the other person is doing with me is suitable for me, and the next moment, entirely different organs of my imagination are testing how my needs–including those which would not have any access to the concrete moment–correspond to this. One moment it is desire that tests, the next moment it is the social meaning of having that tests whether it is actually realistic. Concrete needs have barely established themselves in a human before the moment is disturbed by needs that reach beyond them. Essentially, the point is that the forced economic laws in commodity traffic apply robust reductions to the material relationship–and in the process also provide security against endless fluctuations. It is precisely these forced laws and their reductive effect that are initially suspended in relationships; needs express themselves directly. This leads free-floating, uncontrolled compulsions to enter relationship work. For in a relationship, concrete moments (exchange) can likewise only be brought about through exclusion (reduction). The lack of such reduction creates the picture of an undecided customer who encounters a generally undecided salesperson, because buying and selling are so important to both of them that they cannot reach a conclusion. When the external forced reductions of traffic are doubly suspended–as relationship work and also as child labour–this is known as playing. The protracted and pleasurable transactions in a child's play shop correspond to this picture. For adults, this is only to be imitated when dealing with one another infatuatedly or stubbornly in an environment with a low reality content. As soon as their elements of reality collide more significantly, they can no longer maintain the principle of the play shop. They often wish that chance could determine the result from without, as in a game of dice, making the decision that they, because of the constant fluctuation of their need, find so difficult to reach.

And yet the need for differentiation and measurement is considerably subtler in relationships than in the consumer world. The things that one can produce and buy only enter temporal relationships with one another to a limited extent. Sugar and heat, for example, must act on each other for a certain time to produce jam. Aside from this interaction, the ingredients and the sugar do not have their own temperament. Subjective relationship workers, on the other hand, all possess a specific, unmistakable temporality of their own. Their nerves and all their characteristics all have their own speeds in their internal relationships (one of the thinks slowly, feels quickly, reacts quickly, remembers slowly, etc.) while the same thing happens on the other side to the relationship partner. These different speeds must be subtly brought closer to one another in the relationship, separately at all levels of the person, for mutual contacts to occur in the relationship. Otherwise there will only be a disturbance and the highly roundabout compensation for it. This repeats itself in the degree of nearness or distance, individual or communal ownership, loudness or quietness, power grip or pinch grip, and further characteristics. Thus any exchange first requires subtle controlling actions driven by the one, the other and the habits of the relationship—three subjective locations and productions that are interlocked, but not coordinated. It is pure sensitivity at work, so to speak.

Relationships spontaneously encounter their precursor, which constitutes a power relation, and search the pure relationship to find solutions for the moment: only these measures are sufficiently exact. Perhaps others will already have to be invented a moment later. It is apparent, however, that this fine tuning demands constant attention, and is therefore required at every moment. This control without institutionalization of measures, weights and rules is reminiscent, as mentioned above, of archaic communities composed of relationships. At the same time, the processes requiring regulation are of a modern nature; if control fails, they cannot degenerate into the Celtic-style open slaughter, which did not bring about the end of civilization in its time but would immediately lead humans away from civilization today.[35]

11
The Commodity Character in Relationship Work

For simplicity's sake, we will pass over the question of how the external commodity character affects relationship work; it goes without saying that it involves constant transactions with commodities–the furniture, the car, the home,

35 The less consciously the fine-tuning takes place, the more successful it is. If it is attempted in a clever fashion, then the historical form of spirit first of all suppresses the mimetic capacity, which alone is capable of pushing momentary self-regulation far enough to replace measures and weights. For this to succeed, one must put one's faith in something other than so-called goodwill, because the part of this that is the prevailing consciousness destroys the fine tunings.

the clothes, the knowledge commodities, the erotic commodities.

The people taking part in the relationship are themselves in turn commodities. The special beauty of a woman, the professional qualification of a man, the fact that children are dressed in a sporting, intelligent, polite or orderly fashion: all these are personal commodity characters. One can say, however, that the relationship begins where these commodity characters end or are inverted. The mere addition of commodity characters can look like a family but is a non-relationship if it consists only in this addition: an ideal woman has an ideal man next to her with ideally diligent children. The couple can live alongside each other for many years without constituting a relationship. It would be pure status, like furniture.

Where the relationship begins, it needs an object to work on. Something that any third party would consider a disadvantage has to be present so that love can attach itself to it and, in an inversion of the supposed disadvantage, transform it into something loveable. This conversion of worldly commodity values or non-value into a communally supported relationship constitutes exchange value in relationship work. The commodity's exchange value does not contain any of its utility value. The exchange value of relationship work restores a pure utility value that rules out neutrality as far as possible. That is precisely not the commodity value of the person; love has adapted it to them. But one should not suppose that hatred is not capable of the same thing: it changes all the objective commodity values of a person that they would have outside in the economy, visible to every third party, into enemy value.

FIGURE 79. *The Intervention of the Sabine Women*: detail from a painting by Jacques-Louis David.

We know that in the original society that preceded the classical social formations—in our country these took the form of feudalism—the pure production of utility value dominated and there was only *one* commodity: women, who were irreplaceable for the reproduction of generations. This inimitable commodity and its hazardous exchange bring about special conditions. Not only this exchange itself, but also the integral cohesion of the early domestic community associated with it, in which all relationships have their proper time and place, creates a utopian longing out of the most modern needs.

Fulfilments of this longing for original cohesion are the main concern when attractive and repulsive capacities in relationship work, which have historically been divided in different directions, set about achieving their absolute goals. This absolute goal, for which all other relationship work is merely preparatory, is a commodity that is impossible, unattainable in our society, and it is striven for by sensual methods that ultimately cannot be deceived. The fact that such a goal offers no concrete resistance, being unattainable, makes the corresponding search for happiness impossible to influence or contain. Nor does it relate to the concrete other but, rather, the fulfilment of the history that is presumed to lie within that other. It therefore only succeeds in history, proceeding from that other, and not in the small group with that other.

> The so-called *Liebestod*, for example, is a mystery. Richard Wagner took up this topic with the specific remark that he did not know what love is, and was compelled for that very reason to compose what was incomprehensible to him. The myth tells an entirely different story from the *Liebestod* of Tristan and Isolde. Neither King Mark nor Tristan can bear living with the mighty Irish sorceress. They share the duty: Mark sends Tristan to court her and becomes Isolde's husband, seemingly unaware that the love potion guarantees she will shift her attentions to Tristan. By now the men have long suffered the *Liebestod*; in the fairy tale, once the back and forth between them can no longer continue, Isolde must go through it too.

12
A Peculiarity of Exchange Value in Relationship Work

Exchange value produces images. If, as described above, I identify the pair of boots I have produced in terms of what I can exchange them for–a quantity of grain, coal, cucumbers, tools, friendly eyes–then these images present the exchange value, which tends to mirror my work and its social context in a somewhat displaced manner. Such a pictorial world is also contained in the exchange value that results from the two fundamentally contradictory commodity values in relationship work. But this pictorial production has its peculiarities.

For the commodity objects of goods production, the following applies: nothing will come of nothing. There must always be a material thing, or a clear change of state when services are rendered (for example, the barber has genuinely cut the customer's hair), for an exchange image to attach itself to it. The exchange values are copies of concrete forms of human labour or social wealth. So they can produce many images, but always stem from **one**, namely, the commodity as an element. This element connects them, as a genuine resistance to an infinite abundance of images, to two crisis laws: (1) at the end, all exchange values in the crisis are checked once more for usability; (2) in a crisis, all exponentiated work is traced back to simple work.

Both laws also apply to relationship work; in the objective semblance, however, they cease to be in force.

13
Private Property in Relationships as Opposed to the Historical Principle of Private Property

The **principle of private property**, which was only developed in Western European societies (and exported to the USA or to societies dependent on world powers) is the basic cell of the capitalist system. At the same time, it has historically always been used for entirely different purposes too. Protestantism, for example, is in this sense an attempt to produce private property from one's faith or conscience. Private property contains two different roots. The first is forming property at the expense of the others, that is, exclusion, making something else unsocial and making **oneself** social. In non-economic matters, on the other hand, the principle of private property means an attempt to preserve and defend elements of original property. The latter form of private property comes not from an ownership of land that excludes others but is rather based in the community. The fewer others are excluded from it, and the more others are included, the more it becomes property.

For the worker, as a private owner of the commodity of labour power, these two sides are clearly different. Both roots have a principle of consistent decentralization and autonomy that is indispensable in rich social or individual relationships. Setting boundaries between oneself and the other, controlling nearness and distance, entails a necessary reservation for every self-regulation. It is the historical trick of private property that because of its dual character, its destructive work cannot be made plausible one-sidedly. If I attack private property, I am simultaneously attacking the economy of original property, which I use to decide my own nearness or distance. I cannot abolish private property, because it always means abolishing two things at once: the one thing, which I need to use, and the other thing, which misuses me.

> In the outside economy, the central contradiction is that there is private property. In the interior societies of relationships, the contradiction is that there is no private property.

It is notable that under the exchange conditions of private relationship work, a secured zone of autonomous self-development is extremely difficult to realize. Indiscretion, not leaving the other alone, nagging and symbiotic disturbances at all times are practically considered the principle of a functioning relationship. The illusion of thoughtfulness only heightens the immanent unrest, because this civilized elevation rests on individual effort and, if this effort-making with the other ceases, also comes to an end. Thoughtfulness, paying attention to reservations within the relationship, encompasses the threat that it is artificial and actually contradicts the principle of the situation. It is considered an exception.

An economic relationship like those underlying business or wage labour is expressed in segmented terms: 'Whatever is not expressly agreed on is excluded from the arrangement.' The promises in private relationships are quite different: 'Whatever is not expressly excluded is agreed on.' This dissolves the boundaries between what is yours and mine, meaning that certainties about an original property that could serve as the starting point from which to approach the other are not given any recognition. But one can only become collective on some historical basis. As the self, with all its connected factions and components, must wage complicated internal class struggles and make comparisons with itself, it requires a space that is exclusively its own–in short, private property. Engagement with the traditional fabric of norms, which always reckons with a remainder of such autonomous individual responses, likewise requires this personal reservation. In addition, all notions of community in Western European tradition are based on autonomy, that is, decentralized property structures, that come together thanks to a portion of spontaneity and self-regulation. There is no culturally prepared idea of how such an orientation and agreement on a community is supposed to arise among complete strangers. The disastrous lack of boundaries that characterizes private relationship work, especially in our country, means that in those relationships, the respective foundation and community must be acquired anew on each occasion, ad hoc and bit by bit—and thus gained from the excessively far-reaching promise that whatever is not expressly excluded is included.

14
Property in the History of the Species

The generic history of primates, of which we humans form a socially developed part, goes back to a relatively small order of animals referred to by some palaeontologists as 'tree shrews'.[36]

The pressure of selection and the variety accumulated in evolution create a fixed store of characteristics. These characteristics constitute a particular species-historical property that precedes all later forms of property and must be included in them if those principles of property are to have any power in relation to this special original property. In this *particular* original property, the subjective side on

36 Bernhard Krebs, 'Die Archosaurier' in *Naturwissenschaften*, VOL. 61, pp. 17–24: 'Forms that are capable of development [. . .] are always unspecialized and small in stature.'

which the **revolutionary** development into humans is based deviates from natural conditions as soon as social conditions ensue. This subjectivity is located on the one hand in the objective materiality that brings about separations, and, on the other hand, in the sum of internal and intimate safety rings where subjective answers to separation are found.

This particular property of subjectivity also has the raw form of nest-building, corresponds to the portable nest of the womb, and–duplicating the latter–builds nests during the postnatal incubation periods which, as periods that are safe from disturbances, **respond to the times in which disturbances** make their mark. If one of these conditions is missing–the materiality or the protective ring–**then this raw form of original property cannot come about.** The simplest definition of this specific private property is the category of cohesion. Only in periods of intimacy and protection can times and relationships be arranged next to one another. This produces the raw form of what is later called social wealth. It arranges the rich capacities alongside one another, and the strongest do not exclude the weaker ones; times of separation and happy return are also placed alongside one another; through cohesion–the other side under alienated conditions is a tearing-apart between irreconcilable times–there is return (and not as a mere compulsion to repeat).

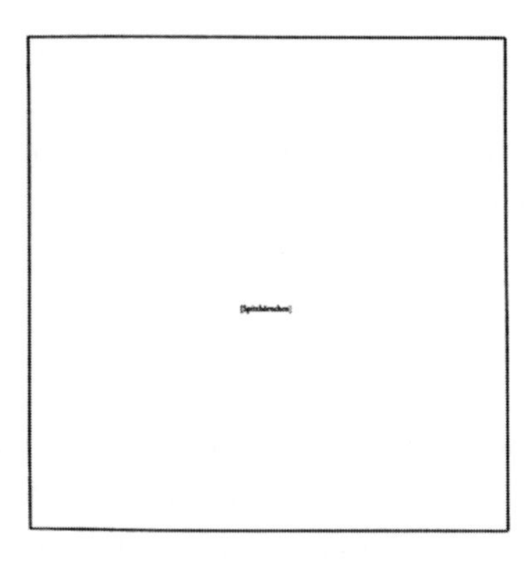

FIGURE 80. Tree shrews: nobody knows what they look like. Apparently mammals emerged in four different groups, independently of one another, from dinosaur-like reptiles. Such *therapsidae* appeared in the Permian (roughly 220 million years ago) and survived until the Middle Jurassic (roughly 150 million years ago). During that time, the mammals, known as *pantotheres*, developed from them. These, it seems, gave rise to almost all later mammals. They were tiny animals that have only survived in fragments, and their size and certain dental characteristics were reminiscent of mice: small, agile, carnivorous and more intelligent than reptiles. The separation of the nasal meatus from the jaws facilitated simultaneous chewing and breathing, as well as sucking up food.

According to one hypothesis, our ancestors were ovivores–that is, egg eaters. Around 300 million years ago, amphibians began laying their eggs on land because they were safe from predators there. The firm shell protected the eggs from drying out. Increasing nutrients were added to the egg in order to develop more robust offspring. These amniotic reptile eggs must have been the ideal prey for predators on land, as reptiles remained unskilled at protecting their brood.[37] Going by this argument, our ancestors accelerated their generative reproduction, or at least kept it constant, by stealing and pleasurably sucking out reptile eggs. The archosaurs were connected to the egg thieves by mutual selection. The egg thieves, small and quick to escape, were put under selection pressure by the introduction of reptile egg shelters: they had to develop stronger teeth and intellects, and become tree-dwellers (trees as safe refuges). For them, hatching eggs in a shady hiding place had to replace the sun's warmth. Giving birth to live young made this superfluous. It was less difficult for the small mother to feed her young if she herself had lived the life of a 'suckling' child by nibbling open (head specialization), sucking out or eating up the dinosaur egg. Natural selection had an especially random effect on such animals; they had no opportunity to adjust their bodily means to their zone of effect in a slow maturation process. Instead, mutations led to radical experiments and chance hits. The rest of the

37 Selection and variety therefore favoured saurians that already had a shell-like structure in the amniotic egg. The firm shell of the egg could always be broken but the flexible shell of its inhabitant could not. But such creatures then had to carry about a shell that was indispensable for birth yet superfluous in daily life, and their armour became a handicap. Palaeontologists have always doubted that such diverse dinosaurs could have died out from mere climate change or in the battle of attacker against armour. The selection of an impractical armour in order to protect the brood is a more plausible explanation for the downfall of the giant reptiles.

development followed two evolutionary rules: (1) a rapid generative reproduction that presupposes small size allows more mutative variants than a slow one; (2) the language of pregnancy and postnatal development, included in incubation times, holds the precondition for cerebralization and the beginnings of learning processes. The mouse builds a nest, the squirrel's is already better, and the beaver turns the nest into a fortress. In this fortress there are aunts that care for the newborn and temporarily replace the mother.

FIGURE 81. Dinosaur

FIGURE 82. *Mus etrusculus*: the Etruscan pygmy mouse is a tiny animal, less than a centimetre long. It is warm-blooded. Almost as soon as it is born, it must feed in order to produce a temperature of around 37° Celsius in its little body. It feeds until the end of its life, unable to pause for an hour without freezing. Its life is pure execution: it is born naked and does not even have time to grow a coat of fur, which would surely protect it from the cold more effectively.

15
What Does Enlightenment Mean in Relationship Matters?

Relationships are stuck in stances. In so far as they display attraction and repulsion, these have degrees of material concretion that overrun the enlightened discourse. They include 'trial actions in spirit' but they themselves, once solidified into relationship work, are not trial actions. They do not reflect in times of crisis.

The primacy of execution (as with the Etruscan mouse) knows two traditions of decision making: (1) the discussion after the fact, when everything is already decided, and (2) forms of previous agreement; they succeed if there is a behaviour that can be called up.

One can reach agreements for shares in relationship work that elude personal wilfulness and the principle of immediacy. The guarantee for the agreement is not the other relationship worker, but rather the chorus, which votes collectively and uniformly for certain agreements—for example, that one should not let one's children go to the dogs.

If we proceed from enlightenment, which lies in an attitude (not in speeches or essays), such a concept can focus on the following: (1) I myself become enlightened, and sit there with enlightened experience. (2) Enlightenment enters the relationship, changes it. (3) Neither I nor the relationship *behave* in an enlightened fashion, but from its crises, the work of enlightenment enters the collective structure of other relationships, the social experience of relationship work.

What we call the process of Enlightenment in the eighteenth century was conservative and affirmative towards relationship work. The rationalists and architects of the houses of enlightenment urged the preservation of morality and establish subjective duties that always led to the consolidation of traditional bonds. Religions were demythologized while relationships were supposed to be mythical.

A

The most frequent stance of enlightenment, the one for which the most means of production are available in a relationship, is this: I enlighten *myself*, I *receive* enlightenment.

This process does not initially affect the relationship but, rather, a person (and within this, it does not affect all operative forces in the same way). While the relationship is maintained, forces leave it. Reservations form, illusions disappear. Such enlightenment work can give rise to stances and inventions that in turn act to reinforce the relationship. Clarity of sight releases forces that balance out the deficits of the other. Insight is translated into cooperation. For the hope of reciprocation can also become enlightened, the true misery is viewed, and this produces a reserve or a departure. This **simple enlightenment** always contains an element of self-alienation. If I give up something that lies in the relationship or leave, some part of me remains in the relationship from which I am now fully or partially separating.

B

To ensure that enlightenment work is not only directed at me–which would impoverish it, de-mythologize it and shift the myth back to the free market–but affects the relationship itself, a specific *form* is required. We had assumed that it must consist of stances, not words, if it is to express itself in the particular mode of speech native to the relationship. This form is the limited rule violation that we know as a political form from the protest movement. It does not leave the relationship but works with its true forces, yet breaks through the law of inertia that has established itself in the relationship. Such rule violations follow the *indirect method* in warfare (surprise). They have all the attributes of the blitzkrieg: dislocation of enemy motives. They must descend into confusion and join to form an altered figure.

Enlightenment work through limited rule violation precisely does *not* attempt to destroy the will of the other but, rather, to produce the other's autonomy. It therefore carries out what the classics call the sublation [*Aufheben/ Aufhebung*] of contradictions. This word *Aufheben*, with its dual meanings of 'cancel' and 'preserve', applies here in a very immediate sense. First one must find the contact area for this work; it always lies where the forces at work in the special power structure of the relationship cancel each other out. The powers have a moment of rest. That is the point to which the immanent productive aspects of the relationship can be moved; one can therefore preserve them there, then put them together in new ways. The forces come from the main battle zones, from the tumult. The places and times that permit their organization lie at the abaric point, in the absence of gravity, and thus in opposition to the point of origin and the primal contact surface of relationship work.

FIGURE 83. The abaric point between the Earth and the Moon (→ 'W. Benjamin, the Stars and the Revolution').

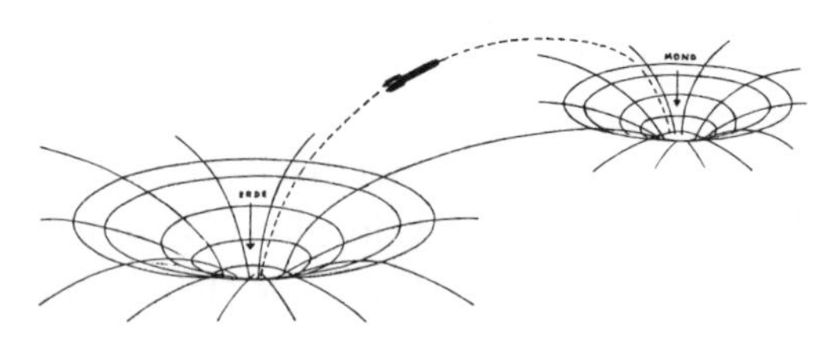

FIGURE 84. Flight from the earth to the moon. Attempt at a graphic representation of gravity.

During the Second World War, women took over the professional duties of the absent men and governed their families. This creates a different kind of self-confidence. After the capitulation, the men came home without any attributes of victory. Their collective, primal patriotism is reduced by the amount of the national loss. The women need peace and quiet, the men need peace and quiet. Beneath the manifold weights, something like an ahistorical (and simultaneously 'abaric') point comes into being. It might last a few days or three months. Without collective awareness and some marking, this point is passed over and the old conditions re-establish themselves. For the overall work in the families, however, something must have happened in that short time which, in the years after the currency reform, caused men and women to undertake a joint rebuilding effort that, however, alienated, showed a different coordination of characteristics than the 30s or 60s.

It is essentially no different in the individual relationship; the components are just entirely microstructural. A man comes home after a long absence. Let us assume that he feels longing. Probably this will quickly lead to intimacy. Once it is over, it is hard to change the relationship from the way it was before he left; it is not even the right moment to talk. Before the rapidly approaching intercourse, there was a moment in which the expectations of the enamoured returnee were met with a reply from the other. This answer provided certainty: something would happen. For a few seconds, the desire to embrace each other and the certainty that this would happen formed a constellation of forces oriented towards equilibrium. That second gets overrun; one should make it discernible, mark it as the point of production at which, if one gathered all difficulties on this point (the only one that can endure it) it would be possible for someone to return in a different state from the one in which they went away.

C

A number of relationships become so thickened in their mutual conflicts that even a practice of conditional rule violation at clearly marked abaric points cancels too little of the product's domination of the producers, with the result that neither simple enlightenment (that of the individual) nor enlightenment in the relationship ensues. That is insolvency. It means distress. It is no consolation but true nonetheless, that most of enlightenment work that spontaneously enters collective forms of relationships is recruited from such 'impossible conditions of production'. This (often invisible result) is called 'understanding', 'consideration'. They have a musical key that demands resolution.

A marriage out of love produced children. After three years, the man was no longer sufficiently in love. He withdrew to his work and let supplies come to him. Like a medieval abbot, he ruled the family context, looking with satisfaction at the plates set before him, and inhabited the rooms extensively. His wife had already lived in celibacy for 10 years. While he amused himself outside with various flings, the constant residence of this abbot prevented her from having friends. She was under surveillance, he was not. The situation was hard to bear. Sometimes she thought that it would be an effective limited rule violation to bring a man home. Perhaps it would also make the abbot realize her original value again. She did not fear his retribution but the thought of the reflections in her children's eyes prevented her from acting. She also considered dissolving everything but felt that this would hurt the children, for children insist egocentrically that the state in which the father and mother live together must remain unchanged. Whatever she ultimately decides, she discussed these matters with numerous female friends who had similar problems; they developed rich ideas in that time; the woman, together with her advisers, was capable of bringing every marriage except her own into a process of change on all sides. If a group set out to gather up this experience on a massive scale, it would be surprised to find that enlightenment work for collective relationship conditions has existed for a long time.

Autonomy = outcome[38]

> **'Enlightenment is man's exit from his self-incurred immaturity.** Immaturity is the inability to use one's own understanding without the guidance of another. This immaturity is *self-incurred* if its cause is not lack of understanding, but lack of resolution and courage to use it without the guidance of another. The motto of enlightenment is therefore: *Sapere aude*! Have courage to use your *own* understanding!
>
> 'Laziness and cowardice are the reasons why such a large proportion of men, even when nature has long emancipated them from alien guidance (*naturaliter maiorennes*), nevertheless gladly remain immature for life. For the same reasons, it is all too easy for others to set themselves up as their guardians. It is so convenient to be immature! [. . .]
>
> 'For enlightenment of this kind, all that is needed is *freedom*. And the freedom in question is the most innocuous form of all–freedom to make *public* use of one's reason in all matters. [. . .]

---

38 Kant, 'An Answer to the Question: "What Is Enlightenment"?', pp. 54ff. The question in the title as found in the *Berlinische Monatsschrift* refers to Johann Friedrich Zöllner's essay 'Is It Wise to Tie the Bond of Marriage to Religion?' Kant's essay was a reply to this. Zöllner writes, '*What is enlightenment?* This question, which is almost as important as *What is truth?*, must surely be answered *before* one starts enlightening! And yet if have not found it answered anywhere!'

‘If it is now asked whether we at present live in an *enlightened* age, the answer is: No, but we do live in an age of *enlightenment.* [. . .]

‘But only a ruler who is himself enlightened and has no fear of phantoms, yet who likewise has at hand a well-disciplined and numerous army to guarantee public security, may say what no republic would dare to say: *Argue as much as you like and about whatever you like, but obey*! This reveals to us a strange and unexpected pattern in human affairs (such as we shall always find if we consider them in the widest sense, in which nearly everything is paradoxical). A high degree of civil freedom seems advantageous to a people’s *intellectual* freedom, yet it also sets up insuperable barriers to it. Conversely, a lesser degree of civil freedom gives intellectual freedom enough room to expand to its fullest extent. Thus once the germ on which nature has lavished most care–man’s inclination and vocation to *think freely*–has developed within this hard shell, it gradually reacts upon the mentality of the people, who thus gradually become increasingly able to *act freely*. Eventually, it even influences the principles of governments, which find that they can themselves profit by treating man, who is *more than a machine,* in a manner appropriate to his dignity.

‘Königsberg in Prussia, 30 September 1784.

‘I. Kant’

'Man's exit from his self-incurred immaturity': in this respect, the child's birth and its separation from its original orientation inwards, its separation from the primal objects, which already begins when it first experiences affection, the separation from its original egocentricity and all later relationships based thereon, are varieties of **going away** or **exiting**. In this sense, the natural process of an **enlightenment for oneself** is contained in the root of relationship work. It repeats itself in the historical separation of soil and original community once the worker becomes fair game, that is, adaptable to wage labour. It is clear that the use of the adjective 'self-incurred' to describe these events does not offer a usable perspective. It is equally apparent that each of these separations is first of all an 'increase of our "desert"'.[39] In that sense, simple enlightenment, which only produces the courage to use one's own mind without the guidance of another, is initially empty of living substance, and it should come as no surprise that the public use of reason 'which anyone may make of it *as a man of learning* addressing the entire *reading public*'[40] is any less attractive for entire collectives than the light dome formed by anti-aircraft searchlights at the Nuremberg Rallies.[41]

---

39 See Friedrich Nietzsche, *The Will to Power* (Walter Kaufman ed., Walter Kaufman and R. J. Hollingdale trans) (London: Penguin, 2017), p. 327: 'That the destruction of an illusion does not produce truth but only one more piece of ignorance, an extension of our "empty space", an increase of our "desert".' [Trans.]

40 Kant, 'An Answer to the Question: "What Is Enlightenment"?', p. 55.

41 One must therefore resort to abbreviation and say, 'Man is mature when he goes out', just as one refers to leisure activities as 'going out'.

One thing that has been overlooked is the 'germ on which nature has lavished most care', the 'inclination and vocation to think freely' that 'has developed within this hard shell': the **tenderness of reason**, which, on the other hand, has far-reaching power because no people can be persuaded or commanded to dispense with it permanently. Another thing has been overlooked: that the *universal* application of the principles of reason separates reasonable human tools from human motives according to their tendencies. In complete contrast to the intended universal application, reason here joins the side of the tools, which already brings it closer to instrumental reason.[42]

But the fact is: it is not the tools that know the escapes and motivate the individual to emerge, for only the subjective material knows forms of assistance and ways out. The tools learn from this subjective material–that is exactly what makes them useful tools–by becoming a series, transforming themselves through deformation and damage. This is the part of them that promises escape, because they themselves are subjective material. Initially, the subjective material (motives) in relationship work is always unreasonably loud: the natural vehemence and expansion of motives. As a result, the tiny pauses and incubation points that are likewise present in this material, and of which all

42 It should come as no surprise if various scientific schools which cite Kant as an authority restrict themselves to pure methodology. They then keep the house clean, and ensure the purity of the methodological instruments, by not exposing them to any friction with the subjective material that might damage or deform the instruments. This does not apply to South German neo-Kantianism or the epistemological Marburg School.

natural exits are composed, are overrun in practice. The tiny pauses take place, they form no less of a real foundation than the pure activities, but they are not noticed and therefore cannot develop material-changing tools, cannot independently control or be controlled. What the overhead electric wire, imposed from the outside, does to the immature is likewise not so much control as a process of appropriating the uncontrolled.

Dealing with reason (the tender core)[43] thus presupposes a *reasonable* distinction between the moments in which it can operate and those in which it can only be a hindrance or a disturbance. To do this, one must take its other manifestations into consideration–those which consist not only in the 'courage to use one's own understanding'. Someone who *goes out* one evening in 1944, only a moment after taking part in the anti-reasonable war, might go dancing, for example. He cannot do this if he limits himself to the tools of understanding.[44]

If it is not a matter of establishing, of setting something in opposition to something else (objectification), but, rather, of movement, contact, rhythm (dissolution of wilfulness[45]), then motive and reason, the natural and the

---

43 We must insist on the fact that Kant speaks of reason as if it were an unborn child.

44 The category of dance is used emphatically by Friedrich Nietzsche, but also by Marx, when he speaks of the particular melody of German conditions. Here, however, dancing is meant literally–in contrast to the dancing lesson, in which the tools of learning are still incompetent.

45 'He wilfully trampled on her feet. She no longer wanted to dance.' This wilfulness (clumsiness) must be resolved. But the

intentional, material and human tools combine in ways that differ from the work of understanding. It transpires that the tender core, as concentrated yearning, has the character of a tool, in a sense, while simple yearning has the character of material. But both of these, the material and the tool, consist not only of yearning but also of life experience and the species history of pre-acquired practice: the relationship to the body, going together, *grace* in the sense of *courage*.

It is not a matter of resolution or courage to draw on one's own traits without the guidance of another. I am guided by the primal objects within me; they are active in all passionate motives. Without the guidance of this other, and only *factual*, I would be: myself and empty. So it is not simply about eliminating guidance as such and celebrating the exit from all relationship networks. The words 'cowardice' and 'laziness' in Kant's text need to be inverted. The inversion of laziness is industriousness (diligence); the inversion of cowardice is solidarity.[46]

---

wilfulness also reveals itself in other ways: public dance events, for example, are forbidden in wartime. This ban does not work in practice, however, because people who are allowed to go out will by no means allow the authorities to forbid them to dance. While Adolf Hitler was putting an end to his life at the bunker in Berlin, a vigorous dance event was taking place at the canteen.

46 One cannot simply posit courage or bravery as inversions. In the Socratic method, bravery is the knowledge of 'what is to be feared and what is to be loved'. Being courageous in a context that lacks solidarity will be disastrous for me. The material core of bravery, like that of knowledge, is therefore trust.

In political practice, people with an inclination towards enlightenment appear as doves and reactionaries as hawks, as if the stance opposed to reason were the 'harder' one. In fact, the material relationship is the reverse. Reasonable inversion is hard material viewed in the long term. For Kant, the paradox lies in the command: 'Reason as much as you want [. . .]; just obey.' But the tender core is practically disobedience itself, both in its laws and as subjective material. The passions closed off from this, however, behave obediently because of the compulsion to repeat that is triggered by the barriers. Because of these different relationships to obedience, the two human materials–both of them are material and tools at once, depending on the moment and the situation–can hardly interact with each other. The specific work in processes of enlightenment consists first of all in provoking the moments of contact that are naturally present or can be brought about through art. Only then does the inherent self-activity of the two materials assist the process. This what is meant by the assertion that contains the central point of the present book: **the tender force probably has independent access to the process of enlightenment.**

[Listening] People at different factual or emotional speeds do not listen to one another, even when exchanging words; first they have to align their respective movements. One can imagine this literally, like spaceships that reach a uniform speed through numerous manoeuvres of braking and accelerating; this alone makes docking possible. Several sleights of hand are required here: (1) acceleration;

(2) braking; (3) control and adjustment of both processes (piloting). In the case of spaceships, these sleights of hand are accompanied by natural forces such as starting speeds, inertia, weight, etc. It is clear that the natural force will be the tool or material in one case, while in another it will be the artificial intervention of the engineers or pilots.

A politician campaigning for election is confronted by a pensioner with a petition and, after the end of the event, goes to his female partner, whose son is lying in hospital recovering from a major operation. But these are clearly irreconcilable temporal forms. The time of a recovery, the time of a relationship, the time of a person who has left the labour process, the time of political currentness. If they want to listen to each other, they must both either brake or accelerate–that is, they must build up a situation through sleights of hand *and* natural capacities. Their capacities in turn originate from earlier roots, depending on who listened to them in childhood, and what kind of listening they came to trust in themselves or among others. One can understand such a process of attentiveness as the primordial cell of enlightenment. It is not a matter of an exit from immaturity *in and for itself*; the politician is departing from his daily routine if he **truly** engages with the pensioner, and he subsequently re-enters it.

The processes thus comprise an abundance of entrances and exits. Maturity, that is, listening and speaking, does not result from going in and out, nor is it produced in the moment by the two parties involved; rather, it ensues collectively and as a side effect of diverse attentions that come about in succession. Third parties, for example, can observe how this works and carry the experience further. Among humans, such primal scenes of listening fail more often than they succeed. 'Now this danger is not in fact so very great, for they would certainly learn to walk eventually after a few falls.'[47]

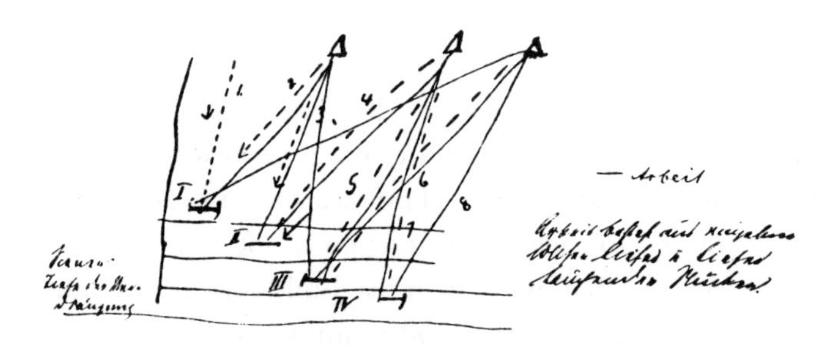

FIGURE 86. Sketch by Sigmund Freud from *Letters to Wilhelm Fleiss*. All the dotted lines, arrows and numbers are in red in the original, as is the word *Arbeit* [work]. Written below that: 'Work consists of separate pieces like this that run deeper and deeper.'

47 Kant, 'An Answer to the Question: "What Is Enlightenment"?', p. 54.

FIGURE 87. At a dance marathon.
A short break.

ANNOTATED INDEX

[The Flash of the Second, the March of Millennia] → The First Seven Seconds, p. 21 → My Maternal Grandfather, p. 15 → In the Magic of Haste, p. 22 → People 6,000 Years Ago, p. 19 → The Hour in Which the 'Self' is Born, p. 18 → Love Comes Soft-Footed, p. 398 → The Most Beautiful Treasure of Evolution, p. 100 → The Law of Love, p. 393.

In the operetta Wedding Night in Paradise, *it is said that 'with a beautiful woman, the exact second counts'. Jacques Fromental Halévy, Georges Bizet's father-in-law, wrote the opera* The Lightning Flash. *The opera paraphrases the following statements: 'love strikes like lightning'; 'love makes us blind'; 'love makes us clear-sighted'. The Theban princess Semele wants to see the lightning-wielder Zeus, who has impregnated her, in the flesh. The sight of the lightning strikes her dead. In this way, suddenness and lobe are correlated. On the other hand, the ability to love—that is, the chance to react in the moment—comes about in a process lasting several millennia; indeed, the tender force, in the seven currents that join to form it, is a result of evolution, primarily the social kind and secondarily the natural kind.*

[Absolute Love, amour pur] → She Never Had Any Doubts, p. 7 → Love Triumphs, p. 6 → Tristan and Isolde after Five Years, p. 435.

Niklas Luhmann calls the passion that dreams of its absoluteness a 'socially improbable institution'. Nonetheless, this idea forms a lasting horizon across the centuries that accompanies the every-day practice of love. At the altar of self-isolated love lie the dead. How could one design a memorial to the UNKNOWN FALLEN ON THE BATTLEFIELDS OF LOVE? Where in the city could one place something like that?

[The Tender Force Needs Some Resistance in Order to Assert Itself Verifiably] → Affection and the Superfluous, p. 281 → The Model from the Art Academy in Beijing, p. 382 → The Imperfect One, p. 13 → Six Veterans, p. 305 → Regine Feiler of the Moonlighters' Brigade, p. 204 ('On the prejudice that a woman markets herself well by having a certain balance of proportions, certain normalities, even though love is the last thing to stick to norms.') → Beauty Is Flawless, p. 12 → Memory of a Romance, p. 132 → He Wanted to Keep Her for a While Like a Preserving Jar and Then Exchange Her for Someone Better at Some Point, p. 194.

The idea that love 'works', that it overcomes obstacles, appears in T. W. Adorno's Minima Moralia. *Elsewhere in his work, Adorno (taking up an observation by Marcel Proust) points out how verifiable the Duke of Nemours' love would be for him if the Princess of Cleves had a wooden leg. After all, the novel deals as much with the concealment of feelings as with their expression and their VERIFIABILITY. That is why, according to Proust, one deprives love of its contact surface—its homeland, its field—if one smoothes out physical circumstances in keeping with a universally accepted norm. → The Mermaid, p. 93. See, on the other hand, the phenomenon of being 'low-ranking and highly gifted' in The Great Velashka, p. 407. It is highly tragic when uncommonly beautiful and admirably talented people nonetheless fail to achieve any significant status. No amount of merit helps.*

[Wildness] → Wildness as a Requirement, p. 14 → The Indomesticability of the Libido, p. 603.

Referring to the often impetuous, transgressive character of the tender force, Niklas Luhmann speaks of the 'logic of excess'. The term 'logic' indicates that the vehement emotions are subject to a schema, an order, which stems from the sociability of humans. If wildness becomes the sole criterion for a relationship, however, then the category of longevity loses its chance. An element of practicality, Luhmann argues, is necessary in order to give the tender force constancy.

[Revolutionary Elan as a Derivative of Eros and Self-Confidence] → A Flying Visit to Davos, p. 73 → A Strong Motive, p. 74 → W. Benjamin, the Stars and the Revolution, p. 368 → The Political Commissar Dashevskaya and Her Brother, p. 373 → Reversal of Conscription, p. 447 → A Leninist of the Emotions, p. 282 → To What Extent Is Love a Republican Virtue?, p. 84 → Social Second, Third, Fourth, etc. Birth, p. 166 → The Concept of Self-Regulation, p. 164 → A Learning Process with a Fatal Outcome for Otto Laube and Fritz Brink, p. 145 ('They thought, now it's the revolution and then everything will be overturned, our private lives too . . . ')

In the French Revolution of 1789, the Commune of 1871 and the Revolution of 1915, it was women who initially determined the events. Evidently revolutions are accompanied by metamorphoses in the role of the sexes and changes in the types of love relationships. The end of the Revolution too, the Thermidor, was assisted and accompanied by the intrigues of couples. At the same time, the tender force as a whole seems strangely indifferent to politics. This indifference does not apply to its individual components. Amour propre, *self-confidence, thymos, the 'self' (the narcissist) and desire all fuel revolutionary elan. Principles, motives and sayings like 'The exact second counts', 'In the magic of haste' or the problem of longevity can, using cross-mapping, be applied as much to amorous matters as revolutionary processes. Benjamin sees the longest-lasting revolutionary movement in the orbit of the centre of the Milky Way by the Sun and planets. The temporal needs of the revolution also follow this metaphor.*

[Anna Karenina, Norma, Princess of Cleves, Tosca, Manon Lescaut, Luise Miller] → 'For Anna Karenina', p. 25 → Commentary on Anna Karenina, p. 401 → Anna Karenina in 1915, p. 385 → 'The Company Thought of Themselves as Metropolitan, Insofar as They Enthused about the Novels of France', p. 88 → NORMA, a Concentration of Magnanimity, p. 468 → An Afternoon with Maria Callas, p. 388 → Princess Turandot, p. 117 → Madame de Lafayette, p. 366 ('She was not learned, yet she read with persistence.').

On a map of love, place names would have to be replaced by the names of women and other lovers. The fact that the fates of ordinary people would be underrepresented on such a map (because they are more rarely the subjects of novels, plays, operas or films) would have to be balanced out by monuments to these, inserted at numerous points. The continents, provinces and landscapes, on the other hand, bear the names of the different currents of desire, just as one names stretches of land after the rivers that run through them. The maps of love from the seventeenth century also indicate the qualities of love that cause amazement: 'Mad Sadness'; 'Lake of Confusion'; 'Wonderful Solitudes'. → Map of Love, pp. 367.

[The Soundlessness of Love] → Love Comes Soft-Footed, p. 398 → The First Seven Seconds, p. 21 → The Siamese Hands, p. 77 → Metallic Happiness, p. 427.

In love, one often encounters an element of inaudibility. Two people meet, spend time together and form a coalition for years, and only then do they realize that they have fallen in love with each other. The tender force operates underground. Because of their subterranean character, the libido's canal systems, barely explored until now, cannot be marked on a conventional map of love.

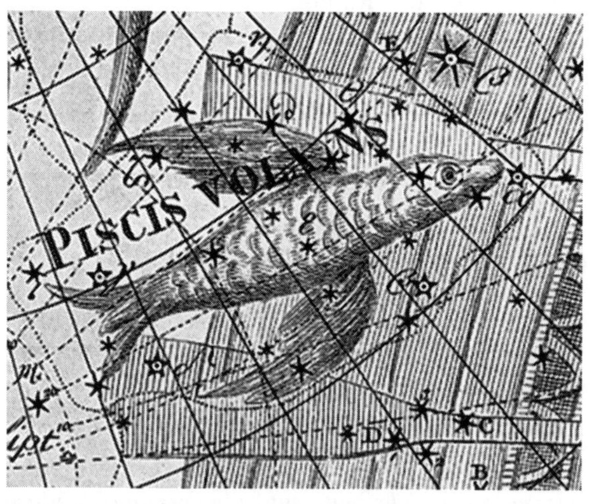

FIGURE 88. *Celestial map of love. In the constellation of the flying fish. The following phrases, invisible in the present image, are inscribed in the sky: 'Sensuality is the basis of all science'; 'The tender force, now at a crossroads'; 'The Enjoyment of Lost Chemistry'; 'Eleonora Duse: if you can't love somewhere, pass by'; 'But the soul is already free, it floats in the sea of*

light'; 'The timelessness of unconscious processes'; 'Flirting'; 'Limbs, just five'; 'Ironing paper money'; 'Anatomy is destiny'; 'The inquisitive nature of children'; 'The adhesion of the first love'; 'Joy of movement'; 'Infectious mistake'; 'Statue of Venus, shattered'.

The words are written over one another, as in a palimpsest. This is possible when entries are made in the firmament at a great distance. How did the writings get there? Who put them there? The observant astronomer must carefully pull apart the different overwritings and read each underlying inscription 'through' those superimposed on it, as it were.

[Work] → Love–Dispensation from Work?, p. 35 → Relationship Work, pp. 584–641 → The Bed Warmer, p. 195 → Bettine G., p. 212 → Semm, p. 215 → The Frontline Fighter, p. 236 → The Monk of Love, p. 442.

[Time Pressure] → A Case of Time Pressure, p. 263 → In the Magic of Haste, p. 22 → The Week of the Engagement, p. 435.

[Murder Ballads] → Then She Called Out: 'Homeland, Sweet Homeland, When Will I See You Again?', p. 52 → Behind Every Indignation There Is the Image of a Woman, p. 55 → Wandering Fates, p. 521 → The Story of the Vengeful Medicine Man, p. 61.

[Love at the Theatre] → Illusion and Reality in Operetta, p. 56 → Death in Theatre and in Reality, p. 59 → The Great Velashka, p. 407 → An Afternoon with Maria Callas, p. 388.

[Love in Cinema] → The Cinema Programme for December 1917 in St Petersburg and Moscow, p. 64 → Children of Love, p. 451 → To New Shores!, p. 343 → Relationships have their public life in cinema. Via surrogates., pp. 606–07.

[Love in Antiquity] → A Sudden Transition of Power, p. 60 → A Female Sacrifice in Antiquity, p. 104 → Murder in the Wedding Night, p. 107.

[Cold] → Cold Is Not Energy, p. 339 → Portrait of a Woman Happy to Have a Cold, p. 141.

[The Tender Force and Social Rank] → A Person Wants to Be Rewarded for Their Own Sake, p. 90 → A Case of Class Struggle Within the GDR, p. 67.

The pilot story for the mingling of desire based on lust and desire based on social advancement can be found in BEL AMI by Guy de Maupassant. It is baffling that the two desires do not diminish but, rather, multiply each other. At the centre of bourgeois society, we find a growing intensity of the capacity for desire, somewhat like a stock market. The motif is foreshadowed in 'A Rake's Progress', a series of copperplates by Hogarth (with commentary by Georg Christoph Lichtenberg). The story tells of two young men (their house and home were burnt down, and they are typical victims of primitive accumulation in England as described by Marx). After arriving in London, one of them becomes a thief and ends at the gallows. The other chooses the path of virtue and is damned to marry the principal's daughter; this is the path of advancement minus lust. → Luise Miller, p. 519, pays for the combination of romantic longing and will to advancement with her life. In the constellations of Balzac's novels, social advancement and love relationships are combined without tragedy; they lead to advantages. See also Proust's precise observations on the meanwhile inherent interconnection of love and social rank. This phenomenon can also be observed negatively in Baron Charlus, who can only love if his partner in love has a shamefully low social standing and coarse manners. Wistful are the stories after the First World War that deal with loss of rank and related love stories. 'That I can show my weakness and still continue to be loved.'

Gigolo

He wore the dapper uniform of a cavalry captain from the Sokolny Hussars. Though original, it could have been taken for a make-believe uniform. Once an artefact of the power of order, it was now without a social context.

So he went every day, except Saturday, to the 5 p.m. dance tea at the Hotel Eden. There he worked as a gigolo. He was paid in advance for two dances; women who wanted him to have further dances with them had to by a five-dance ticket. He shared the profit he made in this way with the establishment. Naturally, he was also suspected of offering his services for a rendezvous outside the dancing event. That was considered disreputable for a former officer. But his services during working hours, accompanied by the sounds of the salon orchestra, were also nothing that an army comrade would have forgiven if he had noticed him.

But there were precious, energetic women who valued precisely this disreputable aspect. One could say that they bought themselves a dominator whom they simultaneously dominated, a servant for a few hours. Essentially they were buying a former master.

At the end of 1921, he had the idea of dropping all that business with the uniform. He arrived punctually at the dance events wearing English cloth, 'just elegant', often only in a Scottish pullover, which was fitting for the foxtrot. Until, in 1932, the national upheaval made a continuation of this 'profession' difficult. After the accession to power, it was even unclear whether his dressing up as a 'gentleman' and 'national', when he was a whore in sexual terms, might be an offence. There was no actual law against it yet, but it did not take a clairvoyant to imagine such activities being punishable. At the time, people were singing in the cities:

'You can't suspect such a thing
Sweet angel that you are!'

Thus the former cavalry captain erased the traces of his temporary professional activities, eked out a living as a waiter and an assistant at a city theatre, and then took up his old rank in 1935 in Germany's new Wehrmacht. Now he could be a master again, and was soon a master in foreign countries too.

[The Genealogy of the Tender Force] *Descent not from the animal kingdom but, rather, from the practices of earlier human societies that already knew music and language. Music, which came first, constitutes the bright element. From the start, language was the 'handmaiden of advantage'. Early violence comes from it. Long speeches were given before the sacrifice of Iphigenia. Myth analysts speak of the original matriarchy. This rule, according to the myths handed down, followed the murder of mothers, followed by patricide and the battle of the brothers against one another. According to an earlier school of analysis, crises and conflicts are located in the transition between the life* *of hunting clans and the status of sedentarism. Here, experts say, human sacrifices took place and religions were born. Drugs, brain-stimulating intoxication, were the means of forming communities. ('First there was beer and mushrooms, then bread.') One must be intoxicated to set up a community.*

In the descriptions of this and similar ORIGINAL VIOLENCE one finds few references to the obstacle course of the tender force over millennia. Evidently it had to adapt to all of these structures and abrupt changes. That, according to Freud, is what causes the diversity in the swarms of the libido: that they come from so many social locations, have forgotten everything and yet cannot forget anything.

[Generosity] → Teatime with Academics, p. 208 → The Beauty in the Voice of the Nightingale, p. 108 → The *Metamorphoses* of Ovid, p. 10.

[The Threads of Ariadne, the Iron Constructions of Daedalus: What Does Flexibility Mean?] → Do People Confuse the Minotaur with an Entirely Different Construction by Daedalus?, p. 115.

The concept of flexibility relates to the elastic curvature of a young tree that persistently defies an overwhelming gust of wind. Once the wind has passed, the tree stands upright again. The opposite would be ataraxia, which is likewise ascribed to trees—oaks, for example. Rigidity is also a characteristic of iron constructions. Monuments of persistence are constructed from iron in the form of bridges and the Eiffel Tower. Machines show how flexibly such iron structures can react. Psychic constructs are neither flexible nor hard as iron; the follow laws that need images of their own. One of these is Ariadne's thread. It was probably not a leash that one would use to lead animals, nor a rope. It was, rather, the inner voice in which the two companions, no matter how far apart, called to each other. This (and not any physical connection) drew Odysseus home, to the bed he had built, a place of pleasure (locus amoenus) *that he himself had carved into the tree.*

[The Tender Force and Its Relationship to the Enlightenment] → A Late Application of Immanuel Kant's Natural Law, p. 23 → To What Extent Is Love a Republican Virtue?, p. 84 → On the Supposed Right to Lie Out of Philanthropy, p. 491 → The Law of Love, p. 393 → Love Triumphs, p. 6 → What Does Enlightenment Mean in Relationship Matters?, p. 625 → Enlightenment in the Case of Immaturity through No Fault of One's Own, p. 414 → An Episode in the Age of Enlightenment, p. 409.

Rationale, reason, emotion, daring and capacity for love are distinguished from one another as if they were separate departments of a government agency whose responsibilities need to be organized. On the other hand, Immanuel Kant speaks of the powers of reasoning, the desire for reason, as the 'tender germ' that nature has planted inside us humans. So there seems to be a central motif whose developmental goal is a universal unfolding of all human qualities. There are indeed strong libidinous forces at work, disguised as rationale. One situation later, those same currents act eagerly as illusionists. It is therefore permissible to assume that related or conspiring forces are active in all these states of matter of the human character. That is why the image contained in the French word ARRAISONNEMENT is so plausible. A ship of life is being loaded and the cargo lists checked. In Kant, this means finding one's bearings in thought. Essentially, the aforementioned human traits are unified by their spirit of resistance: no one has the right to command other humans.

FIGURE 89. *'Aucun home n'a reçu de la nature le droit de commander aux autres.'* (*Diderot*)

[Happiness] → A Lucky Charm, p. 9 → Born under a Lucky Star, p. 402 → Verdun, the Great Trading Centre for Slaves, p. 471 → The Search for Happiness in Private Life, p. 585 → A Guide to Being Happy, p. 267 → The Kitchen of Happiness, p. 560 ('Two Days During the 1968/69 Winter Semester in the Revolutionary City of Frankfurt').

[Commodity Character] The Commodity Character of Love, Theory and Revolution, p. 425 → The Commodity Character in Relationship Work, p. 613 → A New Genotype of Theory, p. 556.

FIGURE 90. *ARRAISONNEMENT: Argo Navis. Constellation in the form of a sailing ship in the southern firmament. Noah's Ark is drawn into this constellation. The ship, according to traditions, contains a 'chest of writings' that must be saved. The completeness of the writings was checked by way of ARRAISONNEMENT before disembarking. Bottom right: Canopus, the second-brightest star in the firmament. Argo is the ship of Jason and his 50 marauding comrades who abducted Medea.* → *'Time and Place Without a Ground Is Violence'* (Aristotle), *p. 535.*

[Crimes of Love out of Depression] → Impotence Increases Violence, p. 331 → Divorce Date, p. 307 → An Attempt at Love, p. 159.

It is in keeping with observations that wars are not started by a bubbling-over of thymos but, rather, by depressive persons and out of desperation. This is true of 1914, for example. War crimes also mount at the moment of defeat, not in times of success. Similarly, situations that bring the capacity of love to an end rarely involve persons with self-confidence and autonomy but, rather, desperate ones. In that sense, impotence increases violence. The guards who pursue their absurd research in → An Attempt at Love, p. 125, likewise behave like depressive persons. Such stories are difficult to tell. Adorno's verdict that one can no longer write poems after Auschwitz can be translated thus: there can be no literature that keeps silent about the depths of depressive cruelty in order to spare the nerves of its readers. → 'Several young men, ugly, impertinent, intrusive, but at once closely observing the impression they were making, drew closer', p. 25.

[The Deadly Triangle] → Adultery and Its Consequences, p. 322 → Death in Theatre and in Reality, p. 59 → The Othello of Luneburg, p. 324.

[A Human Right to Tenderness] → Six Veterans, p. 305 → She Wanted at Least to Be Treated with the Same Care One Shows Towards Objects, p. 462.

[He Could not Bear to Be Separated From His Heard-Hearted Egotism Even for Two or Three Minutes] → The Hiding Place of Her Will, p. 319 → So Incredibly Evil That His Hair Had to Fall Out, p. 542 → Erwin, a Ruin of Clear Egotism, p. 346.

[Property] → A Case of Expropriation, p. 293 → Original Property, p. 170 → Private Property in Relationships as Opposed to the Historical Principle of Private Property, p. 617 → Property in the History of the Species, p. 620, → 'The Sensuality of Having', p. 192.

[They Had Hurtled Towards Each Other and Had No Way of Keeping Each Other at a Distance] → 'I Wish I Hadn't Wanted That', p. 303 → Original Disunity, p. 298.

[All Those Eyes] → That Was the Terrible Thing: They Knew Each Other So Well That They Couldn't Really Afford Conflicts, p. 309 → All Those Eyes, p. 608.

If There Were No Skin, the Bones Would Take On a Life of Their Own

My thighs and the right side of my face, the neck and the shape of my head, one of my eyes and my feet, come from my mother. The ribcage, edge of the ribs (shaped like a hat brim, a peculiarity), shoulders and left hand from my father. The spinal column and top of the rear a mixture of both. Now there's a fine pair, says Schmidtlein, in life they never suited each other but now I'm supposed to bring them together. If the regions of my body agree with what I'm doing at the same time as protesting, then the contrasting parents of my parents are interfering. As far as their possibility and reality go, there are 16, and through them thirty-two are speaking, etc. How could I be interested in being a whole? I would much rather feel real as the mongrel that I am, and I can when I feel strong.

So Schmidtlein was distrustful, even hostile, to any approach along these lines: Now look, you have to close your eyes, relax completely, feel somehow grounded in yourself and concentrate on your voice, the currents inside you. Meditate a little! The goal is for your person to become a whole, if you just accept it deeply enough.

If I attained self-awareness, Schmidtlein replies to such recommendations, I would be true to myself and focus on what was important, that is, all the things I did not want to part with it any cost, and I would whirl away in 32 or 46 directions at once. Do you want to punish me? The way one tore criminals into four pieces in the Middle Ages and had them scattered to the four winds? Every day I hold my diverging traits together with a lot of improvisation. Not in the middle at all. I act as if I liked all my different components equally, for they do not forgive unfair treatment—after all, no one ever asked them if they wanted to be together, or even just if they were suitable to stick together. They are flight animals.[48] *And so I don't want to be* mine *but, rather,* theirs.

['If one can die of it, then let's view it as the enemy and not like your kind smile, which—I'll bet on this—started off as you baring your teeth.'] → In the Trough of Psychology, p. 437 → The *Metamorphoses* of Ovid, p. 108 → The Battle between Conscience and Superstition, p. 312 → *The She-Devils*, p. 607.

[The Person, the SELF] → The Hour in Which the 'Self' Is Born, p. 18 → The Seat of the Soul, p. 467.

PERSONA comes from Latin, from the verb personare, '*to sound through*'. *In the Greek theatre, the term originally referred to the*

48 The mental faculties do not arrange themselves into a white and a black horse, as Plato claims. Nor does the addition of an intermediate grey horse explain the direction in which the different tendencies move. Rather, one should think of the way a herd of horses behaves in stormy weather. The individual horses are as small as fingernails and as large as houses. But they cannot so easily be divided into good and bad or white and black, says Schmidtlein.

masks used by actors, through which the voices of the figures sounded. So the word refers precisely to something non-personal. If one considers that we humans resulted from a mingling of highly divergent ancestors (grandparents and parents), it is reasonable to assume that a love relationship does not involve two individual persons speaking to each other but, rather, that each of the two partners is negotiating with the other as a whole chorus of voices. Those who allow each other this multiplicity, however, are elemental and authentic. The chorus (including the coalitions between the chorus members on each side) is less confusing than the fiction of two monolithic units justifying themselves to each other or exchanging touches. In addition, the 'confederated ancestors' whom we call humans are subdivided according to their capacity for desire; some of this is conscious, some of it unconscious (and this is only the simplest distinction). It is precisely because the SELF is thus–to a heightened extent in love matters–not the master of its own house that the SELF is nonetheless (like all endangered organisms) particularly tough, robust, resourceful and consistent. The danger of breakage ensures resistance to breakage.

On 16 November 1800, Heinrich von Kleist wrote to Wilhelmine von Zenge: 'On the eve of the most important day of my life, I went for a walk in Würzburg. When the sun set, it felt as if my happiness was going down with it. I shuddered when I thought that I would maybe have to part with everything, with all that is dear to me.

'Withdrawn into myself, I went back into the city through the arched gateway, reflecting. Why, I thought, does the arch not collapse, for it has no support? It stands, I replied, because all the stones want to fall at once–and from this thought I drew an

indescribably invigorating comfort that, until the decisive moment, always remained by my side to offer me hope that I too would hold on if everything let me fall.'

[A Guzzler of Lifeblood] → A Leninist of the Emotions, p. 282 → The Reckless Dog, p. 33 → So Incredibly Evil That His Hair Had to Fall Out, p. 542.

[Mother–Child Relationship] → The Robot as Emotional Intelligence, p. 163 → The Concept of Self-Regulation, p. 164 → An Unusually Difficult Birth, p. 168 → Original Property, p. 170 → She Had Resolved That Her Child Would Want for Nothing, p. 172.

['A Good Mind Is Dry'] *Niklas Luhmann's motto for examining complex systems like love and society. Luhmann distinguishes between self-critical reason and the 'lazy reason' of naive rationalists in the eighteenth century.* → Six Stories for Niklas Luhmann, p. 541 → The Kitchen of Happiness, p. 560.

[The Libido and the Self] → The Indomesticability of the Libido, p. 603 → A Libidinous Reason for Matter-of-Factness, p. 231 → In the Shadow Realm of the Libido, p. 250 → Invisible Images, p. 250.

In Three Essays on the Theory of Sexuality, *Freud writes: 'We have defined the concept of libido as a quantitatively variable force which could serve as a measure of processes and transformations occurring in the field of sexual excitation.* [. . .] *In thus distinguishing between libidinal and other forms of psychical energy we are giving expression to the presumption that the sexual processes occurring in the organism are distinguished from the nutritive process by a special chemistry.* [. . .] *We thus reach the idea of a quantity of libido, to the mental representation of which we give the name of "ego-libido".'*[49]

And elsewhere:

'The fact of the existence of sexual needs in human beings and animals is expressed in biology by the assumption of a "sexual instinct", on the analogy of the instinct of nutrition, that is of hunger. Everyday language possesses no counterpart to the word "hunger", but science makes use of the word "libido" for that purpose.'[50]

Freud adds:

'The only appropriate word in the German language, Lust, *is unfortunately ambiguous, and is used to denote the experience of both a need and of a gratification.'*[51]

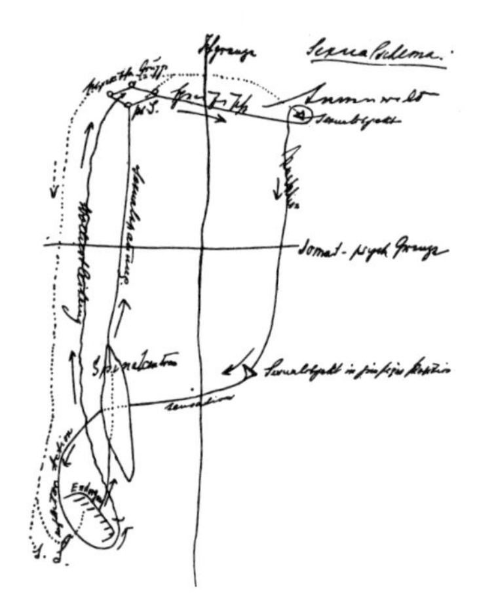

FIGURE 91. *Sketch by Sigmund Freud concerning the sexual schema. 'The battle at the ego boundary'. Vertical line in the centre: ego boundary. On the left: 'lust line'.*

---

49 Sigmund Freud, *Three Essays on the Theory of Sexuality* (James Strachey trans.) (New York: Basic Books, 2000), p. 83.

50 Ibid., p. 1.

51 Ibid., p. 1n.

[Derivatives of Eros] → What Are Derivatives?, p. 228 → Matter-of-Factness, Making an Effort, p. 227.

Other derivatives: intelligence, revolutionary elan, pleasure, art, lightness of touch, cooperation, friendship, generosity, indomitability of libido, loyalty, etc.

[Long-Distance Love] → A Case of Long-Distance Love, p. 478 → Not Public–Public (The Sister's Glance Into the Distance, Where Her Brother is Imprisoned in a Concentration Camp), p. 128 → The Minotaur Looks with Longing into the Distance, p. 103.

'*What I love must be as distant as the kingdom of heaven.' On the Other Side: → The Nature of Love, p. 247 (Skin Contact as the* Oikos *of the Tender Force).*

[When Love Is no Longer Possible . . .] → The Wedding at 'The Steed', p. 125 → An Attempt at Love, p. 159 → Impotence Increases Violence, p. 331.

[*Homo compensator*] → The Peculiar Children Next Door, p. 363 → *Homo novus*, p. 501.

Goethe viewed Homo compensator, *the balancer, as a continuation of* Homo sapiens. *In his many millennia of history,* Homo sapiens *never developed adequate abilities of self-regulation. Essentially,* sapientia *remains unsociable. In amorous matters especially, some balance is required. Only this allows one not to exclude wildness, the passions. The virtue of the middle serves the purpose of permitting the extremes. This is the PRINCIPLE OF INCLUSION. The balancer possesses EQUILIBRISTICS.*

[Love Is a Force That Makes the Stars Dance . . .] → Benjamin and Astral Metaphors, p. 368 → A Strange Kind of Attraction, p. 378.

Freud refers to this claim as a 'poetic overestimation of love'. Walter Benjamin counters that the gravitational forces whereby the heavenly bodies act on one another and keep the others on their orbits are directly comparable to the strong but also long-range forces that govern matters of love.